A NOVEL

We Close Our Eyes

A choice is an act of personal power.

JUSTINE BRASHEAR

Part One

Loving ourselves through the process of owning our story is the bravest thing we will ever do.

Brené Brown

One

S trobe lights blinked in the darkness, revealing flashes of writhing bodies below. Emily held onto the bars of her elevated cage—a fallen angel in captivity on display for everyone to worship. This was her church of choice now, not the evangelical one her mother forced her to attend as a teenager. She traded communion juice for tequila and speaking in tongues for club music. No more judgment and condemnation. Just acceptance and adulation.

She loved having the power to captivate men but hated having to ward them off when they thought she owed them something. Which was why she preferred dancing at gay bars. She had the freedom to let loose and not worry about men falling all over her, thinking she wanted to sleep with them just because she danced with them. In a place like this, she was just another pretty decoration, not a prize to be won at the end of the night.

Eighties Prom was an annual event at Tracks Nightclub in downtown Denver, and Emily never missed an opportunity to dress up. Surrendering to the decadence of "Like A Prayer," she watched herself dance in the extravagant gilded mirror mounted on the wall next to her. Her short black crinoline skirt swayed over footless fishnet stockings, and her black stilettos, paired with neon pink ankle socks, highlighted her long legs. She was slightly horrified to see she resembled a prostitute, but equally intrigued by how salaciously hot she looked.

If only Mom could see me now.

The music paused while the emcee called people to the stage to enter the contest for Prom King and Queen. Emily climbed down from the cage and pushed through the lust-filled crowd, looking for her friends. With none of them in sight, she squeezed in at the bar to order another drink. The shirtless bartender in black leather pants had his back to her while half a dozen men vied for his attention.

When he finally broke away from a conversation, his eyes settled on Emily. She wasn't prepared for the rush of heat that flooded her body as his chiseled abs and bow tie approached her. Shaggy brown hair fell into his green eyes, which were as mischievous as his smile.

"Something tells me you don't belong here," he shouted over the music, handing her a bottle of water.

Why are the most gorgeous men gay?

There was a familiarity about him she couldn't quite place. "Do you?" Her fingerless lace gloves gripped the chilled water bottle as she rolled it across her chest to cool down.

"No, don't tell anyone." He winked. "I'm not really a bartender."

"So, do you even know how to make a good drink?" She opened the water and gulped it down.

"I know a thing or two. I'll make one just for you." He grabbed a shot glass and poured in Baileys and Amaretto.

He wouldn't dare.

Then he topped it off with whipped cream.

"Really? A blow job? That's the best you can do?"

"I have to see what you can handle," he smirked, adding more.

Game on. Emily set the empty water bottle on the bar and tied up her long chestnut curls with the giant bow wrapped around her head. Leaning over, she held onto the multiple long necklaces adorning her neck, hooking her thumb into the bright pink bra peeking out from her mesh tank. She lapped the whipped cream and picked up the glass with her lips. Tossing her head back, the smooth drink flowed down her throat. Everyone around her erupted into cheers. The bartender slowly clapped at her victory as she proudly set the shot glass in front of him.

"There you are!" Addison, Emily's best friend, ran up and grabbed her hand, dragging Emily over to the stage. "Diego got the biggest applause!"

They reached the front and found Todd just as the emcee presented Diego with a glittering rhinestone tiara and a "Prom Queen" sash.

Dressed as Boy George from his Culture Club days, Diego jumped off the stage into Todd's arms, gushing, "They like me. They really like me!"

Todd, channeling George Michael in short shorts and an oversized "Choose Life" t-shirt, wrapped his arms around Diego and kissed him. "I've always said you're a queen. Now, it's official."

Diego and Todd were Emily's favorite couple. She first met them when she started working at Josephina's Trattoria as a hostess five years ago and watched the two servers grow from work colleagues to best friends before finally falling in love. They left the restaurant last year to pursue their dream of opening a camp in the mountains for at-risk foster kids. They were definitely couple goals—even though Emily doubted she could ever find that kind of genuine connection for herself.

"This coronation should increase attendance at the fundraiser next week," Emily said playfully. "Maybe we should raise the price of admission?"

"Were you ever able to book a band?" Todd asked.

"No. No one will play for free. Even for troubled kids. People suck."

"We need Addy there," Diego cried. "There's no way you can come?"

"Shavuot is a big Jewish feast. My family would disown me if I skipped it," Addison said. "But I promise to make it up to you."

A cocktail server approached them with a tray of tequila shots. "Your Majesty," he curtsied. "Courtesy of the bartender."

Emily glanced over her shoulder at the Chippendales man behind the bar. He held up his own shot glass and winked. His dazzling smile ignited a fire in her belly.

"I like the whole Courtney Cox 'Dancing in the Dark' vibe you have going on." The server circled his hand in front of Addison, assessing her rolled-up jeans and white muscle tee. "Very nuanced."

"Thank you!" She threw a smug smile at her friends—her "boring" costume choice validated—and passed the shots around. "Let's celebrate! Drink up, bitches!"

Emily danced in direct view of the bartender. His eyes stayed fixated on her whenever he wasn't mixing cocktails, propelling the fire into her veins. With "Bizarre Love Triangle" blasting, she danced between two women, letting them run their hands up and down her curves, imagining it was him caressing her body.

He held up another shot, beckoning Emily over. She broke away from dancing and met him at the front of the bar.

When he placed his hands around her bare waist, his touch sizzled against her skin. "Ready?" Before she could process what he was doing, he lifted her onto the bar top. The surrounding crowd immediately began chanting, "Body shot! Body shot!"

The bartender stepped between her legs and handed her the glass. "House special." He squeezed lime juice on his chest and sprinkled salt on top. Excitement coursed through Emily as she stared at his glistening pecs inches from her face. With a wicked smile, she leaned in, licked the salt from his skin, and shot back the tequila. He held the lime to her mouth. Staring into his eyes, she bit down.

"My turn." He laid her on the bar. After tracing a wedge of lime across her exposed stomach, he placed it on her lips. Emily watched as he sprinkled salt onto her moistened skin. Her body flinched with excited nervousness as Patrón filled her navel.

She closed her eyes, feeling his warm tongue drag across her stomach. His lips surrounded her belly button, sucking up the alcohol and sending pleasure down into her core. The group cheered loudly when the bartender hoisted himself on top of the bar and straddled her body. Emily's eyes shot open, and he leaned down, biting the lime from her mouth.

He pushed himself up and helped her to her feet. Placing his arm around her back, he pulled her hips into his. Their bodies moved in unison to "Tainted Love" as Emily lost herself in the music, grazing her hands over his bare skin while he did the same to her.

When the song ended, he leaned in and kissed her cheek before jumping down and resuming his bartending duties. As the night went on, the heat between them continued to ratchet up while the tequila rounds kept coming.

At closing time, everyone poured out onto the sidewalk. The bartender walked up to Emily and wrapped one arm around her waist, pulling her into him. "You are not what I expected."

She thought he was going to kiss her. Instead, he leaned toward her ear and said in a low voice, "I'm in."

***

Emily heard a loud knock on her front door. She wasn't sure if she was dreaming or if someone was really there. Ignoring it, she willed herself back to sleep. Another knock. *What the hell?* Her eyes fluttered open, and she slowly sat up, waiting for the room to stop spinning.

After the third knock, she mumbled, "I'm coming." She grabbed her satin robe and wrapped it around her naked body, stumbling to the door. When she opened it, she was stunned to see the bartender from the night before holding up coffee in one hand and a paper bag in the other.

"I thought you could use these."

Shit! Did I sleep with him?

Emily held onto the door for support. Images of the night before played through her mind: groping hands, whipped cream, his tongue on her skin, holding her against his half-naked body.

"Can I come in?"

Still slightly incoherent, Emily moved off to the side, allowing him to squeeze by. She closed the door and leaned her forehead against it, trying to pull herself out of her stupor. The bartender set the coffee and bag down and wrapped his arm around her waist, guiding her over to the stools at the breakfast bar.

Emily pulled the satin across her chest to tighten the robe over her partially exposed breasts. "How do you know where I live?"

He chuckled as he pulled out his phone and tapped on it before sliding it over for her inspection. She cringed as she saw the desperate selfie in front of the club and read her words: *I'd like a nightcap, Mr. Bartender,* followed by her address, complete with the door code to her building.

"I put my number in your phone last night—at your insistence." He winked as he reached into the brown paper bag.

Embarrassment washed over her. She couldn't bring herself to look at him.

"Here's some Tylenol. It's best to take it with a full glass of water before falling asleep after a night of drinking. Makes a huge difference in how you feel the next morning." He set the pills in front of her, along with a bottle of electrolyte water. "Better late than never."

Emily was quiet, partly from the intense hangover but mainly from the humiliation of her behavior the night before. She grabbed the medicine and tossed it into her mouth.

He pulled a round paper container from the bag. "You need to eat this soup to sweat it all out."

Emily's mouth practically burst into flames as she sipped a spoonful. "Oh, my god, this is spicy!"

He laughed and sat down next to her. "You gotta do it if you wanna feel better."

She remembered her friends walking her home from the bar and knew she hadn't slept with this man. Her nose began to run, and she grabbed a napkin, wiping away the dripping snot before speaking again. "Why are you doing this?"

"Because I like you."

Emily's stomach flipped more than it already had done that morning. His candidness surprised her. But then she remembered how she acted the night before and realized he was probably here expecting more.

"Last night," Emily began. She stared down into her lap, at a loss for words. Noticing her exposed thighs, she tried, unsuccessfully, to cover herself.

"Last night, we found out what a little alcohol does to Emily Bisset."

She snapped her head up and stared at him defiantly. "That's not really who I am."

"Someone who likes to have fun?" He placed his hands on her bare thighs, turning her barstool so she was facing him. "I'd love to find out who you really are. As much as I want to take you to your bed right now and…"

Emily held her breath. As she sobered up, she realized how stupid it was to let a stranger into her apartment, even if there was something familiar about him.

"This isn't the time." He stood up and walked to the door. "You need to sleep some more. Sleep this off. I'll see you soon."

She sat there stunned as he walked out the door.

With her bladder about to explode, she raced to the bathroom and saw herself in the mirror. Her sexy, smokey eyes from the night before now made her look like a zombie; her face was flushed and damp from the spicy soup, and her hair tangled and disheveled like she'd spent the night on the street.

No wonder he left.

Two

Emily loved living downtown. Anywhere she wanted to go was within walking distance or a short ride on the free shuttle bus that cruised up and down the outdoor Sixteenth Street Mall. She would forever be grateful to her grandmother for not selling her high-rise condo when she moved in with Emily's dad, allowing Emily to rent it for a third of its value.

Late spring was her favorite time of year in Colorado. The vivid colors of nature swirled together to create a perfect picture as she walked down the tree-lined street, feeling the warmth of the sun against her skin.

Larimer Square bustled with shoppers exploring the boutiques on Saturday afternoon. The line at The Market—the first and oldest espresso bar between New York and Los Angeles—was out the door as usual. Its blue and white striped awnings, combined with flower boxes hanging over patio railings, were reminiscent of a quaint European café.

Emily walked past the line for coffee and up the steps to the deli displaying everything from luscious cakes and exquisite chocolate truffles to an array of salads and freshly sliced meats. She waved at Addison behind the counter and grabbed a table in the back corner.

Addison was the first friend Emily made when she moved downtown five years ago. The Market was two doors down from Josephina's in Larimer Square. And only two blocks from Emily's condo. Every morning, Emily sat at one of their small tables with a cappuccino, pouring over the newest edition of *Westword*, uncovering all the cool places she wanted to check out as she familiarized herself with the city. One morning, Addison was carrying a tray of baked goods by Emily's table when a man in a suit hurried past, knocking Addison out of the way. Her tray went flying, sending pastries raining down all over Emily and causing her cappuccino to spill into her lap. With only a cursory glance back, the man continued out the door. The two women had been inseparable ever since.

When Addison finished ringing up a customer, she joined Emily with a muffuletta and two cans of passionfruit La Croix.

"You look like hell." Addison set the sparkling waters on the table before placing the enormous sandwich in front of Emily and removing the extra plate for herself.

"Thanks."

"Bad hangover?"

Emily moaned. "Why did you let me drink so much?"

"Like I could stop you." Addison grabbed half of her Italian masterpiece and took a big bite.

Emily battled a dull headache despite all the remedies given to her earlier. "So, I had an interesting morning. The bartender from last night showed up at my door."

Addison almost choked on her sandwich. "You're kidding!"

"He brought me coffee and soup. And Tylenol."

"How does he know where you live?"

"He showed me a text I sent him, inviting him over." Emily dropped her head into her hands.

"Well, you did babble on all night about wanting to stick your tongue down his throat. I think you actually tried!"

Emily shook her head as she continued holding it. "I've got to stop drinking so much when we go out."

"So, what happened this morning?"

"Nothing. He told me to sleep it off and left."

"That's it?"

"Yep."

"What's his name?"

Emily shrugged. "I have no idea. He knew my name though. I feel like I know him from somewhere. It's driving me crazy. Did he look familiar to you?"

"I didn't look at him that closely. You probably put your name in his phone though."

"My full name? Seems unlike me."

"Do you think you'll hear from him again?"

"He said he'd see me soon, so maybe." Emily took a bite of her sandwich. *I hope.*

"Well, I have to give him credit for not taking advantage of the situation."

"I must have looked so pathetic."

"Stop it. And don't talk with food in your mouth. It's gross."

"Sorry, Mom," Emily said while still chewing.

"He's obviously interested in you. I don't think a guy looking to hook up would take time to bring you that stuff and then leave without trying anything."

"I guess that's true," Emily conceded, feeling slightly less mortified.

"You deserve a good man, Em. Not the assholes you usually attract."

Emily shot her a pointed look.

"No offense. But come on! You have to admit you're drawn to the bad boys."

"But why?" Emily whined. "Why can't I be attracted to a good man for once?"

"Because they're boring?" Addison laughed. "I'm no expert. I can't find anyone I'm the least bit interested in. But I know you'll find the perfect guy. Probably when you least expect it."

Emily looked at her friend and laughed. "That's such a cliché."

"I know. But there are truths in clichés, or they wouldn't be cliché."

"Maybe I'll meet a sugar daddy at the fundraiser next week. At least I wouldn't have to worry about figuring out a career anymore. Kill two birds with one stone."

"Talk about cliché."

"Speaking of the fundraiser, I have some exciting news," Emily said, perking up. "The manager for The LoDo Dogs called me a couple of hours ago and said they're available."

Addison's eyes widened. "Seriously? Why didn't you lead with that?"

"She told me they had a last-minute cancellation, and they'd be happy to play for free as their contribution."

"I'm so upset I'm missing it," Addison cried. "I can't believe it falls on the same night Shavuot begins. Not only am I not there for Diego and Todd on such a special night, but now I'm missing out on a front-row seat to the hottest jazz band in Denver."

"I know. I'm sorry. It was the only date this month Enzo could get it on the calendar. There's no way you can be there?"

"No. Shavuot is an important holiday to my dad. He makes us stay up all night reading the Torah."

"That sounds... fun," Emily teased. "Maybe I can score us a reserved table at one of their upcoming gigs using my girly charm." Emily batted her eyelashes.

"Oh, please make that happen." Addison glanced at the clock. "I need to get back to work. Shift change is coming up."

"Yeah, I need to get to work, too. Thanks for the food. I don't know how I'm going to get through this night." They gathered their dishes and walked them back to a bin. "I'm training a new bartender."

Addison lit up. "Maybe your mystery guy is the new bartender?"

"Not unless he identifies as female. You read too many romance novels, Addy." Emily rolled her eyes, teasing.

"Wait, he must have put in his name when he added his number to your phone. What's the text show?"

Emily opened the message and laughed. "Not a Bartender."

***

The late nineteenth-century buildings lining Larimer Square consisted of narrow storefronts connected up and down the block. Josephina's Trattoria and Bar stood as the crown jewel, housed in two side-by-side spaces, making it easy to close off one side for private events.

When Emily walked in, her boss, Enzo, was behind the dark vintage bar, talking to a young woman with strawberry blonde hair. He called out to Emily when he saw her.

"Hey, Em, come meet our new bartender. Stephanie, this is Emily. She'll be training you this week."

The two women shook hands as Enzo continued. "My goal is to have you on your own next weekend during the fundraiser. Think you can handle it?"

"Yes, Sir. I'm used to a crazy-busy bar with frat boys who can get a bit wild."

Enzo looked to Emily. "Stephanie recently moved down here from Fort Collins where she was a bartender for a year. I'm sure under your expert guidance, she'll pick things up pretty quickly."

Stephanie looked younger than Emily. She would have guessed maybe eighteen if she was trying to order a drink at the bar. But Emily figured she had to be at least twenty-two if she already had a year's experience. Enzo liked to hire young bartenders. Especially pretty girls. It was good for business in this hip neighborhood that attracted college kids, young professionals, and tourists. And Emily knew how to play the game. She counted on the generous tips from the men who thought they had a chance with her.

"Nice meeting you, Stephanie," Emily said. "Let me put my stuff away, and I'll be right out."

"I'll walk back with you." Enzo came around from behind the bar and alongside Emily. "So, what do you think?"

"She seems great," Emily replied. "But do you really think she'll be ready to be on her own by next week?"

"She's not a rookie like you were," he said, leaning against the lockers while Emily put her purse and hoodie away. "Plus, she'll have help from a couple of servers that night. She'll do fine."

His seductive smile and espresso-colored eyes gave Emily butterflies whenever he was near. Anyone else would probably consider him average-looking. As a thirty-five-year-old married father, he definitely had more of a "dad bod." But there was something in the way he carried himself, the way he spoke. Confidence, maybe arrogance?

Whatever it was, Emily often found herself spellbound by him, which pissed her off.

"By the way, Isabella won't be able to make it to the fundraiser," he told her. "She's out of town."

Emily's mouth fell open. His wife had taken Emily under her wing when she saw her struggling to figure everything out for the fundraiser. She helped Emily reach out to the right people and ask for donations. She seemed very invested in the event's success, so it didn't make sense that she would miss it. "Where is she?"

"Rhode Island. She took the baby back to visit her folks for a while."

Emily noticed what appeared to be irritation flicker across his face. "Is everything okay?" She quickly added, "With her parents, I mean?"

"Oh, yeah, they're good. She just wanted to spend her first Mother's Day as a mother with her mother." He pushed himself off the lockers. "Are you heading up to your dad's place tomorrow?"

"I guess," she said warily, turning toward him.

Enzo placed his hand on her arm, gently squeezing with reassurance. "Just let me know if you need anything. You got this."

She wasn't sure if he was referring to the fundraiser or the fact she was spending Mother's Day at her dad's house. Regardless, she would find something she needed from him.

Enzo turned and headed toward his office, singing along to Taylor Swift playing overhead.

Three

Emily regretted accepting her father's invitation to Mother's Day brunch. Not because she didn't like her stepmom. She did. But it pained Emily to visit her dad's home on any holiday that celebrated parenting—a home filled with a loving, intact family that she'd never had. She adored her little sisters but always felt like an outsider. Like she didn't really belong there, and they were all just accommodating her presence out of some feeling of obligation.

Spotting the Elk Creek fire station, Emily pulled off Highway 285 and headed up the winding road until she reached the familiar mailbox with horses painted on it. She turned her grandmother's old Volvo down the steep rocky driveway and bounced slowly toward the wood-paneled house at the bottom. Reluctantly trading the warmth of her car for the brisk air, she quickly navigated over patches of ice and snow in her high-heeled ankle boots and short bohemian dress, letting herself in through the side door.

This part of the house was cold and closed off from the rest. It had been the original garage before her dad remodeled it into his workspace. He and his new wife bought the six-acre mountain ranch when Emily was eleven years old. An eclectic collection of various half-finished projects sat atop the bed Emily used to sleep in when she first moved to Colorado after high school.

She opened the French door leading into the warm living room, and the smell of incense filled her nostrils. Eva Cassidy played through the speakers strategically set around the house.

"Sissy!" Ten-year-old Summer and seven-year-old Rain threw their arms around their big sister.

"Hi, beauties." Emily kissed the top of Summer's curly golden mane and Rain's silky smooth brown locks. The three of them shared the same brilliant blue eyes—a Bisset family characteristic along with a crooked nose. "I've missed you guys!"

"Hi, sweetheart." Her dad stood up from the sofa where he was sitting next to her grandmother. Being close to sixty years old when her sisters were born, he looked more like their grandpa now with his gray frizzy curls sticking out in all different directions. "How was the drive up?" He hugged her tightly.

"Terrifying. I was not expecting snow." She muffled her answer into his shoulder.

"Snow?" her dad scoffed. "That's just a light dusting. It will be gone before you leave."

Her stepmom, Amy, walked up and hugged Emily. "Such a California girl. So good to see you!" Amy was twenty years younger than her husband and looked ethereal wearing a printed caftan with her blonde hair floating down to her waist.

"You too." Emily pulled a small potted herb garden from her tote bag. "Happy Mother's Day."

"I love it! Thank you." Amy motioned for Summer and Rain to follow her back to the kitchen. "Let's finish setting the table."

"Hi, Grams." Emily walked over to her 92-year-old grandmother and bent down to kiss her cheek.

"Hi, honey. Help me up, will you?"

When she was standing, her grandmother wrapped her frail arms around Emily.

"How are you? Not staying out of trouble, I hope?"

"Of course not."

"That's my girl."

Emily handed her a small pot of yellow baby roses. "Happy Mother's Day."

"Oh, my favorite color!" She took the flowers from Emily. "I'll go put these in my room before we sit down to eat."

Emily turned back to her dad as her grandmother shuffled away.

He gave Emily an empathetic smile. "Have you spoken to your mom today? Your brother called this morning and said he's taking her to lunch."

Emily's throat clenched. "We Facetimed. Yeah, she's pretty happy she gets to go to a fancy restaurant in Beverly Hills."

Emily never quite figured out how to celebrate her mother on Mother's Day, who, in rages, would scream at her she didn't ask to become a mother, and then later, hold Emily for hours sobbing she'd have nothing to live for if she didn't have her baby girl. Her mom had never forgiven Emily for "abandoning her" when her dad offered to help with college. And she made sure to remind Emily of her betrayal in every conversation.

"Come to the table," Amy called from the dining room.

Summer set a bowl of whipped cream next to a larger bowl of mixed berries and proudly announced, "I made this from scratch."

"I mixed the berries," Rain said. "There's strawberries, blackberries, raspberries, and blueberries." She scrunched her face up. "I don't like blueberries, but Mama made me put them in."

"I love berries and whipped cream," Emily said excitedly. "I'm very impressed."

Amy set down the last dish. "We also have creamy parmesan polenta and avocado toast on pumpernickel rye, topped with hard-boiled egg and a sprinkling of sumac."

Even though Emily wasn't a vegetarian, she had grown to love the unusual earthy foods her stepmom made and always looked forward to her cooking. "Wow, this looks delicious. Isn't there some rule though that mothers aren't supposed to cook on Mother's Day?"

"If she left the cooking to me, we'd be having bagels," her father said, helping his mother get settled in her seat.

"Your dad is going to clean up for me." Amy smiled. "Right, honey?"

"I wouldn't have it any other way." He kissed her cheek before sitting down at the small round dining table.

During the meal, Emily's father turned the conversation toward her. "So, how are things going at Enzo's place? Has he made you a manager yet?"

She couldn't help but feel the subtle jab of disappointment from him. Enzo hired Emily five years ago as a favor to her dad, but she knew her father wasn't pleased she hadn't moved on to a real career by now. "Still bartending. I have no desire to go into restaurant management." Emily considered it may impress him to learn about her work on the upcoming fundraiser. "You remember Diego and Todd?"

"Sure," her dad said. "They opened that camp over in Evergreen for at-risk youth, right?"

"Yes, last year. I'm coordinating a fundraiser for them to raise money for a new rec center. Enzo and Isabella have agreed to host it at Josephina's and provide all the food."

"That sounds exciting," Amy said. "So, how are you raising money?"

"I've been reaching out to local business owners and philanthropists, inviting them to purchase tickets to the dinner and donate something of value to the silent auction. So far, we've raised around twenty thousand dollars." Emily glanced at her dad to see his reaction. He bit into his avocado toast.

"That's amazing, Emily," Amy exclaimed. "When is it?"

At least she seems impressed.

"Saturday night."

"How much are the tickets," her dad asked as he finished chewing.

"One-twenty-five a person."

"We'd love to attend and contribute," he said. "What do you think, honey? A night out?" He looked at his wife.

Emily hadn't expected that. Her dad wasn't one to spend money.

"Absolutely!"

"How about you, Mom? Would you like to join us?"

Her grandmother chuckled. "Oh, heavens no. I think that would be a little too much for me. I tire so easily." She patted Emily's hand. "I hope you understand, dear."

"Of course, Grams. I'll send you lots of pictures."

"But I will contribute a little something," her grandmother told her. "I want to support what you're doing."

"That's very generous of you." Even though Emily didn't have the opportunity to grow up around her grandmother, she always seemed genuinely interested in Emily.

"Can we go, Daddy?" Summer asked.

"No, baby girl. It's a grown-up thing. Maybe your mom can arrange a sleepover with your cousins."

Summer and Rain's hopeful faces fell with hard disappointment.

"Hey," Emily said to them, "How about you guys come down soon and we'll spend the day together?"

The girls jumped up and down with excitement. "Can we go to the water park at Elitch Gardens?" Rain asked.

Emily laughed. "It's snowing outside and you want to go to the water park?"

"It won't be snowing in a couple of weeks when they open for the season," Summer informed her. "They just put in a new roller coaster I want to go on!"

"That sounds fun," Emily said. "It's a date then."

"Enzo and Isabella have always empowered people to follow their dreams," her Dad said. "It's no surprise they'd do something like this for their employees."

Ex-employees. And it was my idea.

"I suppose you know he's going to be leading the weekly seminar series after the Symposium Intensive in a couple weeks?"

Emily's chest tightened.

Here it comes.

"Yes, he told me." She reached for more polenta, hoping the topic would change before the inevitable question arose.

"Would you be interested in going?"

Too late.

"Dad, you know it's just not my thing." Her dad first met Enzo at the self-help seminar over a decade ago and periodically tried to get her to attend. But she had no interest in spending a three-day weekend listening to someone lecture her about her life. She didn't tell her dad Enzo said he would cover the cost. She was still trying to figure out how to decline his offer. It was easy to tell her dad no, but her boss was a different story. And she had a stupid schoolgirl crush on Enzo, making it difficult to refuse anything he ever asked of her.

"Yes, I know, I know—it's not your thing." He rolled his eyes. "I just thought you might feel differently with Enzo being one of the leaders."

Emily ignored him as she shoveled food into her mouth.

He continued. "This seminar could give you some focus in your life you seem to be lacking."

Her eyes burned as she held back tears of resentment. She wouldn't have had to drop out of college if her parents had planned for her education like her friends' parents had. She moved to Colorado to attend college because of her dad's offer to help, but once she arrived, she discovered his help never came in the form of cold, hard cash. Paying bills became her priority, and she was unable to balance working late nights with school. She racked up student loans while barely passing any of her classes, so she eventually dropped out.

"I'll figure something out."

"But, when Emily? You're almost twenty-five. This is the time to figure it out. Since you moved out here, you've told me you wanted to be a journalist, a lawyer, even a fashion designer. You're all over the place. It boggles my mind." His voice dripped with condescension.

"I'm just trying to find something I'm passionate about, Dad."

Something that doesn't require a degree, obviously.

"Yes, I know, Emily." He sounded exasperated. "As I've always said, you can be anything you want—you just can't be everything. You need to pick something and stick with it. You're always coming up with some fantastic new career idea and then quickly losing interest."

And therein lay Emily's problem. She had so many things she dreamed of doing. Life offered a plethora of options to choose from, and she had no idea which direction to go.

Four

The black-tie event for the youth-at-risk camp brought out some of Denver's more affluent society. Men donned designer tuxedos, and women showed off stunning evening gowns to the photographers from the Denver Post.

Emily was no exception. Her black Mac Duggal halter dress shimmered with beads and sequins, hugging every curve of her body. With its open back and thigh-high slit exposing her leg, she felt like a movie star. She had spent the afternoon at the salon, taming her wild curls into elegant waves and having her make-up done in preparation for the special night.

While people bid on the silent auction, servers walked around offering champagne and appetizers. Emily, Enzo, Diego, and Todd mingled with the guests until it was time to direct everyone to find their tables for dinner. She was trying not to panic that the band hadn't yet shown up when she spotted the musicians walking through the door.

She greeted them, concealing her stress and subsequent relief. Winding through the tables, she ushered them to the area where, earlier in the day, they had set up their bass and drums next to the restaurant's baby grand piano.

"They're starting to serve dinner now, so we'll have you open with a couple of songs, and then we're going to do a brief welcome and presentation of the check."

"Sounds good," the sax player told her as he pulled out his instrument.

It wasn't until she watched the band members take up their instruments that she realized they were missing the showrunner.

"Where's the piano player?" Her stress level shot back up. As much as she loved the bass and brass, the piano player was the star of the show and a bit of a local celebrity. She hoped their free performance didn't mean only a partial band.

"He should be here any minute," the bass player offered. "He had to take care of something last minute, but he's just around the corner. We can jam a little until he gets here."

Emily took a deep breath as she felt herself relax a bit. "Thank you!"

Spotting her dad and Amy, Emily made her way over to their table. Their giddiness highlighted the fact this wasn't their usual scene.

"Are you guys enjoying yourselves?" She picked up the bottle of wine and refilled their glasses.

"Oh, yes," Amy beamed. "This is so exciting. I feel like we're part of high society."

"We were entertained watching all the wealthy people try to one-up each other at the silent auction," her dad chuckled.

Enzo walked over and shook her dad's hand. "Great to see you, Graham." He took Amy's into his and kissed it. "You look beautiful tonight."

"A classy affair you're putting on here, Enzo," her dad said. "Always so great to visit Josephina's."

Enzo placed his hand on Emily's exposed back, sending chills up her spine. "It's pretty impressive what Emily's done here tonight, isn't it?"

"Yes, it is." Her dad nodded but with just enough hesitation to make Emily feel like he didn't really mean it. "So great of you to open your restaurant and donate all the food and labor."

"That was easy. Emily did the heavy lifting." Enzo subtly stroked his fingers along her skin, leaving trails of goosebumps. "Her dedication and hard work have certainly paid off. She really commits herself when she takes on a project."

"A little different from the Emily I know," her dad looked at her and smiled, "but perhaps she's growing up."

Emily's stomach twisted.

"She most certainly is." Enzo's hand flattened out, its gentle pressure offering silent comfort.

"So, have you convinced Emily to take the Symposium yet?" her dad asked.

Shit.

"I'm working on it," Enzo said. "We'll get her there." He looked at Emily with an assured look of success.

As she so often did, Amy seemed to pick up on Emily's unease and chimed in. "Your dress is gorgeous, Emily. You look stunning."

"Thank you." She heard the keys of the piano and turned to Enzo, eager to leave the table. "Ready? It's almost time."

As The LoDo Dogs played Harry Connick, Jr.'s "A Wink and a Smile," Enzo and Emily made their way toward the back of the dining room until they reached the band. Her heart raced when the familiar man behind the piano sang the last notes to her, ending the song with an actual wink and a dazzling smile.

Enzo stepped in front of them, gesturing for Emily to follow as she stood there frozen, staring in disbelief at the local celebrity whose gaze and roguish grin remained focused on her. She thought she was going to throw up.

Not a bartender, indeed.

Enzo took over the microphone to address the audience. "Thank you, everyone, for coming out tonight to support this wonderful cause. Diego and Todd, can you please come up here?" The crowd applauded as the two made their way to Enzo. Emily broke the stare-down with the piano player and grabbed the large cardboard check propped up against the wall before joining them.

"Since founding the Evergreen Camp last year in the mountains, more than sixty teens have gone through their program," Enzo continued, "and because of your generous donations, we are honored to present this check to them tonight for $22,000 so they can help even more at-risk foster kids who are struggling to find their footing in the world."

Emily tried to calm her racing nerves upon her realization that the man who brought her coffee and spicy soup a week earlier was none other than Dylan Holt, founder of The LoDo Dogs. She stepped forward to present the check to Diego and Todd while everyone stood clapping and the photographer snapped pictures.

Diego picked up the microphone. "Both Todd and I grew up in the broken foster care system. When we met here at Josephina's six years ago, we formed an instant bond. We recognized that while we had been lucky enough to eventually end up with loving families as teenagers, many others fell through the cracks." He choked up.

Todd took over, placing his arm around Diego's back. "We want to provide outlets for these at-risk kids to channel their hurt and anger. This money will allow us to refurbish one of the empty buildings on the property into a rec center. Our mission is to help these kids take responsibility for their lives so they can change the course they're currently on. Really, thank you from the bottom of our hearts. We look forward to seeing all of you at the grand opening in a few months."

Once again, the room erupted into applause. Diego and Todd hugged Emily, leaving the check with her so they could embrace Enzo as well. She stepped back, and the large piece of cardboard hit the drink on top of the piano, spilling onto Dylan's lap. He jumped up, knocking over the bench. Gasps and laughter came from the guests as Enzo, Diego, and Todd turned around to see the commotion.

"Oh, my god!" Emily dropped the check and instinctively stepped toward Dylan, but her foot caught on the edge of the cardboard, causing her to trip and lurch forward.

"Whoa!" He tried to suppress his laughter as he caught her.

Clinging to his body, Emily worked to regain her balance in her four-inch heels until she was looking into the mischievous green eyes of the sexiest piano player in all of Denver.

"So, this is what you're like when you're sober?" He held onto her as she tried to form words.

Enzo addressed the audience again. "Please continue to put in your bids for the silent auction. All proceeds will go directly to the camp. Enjoy the rest of the evening." He picked up the check from the floor and walked over to Emily and Dylan.

Emily stepped out of Dylan's arms, feeling flushed and reeling from her clumsiness.

Enzo looked at her. "Are you okay?"

No! I want to crawl into a hole! "Yes, I'm fine." She hoped to laugh it off. Noticing Diego and Todd's recognition spread across their faces, she said to Dylan, "Come on, let's go get you a towel." She wanted to avoid any conversation in front of Enzo about her and the piano man's previous encounter.

Dylan instructed the rest of the band to continue playing before following Emily. She silently led him through the restaurant to the packed bar on the other side of the open doorway as she sorted through her thoughts and what to say to him.

You're Dylan Holt?!

Thanks for the delivery last week.

You're Dylan fucking Holt?!

She quickly assessed how Stephanie managed the customers sitting around the bar. As Emily walked around and grabbed a hand towel, Stephanie glanced over and smiled confidently. *A natural.*

"Here." Emily handed Dylan the towel and stared at him.

"So, are you surprised?" He pointlessly wiped the dampness on his pants.

Wait.

"Did you know I would be here?"

How?

He seemed to enjoy the bewilderment he was causing. "When you sent me that text inviting me over, your name popped up on my phone. I had you in my contacts to call you back about your email inquiry for tonight's performance. You really didn't know it was me that night?"

Wow. Cocky much?

"No. I had no idea."

"But you said in your email you're a huge fan?"

"Well, I am. I mean, I've seen you guys play a lot. But I've never actually seen you up close. And you don't look the same in person as you do in pictures."

He scowled. "Oh. Are you disappointed?"

"No... I..." Emily was getting flustered. "Can I get you a fresh drink?"

"Sure. I'll take a Jack and Coke. Thanks."

She grabbed the whiskey and soda and began pouring.

"So, having no idea who I was, you let me into your apartment?"

Realizing how desperate she must have appeared, she tried to explain. "You looked familiar to me. I just couldn't place from where."

"Do you often invite over strange yet familiar men that you meet in clubs?"

Irritated at his implication, Emily slammed the glass of ice on the counter, causing other patrons nearby to glance over.

He laughed. "I'm sorry. I'm just teasing you."

She finished mixing and pushed the drink toward him.

He had an amused smile on his face. "Are you going to make one for yourself?"

"I guess I could use a drink right about now." She stirred together an amaretto sour. She was still embarrassed by her behavior at the club and humiliated about the next morning—and now, spilling a drink on him and tripping into him.

He must think I'm a joke.

Enzo walked up. "Emily, do you have the champagne for the boys?" He turned to the piano man and extended his hand. "Enzo Rizzoli."

"Dylan Holt."

"We appreciate you and your band being here tonight, Dylan," Enzo told him. "Sorry about your pants."

"Oh, it's all good," Dylan smiled and gave Emily a wink.

Why does he always wink?

It annoyed her and turned her on at the same time. She was keenly aware of his reputation, and she had no desire to be his next conquest, although she found herself currently having an internal struggle about it.

"Champagne?" Impatience coated Enzo's voice. He watched Emily closely as she grabbed the bottle and set it on the bar. With both men staring at her, Emily stood in uncomfortable silence. Enzo seemed to be waiting for her.

Finally, she picked up her drink and the bottle of Veuve Clicquot. "Sorry again, Dylan. I need to get back in there." She stepped out from behind the bar and headed into the dining room with Enzo.

After the silent auction winners had been announced, the LoDo Dogs played late into the evening, well after her dad and stepmom had gone home. Sitting at a table with Diego and Todd, Emily and Diego were deep in their third bottle of champagne while Todd happily sipped on ginger ale.

"So, any special requests out there?" Dylan asked the thinning crowd from his seat at the piano.

Diego and Todd both looked at Emily, glee lighting up their faces. She knew what they were thinking. "Don't you dare," she warned.

"You know you want to!" Diego's cheeky grin spread across his face.

She shook her head, trying unsuccessfully to hide her laughter. "No, I don't!"

"Nina Simone. 'Sugar in My Bowl,'" Todd yelled to the band. Dylan began playing the first few notes on the piano.

Diego flung his arms out. "It's your karaoke dream."

"Oh, come on, you know you can't help yourself." Todd jumped up from his seat and grabbed her hand, leading her to the band. "Emily wants to sing!"

Laughing, she tried to pull away. The small crowd started clapping and hollering as the rest of the band joined the intro.

"You can't disappoint your fans," Dylan smiled.

Todd handed her the microphone and returned to his table with a look of delighted satisfaction.

Emily had enough alcohol in her to give in to the sultriness of the music. She did her best to sing in a seductive voice as she waltzed through the crowd, hopping from lap to lap. Enzo watched from a table with friends, smiling behind a glass of cognac. She made her way over to him and sat in his lap as she sang about wanting sugar in her bowl. He looked hungry. As she got up, he grabbed her hand, reluctantly letting her go as she sauntered back to the band for the song's conclusion.

Diego and Todd rushed to her as the crowd cheered. "Our Queen!" They both bowed in mock exaggeration.

The band packed up shortly after midnight, and Enzo and Emily walked over to thank them. Enzo handed each musician an envelope. "Thank you again for coming out to play tonight. Everyone really enjoyed your music. There's a little something to show our appreciation, along with a voucher to come back and dine with us any time."

"Thanks, man," they all exclaimed as they accepted Enzo's tip, shaking his hand.

Emily thanked them and shook each of their hands as well. Dylan held onto hers for an extra beat. She felt Enzo reach out and touch her elbow, silently letting her know to walk away with him.

"You did an amazing job tonight, Em," Enzo told her as he led her into his office. "You should be very proud of yourself."

"Thank you. I wish Isabella was here to see it all. It wouldn't have been this successful if it wasn't for her."

"No, this was all you, Emily. She might have had the connections, but you're the one that made it happen."

Silence sat between them as Emily shifted on her heels and looked down, smiling from embarrassment.

"Why do you do that?" he asked.

"Do what?"

"Get embarrassed when someone acknowledges something you've done well?"

She looked down again, giving no response.

"This is why I want you at the Symposium next week," he said. "I want you to get how extraordinary you are."

I don't feel extraordinary.

"I really can't afford to take the time off."

Enzo cocked his head to the side, as if contemplating her words. "This isn't about money. This is about you not wanting to confront what you're most afraid of."

She had no idea what he meant by that. It irritated her, nonetheless. "But it is about money. I count on my tips every weekend just to get me through the month."

"Fine. Let's take care of that right now." He pulled out his wallet and presented her with five one-hundred-dollar bills.

Her stomach dropped. "Enzo, I can't take that."

He walked over to her. "Emily, this is how much I believe in you. You can take this." He picked up her hand and placed the cash inside her palm. "Let's not have any obstacles in your way."

She looked down, avoiding his eyes. "It just feels weird."

"I want this for you, Emily," he replied as he lifted her chin to look at him. "I want to take away your excuses."

Maybe it was the champagne she had earlier or the way he looked at her while holding her face. Butterflies flew into her stomach at his touch, and her breath quickened. His smell was intoxicating. With his face almost touching hers, she thought he might see right through her and discover her inappropriate thoughts about him.

After a moment, he released her and stepped back. "It's been a long day. You should go. I'll wrap up everything here."

Emily nodded as she tried to calm her racing heart and turned to leave.

"You do look stunning tonight," he said as she walked back into the restaurant.

Dylan caught up with her. "A friend of mine is playing at the Crimson Room tonight, and I told him I would swing by. You should join me."

Emily hesitated. She was still rattled by Enzo and a little leery of the womanizing musician in front of her. But it wasn't every day a semi-celebrity invited her out, and he could offer her some much-needed distraction right now.

He grabbed her hand. "Just a quick drink. One song—maybe two."

Dylan's eyes and sexy smile made it hard to decline his offer. "Sure," she relented. "Only because I love the Crimson Room."

"I hope that's not the only reason." His thumb stroked the inside of her palm, and she recalled his words in her apartment, telling her he wanted to take her to her bed.

She looked over her shoulder to see Enzo watching them leave together.

Five

Emily and Dylan headed down Larimer Street and stopped at the tall red door where a big man solemnly stood until he noticed them. "Hey, my man," the bouncer exclaimed as he held up his hand for contact.

"Hey, Maurice… how is it in there?"

"Packed, as usual, buddy. But we got your booth reserved for you." Maurice gave him a big, toothy smile before turning his eyes to Emily. "And who, pray-tell, is this beautiful creature?"

"This is Emily. She works at Josephina's. She hired us to play at a fundraiser there tonight."

"Emily," Maurice reached out and took her hand into both of his. "It is a pleasure to meet you. You two head on down the stairs and have fun tonight." Maurice nudged Dylan with his elbow.

Dylan grabbed Emily's hand as he led her to the booth. She loved the speakeasy vibe of the Crimson Room. It was like being transported back to the prohibition era; high-back velvet chairs, crystal lamps, and jazz music set the retro ambiance. They slipped into a tiny half-circle booth closest to the piano, and the server walked up to take their order.

"I'll have a Jack Daniel's on the rocks, and she would like…" Dylan looked at her for her answer.

"I'll take a Bee's Knees."

"We'll also have a charcuterie board," Dylan told the server. Turning back toward Emily, he asked, "What the hell is a Bee's Knees?"

"A true bartender would know," she told him coyly.

An older gentleman approached their table. "What did you do to land her?"

"Got her drunk," Dylan joked as he reached up to shake hands. "Good to see you, Robert."

Emily cringed inside at the realization that what he said was true.

Dylan explained he met Robert a couple of years ago at Charlie Brown's—an old neighborhood hangout on Capitol Hill.

"Yes, Ma'am," Robert said, "And then he helped me get the gig here." He smiled, taking Emily's hand and kissing the top of it. "I'll play a special song just for you."

"Back off, old man. I've got dibs," Dylan teased.

Emily's heart jumped. She knew she was going down an inevitable path with him, but she had no interest in putting on the brakes now. She needed to get her mind off Enzo.

Robert sat down at the piano and began playing Duke Ellington's "Satin Doll."

"Thanks for the gig tonight," Dylan told her. "A couple of people came up to me, interested in booking corporate parties. And one socialite wants us to play at her daughter's fancy wedding next year."

"That's because you guys are rock stars."

"We weren't the rock stars tonight."

She was suddenly self-conscious about how much she had gotten into the song.

"So, I'm unclear what you do at Josephina's?" he asked. "Are you a manager? An event planner?"

She answered meekly, "No, just a bartender. Diego and Todd are good friends of mine, so I coordinated the fundraiser. We're all like family there."

"Uh-huh."

The server placed water on the table, and Dylan took a drink before asking, "So, is there something going on between you and that Enzo guy?"

The question shocked Emily. "No. Why would you ask that? He's my boss. And married." She sounded like she was trying to convince herself more than Dylan.

He shrugged. "That doesn't mean much to many men. I could see the way he looked at you. He definitely doesn't consider you family."

Emily began to speak but had no idea how to respond. Instead, she took a sip of water.

"I'm glad to hear it's one-sided," he continued. "You make a mean Jack and Coke. I think I may have found my new favorite bar." He winked again.

"One of my many talents," she said with a hint of sarcasm.

His eyes danced at the possibilities. "I bet."

His intense gaze bore through her, making her nerves prickle under her skin.

"So, how long have you been playing in the band?"

"Most of us have been playing together since our senior year of high school, so about six years now, I guess." He sat back in the booth. "But we formed the LoDo Dogs with the drummer three years ago."

"Who came up with that name?

Dylan shrugged. "I did. I wanted something simple to reflect that we're from lower downtown."

"And that men are dogs?"

Dylan lifted his water glass in a toast and smiled.

"Do you ever play here?" she asked, gesturing to the piano.

"Not as much as we used to; maybe once every few months. We're booked up pretty solid for the next six months. We've got regular gigs at Nocturne and Herb's Hideout, along with other shows around the city."

"So, how did I get lucky enough to land you for the fundraiser? On a Saturday night, no less?"

He laughed. "Well, that's kind of a funny story. My mother was supposed to host a fancy birthday party tonight for her best friend, who turned fifty. They've been planning it for almost a year. It was going to be at the Grant-Humphreys Mansion. They were expecting like a hundred and fifty people, I think. Just this ridiculously extravagant party and we were the entertainment."

The server interrupted with their cocktails, setting them down.

"May I?" Dylan asked, pointing to Emily's drink.

"Oh, sure."

"Hmmm... I taste gin, lemon juice, and honey."

"Impressive!"

He laughed. "I was a bartender through college, but never at a fancy enough place where anyone would know what this is."

"Well, that explains a lot," Emily teased. "So, what happened with the birthday party?"

"A couple of weeks ago, my mom stopped over at her best friend's house early in the morning, unannounced, with coffee and pastries. She discovered my dad sitting on the front porch, in his robe, reading the newspaper."

It took Emily a moment to register what he was saying. "Oh, my god."

He took a sip of whiskey. "So, she canceled the whole thing. Sent out formal announcements to everyone, letting them know Debbie was a back-stabbing whore and warned all the women to keep their husbands away from her."

"Wow, I'm so sorry. That's horrible. Your poor mom." Emily couldn't imagine what Dylan was going through. "How are you doing with that news?"

"Oh, I'm fine," he said, chuckling. "My parents have been divorced for twenty years."

Emily was stunned. "Wait… really?"

"Yep."

They stared at each other as their smiles grew bigger and bigger, eventually turning into full-blown laughter.

"So, at what point did you decide you were going to play the fundraiser?" Emily asked.

"Well, I had been sorting through inquiries and honestly called a few of those first. Because, you know… money. But they had already made other arrangements. My mom suggested we do the fundraiser when I mentioned it to her. She liked what it was about and thought it would be good to give back to our community."

"Yay, Mom," Emily cheered.

"Yes. Yay, Mom. I've learned not to argue with her, so I put your number in my phone to call you the next day. Imagine my surprise when the girl I couldn't take my eyes off of in a gay bar texted me to come to her place for a nightcap, and she turned out to be the one who emailed about the fundraiser."

"The girl who made a total fool of herself." She covered her face in embarrassment.

He pulled her hand into his. "The incredibly hot, way out of my league girl who I haven't been able to stop thinking about." He gently kissed her fingertips, sending chills through her body. "After I visited you the next morning and realized you didn't know who I was, I had my mom pretend to be my manager and call you."

"So, you don't really have a manager?"

He shook his head. "Nope."

"And you're not actually gay?"

Dylan laughed. "No, I'm not gay. I covered a shift for my buddy who had a family emergency."

The server interrupted the moment to set their food on the table. Dylan picked up a cracker and topped it with brie and fig jam. "Try this... it's one of my favorite combos." He held it out in front of her mouth, apparently intent on feeding her.

Emily wanted to pinch herself. She couldn't believe she was here with Dylan Holt and that he considered her out of his league. Leaning in, she tried to look sexy as she took a bite. That didn't stop it from falling apart and into her lap. Dylan jumped with surprised laughter. Emily wanted to die.

He picked up the food morsels from her lap and brushed away the remaining crumbs. He casually left his hand lingering where the slit exposed her bare leg. His fingers gently slipped in between the curve of her thigh, leaving Emily trembling inside.

After a few songs, they finished their drinks and food and got up to leave. Dylan walked to the piano and dropped a twenty in the tip jar, nodding to his friend. Grabbing Emily's hand, he guided her up the stairs and out onto Larimer Square. "Thanks for coming with me tonight."

"Thanks for inviting me."

They walked hand-in-hand toward her apartment.

After she keyed in her building code, Dylan held the lobby door open, ushering her inside. "I want to be sure you make it safely to your apartment." He winked.

Ohhhh... what am I doing?

When the elevator doors closed, Dylan grabbed her hips and pushed her up against the wall. His lips immediately closed the space between them—his tongue eagerly devouring her mouth. The slit in her gown allowed him to lift her long leg behind him as his other hand grabbed her ass. Her entire body ignited, and she pulled him in closer.

When they reached the twenty-second floor, she took his hand and led him down the hallway. Stumbling into her apartment, Dylan kicked off his shoes and unbuttoned his pants. He closed the door behind him and grabbed her around the waist. "How do we get your dress off?"

Emily raised her arm, showing him the zipper along the side of her body. He quickly peeled off her gown, letting it crumple to the floor in a sparkling puddle. She was eager to get his pants off, but he pulled her into the kitchen and hoisted her up onto the counter.

"You seem to have a thing for counters," she said as he kissed her neck.

"Easier access."

He took one breast into his mouth and squeezed the other before his hand trailed down and spread her legs open. His fingers slipped inside her silky black panties, sending a jolt of electricity through her body.

He retrieved a small packet from his front pocket. Emily watched with anticipation as he ripped it open and slid the condom onto himself. He pushed her panties to the side, and they both released moans of gratification when he drilled his way in. Reverberating waves of pleasure kept her begging for more each time he slid out and plunged back in deeper.

His hand slid up the back of her neck. He intertwined his fingers with her hair, pulling her head back. Her back arched, her breasts beckoning him. His free hand grabbed her nipple as he buried his face into the crevice between her neck and shoulder. And then he groaned loudly, locking himself into her as he came.

She held him as his whole body quivered in release. His hard breathing warmed her skin as he remained inside of her. She traced her fingers along his back, waiting for him.

When he finally pulled out, he took off the condom. "Where's your trash?"

"Under the sink." She jumped down from the kitchen counter and grabbed his hand. "Come to my bed." She wanted more.

He lifted her hand to his lips. "I wish I could, but you've worn me out. And I have to be up early." He buttoned his slacks and shirt and said, "Let's do this again soon."

And then he left.

As Emily lay in bed alone, staring at the ceiling, she kicked herself for sleeping with Dylan so quickly. *I'm nothing more than another pathetic groupie.*

She closed her eyes and imagined Enzo's hands caressing her body. Guilt and shame washed over her as she brought herself to orgasm.

Six

THE SYMPOSIUM - DAY ONE

Emily was not up for this. It was bad enough that one of the overly enthusiastic volunteers in the hallway made her shut off her phone when she arrived at this ridiculous self-help seminar. But when the middle-aged woman standing outside the double doors to the meeting room told her she couldn't take her five-dollar coffee inside, Emily contemplated turning around and leaving.

Better that than throwing it at her.

Thankful for an aisle seat that would provide a quick escape, she sat down and settled her eyes on one of the whiteboards at the front of the room. She read the words written in perfect penmanship: *"A choice is an act of personal power."*

Looking to the opposite side of the sparse stage that held only a director's chair, she read the message on the second whiteboard: *"You don't know what you don't know."*

What the hell does that even mean?

"Five minutes!"

Glancing back at the familiar voice, she saw Enzo standing in the back of the room. Emily raised her hand in a feeble wave, but he kept his eyes trained forward as if he didn't notice her.

What the hell?

She had tried to back out all week, but he wasn't having it. He told her she was letting her limiting beliefs stand in the way of creating an extraordinary life. He said he cared too much about her to let that continue.

And now he's ignoring me?

Emily looked around at the other poor souls imprisoned with her. The large room housed a couple of hundred people sitting shoulder to shoulder in rows set with the precision of an engineer. It was a diverse group—from suburban soccer moms to big burly men with face tattoos, kids who looked barely out of high school, and people who must have been upwards of seventy years old.

At 9:00 a.m. sharp, a bell rang out, and the back doors shut with an intimidating thud. Volunteers assumed their posts and stood with their hands folded in front of them, blocking the exits. Trapped and freezing, Emily watched an attractive man who appeared to be in his mid-forties ascend the stage. He wore black slacks and a charcoal gray dress shirt, unbuttoned at the top, with his sleeves rolled up. His messy, dark blond hair matched the stubble on his face. Emily loved a man with stubble. Not a full beard. Not a goatee. Just the stubble. Like he had better things to do than waste time shaving.

"Welcome to the first day of the Symposium, a course in transformation." His smooth, British voice broadcast through the wireless mic clipped onto his lapel. "My name is Jack Fletcher, and I am honored to be your leader for the next three days."

Jack explained his commitment to assisting people in having a fundamental shift in their awareness of living a life full of possibility. "By the end of this weekend, you'll have discovered the freedom to be and the power to live your life effectively. Any questions?"

"Yeah, I have a question," a voice yelled from across the room.

"Please stand up and tell us your name and how you found out about the Symposium." Jack nodded to a volunteer who ran over and handed a mic to the man.

"My name is Brian. My wife made me come here. She took this last month, and frankly, she's been driving me crazy ever since. I feel like she's joined a cult or something because she's obsessed with this place. She told me I needed to come here to save our marriage. Is this like a brainwashing thing or what?"

Some people in the audience chuckled, but most were silent, as if they were also worried about what they were getting themselves into. Emily was just annoyed to be crammed into a room with a bunch of strangers hoping to transform their mundane lives.

"Hi, Brian," Jack responded. "First, I want to acknowledge you for being brave enough to stand up and ask your question. Thank you for that." Then he addressed the audience. "How many of you feel forced into being here today by a friend or family member?"

Everyone seemed to squirm in their chairs. A few hands went up.

Emily wanted to raise her hand.

"Okay, got it," Jack said, surveying the room. "If you go talk to the dapper gentleman sitting at the back table, you'll receive a full refund."

Enzo raised his hand to identify himself to the crowd.

No one moved.

"Look, if you aren't here because you choose to be here, this won't benefit you. It will be a waste of your money. So, no hard feelings.

Six-ninety-five is a lot of money to give up for something you're not really into."

Emily felt sick to her stomach.

"And, yes," Jack continued, "we do brainwash you."

More nervous laughter from the crowd.

"We wash your brain of all the rubbish that's been dumped in there over the years. It's going to get pretty bloody uncomfortable. But, if you put the work into it, you will experience a breakthrough in your life. Breakthroughs are uncomfortable. So, if you're not ready for one, please see Enzo at the back table. Not everyone is ready, and that's okay."

Brian sat down while a few other people headed to the back table. The room waited in watchful silence.

"Brian, please stand back up," Jack instructed. "So, you sat down. Does that mean you choose to be here?"

The volunteer handed Brian the microphone again. "I don't have a choice. My wife would be pissed if I left."

"Brian, please leave now," Jack said calmly.

"What?"

"One of the prerequisites for participating in the Symposium is for the participant to choose it for themselves," Jack explained. "Obviously, Brian, you don't choose to be here for you. Staying because your wife will be pissed if you left isn't you making a choice. You won't be able to access the information we present because it's being filtered through you feeling forced to be here. Let's not waste your money and everyone's time. Please leave now."

Brian glared at Jack. Tension suffocated the room.

"Fuck you, man." He dropped the mic on his seat and walked away.

"Anyone else?" Jack asked.

Emily wondered how Enzo would respond if she stood up. *I defi-nitely don't have a choice.*

After a moment of uncomfortable silence, Jack continued. "Okay, let's move on. First, I want to start with an exercise. On my signal, turn to the person next to you and introduce yourself. Tell them a bit about yourself—how old you are, what you do for a living, how you've been wronged in life. Whatever. Just talk to them until I tell you to stop.

"Now, the person doing the listening, grab the piece of paper that's under your seat. I want you to listen to your partner. Don't respond. Don't ask questions. When you find yourself checked out of the con-versation, raise that piece of paper in front of your face. Don't say anything.

"To the person talking, keep talking as if you don't even see the piece of paper—until I say stop. You'll have sixty seconds. Go!"

Emily turned to the guy on her right. She hadn't paid much at-tention to him when he and his friend squeezed in next to her. Now, face-to-face, his startling blue eyes caught her off-guard.

Jesus, he looks like Captain America.

He smiled, causing his eyes to light up even more, slightly disarming her. "Ladies first."

"Wow, thanks," Emily laughed. "Okay, my name is Emily Bisset. I'm twenty-four. I'm a bartender. I live downtown. Let's see... my parents divorced when I was two. I grew up in Southern California with my mom and older brother, but he moved out when he was eighteen. I was twelve, so I pretty much was raised as an only child after that. A couple of years later, my dad remarried and moved to Colorado."

White paper up.

"Ummm... I came out to visit him every summer and winter break. He and my stepmom had two daughters together, so now I'm a big sister. I moved here to go to college, but that didn't really work out as planned."

"Ten more seconds," Jack shouted.

Emily was running out of things to say. It became painstakingly clear she had nothing interesting to share about herself.

"I like to read," she offered. "Anne Rice is my favorite author. I'd be a vampire if I had the choice." She laughed nervously.

Why the hell did I say that? Now he's going to think I'm some kind of goth wannabe.

"Okay, stop!" Jack commanded.

You could hear quiet laughter and chatter throughout the room as everyone brought their attention back to the Symposium leader.

"Now, to the person listening, if you held up the piece of paper while your partner was talking, I want you to tell them why. Be honest. That's what we're all here for. You can't have a breakthrough if you're not honest. Were you thinking about something else? Distracted by something in the room? You'll have ten seconds. Go on."

Her listening partner took a deep breath and chuckled. "I was totally distracted by how pretty you are."

Is he hitting on me? Seriously?

"I'm sorry... just trying to be real here!"

Jack spoke again. "Okay, speakers, without addressing what their reason for checking out was, tell them how it made you feel when they held up the paper. Ten seconds. Go."

Emily spoke up. "Well, it made me self-conscious, like I wasn't interesting enough, so you stopped listening."

"I can assure you that was not the case."

"Switch!"

"Okay, I'm Clay Olson. I'm in Information Technology just up the road in the Denver Tech Center. Kind of always been a computer geek."

You don't look like a computer geek. You look like you belong in a Marvel movie. Well, I guess Steve Rogers started out as a geek, but then he got superpowers. Makes perfect sense, actually.

"I turned twenty-six at the beginning of this month. Um... grew up in Colorado Springs next door to this guy." He motioned to the redhead sitting beside him. "His brother was my best friend, but he passed away from a brain aneurysm when we were in high school."

Oh, shit.

"So, that sucked. Uhhh... what else? I like to go rock climbing..."

White paper up.

I don't see a ring, and he's flirting with me, so I'm assuming he's not married. I wonder if he has a girlfriend? Wait... is he flirting with me? I guess telling someone they're pretty isn't necessarily considered flirting. The leader did say to be honest. He's totally not my type. Clean-cut athletes don't do it for me—even if they do look like Captain America. Give me Damon Salvatore any day... or night. Maybe I am a goth wannabe?

"Time's up," interrupted Jack. "Same as before; listeners, tell them why you checked out of the conversation."

Emily felt bad for holding up the paper most of the time, but she wasn't about to admit what was really going through her mind.

"I was just thinking how awful it was about your friend. I can't imagine losing someone like that."

"Speakers, let them know how that made you feel."

"Oh, yeah... thanks. I thought you just found me boring."

Well, kind of.

"So, how was that?" Jack asked the crowd.

People laughed, blurting out answers.

"Awkward!"

"Interesting!"

"Telling!"

"Brilliant," said Jack. "We need to first acknowledge to ourselves how we listen to others. Most people get so caught up in their own heads, they aren't even hearing what the person talking to them is saying. Do you ever feel like no one gets you? Like really gets who you are as a human being?"

"Yes," came the agreement from the crowd.

That got Emily's attention. She never felt like anyone knew the real her, even Addison, Diego, and Todd.

Jack continued. "Everyone is already listening through their own filters that were formed through their experiences and upbringing. And those filters profoundly influence our relationships with people, circumstances, and even ourselves. But having an awareness of these filters, and acknowledging them, can bring freedom. And that can alter our life dramatically. So, let's unpack all that now, shall we?"

Jack had them break into small groups of four. Emily and Clay partnered up with his friend, Lucas, and a young blonde girl sitting next to them named Tonya. They spent the next five hours dissecting the topic as the seminar weaved from small groups to Jack speaking and individuals standing up to share their life stories and receive coaching.

Finally, it was time for their ninety-minute meal break, the only meal break of the day, and Emily was starving. The four of them decided to stick together and go as a group.

"So, Tonya, what do you do? Are you in school?" Emily asked while they were eating. She always hated that question when directed at her, but it spilled out of her mouth now absentmindedly.

"I work part time at Dillard's in Park Meadows Mall. I'm finishing my general ed at Arapahoe College, but I'll be starting at Denver University in the fall."

Tonya had a mom-like presence about her that Emily found somewhat disorienting on a twenty-year-old.

"Oh, cool," Lucas responded. "I go there. What will you be studying?"

"Social Work. What about you?"

"Psychology. Going into my last year. I was playing football at Kansas State, hoping to go pro. But I injured my shoulder during my sophomore year. Lost my scholarship, so I had to move back home. Luckily, I was able to transfer to DU, and Clay let me move in with him."

"Wow, I'm sorry to hear that," Emily said.

"Me too," Clay scoffed. "I have to listen to him and his girlfriend sweet-talk each other every night on the phone."

"Dude!" Lucas punched him in the arm. "Seriously, though, he's my superhero. Really stepped up when I lost my brother."

The table got quiet. Lucas had broken down crying about his brother during the seminar, but he bit into his cheeseburger now, seemingly okay while Clay patted his back.

Emily wanted to lighten the mood. "Well, he does kind of have this Captain America vibe going on."

Lucas yelled out, crumbs falling from his mouth. "I'm always saying that!"

Clay shook his head, laughing. "I guess my secret's out."

When they returned from lunch, Jack focused on how people experience their lives based on the context they grew up in. "How many of you are angry at your parents for suffocating you? Feeling like they held you on a tight leash? Loved you too much?"

About half of the audience raised their hands, including Emily, as she thought about her overly protective mother.

"Okay, got it," he acknowledged. "Now, how many of you are angry at your parents for abandoning you, not having any interest in your life? No rules or structure to guide you?" He paused. "Just didn't love you enough?"

The other half raised their hands.

Emily also wanted to raise hers, thinking about her dad. Her mom kept Emily from him because he was a weed-smoking atheist and barely paid child support. It wasn't until he left California that he took her mom to court for visitation rights. But, when her sisters were born during Emily's teenage years, they had become her dad's world, and Emily felt his interest in her wane. He hadn't been part of her life much when she was young, thanks to her mother, so she knew she shouldn't fault him for wanting to be a better parent the second time around.

"Don't you see? Our parents will always screw us up," Jack laughed, which allowed everyone else to as well. "Seriously, look around. We all blame our parents. No matter what, they can't do right. They either suffocate us or abandon us. But what you need to understand is that your parents were just being human, and you chose to interpret it the way you did. Your parents lived within the context they knew. They created a life out of their past experiences.

"This is your life. You created it. This is your universe. It's not your parents' fault if you're not happy with how your life has unfolded to this point. No matter what, whether they suffocated or abandoned you, only you are responsible for your life. You don't get to blame anyone. You do, however, get to choose whether you are going to live an extraordinary life."

Seven

E mily didn't get much sleep with all the new concepts rolling around in her head. She wasn't sure she had it in her to return for a second fifteen-hour day. But when Enzo's text came over early Saturday morning stating how exciting day two would be, she reluctantly pulled herself out of bed, hoping she'd have enough time to stop at The Market to grab a cappuccino. She quickly applied some mascara and lip gloss and headed out the door with wet hair.

Emily walked past the long line of people waiting to order coffee and stepped up to the counter where Addison was securing the lid on a to-go cup.

"Perfect timing... large double cap to go."

"You're the best!"

"I know." Addison blithely flipped her dark hair. "So, how's the seminar?"

"Interesting," Emily admitted. "You'd probably love it. It's totally your kind of thing."

"I'll check it out after you've given me your full review." Addison grabbed a croissant from the basket on the counter and handed it to Emily. "Here, take this. It's a day old. I'm getting ready to toss them."

"Thanks. You might need to take on a second job, though, if you want to do it. Or ask your parents for a belated birthday present. It's ridiculously expensive."

Addison laughed, dismissing the suggestion. "There's no way my parents would pay for something like that. As far as they're concerned, I should only ever go to synagogue and listen to my rabbi. How much is it?"

"Seven hundred dollars."

Addison's eyes practically popped out of her face. "Are you kidding? Enzo paid that on top of the five hundred he already gave you?"

"I'm guessing he didn't have to actually pay for me since he'll be leading the series that follows. Maybe he gets freebies."

"That man has a thing for you, for sure."

"No... it's not like that. Both he and Isabella wanted me to do the Symposium."

"Emily, come on. You can't be that naïve. I've seen how you guys flirt with each other every time I stop by."

"I don't flirt with him," Emily protested. "He's just a generous person—and my dad's friend."

Addison shook her head with a patronizing smile. "Okay, Em. Whatever you want to tell yourself. Just be careful."

Emily rolled her eyes.

"I still can't believe you slept with Dylan Holt," Addison said. "Have you heard from him?"

"Nope." A lump formed in Emily's throat at the sting of him ghosting her. "I knew what I was getting into with him."

Addison looked at the ever-growing line of customers. "I better get back over there and help. We're swamped, and it doesn't look good when the manager is slacking."

"I have to take off for the seminar, anyway. Thanks for the coffee and croissant. Love you."

"Love you, too!"

***

The Symposium - Day Two

Emily found Clay, Lucas, and Tonya waiting inside the halls of the seminar center, all looking a little bleary-eyed. They walked into the meeting room together and sat in the same seats as the day before. She wrapped herself in her cozy red throw blanket, determined not to freeze today in her cute sundress.

Jack immediately dove into how identities get created. He said the process begins in childhood, and people gradually adopt practices and characteristics throughout the years that make up their personality.

"So, when you begin to see that your identity was put together in response to how you think something shouldn't be, you find freedom in saying who you are and what you know is possible."

He scanned the room as he let what he had been saying sink in. He then stepped off the stage and walked up the aisle, stopping next to Emily.

"Emily," he said, smiling as he glanced at her name badge, "can you please tell us what identity you've created for yourself?"

Fuck.

She stood up. "Ummm... I'm not sure?"

"Let's start with the basics. Friendly or aloof?"

"Friendly."

"Shy or outgoing?"

"Pretty outgoing, I guess." *But not right now. I want to sit down.*

"Intimidated easily?"

"No."

"Do you think you intimidate people?"

A college dropout bartender who hasn't accomplished anything? Doubtful. "No."

"Really? You must know you're a beautiful young woman. Beauty can be intimidating to some people."

Emily shifted uncomfortably and looked down at the floor, hoping it would swallow her up.

"Do you think there's something wrong with acknowledging you're beautiful?"

She was keenly aware all eyes in the room were on her.

When she didn't respond, he said to her, as more of a command than a request, "Emily, can you please look up at me?"

She lifted her head and found his eyes.

"I'm going to take a guess that somewhere along the way, you got it into your head that acknowledging your beauty isn't acceptable; that it would make you unlikable. And you want to be liked. Would you agree with that?"

Even though his question was mortifying, she could see nothing but kindness and compassion in his eyes as he stared back into hers.

"There's nothing wrong with wanting to be liked, by the way," he said. "It's a basic human desire. It's when you give it power that you lose yours."

He held her gaze momentarily before speaking again. "You really want people to like you, don't you?"

It's all she ever wanted. And she felt like no one really did.

"Of course," she whispered through her constricting throat.

"Got it."

The silence in the room was deafening as Emily grappled with her admission in front of these strangers and her boss who stood in the back of the room.

"Emily, will you join me on stage for an exercise?"

Oh, god. What the fuck? "Ummm... okay."

She wanted to flee from the room to a world that didn't ask her to bare her soul. But instead, she followed Jack down the aisle toward the stage. The weight of the attention from the audience threatened her ability to walk as she concentrated on putting one foot in front of the other.

When they ascended the stairs, he turned to her and said, "I'm going to demonstrate for you what I want you to do, and then you do the same. Here we go."

He yelled out, scaring her, and then ran across the stage, waving his hands above his head, screaming wildly, "Hot tea! Want some hot tea? I really need to give you my hot tea!"

The audience erupted into laughter along with Emily.

He regained his calm corporate-like composure and stepped off the stage. "Your turn."

Fuck, no. "I'm not doing that," she said, laughing.

"Why not?"

Emily stared at him like he was out of his mind.

"Are you afraid of not looking good?"

Yes!

"And then maybe people won't like you?"

She stopped smiling.

"Maybe you need another demonstration." He called out to a woman in the front row. "Shalette, will you please step up to the stage and show Emily what I would like her to do?"

"Sure!" Shalette sprung out of her chair and ran up. With her arms flailing and her colorful beaded braids swinging all around her face, she yelled exuberantly about hot tea.

Everyone cheered.

"Thank you, Shalette." Jack helped her off the stage and turned his attention back to Emily. "Look how much everyone likes Shalette. Now that we've established people will still like you, can you please do that for me?"

As much as Emily admired the uninhibited gregariousness of people like Shalette, she couldn't imagine herself acting like that.

"No, I can't...," she said with an awkward smile.

"Why not?"

She searched for the words. "It's just not me."

"Interesting." Jack stared at her for a moment while he seemed to be figuring out a new approach. "Well, you do sort of ooze sensuality, don't you?"

Emily looked down at her faded, form-fitting black jersey-knit dress and tan, bare legs. She wasn't sure if he had just complimented her or mocked her.

"Let's try something else. I want you to walk across the stage, in your sexiest walk, and say in your sexiest voice, 'Hot tea! Want some hot tea? I really need to give you my hot tea.'"

"Seriously?"

"Seriously."

She glanced at the back of the room and saw Enzo standing there watching without expression. The room was dead silent as the audience stared at her with anticipation. More than anything, she wanted to get off the stage without humiliating herself.

This I can do.

"Okay." She took a deep breath, channeling her performance at the fundraiser, and felt as if another persona took over. Kicking off her flip-flops, she sauntered across the stage, and in her sexiest voice, she breathed out, "Hot tea... I have hot tea..." She scooped her long hair from her shoulders onto the top of her head as she walked toward Jack, her focus locked on him. "Want some hot tea?" Letting her loose curls cascade freely, she slid her hands seductively along her lithe body as she slowly crouched down and looked longingly into his pale eyes. She knew she was giving quite a performance, and it was exhilarating. Inches from his face, she lowered her voice. "I really need to give you my hot tea."

It was silent for a moment as she continued to stare at him, caught up in the moment as if no one else was in the room.

Finally, he spoke. "Bloody hell."

The audience erupted into laughter again, along with a few hoots and whistles.

He stepped up onto the stage, offering his hand to help her stand. Everyone applauded. Emily looked at Enzo, who was now grinning ear to ear.

"My god, even I didn't expect that," Jack said.

The crowd cheered again while Emily reverted to being embarrassed, which Jack noticed.

His expression turned more serious. "Emily, you stood down there as someone who acts oblivious to her sensuality, but you're not, are you? You're like a snake in the grass."

"What? Are you saying I'm evil?"

"No, of course not. I mean, you sneak up on people. You lie low until you see the perfect moment to strike, and they're so caught off-guard, they can't defend themselves from your bite."

"I don't intentionally hurt people."

"I'm sure you don't. A snake isn't lying in the grass looking for someone to bite. A snake is just being a snake, slithering around. But when something—or someone—enters its orbit, the snake goes into protective mode. And to protect itself, it uses the advantage it has of the element of surprise. Intentional or not, people get hurt by snake bites."

Emily was trying to understand what he was saying and how it applied to her.

"You are a powerful woman, Emily. A force to be reckoned with. And yet, you hold back. Why is that? Are you ashamed of your sensuality?"

She immediately thought of when her mom dragged her to an emergency meeting with the church elders once she discovered Emily was sleeping with her boyfriend at seventeen. They were worried about her salvation because her choice to be sexually promiscuous was separating her from God. Her mom had sneered at Emily's short skirt and cropped top. *"Look at you. You look like a walking advertisement for hire."*

Tears sprang into her eyes.

"Why do you feel shame about who you are?"

"Church, I guess."

"Ah, church. The original institution of guilt. Can you imagine what life would be like for you if you acknowledged who you are without shame? If you lived like that confident, unabashedly sexy woman that just walked across that stage?"

A small smile escaped the corners of her mouth as she contemplated what he was saying.

"Life would open up for you!" He beamed. "Right?"

Her smile spread at his enthusiasm.

"Be authentic to yourself and embrace your sensuality, Emily. Hiding who you are makes you a snake in the grass. Acknowledging your beauty does not make you evil. After all, your God created you that way, did he not?"

Embarrassed still, she let out a small laugh and nodded in agreement.

"Stop acting like a little girl who doesn't know what she's doing. You are very much a woman who is aware of her actions. It's time you own them."

She knew he was right. She knew the game she played—and he was calling her out on it.

Jack continued. "Pretending to be oblivious to who you are is holding you back. It's time to stop playing small." His eyes were full of delight. "You need to play big. Get out on the field and shine. Can you do that?"

"I'll try."

"Remember the wise words of Yoda. There is no 'try.' You either will or you won't. Which is it?"

"I will."

"You got it?"

"Got it." Emily threw out the phrase she kept hearing everyone repeat over the weekend. With a big smile, she hoped she looked confident enough to get off the stage.

"I believe we just had a breakthrough. Thank you, Emily." Jack helped her step down. "Everyone, please thank Emily for being brave and putting herself out there."

The applause erupted again, and people congratulated her as she walked back to her seat. She was still a little perplexed by what just transpired, but she felt amazing. There was a shift within her. She felt powerful.

After returning to her chair, Clay nudged her shoulder, smiling as he looked straight ahead and said, "Fire."

Eight

E mily grabbed her phone from the nightstand to read the early Sunday morning text.

Hey, sexy. How did you sleep?

That's new.

Very little.

I had to stop at the restaurant this morning to take care of a few things. Can I give you a ride to the Symposium today? I'll buy breakfast.

Emily

Free gas and food? I'm in!

Enzo

I'll be there in 30 minutes.

When she exited her building, she found Enzo standing next to his black BMW.

"Good morning," he said as she approached him. He placed his hand on her hip and leaned in to kiss her cheek before opening the passenger door. "I like your skirt."

A nervous flutter coursed through her. "Thanks for picking me up."

As they drove South on I-25, they discussed the various aspects of the Symposium. Enzo wanted to know her thoughts on everything. She was relieved he didn't mention her performance on stage.

They pulled up to Urban Egg—a popular breakfast spot around the corner from the seminar center. There was a line out the door.

"That doesn't look good," Emily said.

"A friend of mine runs the place. I called ahead."

When the host sat them down at a window table, Emily commented, "This is nice. I probably would have just grabbed a Pop-Tart on my way out."

The server was rushing by when she abruptly stopped and asked, "Coffee?"

"Please," Enzo confirmed.

She turned over their empty mugs and poured the coffee, nodding toward the other side of the table. "There's cream in that small pitcher next to the sugar."

After she rushed off, Enzo asked Emily, "You like cream, right?"

The glint in his eye alerted her this wasn't an innocent question.

"I do," she responded, probably more provocatively than she should have.

He smiled as he poured the cream into her cup. "By the way, you were amazing up on stage yesterday."

Shit.

Embarrassed, Emily let out a soft laugh and looked down as she wrapped her hands around the warm coffee mug. They hadn't ever had a meal alone together like this, and suddenly, the pressure to banter with him left her mouth dry.

Enzo reached for his mug sitting next to hers. He extended his finger out to caress the back of her hand, sending a shiver up her arm. "There you go again, not owning who you are."

The server returned to take their order. Emily picked up the menu and quickly scanned it over. "I'll have the pancake flight with the strawberry cheesecake, the Hawaiian, and the cinnamon swirl, please."

Enzo seemed amused by her order. "I'll have the classic eggs benedict with melon and prosciutto."

When Emily reached for her coffee, Enzo tapped her fingers. "You need to break this nail-biting habit. Your hands look like they belong to an insecure little girl, not the powerful woman you are."

Emily instinctively pulled her hand back. She had always been self-conscious of her fingernails and hated that he noticed them.

"So, Isabella and Chloe come home tomorrow?" She took a sip of coffee and hoped the conversation would offer a distraction from the fluttering in her stomach.

"They do. I can't wait to see my little princess."

"I'm sure it will be nice to have them home."

Enzo stared at her from across the table and let out a deep sigh. "I'll let you in on a secret. Isabella and I have more of a business relationship."

This shocked Emily. She never got that vibe from them.

"Really?"

Enzo leaned forward, crossing his arms on the table, and looked straight into Emily's eyes. "Really."

Her breath quickened.

So much for distraction. "I... I'm sorry."

"Don't be." He sat back. "The truth is, we've never really been in love. Not the kind of knock-you-off-your-feet kind of love, anyway. When we met in college, we shared a similar vision. In that sense, we've been very good for each other. Helped each other accomplish some pretty big goals. And will continue to do so. But we just discreetly do our own thing."

Is he saying... "You guys have an open marriage?"

Enzo shrugged and sat back. "Why do you think she's been in Rhode Island for so long?"

"I thought she was visiting her parents?"

"And her high school sweetheart."

The server set their food down as Emily sat in disbelief.

"Eat up," Enzo said. "We have to get going."

When they finished, he paid the bill and rushed her out to the car. "We need to hurry. It starts in ten minutes."

He climbed into the driver's seat and turned toward her.

As Emily started to thank him for breakfast, he reached his hand to her face and placed his thumb in the corner of her mouth.

"You have cinnamon glaze on you... from your pancakes." He slowly wiped it away and licked his thumb clean as he began driving.

***

The Symposium - Day Three

Making it inside just before they closed the doors, Emily spotted her new friends. Clay had laid his jacket across her chair, saving it.

"Sleep in?" he asked as she slid in next to him.

"No. Breakfast with my boss."

He glanced at the back of the room where Enzo stood in position, overlooking the participants. "Must be weird having your boss be one of the leaders?"

"A little," she mumbled as she took a sip of her water and wrapped her blanket around her, trying not to think of Enzo's thumb in her mouth.

It was the final day of the weekend. Emily was exhausted and exhilarated at the same time. It had been a long three days, emotionally charged days with little sleep. But she was thankful to have befriended Clay, Lucas, and Tonya. They stuck together through all the breaks to continue their intense conversations. She already felt she had formed a close bond with the three of them in the short time since they had met.

As the day neared the end, Jack asked for a volunteer who loved berries. Clay's hand shot up, so Jack called him to the stage.

"Thanks for coming up here, Clay. Have a seat." He motioned for him to sit in the director's chair. "Now, let's pretend these rubber balls are berries. The red one is a strawberry. The blue one is a blueberry. Which one do you choose?"

"The strawberry."

"Why?"

"Because I love strawberries."

"Great. Why?"

Clay seemed slightly confused. "Because I like how they taste."

"Wonderful. Why did you choose the strawberry?"

Clay chuckled. "Because it's my favorite kind of fruit."

"Got it. Why did you choose the strawberry?"

Clay looked lost. "Because my grandma used to grow them when I was a little boy, so they remind me of her."

"That's very sweet. Why did you choose the strawberry?" continued Jack relentlessly.

Clay shifted in his seat. "Because I want a strawberry," he said, annoyance creeping into his voice.

"Ah... now we're getting somewhere. Strawberry or blueberry?"

Clay looked him squarely in the eye and said sternly, "Strawberry."

Jack looked right back at him. "Why?"

Clay was silent for a moment with obvious frustration. Finally, he said in an exasperated tone, "Because I just choose the strawberry."

"Bingo!" Jack exclaimed.

"What?"

"Everything else you said are reasons, and reasons are based on considerations. You deciding what you think is best based on the reasons you've considered is not a choice. A choice is choosing regardless of the reasons and considerations."

Murmurs came from the audience. Some people were nodding their heads as if they got it. Others still looked a little bewildered.

"Let's try this again." Jack set the red ball down and held the blue one in front of Clay. "Now, choose the blueberry."

Clay tilted his head and raised an eyebrow. "I don't like blueberries."

"I didn't ask if you liked them. Choose the blueberry."

"Okay, I choose the blueberry."

"Why?"

"Because it's my only choice, apparently," Clay snickered.

"That's a reason, not a choice. Choose the blueberry."

After a moment, Clay's demeanor changed as an understanding smile spread across his face. "I choose the blueberry."

Jack returned his smile. "Why?"

"I've looked at and considered my reasons for not wanting the blueberry, and regardless of those reasons, I choose the blueberry."

"Congratulations, you've finally made a choice." Jack smiled with satisfaction as the audience erupted into applause.

He wrote on the whiteboard: *A decision is a result of considering your options,* above the words that had been staring at them all weekend, encircling them together: *A choice is an act of personal power.*

"To choose the life you want to have, you first need to choose the life you currently have. Because once you realize you have an actual choice in the matter, you get to stand in a place of what's possible. That is what we mean when we talk about possibility."

At the close of the Symposium, Jack brought Enzo up on stage to formally introduce him.

"I'm heading back to my day job in New York as a real estate attorney, but I'm leaving you in excellent hands for the next six weeks. I've known Enzo Rizzoli for the better part of a decade. He is committed to making sure each and every one of you continues to have breakthroughs in your life.

"Go out this week and put into practice what you've learned here, and then come back next Tuesday night ready to begin the real work under Enzo's leadership."

When they dismissed everyone, people rushed to the stage to talk to both men. Emily said goodbye to her newfound friends and waited off to the side to thank Jack while Enzo engaged in conversations.

She listened to people praise Jack for his coaching over the weekend and noticed how he gave every person his undivided attention. He seemed genuinely interested in them, not rushing any conversations.

When the last person left his queue, he approached Emily. "Ah, the snake in the grass."

She smiled. "You know, that doesn't sound very flattering."

"Really? Snakes are symbolic for healing and transformation. Sounds pretty flattering to me."

"Well, according to my pastor back home, snakes are symbolic of evil because the serpent tricked Eve into eating the forbidden fruit, condemning humanity to a life of sin."

"I suppose it depends on how you look at it," Jack said. "The way I see it, Eve finally made her own choice by accepting the succulent gift. But with choice comes personal responsibility, and it's much easier to blame that wretched woman in the garden when anything goes wrong."

"Interesting perspective."

"Personally, I'm more of a Lilith fan. Now there's a woman who unabashedly embraced her power."

Emily laughed. "Yeah, they didn't teach us about Lilith in Sunday school."

"I imagine they didn't. She doesn't fit their agenda."

"So, I'm confused... is being a snake in the grass a good thing or a bad thing?"

"It's neither. It just is what it is. The interesting thing about snake venom is it's both a deadly poison and an antidote. The difference is in how it's used." Jack looked at her affectionately, as if considering something. "Emily, I'd like to give you some homework. Would that be okay with you?"

"Sure."

"Great, I have a redeye flight to catch right now, so I need to head to the airport. Can I text you this week?" He pulled out his phone.

"Okay," she said, surprised he would take the time to continue to work with her.

He asked for her number and told her to smile so he could snap a quick picture to put into his contacts.

"It was a tremendous pleasure meeting you, Emily. Thank you for the contribution you brought to the seminar."

Enzo came up to them and placed his hand on Emily's back. "Can you give me five minutes with Jack, and then we'll head out?"

"Of course."

She sat down and closed her eyes while waiting for the two men to finish talking. She was exhausted and wanted nothing more than to climb into her bed.

"Ready, Sleeping Beauty?"

The late-night drive back to her apartment was quiet except for Jeff Beck's hedonic guitar coming through the stereo. Emily stared out the window as she struggled to keep her eyes open.

"We're here." Enzo's hand stroked her exposed thigh to wake her. He came around and opened the door, helping her out.

"I'm so proud of you, Emily," he said, bringing her into his arms. "Watching the transformation in you this weekend has been profound."

She breathed in his intoxicating scent. He rested his cheek against hers. She could feel his hot breath in her ear. The back of her neck tingled with apprehension. Then his lips pressed gently on her cheek, grazing closer to her mouth.

She was trembling, a thrilling mixture of panic, exhaustion, and exhilaration.

And then his lips were on hers. Slow and sensual. His tongue lapping at them, begging for hers, until it demanded it. And she succumbed. Fully and passionately.

But then Isabella flashed across her mind. *Isabella*, who treated her like family. *Isabella*, who had been nothing but kind to her.

She pulled back. "I'm sorry. I can't do this."

As much as she had fantasized about this moment, she hadn't believed it would actually happen. She assumed their flirtations were innocent play. It hadn't occurred to her that Enzo would act on it, especially after all these years.

"I can't do this to Isabella." She broke away, filled with shame.

"I told you... she has her own indiscretions."

She wanted to believe him, despite the alarm sounding in her head. She couldn't think clearly.

"I'm sorry." She pushed past him and ran into her building to escape the temptation of the forbidden fruit.

Nine

Emily's stomach dropped when she walked into the restaurant Monday afternoon.

"Darling," Isabella exclaimed, rushing to embrace her. "I just got back into town. Enzo has been filling me in about everything that happened."

I bet not everything.

"Welcome home." Emily returned her warm embrace and glanced at Enzo, who was making funny faces at baby Chloe, causing her to burst into giggles.

"I'm sorry I missed the fundraiser and didn't get a chance to talk to you before I left," Isabella told her. "It was last-minute, and I just had so much to take care of before leaving."

"It's okay," Emily said. "Did you have a good trip?"

She pushed away the memory of Enzo's mouth on hers and wondered about the man from Isabella's past.

"I so wish I could have been there, but it sounds like you had everything under control. And you raised almost $25,000?"

"Thanks to you," Emily said. "I can't believe the silent auction brought in almost three grand."

"I'm so proud of you," Isabella clasped both of Emily's hands. "Listen, I have something important I want to talk to you about. Enzo told me you're not working tomorrow. Are you available for lunch?"

I'm a horrible person.

"Of course. What time?"

"Let's say noon at Bazille in Nordstrom at Cherry Creek. I do get tired of this place." Isabella smiled at Enzo. "No offense, my love."

"None taken. I'm sure you ladies will have a good time."

Oh, god... maybe they're actually polyamorous?

"We're taking off," Enzo told Emily. "Do you need anything from me before I leave?"

An explanation. "No, I'm good."

And with that, Emily watched the beautiful little family walk out the door.

***

Emily steamed the sparkling evening gown and carefully reattached the tags with the tagging gun she purchased on Amazon for less than twenty dollars. Even with the extra money Enzo had given her to cover her lost tips, she was still scraping to pay her bills.

As luck would have it, Isabella wanted to meet at the same department store where Emily had purchased the gown. It looked brand new; no one could even tell she had worn it. And thanks to Nordstrom's stellar customer service, she was confident she would get her four hundred dollars back.

The clerk gave Emily a dirty look when she told her it didn't fit right—clearly onto her scheme—but still handed over the cash, which was all that mattered. Emily pocketed the money and headed towards the restaurant.

While waiting for Isabella, she browsed the clothing racks nearby. But knowing their luxury prices were well beyond her reach only depressed her.

"Hello, darling!"

Isabella and Emily walked into Bazille and sat at a table near the bank of windows overlooking the Cherry Creek Shopping District.

"So, tell me about your weekend at the Symposium," Isabella said. "What did you think about it all?"

"It was amazing. A lot to take in. But I enjoyed it and made some new friends."

The memory of Enzo's tongue caressing hers sparked nervous energy throughout her entire body. She tried to swallow down her guilt as she smiled back at Isabella.

"It is a lot to take in. I'm so happy you enjoyed it. Transformation doesn't happen overnight. It's a journey. But now that you have a new space to operate in, you'll begin to see things differently."

Do you and Enzo really operate in the space of an open marriage?

"Plus, Jack Fletcher makes everything easier to swallow, doesn't he? Like a spoonful of sugar." Isabella smiled lasciviously.

Emily laughed at Isabella's unexpected display of lust.

'She has her own indiscretions.'

"Yes, he most certainly does," Emily agreed.

After the server delivered their food, Isabella eagerly began sharing her plans with Emily. "As you know, before I married Enzo, I was planning to become an event planner. I got my degree in Hospitality, but Enzo had this dream to open a restaurant. So, that's what we focused on in those first few years. It took so long to get Josephina's off the ground and running successfully and then Chloe was born. But now that she's a year old, I refuse to wait any longer to pursue my dream. At thirty-three, I'm not willing to let any more time go by."

Emily thought she detected a glimmer of resentment in Isabella's tone and facial expression, but it was quickly concealed as Isabella took a sip of her Prosecco.

"So, I've decided it's time to pursue my passions now, and I'm interviewing nannies."

Oh, god... is she going to ask me to be their nanny? "That sounds exciting," Emily said with slight trepidation.

"It is! I'm hoping to hire one by the end of the week."

This can't be happening.

"Anyway, I've been talking with an old friend from Rhode Island who's an event planner. We spent some time together while I was there, and he let me pick his brain."

High school sweetheart?

"I've decided to open my own event planning business. I think there's a large market here for it. I'll be focusing on smaller events at first—birthday parties, baby showers—that kind of thing before eventually tackling corporate events and maybe even weddings."

"That sounds awesome. I think you'll be great at it." Emily's breath was constricting as she waited for the question.

"Thanks. I already have a couple of things lined up, and my Rhode Island friend has offered to coach me along the way."

I bet.

"But I'm going to need some help. An assistant. And I'd love for that person to be you."

Not at all what I was expecting. Relief washed over Emily as the tension in her shoulders melted away. "Really?"

"Yes! You did such a fantastic job coordinating the fundraiser. I think this could be a great career choice for you, eventually. I know being an assistant isn't glamorous; you'll be running errands for me and helping with set up and tear down. I can only pay you minimum wage, but it's a great way to learn the industry and gain experience. Like an internship. What do you think?"

Emily wasn't sure she'd have time to take on a second job. She knew Isabella had high standards and could be demanding. And then there was the fact she'd made out with her husband, which complicated things. But Emily did enjoy organizing the fundraiser.

Maybe doing events could be my thing?

It seemed like fate had brought this all together.

A sick, twisted fate, but nevertheless, fate.

"What about me working at the bar? Will it conflict with that?"

"No, I promise," reassured Isabella. "I'll utilize you during the days, and then Enzo can have you at night."

Emily almost choked on her pizza. "It sounds like a great opportunity," she replied once she could swallow. "I'd love to."

When they finished lunch, Isabella told Emily she wanted to celebrate their new arrangement by buying Emily an outfit. She explained to Emily how it's essential to dress for success and not always try to be sexy.

But I just spent an entire weekend being told to embrace my sexiness.

As they perused the clothes, Isabella gathered slacks and blouses. Emily paraded out in each outfit for approval.

"The first one is my favorite," declared Isabella.

Emily didn't care for the style but didn't want to insult Isabella. She brought out the black slacks and cream-colored button-down blouse. Though she was grateful for the gift and admired Isabella, she had no desire to dress like her.

"Now, to find you some shoes." Isabella chose a patent-leather crocodile loafer—not the strappy high-heeled stilettos Emily was eyeing.

When they finished, Isabella gave Emily a big hug. "This was so much fun. Let's plan to start our venture together next week. Do Monday mornings work for you to meet on a weekly basis?"

"Yes, that's good. I usually work in the evenings that day."

"Perfect. I'm going to get everything lined up. Our first event is in a week and a half. My friend's baby shower." Isabella hugged her tightly.

Emily returned the hug, trying to ignore the guilt brewing in her stomach. "Thank you so much. I really appreciate everything."

"Of course, darling." She lovingly placed her hand on Emily's cheek. "See you soon!"

***

Jack

Hi Emily. This is Jack Fletcher. How have things been going for you these past couple of days?

Confusing.

Emily

Pretty good. Still processing I guess. Back to lawyering?

Jack

Yes, I am. But never done being a Symposium leader. Our conversations have really stuck with me. I'd like to continue assisting you if that's all right? Still up for some homework?

I've stuck with him? That's kind of cool.

Emily

Sure.

Jack

I want to empower you to be completely authentic with yourself and the people in your life this week. Get comfortable embracing who you are. Don't hold back. See what happens when you stop limiting yourself. And notice what happens when you aren't being authentic. Can you do that for me?

Emily still wasn't sure what that looked like. She knew he wouldn't condone her behavior with Enzo, no matter how "authentic" she was being. And she certainly wasn't being authentic with Isabella.

Emily

I'll try.

Jack

Remember, there is no try.

Emily

Yes, Yoda. Just figuring out how to manage it.

Jack

I'm honoured to be your Jedi Master. Let's touch base next week and you can fill me in on what occurred for you. In the meantime, I want to share this quote by Nelson Mandela:"There is no passion to be found playing small—in settling for a life that is less than the one you are capable of living." STOP PLAYING SMALL.

***

Emily met up with Addison at The Market Wednesday afternoon to grab a bite to eat before work. As they sat outside on the patio, Emily filled her in on Isabella's offer.

"That's so exciting! I agree with her. I think you'd be perfect doing events." Addison's smile turned into a frown. "So, why don't you seem as excited as me?"

"I need to tell you something."

Addison set her sandwich down. "Oh, no... really?" Her instincts were always spot-on. She already knew without having to be told. Emily loved that about her.

"Well, I mean, we didn't sleep together or anything," Emily tried to reassure her. "It was just one kiss."

"Oh, Emily. This isn't good."

"He told me they have an open marriage. Apparently, Isabella has her own flings, too." Emily offered the explanation as some sort of justification.

"Do you really believe that?" The tone in Addison's voice told Emily she shouldn't.

"I don't know what to believe."

"So, what are you going to do?"

Emily looked down again, ashamed to be admitting all of this. "I don't know. You know I've always had this stupid crush on Enzo. I never expected him to feel the same way, and knowing he does..." She didn't finish her sentence as she looked at Addison, hoping she understood her dilemma.

She could tell she didn't.

"But I've made it clear I'm not up for it. Especially now that I'll also be working for Isabella. And thankfully, he hasn't tried anything else."

"That's good to hear," Addison said. "When does his seminar series start up?"

"Tuesday."

"Well, it's certainly going to be interesting for you to navigate it all."

"That it will." Emily took a bite of her sandwich to settle the nausea that was stirring.

"What will be interesting?"

She looked up and saw Dylan standing over them. Her breath quickened at the flashback of their night in her kitchen. And then she cringed from the humiliation that he hadn't reached out since. She covered her mouth to hide her chewing. "Hey, what are you doing here?"

"Getting my hair cut next door."

Addison stared, wide-eyed.

"Dylan, this is my best friend, Addison. Addison, this is Dylan."

"Hey, Addison. So, what's so interesting?"

"Oh, this seminar series my boss signed me up for," Emily said. "It's pretty deep stuff."

"You like deep, right?" Dylan winked.

A giggle escaped Addison's mouth.

The nausea was gone. Hurt and anger simmered inside of Emily now.

"So, where have you been?" She mustered the courage to ask, hoping she didn't sound as pathetic as she felt.

"Just busy with gigs and meetings. We're playing at the Pec tomorrow night. You guys should come."

"I have to work," Emily told him, a little too quickly.

Addison kicked her under the table.

"I get off at nine, though. We can probably head up after that."

"Great," Dylan said. "I'll save you the front booth. See ya."

As soon as he was out of sight, Addison squealed like a little girl.

"You know I haven't heard from him in a week and a half, right?"

"I know," Addison said. "But you need him to keep you distracted from Enzo. Just have fun... I mean, it's Dylan Holt! We're in the inner sanctum now. He's saving us a table!"

"Speaking of fun," Emily interjected. "What's going on with that guy you've been talking to on Hinge? What's his name?"

"Barry." Addison rolled her eyes dramatically.

Emily laughed. "What? You don't like his name?"

"It's just so..." she scrunched up her nose, "fatherly."

"Or presidential. Addison, you can't write a guy off just because of his name. Invite him tomorrow night. Meet him in person and then decide."

"I don't know. He just seems so vanilla. And not that attractive."

"You should at least give him a chance. Maybe it's just a bad picture?"

"Ha! Ever the optimist you are. We Facetimed. I confirmed it."

"I think you need to put yourself out there more, Addy. You'll never meet anyone if you don't."

Addison was still a virgin and had lived a very sheltered life raised in a strict Jewish home. Their fundamentalist backgrounds were one of the things that bonded the women. It wasn't until she and Emily became friends that Addison started truly discovering the world around her. But she was still pretty shy when it came to dating and tended to live vicariously through Emily.

"I promise I'll be there to protect you," Emily assured her.

Ten

Addison met Emily at Josephina's after her shift, and they grabbed an Uber to El Chapultepec, Denver's most historic jazz club.

Pulling up, Addison pointed out a tall, lanky man standing isolated from the crowd on the street corner. He wore khakis and a lime green polo shirt. "That's him."

"He's not bad looking, Addy," Emily said. "What don't you like?"

"I don't know. I guess he's fine. I'm just weird."

Emily followed Addison as they stepped out of the car and approached him.

"Barry?"

"Yes. Oh, hi... Addison?"

"That's me. This is my friend, Emily."

The small bar was packed, and the LoDo Dogs were already playing. Emily, Addison, and Barry made their way through the crowd, stopping at the bar to order drinks before they reached the booth in front of the tiny stage. A piece of paper was taped down on the table with the words "Reserved for E.B." scribbled in messy writing.

Dylan flashed his sexy smile at Emily as he pounded out "Moanin'" on the piano keys.

She slid into the booth across from Addison and Barry. Being so close to the music, combined with the noisy bar, made it too difficult for all of them to carry on any sort of conversation with each other. Emily was content watching Dylan play and looking at all the black and white photos surrounding them; legends that had played at the Pec over the decades. From Ella Fitzgerald, Frank Sinatra, and Count Basie to Paul McCartney, Mick Jagger, and even Bill Clinton on sax.

But when Emily's eyes settled back on the scribbled words taped on the table, she couldn't help but wonder how many other girls Dylan had reserved this booth for. She glanced over at Addison and Barry occasionally, seeing them talk into each other's ears. Eventually, Addison leaned over, asking Emily to go to the bathroom with her.

Addison told Emily she and Barry were going to go some place quieter where they could talk more.

That surprised Emily. "Really?"

"I'm putting myself out there and giving him a chance."

Emily was concerned about her safety, but Addison insisted he was harmless and promised to call her when she got home.

"No texts," Emily said firmly. "An actual phone call."

"Promise."

Emily took a picture of the two of them "for fun" before they left. She wanted to have a way to identify the guy if something went wrong.

After the band finished their set, and the bar was closing, Dylan made a beeline to Emily. "Come with me." He took her hand and led her into a back storage room, locking the door behind them. The room was pitch black except for a cart full of glow necklaces that had been out in front of the bar earlier. Dylan kissed her, backing her up into the cart. He immediately began unbuttoning her pants. "You have on way too many clothes."

"I did just come from work." She was kicking herself for not going home to shower and change. All she could smell was Italian food emanating from her body. Then again, she didn't expect the night to end like this. But as much as his ghosting hurt her last time, she still wanted him.

While he yanked down her pants and lifted her onto the cart, she fumbled to get his zipper undone, enthusiastic at the prospect of secret sex in a back room. He spread her legs open, stepping in between, and pulled her hips toward his until she felt him pressing against her.

"I don't have a condom on me," he groaned. "I left my wallet in my car."

Seriously?

He held himself in his hand, rubbing his tip against her wet entrance. "God, you feel incredible."

A man's voice on the other side of the storage room came through. "Where did Dylan go?"

"I have no clue," said another. "He just totally disappeared."

Dylan continued his rhythmic movements against her clit, listening intently. Emily tried to focus on remaining silent as electricity coursed through her body.

A loud knock caused her heart to drop into her stomach.

"Dylan? You in there?"

Another knock.

"I don't know, dude. Maybe he went home."

"But his car is still here." The voices trailed off.

Emily had to force herself to remain silent as Dylan continued to rub against her, which made the entire experience in the dark even more erotic. All she could see was the colorful glow from the necklaces surrounding her as if she were in a dream. So, when the ring of her phone pierced the silence, Emily answered it in a panic to make it stop.

"Hello?"

It was Addison letting her know she was home safe and sound.

"How was the rest of the date?" Emily asked quietly. While Addison proceeded to tell her how boring Barry was, Emily felt Dylan push inside of her. "Mm-hmm," Emily mumbled, trying to remain present in the conversation as he slowly slid in and out while his thumb circled her clit. Her pleasure was building, but her mind was racing, realizing he was inside of her without a condom.

"Were you sleeping?" Addison asked. "I'm sorry. I didn't mean to wake you."

"Yes," Emily managed to say. "Can I call you tomorrow?"

"Oh, of course. Sorry."

Emily hung up the phone.

Dylan pulled out and zipped up his pants. "They're going to be closing any minute. We need to get out of here," he said. "I'll go first and you follow behind me."

As Emily finished putting herself back together, Dylan leaned his ear against the door. He slowly opened it and peeked his head out. With no one around, he motioned for Emily. They darted for the back exit.

Once in the parking lot, Dylan walked over to his car. "Need a ride home?"

"Sure, that would be great," she said, climbing into his old Mustang, eager to bring him back to her place for more.

When they pulled out of the parking lot, he unzipped his pants and grabbed his semi-erect cock. "I didn't get to finish," he said with a devilish grin.

Surprised at his bold declaration, she found the thought of driving around the city, sucking him off, kind of exciting. Unbuckling her seatbelt, she stretched across and took him into her mouth. She could taste herself and wondered if it was a normal taste. *Maybe I should start eating more pineapple?*

She felt him grow harder, and he placed his hand on the back of her head. "Oh, yeah, baby... just like that..." His fingers wrapped around her hair as he took control of her movement. Yelling out, he let his saltiness flood her mouth. Emily was caught off-guard but knew it probably wouldn't be very sexy to let it spill back onto him. She swallowed, trying not to gag.

"That was amazing." He flashed his megawatt smile at her. After a few moments of awkward silence, he said, "I guess we weren't very smart back there. Are you on the pill or anything?"

We?!

As Emily wiped the corners of her mouth, she quietly answered, "Yes, the pill."

"Oh, thank God. I hate condoms."

"Well, it's not just about me accidentally getting pregnant--"

"I'm clean," he cut her off. "I get tested every six months. What about you?"

"I'm good," she replied, uneasy with his revelation as they pulled up in front of her building.

"Thanks for a great night." He leaned over to kiss her, but suddenly diverted his lips down to her neck. "I'm sorry. You just had me in your mouth. I can't handle the thought of tasting myself."

Emily was stunned. She didn't know what to say. "Oh."

"I'll call you later."

As she exited his car, she tried to brush off the feeling that she had just been dismissed after providing a service.

***

Emily heard her sisters running down the hall before they reached her apartment. She shoved a towel and sunscreen into her tote bag and opened the door to greet them.

"Sissy!" they shrieked, crashing into her.

"Hi, beauties!"

"Thanks for doing this, Emily," Amy told her. "The girls are so excited."

"Of course... so am I."

Summer and Rain ran over to the sliding door that opened onto the Juliet balcony, plastering their foreheads to the pane of glass to see the city life below.

Emily's dad hugged her. "I'm so thrilled you did the Symposium. Enzo told me Jack Fletcher led it. I met him once a few years ago. Seemed like a great guy. What did you think of him?"

"Oh, he was amazing. He texted me afterward and gave me homework this week."

"Really? I didn't know Symposium leaders did that. Isn't that what the seminar is for?"

It hadn't occurred to Emily that it wasn't something normal for a Symposium leader to do.

He did say I stuck with him. "I don't know. He brought me up on stage for an exercise, so the homework was an extension of that."

"Oh?" That piqued her dad's interest. "What was the exercise?"

"Um... just about me being authentic."

He seemed to be waiting for more of an answer, but when she didn't offer one, he said, "Well, that's fantastic. I bet Enzo's thrilled to have you be a part of it."

More than you know.

His smile radiated with pride. "Here, I picked this up for you from The Tattered Cover." He handed her the blue square book: *Be Here Now* by Ram Dass. "It's known as the counterculture bible. I thought you'd appreciate it as you embark on this new journey."

Emily flipped through the brown pages. It looked more like someone's scrapbook, with drawings and large block lettering. "Thanks. Looks interesting."

"It's life-changing stuff. I hope you take the time to look it over."

"I will." *Just as soon as I get to all the other books you've given me on how to change my life.*

"Did you guys enjoy the fundraiser?" Emily placed the newest book on her coffee table.

"Yes," Amy said. "You did such a great job. Was it as successful as you had hoped?"

"Beyond what I had imagined. Diego and Todd are ecstatic. And Isabella was really impressed. She took me to lunch this week and asked me to be her assistant in her new event business."

"So, you're leaving Josephina's?" her dad asked.

"No. This would just be part-time. But she thinks I should consider becoming an event planner. She's willing to teach me."

Her dad nodded. "That sounds promising."

He never reacted enthusiastically anymore whenever she told him about a new career idea. But this time, she heard a different tone in his voice. One that sounded almost optimistic.

A text from Addison dinged Emily's phone, letting her know she was in the lobby.

"Guess who's waiting for us downstairs?"

"Addy!" the girls screamed and ran for the door.

***

As the afternoon sun beat down on them, Emily and Addison let the girls run through the splash zone while they sat down to take a break. Emily drilled Addison for details about Barry. "Where did you guys go when you left?"

"We just drove around in his car for a while."

She didn't seem very forthcoming with information.

"Drove around? You didn't go anywhere?"

"We ended up at a park, but we stayed in the car."

"Well, do you like him?"

Addison shrugged and crinkled up her nose. "I don't know. He's okay, I guess."

"Do you want to see him again?"

"I don't think so."

Emily knew something was off. "What are you not telling me?"

Addison didn't say anything as tears filled her eyes.

"Oh my god, Addison, did he hurt you?"

"No."

"Then what is it, Addy? What's wrong?"

After a long pause, Addison told her, "We had sex in his car."

Momentarily stunned, Emily finally said, "Wow. I did not see that coming."

"Neither did I." Addison laughed nervously, wiping a tear from the corner of her eye.

"Did he force you?"

"No, it wasn't like that. I wanted to do it. I was curious."

"How did it get to that point? You said he was boring."

"He is." More nervous laughter. "While we were driving, we talked about random stuff; nothing really interesting. He asked if I wanted to park the car and talk some more before going home. While we were sitting there, he told me he wanted to kiss me. So, I let him. And then one thing led to another..." Addison looked down.

"Did you enjoy it?"

She crinkled her nose again. "Not really."

"Oh, Addy, I'm so sorry. That's not how your first time should have been." Emily was devastated for her.

"It's fine. I don't know... it was just... weird."

"Sissy! Addy!" Rain and Summer came running up to them. "Can we go on the Ferris wheel?"

Emily gave Addison a long hug. "I love you, Addy."

Summer and Rain wrapped their arms around both women. "I love you, too!" they shouted together.

Eleven

T he ding of the text woke Emily up just after 8:30 on Monday morning.

Emily's heart sank that the text wasn't from Dylan. She hadn't heard from him since Thursday night. *I'm such an idiot.* Rolling back into bed, she closed her eyes and thought about how much he wanted her that first night. The thrill of him lifting her onto her kitchen counter, pushing inside of her as he pulled her hair and kissed her neck.

She slid her hand between her legs and found her sweet spot. As her climax was building, the image suddenly shifted to Enzo. Briefly wrestling with her guilt, she ignored it as she imagined him thrusting inside of her until her hips began bucking, and she felt the wetness soak her hand.

***

At 9:55 am, Emily rang the doorbell. After a moment, she found herself face-to-face with Enzo. Warmth rushed to her cheeks, remembering her morning session with herself.

"Good morning, come in." He held the door open for her and stepped aside. "Isabella is still getting ready. She'll be down soon."

"She asked me to bring these." Emily avoided looking at him as she handed him the baby wipes.

He set them on the stairs and walked toward the kitchen. "Can I get you some coffee?"

"That would be great. Thanks."

"So, how are you doing since the Symposium? We haven't had a chance to talk."

A nervous flutter jumped into her breath. *About the seminar or the kiss?* "I'm good. Just, you know, processing things." *Like you kissing me.*

He handed her a mug of coffee. "With cream... just how you like it."

She took a sip and looked away from his intense gaze.

Enzo leaned in closer and whispered into her ear. "I want to kiss you again."

The feel of his body against hers—his lips grazing her earlobe—almost made her crumble to the floor.

"Good morning," she heard Isabella sing from around the corner.

Emily jumped, causing the hot coffee to slosh out of the cup onto her hand.

Just as smoothly as he had moved in, he pulled away and stepped back. "Can I get you something to eat?"

"No, I'm fine." Emily focused on slowing her heart rate. "Can I please get a paper towel?"

Isabella appeared in the kitchen and hugged Emily before pouring herself a cup of coffee. "Thanks for picking up those wipes. I'll send you the money. Let's sit at the table to go over everything."

Emily wiped up the spilled coffee, trying to ignore the searing pain on her skin.

"I'm off to work." Enzo kissed his wife's lips and Emily's cheek before heading out the door.

Maybe he actually is trying to bring me into their relationship?

She had a friend in college who was in a polyamorous relationship with a married couple, so it wasn't out of the realm of possibility.

"We have three events coming up." Isabella pushed folders in front of Emily. "Each folder has a to-do list for you with the dates the task needs to be completed by. I have a Google doc that I'll send over, but for our meetings, I like to have everything on paper. The folders can also hold any receipts or other paperwork associated with the events."

Emily opened the top folder titled MONTGOMERY BABY SHOWER. The left pocket held a list with boxes to be checked off this week. Her tasks consisted of picking things up from various stores and assembling games and activities. It didn't look too hard; just a lot of running around and tedious work.

"I'll need you to meet me here Sunday morning by seven. That should give us enough time to get the cars loaded up and be at the venue by eight-thirty."

Seven in the morning? After working a closing shift at the bar on Saturday night? What have I gotten myself into?

"We'll have two-and-a-half hours to set everything up before guests start arriving."

Emily heard a baby's cry approaching from the hallway. The young nanny, who looked like she was still in high school, walked into the kitchen carrying Chloe.

Isabella excused herself and lifted Chloe into her arms, kissing her. "What's wrong, baby girl? Are you hungry?"

Isabella addressed the nanny. "Carrie, it's important that she stay on her feeding schedule so we can avoid her getting this upset. It's thirty minutes past."

"Sorry, Mrs. Rizzoli." The young girl looked stressed as she began preparing Chloe's food. "She seemed content in her playpen while I was cleaning the bathroom, so I thought I'd finish up before it was time to feed her."

"Got it," Isabella told her. "But we need to work on time management. Perhaps start cleaning a little earlier?" Isabella suggested with a sweet but authoritative smile. She kissed her baby and placed her in the highchair for Carrie to feed.

After discussing the remaining events, Isabella handed Emily a planner, instructing her to keep track of her hours worked so she could pay her every week. "I think a physical planner will work better than digital to keep track of activity. You can just jot it down and the time it took to complete. Please bring the planner and folders with you to our weekly meetings."

Carrie cleaned up from the feeding and announced she would put Chloe down for her nap.

"Thank you, Carrie," said Isabella. "While she's napping, please sort through her clothes, and set aside any that are nine months or smaller. You'll find a basket on top of her closet you can put them in. Any that have stains on them can go into a trash bag."

Isabella picked up her purse and turned to Emily. "I'll walk out with you. I have an appointment at the spa."

***

Jack

Hi Emily. This is Jack Fletcher. How was your week? Any breakthroughs to share?

Emily

Not really. Honestly, it's been a little rocky. Working on being authentic, but it's been a bit of a struggle.

Jack

Breakdowns are to be expected before breakthroughs so don't make anything wrong about that. Can we plan a phone conversation this week?

Emily

Sure. What's a good day for you?

Jack

Weekdays are a little tough. Are you available in the evening?

Emily

I'm a bartender so usually work evenings and weekends. What about Sunday night?

Jack

Perfect. How about 4 pm your time?

Emily

Oh, forgot about the time difference. I won't be home until later. Working an event that day. Would 8 pm my time be too late for you?

Jack

I live in the city that never sleeps. I'll be fine. Looking forward to speaking with you on Sunday. Take care.

Jack

Here's another quote for you to think about this week: 'Change and growth take place when a person has risked himself and dares to become involved with experimenting with his own life.' TAKE RISKS. Talk soon.

***

Emily quickly found Clay, Lucas, and Tonya already seated, saving her a spot. It surprised her to realize she actually missed them, missed their conversations. They weren't people she would normally gravitate toward but sharing each other's stories created a special connection between them.

"Welcome back, everyone." Enzo took the stage. "Let's talk about integrity. I want to hear from some of you. Tell me what you think integrity means."

Hands shot up, and Enzo pointed to a woman in the front row.

"Being honest and telling the truth."

He nodded and pointed to a man sitting behind her.

"Having strong moral principles."

"Okay." He scanned the room. "Emily?"

Emily's hand was not up. *What the hell?*

"Doing the right thing, even when no one is watching." She recited a meme she saw on Instagram and wondered how he reconciled this topic with kissing her.

"Right. Good. Thank you."

He looked out at the audience again. "If you open the dictionary and keep reading beyond those first few definitions, you'll see another: the state of being whole, entire, complete.

"Think about a bridge for a moment. Sediment being carried by swiftly moving water causes damage which, if left unchecked, can eventually lead to the bridge's collapse. Why? Because the erosion and cracks that formed as a result of the water and sediment constantly hitting the bridge affected the structural integrity.

"In the Symposium, when we talk about integrity, what we're really talking about is workability. The secret to making things work is simple. Do what you say you're going to do. Every time. Even the little things. Even when you don't want to. Everything matters.

"Now, obviously, there will be times when things happen, and we can't keep our word. But we can honor it, which restores integrity. What that means is we can acknowledge that we didn't keep our word, and that allows us to create a new promise if appropriate. Because when we don't keep our commitments and we don't acknowledge our broken promises, cracks form and structures collapse.

"When we talk about 'being in and having integrity,' what we mean is honoring your word. Who you are is your word. Your word is you being authentic. Being true to who you are is being in integrity. Integrity is what gives us power. Without integrity, nothing works."

For the next two hours, Enzo was just as engaging as Jack. The audience held onto his every word, soaking up his wisdom.

"Living a life full of passion means stepping outside of your comfort zone. It's easy to stay within the limits we've set for ourselves. We know what to expect. Every day we wake up and remember how to be safe. Do you know what happens to us when we're safe? When we always do what's expected of us?"

Enzo scanned the audience, their eager faces waiting for the answer.

"We die."

The room let out a collective chuckle.

"Yes, we all die. That's how all of our stories end. There's no way of getting around it. There's nothing you can do to stop it from happening. What you can do is live life passionately. Welcome the unexpected. Be open-minded and curious because curiosity is how inspiration begins.

"Our goal throughout this seminar series is to practice being inspired and passionate about living. For the next six weeks, I want you to step out of your comfort zone. Be creative. Do something spontaneous."

At the end of the evening, Emily avoided Enzo and walked out with her friends.

"Okay, I'm going to get out of my comfort zone," Tonya announced. "Would you guys want to come over for an early dinner next week before the seminar? I'm only about five minutes away, and I make a pretty good lasagna."

Lucas lit up. "Lasagna's my favorite food. You don't have to ask me twice."

"I'd love to," Emily said.

"Clay?" Tonya's voice was full of hope.

"Yeah, sure. I get off work at five. What time are you thinking?"

"Five is perfect. Just come over after work."

"Sounds good."

Emily said goodbye and was walking toward her car when the text came over.

Dylan

> Went to Josephina's, but you weren't there. I'd love to see you tonight. Are you free?

She stopped in her tracks. *Finally. He went looking for me!*

Emily

> Just leaving the seminar I was telling you about. What did you have in mind?

Dylan

> Pleasing you.

Emily bit her lip, trying to rein in her smile as she stared at the phone.

"Hey, Emily... wait up."

She turned around to see Clay jogging up to her.

"I know it's late, but do you want to grab a drink at Slattery's before you head home?"

Is he asking me out? "Oh, um...," she was caught off guard by his invitation. "I'm meeting my boyfriend." She knew Dylan wasn't her boyfriend, but she needed that excuse right now. She didn't want Clay to get the wrong impression about her friendship.

"Oh, I didn't realize you had a boyfriend?"

She was racking her brain, trying to remember what she had said about Dylan during the Symposium. "Well, it's pretty new. We just started seeing each other."

"Fair enough. I can be patient." He smiled. "See you next week."

Shit. Why does he have to ruin a perfectly good friendship?

Twelve

When Emily arrived home, Dylan was sitting on the floor in the hallway, leaning against her apartment door. She hated that she seemed to be at his beck and call, but she wanted him. And she wanted him to want her.

He stood up and took her face in his hands. "Hi, gorgeous." He kissed her deeply. "I've been thinking about you all week."

A text letting me know that would have been nice. "Did you have a gig tonight?" She turned away from him to unlock her door.

He wrapped his arms around her from behind. "No. Just been working on some new songs. Wanted to see you."

Once inside, he began pulling her clothes off. "How about a shower?"

Now, that sounds fun. "Yes, please."

She led him around the corner of her dark apartment, guided by the moonlight that shone through her windows. While he undressed, she lit the candle on the bathroom counter and turned on the water. This was exactly what she wanted. Something sensual. Intimate. Something to distract her from fantasizing about Enzo.

She stepped under the warm waterfall, and he followed behind. He pumped soap onto her body sponge and swirled it across her backside, gliding over her ass, and then wrapped his arms around to clean her breasts and belly. Emily rested her head on his chest as one of his hands slid down between her legs, bringing her to a quick orgasm.

Once she recovered, she turned around and guided him under the water. She stood behind him and soaped up his body, reaching around to clean his erection as she laid her face against his wet back. He stopped her before he came.

"I want to be inside of you," Dylan told her as he turned the water off.

She grabbed towels for each of them and led him toward her bed. She had forgotten just how messy her bedroom was until she realized they were stepping on dirty clothes.

When she lay down, he climbed on top of her and kissed her; his fingers played between her legs. She was delirious with another impending orgasm when he stopped and began entering her.

"Wait." She placed her hands on his chest. "Do you have a condom?"

"Why? You're on the pill. And we're both clean."

What? "We still need to use condoms."

"But we didn't last time. What's it matter now?"

Her heart thudded against her chest. She was too nervous to speak up, fearing he would just leave. But she didn't move her hand as she stared at him.

"Fine." He rolled his eyes and pushed off to retrieve the condom from his pants pocket in the bathroom.

Emily wondered if she was overreacting. *Maybe I should have let it go? Now he seems upset. Damn it... why did I say anything? But why is he okay to not use one? Is this a sign he wants to be exclusive? But he hasn't said that. God, I hope he's not mad at me.*

When he returned, he stood in front of her. "Can you suck me for a minute so I can get hard again?"

She could hear the hint of irritation in his voice. Her breathing was shallow as she tried to recover from the momentary humiliation she felt. She took him into her mouth, hoping she could make him feel good enough to want to stay.

He climbed back on top of her and pumped feverishly until he yelled out, pushing in deeper before rolling off.

His hand rested on her belly. *Please move those fingers down...*

"I'm so glad I got to see you tonight," he said. "That was great." He propped up on his side and kissed her, his hand sliding over her hip as she turned into him.

"Me too." She ran her fingers across his chest, silently pleading for his hand to spread her legs.

Instead, he gave her one more quick kiss and pushed himself off the bed. "Wow, it's late. I better get going."

Emily glanced at the clock. 11:33 pm. He had been there for an hour.

"You have to leave already?"

"Yeah, I have an early morning meeting."

She couldn't hide her disappointment. "You keep leaving me."

"I know, I'm sorry. It's just really busy right now. Are you working Thursday night?"

"Yes, until nine." She rolled onto her stomach, hugging her pillow while she watched him get dressed.

"Why don't you come over to my place after for dessert? My mom gave me a lemon meringue pie today. I'm sure we can find some creative ways to eat it." He winked.

Emily perked up and rose to her knees, moving toward the edge of the bed. "Ohhh, I love lemon meringue pie."

He leaned down and kissed her, caressing her breast. "I'll text you my address."

***

Emily met Addison for lunch at their favorite poke place off the Sixteenth Street Mall. She was worried about her ever since she learned what happened with Barry and wanted to make sure she was okay.

"Emily, I'm fine," Addison reassured her. "It just wasn't what I had it built up to be in my mind. It was eye-opening, actually."

"Okay," Emily responded reluctantly. "I just want you to know you can talk to me about it. I won't judge you." She couldn't help but feel Addison was keeping something from her.

"I know, thanks. I'm just glad to have it out of the way."

Emily knew that feeling. She experienced it her first time as well.

"So, how are the seminars going with Enzo?"

Master of the subject change. "Oh, good. He's a great leader."

Addison didn't say anything. She just nodded in acknowledgment—a nod heavy with unspoken advice. "What's it like working with Isabella?"

"It's been fine. Keeps me busy. I spent all day yesterday running around and putting things together. Our first event is this Sunday. A baby shower for one of her friends."

"That should be fun… I mean, if you're into bougie women and the babies they have so they can justify years of extravagant parties just to outdo one another."

Emily burst out laughing. "Wow… I had no idea you had such strong opinions on this."

"I grew up around it. I've seen the ridiculous extremes women like that go to. But they sure do keep event planners employed, so you should do well. Take all their money, I say!"

While they finished eating their bowls, Emily told Addison about her night with Dylan.

"And you're seeing him again tonight? Wow… two nights in a week. That must be a record for him."

Emily threw an edamame pod at her. "You're extra sassy today. What's going on with you?"

Addison sighed. "I don't know. Just restless, I think."

"Are you sure you're okay about what happened with Barry?"

Addison threw the edamame pod back at Emily. "Yes! Jeez… stop already."

"Okay, okay. We need to plan another night out soon with Diego and Todd. Blow off some steam. You're so cranky these days," Emily teased. "Come on, let's go get some Boba."

***

Emily took her second shower of the day. She shaved her legs and massaged cocoa butter all over her body to ensure sweet-smelling, silky-smooth skin. A matching lacy red thong and bra hid under her black slacks and white dress shirt.

But by the end of her shift, Emily still hadn't heard from Dylan. She texted him she was about ready to leave and needed his address. Stalling for more time, she stepped into the bathroom to take her hair out of the braid and spritz on vanilla body spray.

Staring at her phone, which still didn't have a response, she walked back toward her locker to grab her water bottle.

Enzo stepped in front of her. "Plans tonight?"

Emily looked up to find him inches away. "Yes."

"With that piano man from the fundraiser?"

She didn't answer.

He looked at her longingly and pushed a strand of her hair from her face. "You look beautiful. Have fun."

"Thanks," she said, relieved. "Goodnight."

Between Enzo and Dylan, Emily felt like she was riding a roller coaster without a safety belt. With still no word from Dylan, Emily slowly walked back to her apartment.

She peeled off her clothes and tossed them on the floor. Grabbing her favorite book, she settled under the freshly cleaned sheets. She ignored the tears that fell as she read about the vampire Lestat turning a little girl into a bloodsucking immortal.

Thirteen

T he baby shower was a success. Isabella praised Emily for being organized and efficient and treated her to dinner that evening. "By the way, you look very elegant."

"Thank you. I really appreciate you getting the outfit for me." Even though it wasn't something Emily would typically choose to wear, she had to admit she felt professional; a nice change from the college dropout bartender in ripped-up jeans and flip-flops.

"How we dress makes a statement about who we are, and it can give you the confidence to help you through certain situations."

Emily could relate to that. She realized she based much of her wardrobe on how certain pieces of clothing made her feel.

"There's nothing wrong with dressing sexy, but you can achieve that appropriately and remain classy and elegant."

Wait. Is she saying I dress inappropriately?

"So, Enzo tells me you're dating a piano player? What's his name?"

It surprised Emily that Enzo had mentioned her dating life to his wife. She hoped Isabella didn't notice the shame and embarrassment on her face that welled up inside.

"His name is Dylan. We've hung out a few times, but I have no idea where it's going—if anywhere."

"Does he treat you well?"

That question hit Emily hard.She felt a heaviness in her chest, reliving him ghosting her yet again. She was angry at herself for falling for his predictable charms, cast aside like all the other pathetic groupies before her. "It's still so new."

"Well, I'm happy for you. Just remember, make him work for it a bit. He should take you out to nice dinners, woo you. Don't settle for anything less than what you're worth."

Emily didn't know what that world was like. She had never been "wined and dined." She only ever met guys in bars and clubs who had no interest in wining and dining; just drinking and fucking. She was acutely aware that the only time Dylan took her out was the night she first slept with him.

"Anyway," Isabella folded her napkin and laid it on the table, "I'm exhausted. I'm sure you are too. Let's skip our meeting tomorrow morning. You have your task list for the thirtieth birthday party next month, so just work off that. I'll Venmo over your pay."

"Okay, sounds good. Thanks for dinner," Emily said. "Reach out to me if you need anything before next week."

"Of course, darling." Saying their goodbyes, Isabella kissed her on both cheeks. "See you soon."

***

Emily's phone rang just as she walked into her apartment. Eight o'clock sharp.

"Hello?"

"Hi, Emily, it's Jack Fletcher. How are you?"

She had forgotten how sexy his British accent was. "I'm good. Just getting home from having dinner with my boss."

"Oh, Enzo?"

Interesting he knows that.

"His wife, actually. I recently started helping her with events."

"Enzo and Isabella are good friends of mine. We've been participating in this work together for years. Enzo mentioned to me he was the one who enrolled you in the Symposium."

Makes sense, I guess. "Yeah. He's friends with my dad, and they've both been on me about it for years." She chuckled, kicking off her shoes. "It was inevitable, I suppose." *I wonder what else Enzo said about me?*

"So, how's that going for you—working for both of them?"

Awkward. "Good," she said lightly. "They're both great people to work for."

"I imagine so. They can be wonderful mentors for you."

"They are." She felt very much like the snake in the grass.

"So, tell me about these past couple of weeks," he moved on. "Have things occurred differently for you? Are you noticing your rackets?"

"What are rackets again? I didn't really understand when you were talking about them during the Symposium."

"It's a way of being that's unproductive, yet it's persistently how you respond to life. It has some kind of payoff. It works for you. Maybe justifies your behavior. But you complain about it, and it's costing you something... like self-expression or love and fulfillment."

Emily put the phone on speaker and began undressing. "Okay... I think I understand. I did actually notice something I did earlier this week that's been bothering me."

"Tell me about it."

"It was on Tuesday night, after the seminar that Enzo leads. I was sitting with a group of friends I had met during the Symposium. As I was leaving, one of the guys came up to me in the parking lot and asked if I wanted to get a drink. But I was meeting up with the guy I'm sort of seeing--"

"What does that mean?" he interrupted. "'Sort of seeing?' Like, you're dating or just shagging?"

Emily was taken aback by his directness. "Well, that's the thing... I don't really know what we are yet, but I told Clay I had a boyfriend."

"Clay? My berry mate?"

"Wow, yes. You have a good memory."

"So, if you don't know the status of the other guy, why not have a drink with ? He seemed like a nice guy."

"I don't know. It actually kind of irritated me," she admitted.

"Why would it irritate you?"

Emily walked into her kitchen, wearing only her panties and bra, and poured herself a glass of red wine. "I guess, on some level, I felt a little betrayed."

"That's interesting. Why?"

She was trying to put her feelings into words. "It made me feel like his friendship toward me is just a sham. Like he has ulterior motives."

"Okay, I get that. Most men do. So, you told him you had a boyfriend. How did he respond?"

"He said he could be patient."

Jack laughed. "Well, you've got to give him credit. He's not going down without a fight."

"I guess. But now, it will just make things awkward between the four of us. It changes the dynamic of the group."

"Okay, got it. Clay has been relegated to the friend zone. What did you notice about yourself in that situation?"

She climbed into her bed, propping herself up against her big pillows. "I realized that my go-to response was to lie instead of being truthful—and that bothers me. But I just didn't want to hurt his feelings."

"So, you think being straight with him by letting him know you aren't interested is hurtful?"

"Well, yeah." Emily took a sip of her wine before setting it down on the nightstand.

"I can tell you, from a man's perspective, we would much rather know upfront if the woman isn't interested. It will be more hurtful to him later on to find out that he never even had a chance. As it sits now, he thinks if he's patient enough, you'll come around."

"But I don't see how that's on me? I told him I'm not interested."

"But you didn't," he pointed out. "You told him you had a boyfriend. You gave him a reason why you couldn't have a drink with him on Tuesday night. You didn't make it clear that you chose not to have a drink with him simply because you didn't want to. By telling him you choose not to, you're remaining in integrity. Otherwise, you're just a liar."

Emily struggled with that idea. "But that just seems so harsh. Why not spare his feelings and let him believe I can't go out with him because I have a boyfriend?"

"Because you can go out with him, even if you have a boyfriend. You have free will. No one is holding a gun to your head, saying you can't go out with him. Being in integrity about it is another thing, but you most certainly have a choice."

"But if someone tells you they have a boyfriend or girlfriend, shouldn't that shut down the conversation?"

"Look, there are plenty of people who would date—even fuck—more than one person at the same time. You having a boyfriend is just a reason you can give as to why you don't want to go out with someone else. A reason likely based on considerations of behaviors you learned growing up. I'm guessing you were told it's wrong to date—and fuck—more than one person at the same time?"

Emily was stunned at how he was speaking and didn't respond.

"Here's the thing, Emily; there is nothing inherently wrong with fucking more than one person at the same time. It's a choice people make. Some people choose to be monogamous, some people choose not to be. One isn't better than the other. What it comes down to is being in integrity about it. If you've agreed to be monogamous, and then you're not, you've broken your word, and now you're out of integrity. Do you get that?"

Emily thought of Enzo and Isabella. *They must have an open marriage. That's the only explanation for his behavior.* "I think so."

"You having a boyfriend doesn't affect your power to choose whether you want to have a drink with Clay. And Clay understands this. He worked through this exercise up on stage. A lightbulb went off for him two weeks ago. He gets it; it's strawberry or blueberry. He gets that you gave him a reason, but that you still have the power to choose. And he's let you know he will be patient until you wield that power. Unless you're honest with him, you're just leading him on."

Emily grabbed her wine and took a drink, trying to understand everything he was saying.

"Let me ask you this; if you weren't seeing the other guy, would you have wanted to get a drink with ?"

Emily thought about it. "I don't think so."

"Why?"

"He's not really my type."

"Why not? He's a good-looking bloke... pretty enlightened to have participated in the Symposium, right?"

"I'm not sure. I think maybe he's too nice." She laughed at how ridiculous she sounded.

"Ah. I'm going to go out on a limb here and assume the wanker you're currently shagging doesn't fall into the nice guy category? What's his name?"

"Dylan."

"Do you expect to have a relationship with Dylan?"

"I mean, I guess I typically always have somewhat of an expectation for a relationship if I'm having sex with the guy."

"Really? You never have sex just to have sex? Do the men you shag know that?"

"Well, I don't necessarily expect a relationship if I have sex with them, but I guess I hope for a relationship."

"Why?"

"Don't most people ultimately hope for a relationship?"

"Sure, some do," he conceded, "but not all, and certainly not at every point in their life. So, your hope when you have sex with a bloke is to find one that will lead to a relationship?"

"I guess."

"And do you think Dylan shares that same hope?"

Emily thought of all the groupies Dylan had following him from gig to gig. He had probably already moved on to someone new. "I just met him right before the Symposium. We've gotten together a few times, but I don't know what he's hoping for." She knew she was lying to herself, but the truth hurt too much to admit out loud.

"By 'gotten together,' do you mean shagging or actually getting to know one another?"

She had to face the reality that she and Dylan only ever had sex when they got together. There was no getting to know each other. She was silent, pulling her down comforter up over her body.

"Emily, if you were to find out that all Dylan was hoping for was a good shag, would you be okay with that? Because, at this point, I'm getting the impression that's probably all he wants. Again, nothing is wrong with that if you're both on the same page, but it sounds to me as if you need to manage your expectations."

"Maybe."

"Let's go back to Clay for a minute. If you're looking for a relationship, don't the nice guys typically make better relationship material?"

She laughed. "Probably."

"And I'm guessing when you think of Clay being a nice guy, you can't imagine him fucking you the way you want to be fucked? Because, again, I'm going to go out on a limb here and assume you like to be fucked a little hard and dirty?"

Emily's mouth fell open. She couldn't believe he just said that so casually. And, yet, she also found it very titillating. *How do I even respond to that?*

"Have I upset you?"

"No."

"You've gotten very quiet."

She remained silent. Her head was spinning with everything he was saying.

His voice softened. "I know this is a very confrontational conversation for you. Would I be right in saying that?"

"I've just never had this kind of conversation before."

"Does it make you uncomfortable?"

"A little."

"Do you want me to stop?"

"No." She reached over, set down her wine glass and turned off the bedside lamp. The lights of downtown Denver illuminated her bedroom as she settled under the covers.

"Emily, you know you are incredibly sexy. You even relish in that at times, yet it's like you're afraid of it. Why is that?"

She was quiet for a moment before she finally answered. "I guess I don't want people to think I'm a whore."

"Got it. And why do you think people would think that?"

Emily contemplated how to respond. He called her out on things that she never acknowledged to herself. Part of her wanted to hide from this, embarrassed by the things he said to her—about her—but another part of her wanted to keep exploring where this was going. And she felt safe doing that with him.

"Because I love sex," she finally admitted, "but if I'm sleeping with different men all the time, I'm essentially a whore."

"Says who?"

"Society."

"Bollocks! You can't live your life based on how society dictates it should be. Most people are fucked up. They're hypocrites. They pass judgment on someone because they don't have the courage to be authentic themselves." He paused. "Seriously, Emily, embrace who you are. Enjoy being a sexually provocative woman. It's who you are at your core, and you shouldn't be afraid of that."

"But then some men think it's an open invitation for them. And it's not."

"That's on them. You can't be responsible for how they choose to react to you."

"I know, but there's a lot of unwanted attention, and that's the stuff I have a hard time with."

"Like from Clay?"

"Well, kind of," she agreed, "but as an example, I love to go dancing. I love being up on stage and having men watch me. I love knowing I have the power to drive them crazy. But then they think it's okay to grab my breasts or ass while we're dancing—or even just as I'm walking by them. Some even get angry that I won't go home with them, claiming I was implying I would by the way I was acting. I mean, it's not too far-fetched to see why they would be upset."

"Hmmm... so, it sounds like you think if you dare to be this sexual woman, and dress provocatively, dance provocatively, men get a free pass in being pigs?"

"Well, I've had many guys accuse me of being a tease," Emily told him. "So, how do I balance being authentic to myself while not sending a message to all men that I'm here for their taking?"

"Emily, don't give your power away. Owning your sexuality is being responsible for yourself and your choices. You are not responsible for others' reactions. Just because you're a sensual person doesn't give men the right to say or do inappropriate things to you."

Emily was quiet as everything he said swirled through her head. "But this is where I'm really screwed up. Because, sometimes, with certain men, I do want them to just take me and do whatever they want. I fantasize about that. I guess that's what makes me a snake in the grass, like you said."

"Only because you don't own it," he responded. "Look, you've got to get out of your head. It's okay to want to be fucked. You need to let go of these preconceived notions that you're a whore for wanting to shag for the sake of shagging. It holds you back from truly being authentic to yourself. You also need to let go of taking responsibility for what others think about you. People project their own insecurities, anyway. It's human nature. At the same time, you get to hold men accountable for their actions towards you."

"Okay..." she said slowly, trying to choose her next words carefully. She had a nagging curiosity about his intentions with her. "Can I ask you a question?"

"Of course."

"Do you have these kinds of intense sexual conversations with a lot of your seminar participants?"

Jack chuckled softly. "No, I can't say that I do."

Emily was feeling empowered. "So, in the spirit of holding you accountable, is this purely a professional conversation?"

"Well, I'm a lawyer, not a therapist—so, no, I can't claim this is purely professional. But I do have an interest in helping you explore all of this."

"Why?"

"I find you fascinating."

"How so?"

"I think it's the duality I see in you, this transition from a girl into a woman. One moment, you seem very young and naïve—the next, like this incredibly powerful woman. But I think you get overwhelmed with it and are looking for direction."

"And you want to be my guide?"

There was a pause. "I suppose I do."

Emily smiled. "Can I ask you another question?"

"Sure."

"Does this conversation turn you on?" She held her breath, butter-flies dancing in her stomach.

"It does."

"Does that mean I turn you on?"

Jack took in a deep inhale and slowly exhaled. "Yes, you do."

"Good."

"You like knowing that you turn me on?" His voice was softer and lower.

"Yes. Can I ask you another question?"

"Of course."

"Have you fantasized about me?"

Another long pause. "Yes."

"Will you tell me about it?" Her heart was racing.

She heard him draw in another deep breath and exhale. "Yes, but I'd like for you to be lying down."

"I'm already in bed."

"What are you wearing?"

"My bra and panties."

"Of course you are," he chuckled. "Would you take them off for me?"

"Okay." She unclasped her bra and pulled it off. Lifting her hips, she slid the panties down her legs.

His seductive voice filled her ears in the otherwise quiet darkness. "I've imagined caressing your soft skin as my hands glide over your body, over your breasts, down the curve of your waist. I think about sweeping my tongue in circles around your nipples before sucking them in one at a time as they harden at my touch, moving my hands down past your belly, searching for your wet cunt."

Emily's fingers began softly stroking her lips and clit. Her breath quickened.

"Are you wet, Emily?"

"Dripping," she breathed.

"Good, just the way I want you. I want to taste you. I want to lick up every last drop with my tongue and suck on you so I can get more."

Emily's fingers were moving faster in circles as she panted.

"I want to fuck you, Emily. Do you want me to fuck you?"

"Yes," she moaned.

"Tell me you want me to fuck you, Emily. I want to hear you say it."

"I want you to fuck me, Jack." Emily didn't hesitate, though she had never spoken like that to anyone before. She could feel her body tensing up with pleasure, and she heard his breath catch.

"I want to slam into you and hear you scream. I want to feel your hot cunt surrounding me... your juices flowing over me as I keep pounding into you." His voice was deep and gravelly.

"Ohhhh my god," Emily's orgasm was about to explode.

"I want to make you come over and over again, Emily. I want to fuck you like you've never been fucked before."

Emily screamed out in pleasure as her hips arched toward the sky, and she allowed her hand to stop moving. Relaxing back down into bed, she could hear Jack breathing sporadically and the soft rhythmic sound of skin smacking skin.

"Fuck me hard, Jack. I want to feel you deep inside of me. I'm aching for you." Emily couldn't believe what she was saying. She had never talked like this with a guy, but she didn't want to stop. "I can't get enough... keep fucking me, Jack."

She was so turned on by their conversation—so turned on imagining him jacking off to her. She breathed heavily into the phone, moaning and whimpering as she stroked her drenched pussy.

Jack groaned loudly and then went silent.

After several seconds of heavy breathing, his gravelly voice broke through. "You need to come to New York."

Fourteen

When Emily checked her email Monday morning, she found a message from Jack with the subject line, *"In-person Homework."* The airline itinerary showed he was flying her out first class on Friday for the weekend. She hoped and prayed someone could cover her shifts again.

Is this really happening?

With no word from Dylan, she felt foolish for letting herself believe she meant any more to him than the dozens of other women at his fingertips.

At the Market, Addison handed Emily a cappuccino and told her she would take a break in a few minutes.

Emily grabbed a table in the back corner.

Ding!

Jack

Did you get the itinerary?

Emily

Yes.

Jack

I have a lot planned for you. You better rest up this week. The weekend will be an immersive lesson in owning your sexuality.

Emily

Sounds a little confronting.

Jack

Very.

Emily smiled. She couldn't believe she agreed to spend the weekend with him in New York. Isabella would be proud. But Emily knew this wasn't something she could share with her.

Addison slid in on the other side of the table. "Here's a chocolate croissant for you."

"Thanks!" Emily bit into the buttery, flaky piece of heaven.

"So, nothing from Dylan?"

Emily shook her head.

"I'm sorry. What a dick. How was the baby shower yesterday?"

"Great. Everything went smoothly. They were happy. Isabella was happy. She took me out to dinner afterward."

"That had to be awkward."

"It wasn't too bad. I mean, there were certainly my moments of guilt, but I just need to let it go. Nothing else will happen with Enzo."

"Does he know that?" Addison bit into her croissant as she scanned Emily's face.

"I think I've made it clear."

"Well, to hell with these men! Let's go out this weekend with Diego and Todd, get drunk, and get your mind off those assholes. What's your schedule like?"

"Actually, I'm going to be out of town."

"Where are you going?" Addison asked, surprised.

Emily smiled coyly and casually said, "New York," before taking another bite.

"Um, what?"

"I'm going to spend the weekend with Jack Fletcher."

"Who's Jack Fletcher?"

"The Symposium leader." Emily glanced at her friend with a look that pleaded for approval.

"Okay, I'm lost. I can't keep up with your men. When did this happen?"

"When I was saying goodbye to him at the end of the Symposium, he asked if he could give me homework—"

"Homework?" Addison raised her eyebrows.

"Yes, homework. He wanted me to notice when I was being a snake in the grass."

Addison's laughter was boisterous.

"So, last night he called to check in with me, and I was telling him about Clay wanting to go get a drink after the seminar last week--"

"Captain America asked you out?"

"Yes." Emily rolled her eyes.

Addison put her hands to her temples as she shook her head. "Let me get this straight... four men have hit on you in the last... what... two or three weeks? What kind of juju are you putting out there?"

Emily gave an exasperated sigh. "Anyway, I was telling Jack how it irritated me that Clay asked me out and--"

"Why would that irritate you?"

"Can we please stay focused on Jack?"

"Fine, fine... sorry. Go on."

"Anyway, the conversation turned to my sex life, and then, some-how—I'm not really sure how—it turned into phone sex."

That elicited another boisterous laugh from Addison. "You're not sure how? You really are a snake in the grass. I'm sure you knew exactly what you were doing."

"Maybe." Emily smiled, still struggling with owning up to her actions. "Spending a weekend with him in New York should definitely get my mind off of both Enzo and Dylan, though."

"How old is this guy?"

Emily bit her lips before answering. "Fortyish... I think?"

Addison's eyes widened. "So, he could be your dad?"

"Ew, gross... don't say that."

Addison sat back, shaking her head. "That must have been some insane phone sex."

"Hopefully, he's not a serial killer." Emily laughed as she stood up to leave. "And now I need to go talk to Enzo about taking the weekend off."

"Good luck with that!"

Emily walked down to Josephina's. The staff was setting up the outside tables for the dinner crowd while Stephanie was inside stocking the bar. She had her strawberry blonde hair piled on top of her head in a messy bun. It was very striking against her pale skin and green eyes. Emily had never noticed before how she resembled Drew Barrymore and wondered what her story was. She didn't know much about her.

"Hey, Steph," Emily approached her.

"Hi. You can't get enough of this place?" she teased.

"I get way too much of this place," Emily laughed. "Which is kind of what I wanted to talk to you about. I need to go out of town this weekend, unexpectedly. Would you be able to close for me on Friday and Saturday? I can return the favor when you need it."

"Sure. I hope everything is okay?" Stephanie looked at her with concern.

"Yes, just an unexpected trip. I appreciate it. I'll go tell Enzo now."

Emily knocked on the open door. Enzo looked up from his paperwork, a smile appearing on his face.

"Hi." She stepped into his office. "I'm going out of town this weekend, and Stephanie said she would cover for me. I'm sorry for the last-minute notice. It was unexpected."

"Is everything okay?" He also seemed surprised and concerned.

"Yes, just a weekend trip that came up."

"Oh, where are you going?"

How am I going to explain this given I'm always complaining about how broke I am? "New York."

Enzo looked slightly stunned. "New York?"

Emily maintained eye contact as she focused on slowing her racing heart rate. She didn't want to give him too much information. "Yeah, visiting a friend."

She could see his wheels turning.

"Wow, that will be quite an experience. Your first time, right?"

"Yeah, should be fun. Thanks, Enzo."

"Of course."

When he looked at her like that, it still made her stomach do flip-flops. She felt ashamed of her desire to climb into his lap and kiss him. "Okay, well, see you tomorrow night."

***

Emily was the first to arrive at Tonya's. She brought a bottle of Merlot, forgetting Tonya was underage.

"Glasses are in the upper cupboard to the right of the fridge, and the wine opener is in the drawer below. I'll be right back." Tonya walked to the back of the small house with a plate of food to get her father set up in front of the television in his bedroom.

"Would your dad like some wine?" Emily called out.

"No, thank you, honey," came his gruff voice from down the hall.

When Tonya returned to the kitchen, she pulled down dishes from the cupboard. "So, do you think Clay has any interest in me?"

Uh-oh.

"Oh, I don't know. I didn't know you liked him?"

"Yeah, I'm not very good at flirting."

"I don't think flirting should be something you try to be good at," Emily told her while they set the table together. "You just need to relax around him, smile a lot. That exudes confidence."

"That's easy for you to say. I have no self-confidence."

"That's the beauty of it; you don't need to have it. You know the saying—fake it 'til you make it?"

"I don't think I can do that."

"Well then, forget the wine—you'll need something a little stronger."

"Too bad we don't have anything here," Tonya laughed. "My dad isn't much of a drinker."

"I'll have you guys over to my place soon when we don't have to rush off to the seminar," Emily promised. "It will help you relax and have fun around him so he can see your playful side."

Tonya looked worried. "I don't think I have a playful side."

"Well, vodka will certainly help you find it."

The boys finally showed up and scarfed down Tonya's lasagna.

"That was delicious," Clay said as they all took their dirty dishes into the kitchen. Tonya beamed.

Emily spoke up. "I thought it would be fun if you guys came over to my place for dinner and drinks sometime—a night different from the seminar, of course, since I'm downtown."

"That sounds awesome," Lucas said.

Clay lit up. "Looking forward to it. Just say when."

***

Enzo sat back in the director's chair at the end of the evening. "If you remember back to the first day of The Symposium, Jack had you hold up a piece of paper when you checked out of the conversation with your partner. That exercise highlighted how we live in two different worlds; one is in our thoughts, and the other is when we are present to what we are actually experiencing in the moment.

"We find freedom when we spend less time trying to understand and explain our thoughts, and more time experiencing the present. Freedom is what's left when you're in the present.

"Go out and create experiences. Be present in the moment. Be present to your life. See you next week."

As Emily and her friends gathered their things, Enzo came up to them and introduced himself personally to Clay, Lucas, and Tonya.

"Emily, can I talk to you before you leave?" Enzo asked her.

"Sure." She said goodbye to everyone and walked with Enzo over to a corner of the room as her heart beat faster.

"I'm glad to see you making friends here," Enzo told her.

"Yeah, they're great."

"So, you're heading to New York Friday morning?"

"Yes."

"Do you need a ride to the airport?"

Why would he ask that? "No. Addison is taking me."

"So, the piano man isn't going?"

The pit in her stomach grew heavy. "No."

Enzo nodded thoughtfully. Emily could feel the tension building between them.

"You know, Jack Fletcher lives in New York."

Somersaults sprang in her stomach.

"You should reach out and say hi." He stared at her defiantly like he just threw down the gauntlet.

Did Jack tell him??

There was an uncomfortably long moment of silence between the two of them.

"Maybe I will," she finally said. "I need to go. Goodnight."

Emily couldn't stop picturing Enzo's face on the drive home—a mixture of hurt and anger, jealousy and sadness. As wrong as it was, she felt connected to him. She hated knowing she was hurting him, but she was also angry that he had any expectations of her.

***

Addison stopped by the bar at the beginning of Emily's shift on Thursday. "So, are you all packed for New York?"

"Pretty much. I don't know what to take. He said to pack light—whatever that means."

"I think it means don't bother bringing too many clothes."

Emily smirked.

"So, are you staying at his place?"

"I guess. He asked me if I wanted him to get me a hotel room, but I didn't know what to say. It's just so awkward. At the time, going to see him in New York sounded amazing. But now, thinking about the logistics is making me a little sick to my stomach. He and I both know the whole reason I'm going there is for us to..." Emily lowered her voice to a whisper, "have sex—which when planned like this is..."

"Awkward," Addison finished Emily's sentence, repeating her sentiment. "So, what did you tell him?"

"I just told him it's up to him. I mean, a hotel room in New York City for two nights would be hundreds of dollars."

"Emily, money obviously isn't an issue for him if he's flying you out first-class, spur of the moment."

"Yeah, I guess. I just wish he had said he was going to get me a room—not leave it up to me."

"Do you really want your own room?"

Emily hesitated. "No. But then, what if it sucks? What if I can't stand him? I really know nothing about him."

"Well, just make sure you have money for taxis and a hotel room. You don't want to be dependent on him or feel obligated to anything."

"I will, but I really can't afford it. This is the third weekend in a month that I haven't worked. My funds are pretty low, so hopefully, it all goes well. I mean, what the hell am I even doing?"

Addison stared at her with a helpless smile on her face. "Well, it should be an adventure."

"Yes, it should," Emily laughed.

"What time do you want me to pick you up tomorrow morning?"

"I have to be at the airport by eight. Can you pick me up at seven?"

"You owe me big, girly," Addison said. "See you in the morning."

***

It was a busy night at the bar with a live band playing. As closing drew near, Emily looked up to see Dylan sit down in front of her. Her stomach dropped.

"I was hoping to get some of that creamy tiramisu you told me about," he said, smiling with his stupid, mischievous grin.

Emily stared at him. *What the fuck. You stood me up last week and now you just walk in here at closing time so you can get laid?* "Sorry, kitchen is closed."

"Well, I can think of other creamy desserts that don't require this kitchen."

He's not even trying to hide what he's after. "Seriously?"

"What?"

She shook her head and picked up a rag to wipe down the bar.

"Sorry I haven't been around. I've had a lot going on," he said.

"Good for you." She refused to look at him.

"Not like that. Family stuff."

I'm not even worth a text, apparently. She continued cleaning in silence.

"So that's it?"

No, that's not it! I want you to come to me with your tail between your legs. Tell me how sorry you are that you stood me up and haven't bothered to reach out since. I want you to tell me how much you've missed me and beg me for another chance—that you've realized I'm amazing and incredible, and you don't want to lose me. I want you to want to take me out to dinner and make me feel special. I want you never to want to leave at the end of the night.

After a few more moments of silence, Dylan Holt walked out the door.

Emily was hurt—hurt he stood her up, hurt he didn't fight harder for her forgiveness. And hurt that he didn't want anything from her other than sex. But mostly, she was angry at herself for believing he would think she was different from all the other girls. She was angry at herself for expecting anything more than what he offered.

Enzo walked up to her. "I take it he's not happy you're going to New York?"

Emily didn't look at him while she started restocking the bar. He stood there for a few moments before walking away. "I hope you enjoy your weekend, Emily."

Part Two

When we were children, we used to think that when we were grown-up, we would no longer be vulnerable. But to grow up is to accept vulnerability. To be alive is to be vulnerable.

Madeleine L'Engle

Fifteen

The incident over the phone seemed like an alternate universe to Emily. Bringing the disconnected fantasy into real life, she didn't know how to act upon seeing Jack since their explicit conversation.

Do I shake his hand? Hug him? Kiss him?

She walked out of the airport and spotted him casually leaning against a black limousine. He looked different to her than when she saw him at the Symposium. Scruffier. Hotter. He was wearing expensive-looking distressed jeans with an old, faded Oingo Boingo t-shirt.

"Welcome to New York." He smiled as he pushed himself off the limo and walked toward her. Taking her bag, he slid his other arm around her waist and kissed her cheek.

"A limo?" Her giddiness momentarily broke through.

"You mentioned you were robbed of the opportunity at your high school prom, and since this weekend is all about trying new things, I thought we'd start with the most basic."

She regained outward control of her expressions despite the apprehensive exhilaration she felt. "I didn't realize that was the focus for this weekend?"

"Of course it is. For you to embrace who you are, you need to experience new possibilities."

"Thank you for the limo." Emily smiled graciously and climbed in, trying to be mindful of her short skirt as he followed behind. She took a spot on the long luxurious leather seat across from the bar, while Jack sat on the short side, perpendicular to her.

"How was your flight?"

"Very nice. My first time in first class." Her nervousness constricted her throat, making her voice low and quiet.

"Hopefully, this weekend will be many firsts for you. Can I get you a drink?"

"Yes please." *An entire bottle.*

"Let's see," he crawled over to the bar on his knees. "I believe you said you like tequila, yes?"

"I do."

"Here's some Don Julio 1942. Are you familiar with that?"

"I'm a bartender," she reminded him. "That's a nice sipping tequila."

"Right." He pulled out two shot glasses and poured, managing not to spill a drop in the moving car.

He handed Emily a glass and raised his. "To Emily connecting with her authentic self."

They clinked just as the car suddenly hit the brakes, causing Jack to lose his balance and fall into Emily. Tequila splashed onto her wrist.

"Can we shoot a sipping tequila?" Jack asked.

"When the time calls for it."

"Well, I think this time may call for it because you seem slightly nervous."

"Just a little."

Jack took her wet wrist into his other hand and brought it to his mouth, licking up the spilled tequila. Her entire body shivered which she was sure he could feel.

After they each had a second shot, Jack placed the glasses on the rack and turned back toward her, remaining on his knees. He wrapped his hands around her calves. "I make you nervous?"

She could hardly breathe. "Not you. Just the circumstances, I guess."

"I understand. Can I help you relax?" He slowly ran his hands up her bare legs, his fingers grazing the outside of her thighs. She couldn't form words, so she nodded, staring into those same compassionate eyes she found comfort in up on stage three weeks earlier.

Gently pushing her knees apart, Jack moved in closer.

Goosebumps scattered across her body.

"Can I kiss you?"

She nodded again.

His lips were the softest she had ever felt, like satin pillows caressing hers. His tongue coaxed her mouth open while redirecting her body to lie down on the seat. His hand slid up her skirt and caressed her satin panties, his fingertips skimming underneath the sides.

Her body tingled with anticipation.

Sitting up, Jack used both hands to pull her panties off. He moved her outside leg to the floor and buried his face.

His warm mouth was magical and gentle as he took his time tasting her. There was no instant climax, no hurry to get her to come quickly. It was as if he were sipping her, savoring every drop.

Emily was startled out of her dreamlike state by a knock on the window.

"We're here." Jack sat up, smiling as he reached his hand out to help her sit up. "You seem a little more relaxed now."

Heat radiated from her body as she pulled herself back together.

"I love how you taste." He kissed her lips softly. "Don't forget these." Picking up her panties, he stuffed them into the outside pocket of her bag.

It was dark now, and Emily stepped out from the limo in front of a massive old building. Lights poured from the revolving door.

"Are we at a hotel?"

"No, although it used to be. Now, it's apartments. This is The Ansonia." Jack placed his hand on the small of her back as he guided her inside. The black-and-white-checkered marble floors and high ornate ceilings lined with chandeliers were breathtaking.

"You live here?"

"I do."

"It's gorgeous."

"I'm glad you like it. I think so, too. It's one of the most historic buildings on the Upper West Side. Pre-war."

Denver had some beautiful, historic buildings that Emily loved, but she hadn't seen anything of this magnitude.

"Many scandalous things have taken place here over the years. Used to be home to a swingers club and a gay bathhouse where Bette Midler and Barry Manilow started their careers." He pulled her into him for another deep kiss as the elevator doors closed.

His apartment was elegant and understated—*much like him*—Emily thought to herself. Dark hardwood floors, white walls, and floor-to-ceiling windows were a beautiful backdrop for his tasteful, modern furniture.

"I need to finish up some things for work. I assume after a long day of traveling, you may want to unwind a bit and take a shower. We'll go out and grab a bite to eat in about an hour. Sound good?"

"Perfect, thank you."

Walking her back to his bedroom, he kissed her again before closing the door on his way out. Emily fell back onto his white bed, the down comforter cushioning her fall. She couldn't believe she was in New York City with Jack Fletcher. She wondered what her friends from the seminar would say if they knew. Would they think less of her?

After her shower, Emily finished getting ready and pulled on a short black skirt and a white billowy blouse tied at her waist. Not wanting to bother Jack while he was working, she looked over his bookcase: *Welcome to the Monkey House, Daring Greatly, Tropic of Cancer, Become What You Are, The Great Gatsby.*

She recognized one and pulled it off the shelf. *Fear of Flying,* by Erica Jong. She remembered seeing this book in her mom's room when she was a little girl. She laid down on Jack's bed and began reading.

My mother read this??

A little while later, she heard a knock on the door. Jack slowly opened it. "Emily?"

Rolling onto her side, she looked up at him and smiled. "Hi."

"I'm sorry that took so long. There's a big case my firm is working on, and I needed to answer some emails. Thanks for being patient with me."

"Of course."

"What are you reading?"

She held up the book to show him.

He chuckled. "I couldn't have chosen a more appropriate book for you if I tried. I want you to have it." He approached the bed and took the book from her hand, placing it on the nightstand. "But I'm afraid you'll have to read all about the zipless fuck on the plane ride home. You'll have no more time to read this weekend." He looked down at her with his hands on his hips. "We have a problem."

"What's wrong?" She thought maybe he had changed his mind about having her in his space instead of a hotel room.

"I came in here prepared to fetch you for dinner, but now I'm too distracted." He crawled onto the bed and pulled her onto his lap. "Perhaps we could have an appetizer here?" Lifting her shirt over her head, he admired her small breasts tucked into a black lace de`mi bra. "I want to fuck you, Emily."

Her heart jumped.

"Do you want to fuck me?"

She nodded her head.

"I want to hear you say it."

She remained quiet.

"Emily, I want you to tell me you want to fuck me."

"I do," she whispered.

"Say it, Emily. Tell me what you want. Own it."

Emily's brain was racing. She did want to, but she couldn't say it to his face. She didn't want to sound like a slut. She remembered their conversation over the phone and how he demanded it then. It was easier when he wasn't in front of her.

"Emily," he took her face in his hands, "Get out of your head. You are not a whore for wanting to fuck me. Do you want to fuck me?"

"Yes."

"Tell me."

She looked into his eyes and found the courage to speak the words. "I want to fuck you, Jack."

"Make me believe it."

Moving down his legs, she unbuttoned his jeans and reached inside to massage him. "I want you to fuck me, Jack."

"Mmmm..." He watched her for a moment before he pulled out a condom from his nightstand drawer. "Put this on me."

Emily must have looked surprised.

"Rule number one about embracing your sexuality, Emily, is being responsible. Fuck as many men as you want but be safe about it."

She took the little package in her hand and slid his pants off. "I want to taste you first."

Jack moaned when her mouth enveloped him. "That feels incredible." But he stopped her after a couple of minutes. "If you keep this up, I'm going to come. And I don't want to come before I fuck you."

Emily stood up to take off the rest of her clothes. She tore open the condom wrapper but struggled to get it on him; she had never put one on a man before. He was patient, with an amused smile, while she figured it out and climbed back on top.

He filled her up as they both groaned in pleasure at the joining of their bodies. His thumb circled her clit while she moved up and down, bringing her to a quick orgasm.

Emily collapsed on top of him allowing the bliss to spread through her whole body.

He wrapped his arms around her. "I'm looking forward to making you come over and over again these next couple of days."

She peeled herself from him and climbed off. "Wow... how did I get so lucky?"

He rolled over and placed his hand on her belly. "Well, I'd be lying if I didn't admit there's something in it for me too." He leaned over and kissed her. "Let's go grab some dinner."

"I think I'm going to need another shower first."

"No. I want to smell sex on you all night." He picked up her bra and panties. "And none of these," he said, tossing them onto the chair in the corner.

"You're kidding?"

"Part of your training." He helped her up from the bed.

Emily pulled on her clothes and walked into the bathroom. Her curly hair was wild, and she could see her nipples through her blouse. Jack walked in behind her and reached around to unbutton two more buttons, leaving her shirt open down past her breasts. Sliding his hand in, he cupped one. "Perfect."

"I can't go out like this," Emily laughed.

"It's New York. You'd be surprised what you can do. Let's go." He took her hand and led her into the living room, where he grabbed a blanket as they headed out the front door. "I thought we'd walk through Central Park after dinner. There are a lot of outdoor concerts going on right now."

"That sounds perfect."

"Do you like Moroccan food?"

"I don't know. I'm not sure I've ever had it."

He looked at her in disbelief and shook his head. "You need to get out more."

***

They were seated at a low table at the restaurant in a corner surrounded by flowing fabric and tapestries hanging from the ceiling. There were no chairs—only big pillows to sit on. Jack chuckled as Emily tried to carefully navigate down to the ground in her short skirt without flashing the host. He handed her the blanket to cover up with and sat down next to her.

The server brought them sweetened mint tea with small bowls of olives and nuts before returning with a large silver teapot and basin. Raising the pot high above them, he poured rosewater over their hands to prepare them for eating and explained they were to eat with their right hand using only their thumb and first two fingers. "Using more would be considered gluttony."

The first course was Vegetarian Bastila—steamed vegetables with chopped almonds, raisins, and cinnamon, baked in phyllo dough and dusted with powdered sugar.

"This is delicious!" Emily's taste buds were lighting up receptors she never knew she had.

"And the view is phenomenal," Jack added, looking at her almost-exposed breasts.

Next, the server brought Chicken Tagine, bread, and couscous. Jack encouraged Emily to sop up the food and sauce with a piece of bread.

"So, what's going on with you and that bloke? What's his name again?"

"Dylan. And nothing much."

"Are you still seeing him?"

"No. He stood me up last week and then showed up at my work last night—at closing time—completely unapologetic."

"And you shut him down?"

"Pretty much."

"So, safe to say, you and he were on different pages? He was just looking for a good shag while you were expecting a relationship?"

"I wasn't expecting a relationship. Just respect."

"As you should," he agreed. "So, what does that look like to you?"

"In that situation, communication, I guess."

"What would you have liked him to communicate? A couple of weeks seems like a pretty short amount of time to have any kind of expectations."

"He told me last night he had family stuff going on. If that were really the reason, he could have sent a text at any time—just to say hi, tell me why he's not around."

Jack stopped eating for a moment. "But if that weren't really the reason—and I suspect it wasn't—what would have been a better thing for him to say? What if he's fucking other women? Would you want him to tell you he can't see you that night because he's shagging someone else?"

"No."

"Why not? You're not okay with him fucking other people?"

"I guess I don't want to think of him being with other people while he's with me."

"And yet, you're here." He looked at her matter-of-factly. She didn't respond as shame hit her. "Emily, there's nothing wrong with you being here. Don't get back in your head. All I'm trying to get you to see is if you're staying in integrity about it. Did you tell him you were coming to New York to spend the weekend with me?"

"Well, he and I aren't in any kind of relationship, apparently, so I didn't feel obligated to."

"Exactly. Do you see the double standard going on here?"

"How is expecting him to send me a text creating a double standard?"

"Emily, let's say he was banging some other girl last week. What would you want his text to say?"

She was silent.

"He can't win here; you know that, right? Unless you both had an agreement that there were some expectations of your relationship, he owes you nothing."

"How about just courtesy?"

"Courtesy to let you know he's fucking someone else? Did you give him the same courtesy? I'm assuming you thought you and he were still a thing when we spoke on the phone last week?"

She was silent again. Even though Dylan had stood her up, she had hoped he would call with some excuse, apologizing profusely.

"Let me ask you this—why did you agree to come here?"

Emily flushed with embarrassment. "Because I was curious about you," she admitted.

"Okay, got it. Can Dylan be curious about other women?"

She thought for a moment and finally smiled in defeat.

"You are living in the moment right now, Emily, and that's exactly what you should be doing at... twenty-four?"

"Yes. Almost twenty-five."

He laughed. "Blimey! What the hell are you doing with me?"

"Because you said you would be my guide."

He looked at her thoughtfully. "That's right... I did."

For dessert, the server brought them fresh oranges sprinkled with orange flower water and cinnamon.

"How can such a simple dessert be the best thing I've ever had?" Emily asked in amazement.

While they watched the belly dancer and ate the fruit, Emily lay back in Jack's arms, feeling as if she had known him for years.

After dinner, they walked through Central Park until they found some live music. Standing on the outskirts of the venue, Emily leaned back against Jack and held the blanket around them to keep warm.

Jack slid his hand under her skirt and slowly massaged her until she came, crumbling into his arms for support.

Back at his apartment, he bent her over the dining table, facing a mirror. Jack's eyes locked onto hers. "Tell me what you want me to do, Emily."

"Fuck me, Jack," she pleaded.

He slammed into her, and she cried out, closing her eyes as she relished in the submissive position he had her in.

"Look at me."

She found his eyes once again in the mirror.

"Do you like getting fucked hard, Emily?"

"Oh, my god, yes!" Emily's eyes closed.

"Look at me," he commanded. "I want to look into your eyes as I make you come."

The velocity he pounded her with made it difficult to keep eye contact.

"Tell me what you like, Emily."

"Fucking you, Jack," she said breathlessly. "Fuck me harder!"

He increased his intensity, pulling her hips into him with every forceful thrust.

"Play with yourself," he growled.

Emily knew not to ignore him.

"Oh... my... god..." Her entire body shuttered in spasms, and she collapsed onto the table.

Jack pushed in one final time, letting out a grunt. He folded himself over her as they both tried to catch their breath.

When they crawled into bed that night, he pulled her into him and kissed the top of her head. "I'd say day one of your training was a smashing success."

Sixteen

E mily woke up to Jack's hand caressing her cheek.

"Good morning."

She smiled, blinking away the sleep and taking in the golden sunrise pouring into the room.

He straddled her and left a trail of kisses on her body as he slid down and nestled between her legs. She ran her fingers through his hair until her body burst into waves of pleasure.

He put on a condom and slid inside of her. They stared into each other's eyes as they took their time moving in unison. She wondered what he was thinking and how he was feeling about her. She watched his face closely, noticing every flicker of bliss. The corners of his mouth slightly curved upward into the faintest hint of a smile, and droplets of sweat appeared on his forehead. His eyes widened in ecstasy before he shut them and let out a subdued groan, pushing into her. Emily loved that he couldn't seem to get enough of her. She loved the sense of power she experienced knowing she could bring him such pleasure.

"That's a nice way to start the day." He kissed her and rolled off to the side. "How do you feel about helicopters?"

She turned her head towards him. "Why?"

"I figured since it's your first time in New York, there's some required sightseeing that needs to take place." He looked back at her and smiled.

***

The helicopter ride was exhilarating. Emily saw famous buildings she had only seen in movies and pictures. The views of Central Park and the New York skyline were stunning. When they landed and exited the helicopter, Emily threw herself into Jack's arms.

"That was one of the most amazing experiences of my life!" She kissed him. "Thank you."

"You're welcome." He kissed her back. "Now, time for shopping."

"Shopping?"

"Well, you can't very well come to New York and not shop," he stated. "Besides, I figured that would ease the blow of telling you we need to have dinner tonight with a client of mine before you and I attend the show."

"What show?"

"I'm taking you to see *Phantom of the Opera*. You need to see a Broadway show while you're here, and there's nothing like a timeless classic."

He hailed a taxi and whisked her off to Saks Fifth Avenue—the original flagship store in midtown Manhattan. Walking past the iconic window displays, Emily was in awe. As Jack held the door open for her, she stepped into a glorious world of luxury that she hadn't known.

They walked past the iridescent escalator and took the elevator to the third floor.

Emily felt very much out of place, but the sales associate, Simone, put her at ease with her comforting smile and friendly demeanor. Jack informed Simone that Emily needed to find a dress to wear for dinner that night at The View before heading to Broadway. Simone walked around with them, gathering six little black dresses before escorting Emily back to the fitting rooms. Three pairs of black heels were promptly delivered to try on with the LBDs.

After parading out in each dress for Jack's opinion, it was the last one that prompted him to say, "that one." Unlike her shopping experience with Isabella, Jack chose the sexiest dress—a slinky one-shoulder dress that hugged her curves. Its asymmetrical hemline began at the top of her right thigh and stretched down to just above her left knee. Simone helped her pair it with black, thin strappy stilettos that wrapped up her ankles, enhancing her long legs.

To complete the look, Simone chose a set of rhinestone stud earrings for Emily. "Simple and elegant. Do you have a favorite perfume?"

"Not really."

"Might I suggest picking up a bottle of Chanel No. 5? It would perfectly complement this classic look."

Jack arranged with Simone to have everything delivered to his place. He took Emily across the street to Rockefeller Center, where they grabbed some lunch on an outdoor patio.

"So, you consider California your home then?" Jack wanted to know more about Emily's life growing up.

"I guess." she contemplated. "My mom liked to move around a lot, so I never really got too comfortable in one place. We lived in a few different states but always ended up back in California."

"What was that about?"

"She was diagnosed as bipolar when I was seventeen, so that probably had something to do with it."

"Ah, yes," Jack nodded. "What was that like for you?"

"Moving around?"

"Yeah, that and having a bipolar mum."

"When I was little, I adored her. She was a great mom. We had a lot of fun together, and I actually kind of liked finding new houses to move into. It was like an adventure. But after my brother moved out, and it was just me and her, I guess I started to resent her more."

"Why? What happened?"

And just like that, Emily was thirteen years old, standing outside of the empty middle school for three hours on an early release day waiting for her mom. "I was convinced she was dead on the side of the road somewhere but then she pulled up, smiling and waving as if nothing was wrong. Turned out she was having a long lunch with her friend and forgot me. That happened a lot."

"I see," Jack said. "And what did you make that mean about you?"

She pushed down the lump that was forming in her throat. "Well, clearly I wasn't a priority to her."

"Ah. You weren't important enough to remember to pick up. Right?"

Emily's chest tightened, and she gripped her fingers, taking in a deep breath.

"Emily, you've collapsed what happened with a story about what happened."

"What do you mean?"

"Well, the facts are that your mom forgot to pick you up. She's human. Single mom struggling with a mental disorder, right?"

"Right."

"But you made it mean that you weren't important enough. You made that up. Can you see other areas in your life where you've collected evidence for not being important enough?"

Emily sat with this as bubbles popped in her head about friends, school, jobs. She began to see the common thread.

Jack continued. "I'd like you to consider that you've been living your life out of a story you made up at thirteen that you're not enough."

Emily nodded as that soaked in.

"Can you let it go?" Jack asked. "Let go of the story that you told yourself at thirteen years old that you're not enough?"

As she stared back at him, she smiled at the realization that he was right. "Yeah, I can."

He took her hands into his. "Call your mom when you get back to Denver. Acknowledge her and get complete about all that, okay?"

"I will."

"Brilliant." He stood, guiding her up with him. "Time to move on to the next destination."

The black two-story boutique had six large panes of glass that showcased scantily-clad mannequins in the most beautiful lingerie Emily had ever seen. *"Agent Provocateur"* was scrawled across the middle in gold script.

Inside, the pink walls and black furniture highlighted the exquisite bras and panties hanging on the walls. Mannequins strewn about the store displayed some of the more provocative styles.

A young, gorgeous woman named Darla greeted them, wearing a short pink nurse's uniform unbuttoned to her stomach and resting high on her thighs. A black lacy bra and garter belt with stockings peeked out from underneath. Jack told Darla they were looking for the right piece to wear under a dress for Emily. Once Emily described the dress, Darla took them around to choose some items for her to try on.

Leading them both back to the fitting room, Darla handed Jack a glass of whiskey and Emily a glass of champagne before closing the curtain and leaving.

Emily was shocked.

He's going to watch me try on lingerie?

"Well?" He took a sip of whiskey, settling into a smoldering smile.

She pulled her sundress over her head and tossed it to him. Keeping on her red satin thong, she slipped on a strapless sheer lace bodysuit. She took a sip of champagne and slowly turned around for Jack so he could assess the outfit.

"Beautiful. How does it make you feel?"

"Sexy."

"Good." He nodded as he took another sip of whiskey. "Next."

Jack watched her naked body maneuver out of the ensemble and reach for the next piece. Fastening the black strapless bra behind her, she adjusted her breasts in the cups.

He smiled. "How does this make you feel?"

Emily didn't feel much different than she did every day. She had strapless bras at home, and while this one was beautiful, it didn't excite her. She shrugged her shoulders.

"Next."

She looked at the last piece. The intimidating black lace corset hung in front of her. Reaching up, she undid the hook and eye fasteners before taking it from the hanger. She pulled it around her chest and hooked the top loop as she slowly began moving down, closing up the corset around her body until all that was left to do was tighten the ribbons hanging down her back. Jack was staring at her, sipping his whiskey. She bent over, facing him, to adjust her breasts, giving Jack a nice mirror view of her ass.

"How are you doing in there?" Darla asked on the other side of the curtain.

Standing back up, Emily answered, "I'm good, thanks."

"Okay, great," Darla responded. "I'll check back in a few minutes."

"I think I'm going to need your help with this," Emily told Jack.

He set his glass down and put her sundress to the side as he stood up. Walking over to her, he turned her around, so she was facing the mirror. He pulled the laces tight, causing Emily to gasp. When he finished lacing her up, he whispered in her ear, "How does this make you feel?" He caught her eyes in the mirror, resting his hands around her waist.

"Powerful," she said softly, looking at herself.

Jack brushed her hair to the side as he kissed her neck. Sliding his hand into her panties, it didn't take much to get Emily shaking. She covered her mouth so no sound could escape. As her body started to convulse with pleasure, she pushed his hand away. Leaning against the mirror, she tried to return her breathing to normal.

"This one," Jack said as he licked his fingers and smirked.

Once they left the dressing room, Darla approached them with a big smile. "How was that?"

"I'll take this." Emily blushed as she handed over the corset.

Jack walked around the store, looking at panties until he found a pair he liked and brought them up to Darla to ring up.

"One last stop before heading back to my place for a nap."

Jack took Emily into an understated-looking boutique called, *The Pleasure Chest*. Everywhere Emily looked, she saw dildos and vibrators of all shapes and sizes. She had never been in a store like this before and was slightly embarrassed. Jack picked up on her nervousness.

"Ah, sweet Emily. Another step in your training is to set you up to enjoy pleasure of all kinds." He held her hand as they walked around, looking at everything the store offered. Walking past a wall of whips, chains, and handcuffs, Emily felt her core tingling as she imagined herself being restrained.

"Does that excite you," he asked her, leaning in closely.

"A little."

"Sometimes, embracing your power means choosing to surrender to someone else."

Emily felt electricity surge through her.

Jack looked at the wall of pain. "But this is probably not something you're ready for right now. Let's start smaller." She wasn't sure if she was relieved or disappointed when he led her away to another section.

Looking over the vibrators, he picked up a box showing a picture of a purple u-shaped object.

A woman approached them. "Ah, you've found our best-selling toy."

"How does this work?" Jack asked.

The woman took the box out of his hand and opened it up, taking out a plastic case. Lifting the lid, she revealed its purple silicone gift.

"You would insert this thinner part inside so that it rests on your g-spot," she explained to Emily, "while this thicker part would press against your clitoris. See the ridges here? That's where the magic happens. When you press this button..." With that, she did, and the little thing started vibrating. "You can change the intensity, too. Couples can even use it during intercourse so the man can also feel pleasure." She smiled at Jack.

Emily was mortified to be having this conversation with a stranger.

"I see," Jack said thoughtfully.

"Oh, and the best part," the saleswoman continued, looking at Jack, "It comes with an app you download onto your phone so you can control it from anywhere in the world."

Emily's stomach flipped.

Jack clapped his hands together. "Sold!"

Seventeen

When they returned to the apartment, Jack told Emily they would be leaving in two hours to meet his client at the restaurant. Emily decided to use that time to shower and get ready while Jack rested on the sofa. She used her big barrel iron to tame her wild curls into smooth waves and glammed up her make-up with smoky eyes and red lips. Opening the pink bag from Agent Provocateur, she pulled out the panties that Jack had thrown in at the last minute.

Of course. Emily laughed.

The sheer black tulle in the front wrapped around her hips and disappeared into thin straps that perfectly outlined her bare ass. There was no crotch.

After spritzing on Chanel No. 5, she pulled out the corset and slipped it on, fastening it closed. Now, she just needed Jack to tie the ribbons in the back. She put on her black heels, wrapping them up around her ankles, before walking out into the living room to find him asleep.

Happy to see he had changed into pajama bottoms, she dropped to her knees on the floor next to him and slipped her hand into his pants.

He opened his eyes and smiled at her.

"Sorry to wake you," she teased as she massaged him.

"You look beautiful," he said sleepily. "Stand up. Let me see you."

When she stood, she turned around and said, "I need your help."

His hand caressed her bare cheek. "Sublime."

She turned back toward him and crawled into his lap, straddling him. "I want you now."

He kissed her neck and chest, breathing her in. "Mmmm... sadly, it will have to wait."

Emily pouted. "Fine, but I do need your help."

He carefully pulled and adjusted the ribbons and corset while she watched in the reflection of the mirror. "One more thing." Reaching into the bag from the Pleasure Chest, he handed her the vibrator. "I'm getting into the shower. The car will be here in thirty minutes."

Emily held the purple object in her hand, pressing the button to feel the different intensity levels. *Oh. My. God.* Turning it off, she slipped it inside and positioned it the way the sales lady explained. She felt it just enough to remind her it was there, but not so much that it was distracting.

A few minutes later, Jack appeared, wearing a black suit with a white dress shirt—the top few buttons undone. Butterflies rushed into her stomach.

"You are breathtaking." He walked toward her and kissed her softly. "Ready?"

A black Cadillac waited out front. The driver opened the door for Emily, and Jack slid in after her.

"So, tell me about this client of yours we're meeting." Emily was curious about how this was going to go. She had never tagged along on a business dinner as someone's date.

"His name is Steven Briggs. He owns several properties around the city. He's a good guy."

"What will you be discussing tonight?"

"Don't worry, no business tonight — just a nice dinner. When your biggest client invites you out, you accept." He took her hand into his.

"Will it just be him?"

"He's bringing a woman he's just started seeing. I've never met her."

Emily ran her fingers along the inside of his thigh. "So, do your corporate clients know about the secret life you live as a sexy seminar leader?"

He chuckled. "They are aware I lead seminars around the country, yes. A few have even taken them."

"Has Steven?"

"Yes, he has."

He pulled out his phone and appeared to be working on something. Emily felt the sudden vibrations, causing her to jump.

Jack laughed. "It works." He tapped the phone again, and the vibration accelerated. Fully aware of the driver's presence, Emily tried to keep it together, squeezing Jack's hand. She was sure sparks were going to start flying out of her any minute as she shifted in the seat, audibly gasping. She caught the driver glancing back at her in the rearview mirror, and she quickly looked away so she wouldn't have an orgasm staring into his eyes.

As they pulled up to the Marriot Marquis, Jack tapped his phone, and the vibration mercifully stopped. He leaned over and kissed her before getting out of the car. Walking into the lobby, he explained to Emily that The View was Manhattan's only revolving restaurant. It sat perched atop the hotel with the best views of Times Square. They took an escalator one floor up, where they checked in at a podium that stood in front of an exclusive glass elevator that whisked them up to the forty-eighth floor.

Stepping out, Emily took in the scene. The circular restaurant was wrapped in windows, showcasing the brilliantly lit buildings outside as it slowly rotated around the cityscape. Fashionably dressed men and women sat at the small tables sipping cocktails and laughing while servers, clad in black and white tuxedo-style uniforms, walked in between the groups.

Jack spotted Steven and his date waiting for them in the lounge. "You've got to be kidding me."

"What's wrong?"

"His date."

"What about her?"

"We dated for a bit."

Emily couldn't help but let out a little laugh. "Really?"

"She's a psychotic cunt."

It surprised Emily to hear Jack talk about someone like that. It seemed so out of character for him.

Well, this should be fun.

Emily saw a man raise his arm and wave to Jack. The woman sitting next to him opened her mouth in disbelief. She looked to be in her late forties, very put together and polished with her blonde hair pulled back into a sleek bun at the nape of her neck. Emily found her classic beauty and elegance somewhat intimidating. Jack took Emily's hand and walked over to the lounge.

"Hi, Jack." The man stood up and greeted him with a big smile, shaking his hand. "Glad you could make it."

"Of course, Steven. Great to see you," Jack responded with uneasiness in his voice.

Steven turned his attention to Emily, absentmindedly eyeing her up and down. "Hi, I'm Steven." He extended his hand to her.

"Hi Steven, I'm Emily."

Steven reached out toward his date, beckoning her to stand, which she did, reluctantly. "This is Vanessa."

"Yes, Jack and I already know each other," she said curtly, noticeably not extending her hand or acknowledging Emily.

"Oh, you do?"

"Yes, nice to see you again, Vanessa."

"I'm sure," she responded, acid dripping off her tongue.

Emily noticed the reality dawning on Steven. He looked like a deer in headlights as his eyes met Emily's. She smiled in uncomfortable sympathy.

"Well, shall we?" Jack turned to walk down the stairs to the restaurant area, where the host quickly took them to their table. The men stood as the women sat down next to the window, across from one another. Jack and Steven sat next to their respective dates. Emily noticed Vanessa avoided looking at her.

The server approached to take their drink orders. Vanessa spoke up first. "Belvedere dirty martini." She didn't look at him as she barked her order.

He then turned to Emily. "And for you, Miss?"

Emily looked up and smiled warmly. "I'd like Clase Azul, neat, please."

"Reposado or Gold?"

Emily hesitated. A glass of Gold at Josephina's was fifty dollars and likely cost more here. But Jack had told her this weekend was about indulgence. "Gold, please."

He nodded graciously and turned to Jack. "And you, Sir?"

"I'll have the same."

"Sounds good to me," Steven exclaimed. "I will, as well."

"Are you sure she's old enough to drink, Jack? Tequila shots? Really?" Vanessa stared at Jack like he was a child she was reprimanding.

Emily was stunned by Vanessa's acerbic comments. "I'm sure as I age, my taste will grow into martinis," she said sweetly.

The men quietly chuckled. Vanessa finally looked at Emily and rolled her eyes.

After the drinks came out, Steven raised his tulip glass. "Here's to a lovely evening."

Everyone lifted theirs toward the center except for Vanessa, who aimed only at Steven.

"Oh, that's smooth," Steven commented. "I've never sipped tequila before."

"I'm glad I could turn you on to something new." Emily knew her tequilas, and she was thrilled she had something of value to share with these successful people who were almost twice her age.

Vanessa shook her head as she looked away.

Jack explained to Emily that the restaurant served a three-course prix fixe menu. He went over the options with her and asked if she would like him to order for them both.

"Yes, please." She had seen movies where the man ordered for the woman. Emily's aunt always said it was controlling, but Emily thought it was very romantic and sophisticated. And she certainly felt like she was in a movie right now. Plus, she had no idea what half the things were on the menu.

Jack told the server they would both start with the Cream of Shellfish Bisque. Emily would have the Seared Black Sea Bass, and he would have the Filet Mignon, medium-rare. They would share Haricot Verts and a Chocolate Souffle for dessert.

Vanessa said to the server, "I can order for myself. Fois Gras to start followed by the salmon."

Steven ordered crab cakes and the New York Strip Steak, and another round of drinks for the table.

Emily attempted to break the ice with Vanessa. "So, Vanessa, what do you do?"

"I'm an Interior Designer," she said flatly and then looked at Jack. "Where did you meet her? Speaking engagement at her high school?"

Wow. "Actually, I took one of his seminars. Have you ever participated in them?"

"Pffft, no way you'd catch me listening to all that new-age psycho-babble."

"I find them very enlightening," Steven interjected.

The conversation through dinner was mostly between Jack and Steven, with both men making attempts to include Emily and Vanessa. As the drinks made another round, Vanessa continued to spit out rude comments aimed toward both Jack and Emily. By the end of their meal, Emily had enough of Vanessa's condescending attitude toward her and her vitriol toward Jack—and just enough tequila to embolden her. When the server brought out their souffle, Emily asked him for some hot tea with extra cups for the table.

"I don't want any tea," Vanessa snapped.

Emily smiled.

The server brought out a beautiful teapot with three delicate teacups. Emily picked up the teapot and looked Steven in the eyes. "I have hot tea. I'd like to give you some of my hot tea."

A smile spread across Steven's face as Jack chuckled. "I would love to have some of your hot tea."

She happily filled his cup before turning to Jack. "I really need to give you some of my hot tea."

"Yes, you do."

After she poured for both of them, she picked up a fresh strawberry and dipped it in the chocolate sauce. Very slowly, she opened her mouth, exposing her tongue to delicately lick the chocolate off before placing the whole berry in her mouth and biting down, sealing her lips around it.

"Mmmm...." she moaned, closing her eyes. Setting the stem down, she wiped the dripping juice from the corners of her mouth and looked at Jack. "I want more."

"You're insatiable." He smiled.

"I am."

"Oh, this is ridiculous," Vanessa interrupted. "Are you having fun with this child, Jack? Does she stimulate your mind?"

"No," Emily slowly broke her gaze away from Jack and looked directly at Vanessa. "Just his dick."

Both men almost spit out their tea.

Vanessa's eyes filled with rage. "Don't think you're the first young plaything he's had!"

"I wouldn't be surprised," Emily remained calm. "He's an exceptional fuck." She looked back at Jack with a smug smile.

Vanessa stared incredulously at Emily before throwing her napkin down on the table and getting up to leave.

"Goodbye, Vanessa!" Steven yelled after her. Raising his teacup, he said, "More hot tea, please."

***

Phantom of the Opera was spectacular. Emily sympathized with Christine's torment between the seductively dangerous draw of the Phantom and the security and stability of Raoul. She often felt that duality within her. Something that Jack seemed to recognize.

As they stepped out of the Majestic Theater, Jack told Emily he wanted to show her one of New York's underground sex clubs. "How would you feel about that?"

"That sounds... interesting."

He pushed her into a small alcove on the outside wall of the theater, shielding her from the crowd. Pulling her into him by her waist, he kissed her deeply and passionately. She couldn't get enough of his mouth.

He pulled away and held up his phone. With a tap, Emily felt intense waves of pleasure shooting through her. Jack enveloped her lips again, holding her tightly. She couldn't follow his tongue with hers. She couldn't focus on anything but the orgasm that was quickly building. Tilting her head back against the wall, he began fervently kissing her neck and ears as her entire body cinched up and released itself in rapture.

She grabbed onto him as tightly as she could, burying her face into his chest, breathless cries escaping her mouth as the crowds walked past them, oblivious to her ecstasy. The vibrations stopped. Jack held her while her body recovered, and her breathing slowed.

"I like that toy," he growled.

"I can certainly understand why it's their best-seller."

After walking a couple of blocks, Jack took her hand and guided her down a nondescript stairwell and through a door, where they found themselves in a small lobby. He approached the counter to talk with the man while Emily stood back, looking at the vintage pictures of orgies hanging on the wall. She was nervous about what she was going to walk into.

Does he expect me to participate in an orgy?

Emily knew she wasn't ready for that, and it worried her that Jack might want that from her.

"Ready?" He reached his hand out for her.

Probably not.

Stepping through the simple door, Emily was surprised at what she saw. Crystal chandeliers provided dim lighting. Velvet chaise lounges and sofas scattered throughout held writhing, naked bodies. Music blasted while people danced—some with their clothes on, some without. It looked like a swanky, upscale club, aside from the people having sex out in the open.

Jack took her over to the elegant mahogany bar. "I'm thinking this would be one of those times to shoot tequila?"

She laughed. "I agree!"

He ordered Patrón Silver, and they quickly slung it back.

"So, how often do you come here?" Emily was curious but not sure she really wanted to know the answer.

"I don't. I just thought this would be an invaluable part of your education this weekend, so I did a little research online."

Thank God.

"One more shot?" He held up his empty glass.

"Definitely!"

Afterward, she grabbed his hand, pulling him toward the dance floor. "I want to dance!"

"I don't dance."

Emily didn't care. "Play That Song" by Train was filling her body with the desire to move. She placed her arms over his shoulders as she danced against his body. Turning around, she positioned his hands around her waist, pushing her ass into his crotch. His mouth grazed her neck as she reached her hand up and grabbed his hair. Emily could feel his craving for her. Turning back around to face him, she teased her lips over his. She wanted to drink him up. She wrapped her arms around him and guided his body to move in unison with hers.

As the song ended, he took her hand. "Let's go explore."

They went through a door down a hallway with small rooms. Black velvet curtains closed off some while others were wide open, showing people engaged in all kinds of sex acts. Emily stopped as they walked by an empty room with a majestically high, regal-looking twin bed covered in dark red satin sheets. Shackles hung from the painted black wall and a leopard-print velvet chair sat tucked in the opposite corner.

"How does this work? Can we just go inside and play?" she asked.

A woman directly out of Penthouse magazine approached them from behind, surprising Emily. "You're able to have the room for one hour. These are the rates." She handed Jack a piece of paper. If you'd like to use it, just sign here, and we'll charge it to the card you gave at check-in."

Jack quickly signed and led Emily into the chamber, pulling the curtain closed. While he hung up his jacket on a wall hook, Emily connected her phone to the Bluetooth speaker and found a *Sexy Songs* playlist on Spotify.

As Sarah McLaughlin sang "Ice Cream," Emily returned to Jack. After removing his belt and tossing it on the bed, she undid his pants and unbuttoned his crisp dress shirt. She ran her hands across his chest and around his back, gently scraping her fingernails along his bare skin. He closed his eyes and breathed in deeply.

Emily wanted to make him feel as good as he had made her feel all weekend. She dropped to her knees and pulled his pants down. Surprised to discover him wearing cosmic-print bikini briefs, she smiled up at him and took him into her mouth.

"Bloody hell," he moaned.

She moved her hands to his backside and let her fingers graze in between his cheeks as she squeezed and heard him breathe in quickly.

He pulled her up. "Come here." Stepping out of his shoes and pants, he slid off her dress, revealing her corset, and led her to the wall with the shackles. Pulling down a small cushioned bench protruding from the wall, he lifted her so she could sit high. He raised her arms above her head and placed her wrists in the restraints, locking her into place.

The determination on his face sent a ripple of deep desire through Emily. He pushed her legs towards the wall as he guided each one through a black strap that kept her spread open. Picking up a silk sash, he tied it around her head, covering her eyes. She felt very exposed and vulnerable, but she trusted Jack. And she remembered his words to her earlier in the day: *"Sometimes, embracing your power means choosing to surrender to someone else."*

The vibrations from the toy began pulsing inside her. Jack pulled her corset down to rest under her breasts as he took her flesh into his mouth, twirling his tongue around and sucking it in before moving on to the next. She felt something clamp down around one nipple and then a cold chain dragged across her chest and clamped onto her other. She cried out, unable to decipher between pleasure and pain.

He kissed her and then pulled out the toy. His hand smacked her exposed clit, sending waves of electricity coursing through her body. She cried out again. She had never experienced anything like it. The darkness over her eyes took away her awareness of what his next move would be while she sat there in breathless anticipation.

He smacked her clit a second and then a third time. Shockwaves reverberated through her. Emily felt his tongue moving softly up and down to soothe the sting. And then he sucked her clit into his mouth mercilessly. She was screaming. She couldn't move. She couldn't push him away. He just kept going until her hips were bucking violently. He stood up and placed his hands over her shackled arms against the wall, slamming his cock into her—her body still in spasms from her intense orgasm.

Jack undid the restraints, released her, and lifted her from the bench. Carrying her across the room, he sat down on the chair. Her long legs straddled him with her feet on the floor. She gasped at how much deeper he went into her. As she began moving up and down, he smacked her ass. Hard.

"Do you like that, Emily?"

Oh, god, yes!

"Get out of your head, Emily," he commanded and smacked her ass again. "Do you like that?"

She was breathless as she bounced up and down, her pace increasing.

"Yes! Again!"

He spanked her again and again until she came once more, screaming, and collapsed into him.

Removing the clamps from her nipples and the sash from her eyes, he kissed her deeply.

She wanted to devour him. She kissed him back passionately before stepping off. Grabbing his belt, she wrapped it around his wrists and buckled it. He looked shocked. She pulled the condom off and sucked him into her mouth, moving up and down as the grip of her fingers followed her lips.

"Emily, I'm going to come!"

She kept going, only increasing her pace.

"Oh, my god... Emily... I'm coming!" And with that, he shot into her mouth, letting out a loud groan. Emily swallowed her victory, licking up the last drops.

"You are unbelievable."

She sat up higher on her knees and undid the belt from his wrists, gently kissing his chest as he stroked her hair.

"Let's go," he whispered.

Back at the apartment, they peeled off their clothes and stepped into the shower, where they quietly soaped each other up, cleaning their bodies. After drying off, they climbed into bed, exhausted from such an eventful day, and quickly fell fast asleep.

***

Sunshine filled the room as Emily looked over to see Jack was not lying next to her on her last day there.

Pulling herself out of bed, she went into the bathroom to freshen up and brush her teeth. She grabbed his dress shirt from the night before and slipped it on. When she walked out into his living room, she found him sitting at the dining table with his laptop.

He looked up at her. "Well, good morning."

"Good morning. When did you get up?"

"I've been awake for a couple of hours. I had to take care of some stuff for work." He stood up. "That's a good look on you." Taking her into his arms, he kissed her. "I made coffee and picked up some almond croissants. We have a great little patisserie in our building that's famous for them."

"Sounds delicious." She had no idea what a patisserie was.

"How do you take your coffee?"

She noticed the delicate white porcelain creamer pitcher and sugar bowl sitting on the counter. "Cream and a little sugar would be great."

Carrying their breakfast to the sofa, Emily curled up under the blanket in the corner.

"You were amazing last night, Emily. This whole weekend, actually. More than I expected."

She looked at him and smiled softly. "I've had an amazing time." She could feel the pit in her stomach grow at the thought of having to leave in a couple of hours.

"I'm glad. It's good to see you embrace who you want to be."

"Well, you make that easy. Denver is going to be pretty boring after all of this."

"It doesn't matter where you are or who you're with, Emily. You command a room when you walk into it. Don't forget that." Jack took her hand into his. "I got as much out of this weekend as you did, if not more."

She smiled at the thought. "How so?"

"Well, you know how we have assistants at the Symposium?"

"You mean the free labor?" she smirked.

He chuckled. "Assisting is essentially a hands-on training program on the actions and principles of making a difference. The training empowers people in many aspects of their lives, the most important one being a contribution to others." He brought her hand to his lips. "Though this is obviously not the norm, I was like your assistant this weekend in your transformation. In doing so, I became better at being myself as well. And I had the best time watching you triumph over your shame."

Emily loved who she was with Jack. She loved what he brought out in her. She believed him and she believed in herself. And she knew she would never be the same.

Eighteen

Emily walked out of baggage claim to see Addison pull up. When she got into the car, she leaned over to greet her with a hug, and inexplicably, broke down crying.

"Oh, my god," Addison held her. "Are you okay?"

After a few moments, Emily pulled away, wiping her tears from her face, and laughing at the ridiculousness of her outburst. "Yes. I don't know what came over me."

On the drive home, Emily filled Addison in on her weekend get-away—everything from the limo ride to the dinners, shopping, and Broadway, the visit to the sex club, and their last tender moments together that morning.

"Wow... it's almost like a real-life Pretty Woman."

"Are you calling me a prostitute?"

"No! Oh, my gosh... no! I..."

Emily cracked a smile. "Well, he didn't pay me $3,000, but I did get to keep the clothes."

Addison laughed, seemingly relieved she didn't offend her friend. "So, what's next?"

"What do you mean?"

"When will you guys see each other again?"

Emily's tears briefly returned to her eyes. "It's not like that."

"I don't get it. If you guys had that kind of connection, why wouldn't you continue seeing each other?"

It was hard to explain. Emily knew it would be hard for others to understand. Though a part of her fell a little in love with Jack over the weekend, she knew his role in her life was one of mentorship. Admittedly, an unusual kind of mentorship. She did wish their lives could have aligned in a way where their relationship could exist differently, but she was grateful to have even crossed his path, regardless of how brief their interlude was.

When they arrived at Emily's apartment, Addison came upstairs.

"Enough about me. How was your weekend?" Emily asked.

"Well," Addison said reluctantly, "I guess you could say you're not the only one who had a transformation." She pulled off her baseball cap and slowly turned around for Emily's inspection.

It took Emily a moment to realize Addison no longer had a long ponytail extending from the base of her neck. "Oh, my God, Addy! You cut off your hair!" She jumped with excitement and ran her hand along the soft short hairline outlining the back of Addison's head. "I love it!"

Addison beamed. "Thanks! I do too."

"You look like a little pixie. It really suits you."

Addison's expression quickly turned to one of concern. "So, I need to tell you something else."

"Okay." Emily sat down to give her full attention.

Addison sat next to her and took a breath before blurting out, "I'm gay."

Emily stared at her without expression as she tried to process what she just heard. "What? Since when?"

"I think I've known for a while," Addison began explaining. "I was just having a hard time admitting it to myself. But after the night with Barry, things became clearer for me."

"You shouldn't let one bad experience ruin all men for you."

Addison laughed. "Em, I'm not gay because of Barry. Being with Barry just confirmed for me that I'm not into men. And this weekend solidified that even more."

"Why? What happened?"

"Let's just say... I met someone who made it abundantly clear for me." A slight smile appeared in the corner of Addison's mouth.

Emily was still trying to wrap her brain around what Addison was saying. How could she not know this about her best friend of five years?

"Are you okay?" Addison looked nervous about her revelation.

Emily gave her a reassuring smile when she realized she must have looked upset. "Of course, I am. You know I'll always love you, no matter what. I'm just surprised because I never suspected it, which kind of makes me feel like a shitty friend for not knowing you as well as I thought I did."

"Don't feel that way, Em." Addison now tried to reassure her. "I didn't even know for myself until just recently. And I've purposely kept it from you because I didn't want you to feel weird around me. I had to sort through my own feelings about it. But after this weekend, I'm comfortable with accepting who I am and ready to share with you."

Emily wrapped her arms around Addison. "Well, then you better tell me what happened to give you such clarity."

Addison laughed, a huge grin taking over her face. "Oh, my god, Emily, it was incredible! I went dancing with Diego and Todd Friday night, and this person came over to me, and we started dancing. We danced together for probably an hour until we needed a break. They bought me a drink, and we sat out on the patio and talked the rest of the night. When it was closing time, we walked out together, and they asked if I wanted to come to their place for another drink. I was just so drawn to them—so I did!"

Addison's smile somehow got even bigger.

"Once we got inside their place, they kissed me. And everything finally just made sense, ya know?" Addison was glowing. Her brown eyes had a sparkle in them that Emily had never seen before. "I didn't leave their place until today when I came to pick you up."

"Oh, my god, Addison!" Emily laughed. "Seriously? Well, what's her name?"

"Shelby. Their pronouns are they and them."

"Well, I hope I get to meet them soon," Emily grabbed her friend's hand. "I'm so happy for you, Addison."

"Thanks, Em. You're my best friend, and I don't ever want to lose you."

"You will never lose me, Addison Greenberg. You'll always be my best friend."

***

The following day, Emily awoke to the reality of her life. Pulling on jeans, she headed over to see Isabella for their Monday morning meeting.

"I heard you went to New York for the weekend?" Isabella's face was full of excitement.

"I did," Emily smiled, trying to hide her nervousness. She had hoped her cover story would sound believable.

"Were you visiting a friend?" Isabella asked as Enzo walked into the room, his eyes penetrating Emily.

"Uh... yeah." Emily stumbled a bit under Enzo's glare. "A guy I met online."

"What's his name? I want details!"

"Steven. He's in real estate."

"I'm impressed. Will there be another trip anytime soon?"

"I don't think so." Emily masked her sadness with annoyance. "We didn't really hit it off."

"Oh, that's too bad. I'm sorry. Well, tell me where he took you. What did you do while you were there?"

"I'm heading out," Enzo interrupted. "See you tonight," he kissed Isabella on the cheek and walked toward the door. "Welcome home, Emily."

***

That night at work, Emily caught Enzo looking at her often. The knots in her stomach were making her queasy every time their eyes met.

Damn it! She was mad at herself for feeling as if she had betrayed him somehow.

While they were closing up, he came behind the bar to help her restock. "So, a realtor you met online?"

She didn't respond.

"I thought for sure you were going to see Jack Fletcher." He watched her for a reaction. "He seemed pretty enamored with you."

Emily's heart raced. "Why would you say that?"

"I saw him add you as a contact on his phone. And he specifically asks about you whenever I speak with him."

"Enzo, I don't want to talk to you about this."

"So, you did go see Jack?"

Own your shit, Emily. She heard Jack's voice in her head.

She turned to look Enzo directly in the eyes. "Yes."

"I see." He stared at her coldly.

"What do you want from me, Enzo?"

He looked at her for a long moment. "Nothing, Emily," and walked back to his office.

***

"Being responsible for one's life means taking a stand that you, not the circumstances, are the cause in the matter of your life," Enzo said to the group at the seminar the next night. "I'm not talking about blaming yourself or feeling guilty. Rather, deciding that you're up to dealing with the matter because you're the author of it. When you can authentically own what's going on at that level, only then do you have the power to do something about it."

Even though Emily knew the seminar was following a course syllabus, she felt as if Enzo was directing every topic toward her, secretly sending her coded messages she was expected to decipher.

At the end of the evening, Tonya asked Emily when they would all be getting together for that promised night of dinner and drinks.

"I have to work the rest of this week, but how about Sunday night?" Emily suggested.

Tonya and Lucas quickly agreed.

"I can come for dinner but can't stay and drink with you guys. Some of us have to work for a living," Clay said sarcastically.

Emily saw Tonya's face deflate.

"Can't you just call in sick the next day?" Lucas asked him. "You seriously work all the time, dude. People do get sick—even you Captain America."

Emily loved how her little nickname for Clay had caught on.

"Lying about being sick doesn't keep me in integrity," Clay pointed out.

"Can you take a vacation day then?" Tonya asked, hopefully.

Clay seemed to be mulling things over.

"Oh, come on," Emily encouraged cheekily. "That's what this course is all about—being spontaneous, living a life full of passion. You never know who you'll inspire."

Clay looked around at their eager faces. "It's also about being responsible for our lives. So, what's the plan for everyone getting home if we're all shit-faced?"

"You guys can spend the night at my place. I have a sofa and giant beanbag and lots of blankets and pillows for the floor," Emily assured him.

Clay smiled. "You make a compelling offer. I'm always up for a slumber party. Fine, I'll be there."

Nineteen

Emily made balsamic chicken breast with garlic mashed potatoes and roasted asparagus. She enjoyed cooking for her new friends and hosting her first dinner party. After setting the table, she lit candles, dimmed the lights, and turned on some vintage jazz music. She realized she had a newfound desire for sophistication since spending time with Jack.

Tonya arrived first. "Holy cow!" she exclaimed as she looked around at Emily's eclectic apartment. Her eyes settled on the small round dining table covered in a blue Batik tablecloth. An antique silver candelabra sat in the center. "I thought we were just coming over for a casual dinner and drinking."

"I know. I just wanted to do something extra."

"This is definitely extra," Tonya laughed.

"Here," Emily handed her a shot glass filled with chilled Absolut Citron and set down a small plate of sugar-covered lemon wedges. "Tonight is about relaxing and having fun." Raising her glass to Tonya's, they slung back their drinks and bit into the sugared lemons.

"Wow... that was good!"

"Just be yourself tonight, Tonya, and see what happens with Clay."

When the boys arrived, they also seemed a little taken aback by the scene.

"Great place," Clay said, looking around at Emily's things. "Oh, I brought this." He handed her a bottle of Skrewball peanut butter whiskey along with a tub of Häagen-Dazs vanilla ice cream. "You pour the whiskey over the ice cream. Best dessert ever."

"Sounds delicious." Emily was impressed by his contribution. "We'll have it later tonight."

She poured vodka shots for the four of them and instructed the boys on the art of biting the lemon at just the right moment. "You guys need to do another one to catch up."

As Emily was dishing up the food, Clay walked up behind her. "Need help?"

She put two plates in his hands. "Sure, you can take these in for you and Tonya."

Picking up the other two plates, she followed him out to the table.

"This is awesome. I've never been to a dinner party my parents didn't throw," Lucas said.

"I've never been to a dinner party at all," Tonya laughed.

"Yeah, we're not as fancy as you," Clay teased Emily.

Emily loved that she could do this for her new friends. It made her feel good that she could show them something they had never experienced.

This must be how Jack felt on some level.

After dinner, everyone took their plates to the kitchen, and Emily poured more lemon drops. She brought out the box of macarons she had gotten that morning from Drunken Bakery, a whimsical little place that recently opened in Larimer Square.

"What are these?" Tonya picked one up to examine it.

"Delectable clouds of French bliss." Emily bit into a pistachio one—her favorite.

The four of them spent the rest of the evening drinking vodka and eating macarons while dancing to all of their favorite songs. When Shania Twain came on, Tonya tried to give a line-dancing lesson to Clay, but he broke away from the group and headed to the kitchen.

"Time for whiskey and ice cream."

"Yes!" Emily chased after him, feeling the effects of the alcohol. "Show me how to do this."

She pulled out small dishes and the ice cream scoop while he retrieved the Häagen-Dazs from the freezer.

"It's a very precise recipe," he explained, spooning the vanilla into four dishes and making a little indentation on top of each one. He reached behind Emily to grab the whiskey, his arm brushing up against her waist. "Excuse me." He looked into her eyes. "You need to watch closely."

God, he has incredible eyes. Crystal blue. Is that a ring of gold around them? Amazing.

Emily nodded as he unscrewed the cap. She broke her attention away from his face to follow the bottle of whiskey as the caramel-colored liquid filled each small indent, cascading down the creamy mounds of ice cream.

"As the hostess, you should be the first to taste it." Clay offered a bite, and she opened her mouth as he guided the spoon in. After she closed her lips around the whiskey-covered ice cream, he slowly pulled the spoon back out.

"Mmmm..." She moaned, closing her eyes as she savored the ice-cold creamy peanut butter taste. "That's amazing!"

"Glad you like it."

Emily opened her eyes to find herself captivated by him once again. She couldn't look away.

There are even tiny white flecks sprinkled in like stars. Like a dusting of magic. He has magical eyes.

Clay's amused smile dissipated some as he cleared his throat, snapping Emily out of her drunken trance.

Grabbing two of the bowls, she ran back to Lucas and Tonya just as they finished their line dance, laughing and stumbling into each other.

"I have the most amazing thing ever!" Emily handed them each ice cream. "Clay made these."

They all dropped onto the floor to enjoy their second dessert.

It was 3:30 am, and everyone was falling asleep. The whiskey bottle was empty from the boys' continued drinking. Emily turned off the music and grabbed some blankets and pillows for Clay and Lucas to crash in her living room. She and Tonya dragged themselves to her bedroom where they fell fast asleep.

Feeling a hand stroke her face, Emily opened her eyes. Clay was on his knees at the side of the bed, looking at her, the moonlight barely illuminating his face. They stared at each other before he brought his mouth to hers, his tongue gently parting her lips.

Half-asleep, she reached her hand up around his neck, losing herself momentarily in the sensual kiss before she realized what was happening and pulled away.

"Clay, we're just friends," she whispered.

"I don't want to be just friends."

"We can't do this."

"Why not?" His inebriated eyes searched hers for answers.

Part of her wanted to give in and kiss him again. It felt natural. Like home. But then Tonya stirred, and Emily remembered her friend's feelings for him.

Let him go, Emily.

She shook her head, no.

His gaze lingered before eventually standing up and leaving her room.

Emily woke up just before eight in the morning, her hangover hitting hard. Remembering she was supposed to be at Isabella's for their Monday morning meeting, she sent her a text saying she was sick.

Isabella

Sorry to hear that. Hope you feel better soon. xoxo

After a couple more hours of sleep, Emily stumbled into the kitchen.

Thank god I bought coffee yesterday.

She hadn't considered the thunderous roar the grinder would make when she pushed the button down.

"Make it stop," someone moaned.

She brewed a full pot, kicking herself for not remembering to drink water and take Tylenol the night before like Dylan had taught her.

"Coffee," she mumbled when it was ready.

As they all sat around nursing their hangovers, Emily had a brief flash of Clay kissing her.

Did that really happen?

When everyone was ready to leave, they each hugged Emily good-bye—including Clay—who didn't act like someone who had been rejected a few hours earlier. She wasn't sure if it was real or a dream.

However, later that night, she received a text confirming it.

Clay

> Hey Emily, I owe you an apology. After I left today, I remembered what I did. I am soooooo sorry!!

So, it did happen. She was relieved for his apology.

Emily

> It's okay. We all had a lot to drink.

Clay

> True. But I still should have never done that. It crossed a line and I hope you don't hate me for it.

Emily

> Of course I don't. I'm just really enjoying our friendship and want to keep it that way.

Clay

> I totally understand. I'm glad we're friends!

Emily

> Me too.

Emily's stomach fluttered as she touched her fingers to her lips, remembering the softness of his tongue in her mouth.

***

As she pulled into the parking lot at the seminar center Tuesday night, she drove past Clay who was walking toward the building. When he noticed her, he stopped to wait while she parked and met up with him.

"I'm so embarrassed." He smiled, shaking his head.

Emily was embarrassed too, but she didn't want things to be awkward. "Hey, alcohol has made us all do stupid things."

Clay laughed. "Right? I don't know what I was thinking— kissing you for the first time with Lucas and Tonya right there." She could tell by the playful tone he was trying to make light of the whole thing.

"Funny," she smirked.

His voice dropped. "But seriously, it was creepy of me to do that the way I did. I know we're just friends, and I want to keep being friends. You forgive me?"

"Of course I do." She could still see the embarrassment in his eyes, so she reached up to give him a reassuring hug.

He wrapped his arms around her and held her. "You have to admit, though, it was a pretty amazing kiss."

Butterflies flew into Emily's stomach as the memory came rushing back. Pulling away, she smacked his arm and headed inside while he followed behind, laughing.

"Let's talk about happiness," Enzo began. "We all want to be happy—after all, it's one of our inalienable rights to pursue as Americans. But what defines our happiness? We often believe that external things will make us happy: A high-paying job, a luxury house with a matching luxury car, a beautiful woman, a rich man. And when that doesn't come together fast enough, we start to dial down our expectations; we settle for what we already have and hope it won't go away. We begin to protect what we seem to have won: the job we are miserable in but pays the bills, the partner who doesn't treat us well and gaslights us–but hey–at least we're not alone. But being truly happy means more."

He scanned the room, making sure he had everyone's attention. "If you get nothing else out of tonight's seminar, get this: Happiness is not dependent on circumstances. Happiness is a possibility. Happiness is a choice about where you're coming from."

Twenty

Colorado prides itself on its nature and beauty, so it's to be expected that most of its inhabitants would opt to spend the Fourth of July holiday outdoors barbecuing and picnicking. The city's parks all had events scheduled, including live concerts. Emily saw the posters around town promoting the LoDo Dogs at Civic Center Park, so she was thankful her family opted to go to Washington Park this year instead. They drove down early in the morning to stake out their spot near the pond at the boathouse.

Her stepmom, Amy, brought her famous guacamole and sprouts sandwiches on rye. It was one of Emily's favorites; so different from anything she had grown up on. Her mom's side of the family was all about surf 'n turf, including her brother David who never developed the same appreciation as Emily for sprouts and whole grains.

They would all be at the annual barbecue at the beach today. She did sometimes miss her mom and California. Every year, they would gather at Newport Beach with their friends to watch the fireworks and the boat parade after spending the day on the sand. Their large group would bring in steak, chicken, lobster, and bacon-wrapped scallops to cook over the grill throughout the day while the teenagers and younger kids body-surfed in the ocean or walked around Balboa Fun Zone and rode the carnival rides.

Emily grew to love the holidays in Colorado with the other side of her family. Their traditions were different from what she was familiar with, but she enjoyed the simple family gatherings that were more about the people than the food.

"Sissy! Can you take us on a paddleboat?" Summer pleaded with her.

"Of course. Let's go!"

Holding hands, the three girls skipped toward the pond. After taking a spin around the water, they jumped in the bouncy houses, ate cotton candy, and had their faces painted with sparkly stars.

"Do you really have to go to work tonight?" Summer pleaded.

"I do. I'm sorry."

"But you'll miss the fireworks." Rain wrapped her arms around Emily's waist.

"I know. I'm sad I won't be here to enjoy them with you. Will you both do me a favor?"

They nodded their heads enthusiastically.

"Will you draw and paint pictures for me of what they looked like?"

"Okay," they said in unison, hugging their big sister goodbye.

***

Dinnertime was slow at Josephina's for a Saturday night, but everyone knew to prepare for the influx of partiers after the fireworks displays were over and the community events closed down. Enzo came behind the bar to help Emily stock.

"How are you, Emily?"

"I'm fine," she bristled.

It had been two weeks since they had spoken privately with each other after her admission of visiting Jack in New York. She still felt guilty whenever she saw Enzo. She wondered if he now regretted signing her up for the seminar—which she was now immensely grateful for. *Funny how things change.*

They stocked the bar together in silence until they found themselves standing next to one another, lining up glasses.

"Nice stars."

She looked at him, confused, and he pointed to her face, reminding her of the sparkles she had painted around her eyes earlier.

"Oh, I'm sorry. I got it done with my sisters today at the park. I'll go wash them off."

"No, it's okay. I like them."

They both resumed stacking glasses silently.

"Look," he finally spoke up, "I don't want there to be this tension between us. Yes, I hate that you spent a weekend with Jack instead of me. But I get it."

Emily's breathing quickened. *Shit, this is uncomfortable.*

"Do you have plans to see him again?"

"No." She could barely get the word out.

After another couple of minutes, he asked, "Are you enjoying the seminar?"

"I am," she told him truthfully.

"I'm glad to see you're creating happiness for yourself. It's exciting to watch the process."

"I really do appreciate what you've done for me." Emily finally relaxed. "I do find it all fascinating. I look forward to it every week."

Enzo smiled.

"Who knew you were so wise?" she teased.

"Everyone!"

Once the sun set and evening took over, Enzo came through the bar area with four other servers. "Emily, come with me."

There were only a few people in the bar, so she left Stephanie to manage them and followed Enzo and the others up the back stairs. Walking past unused furniture that was stored away, Enzo went behind the small bar and pulled out a bottle of Remy Martin XO Excellence Cognac, pouring some into six brandy snifters.

He handed Emily her glass, and they all walked over to the large windows overlooking Larimer Square. An annual tradition. Enzo stood behind her as the fireworks lit up the night sky, and the cognac warmed her chest. The small crowd oooo'd and ahhhh'd at the spectacle of the brilliant explosions of light before they headed back down into the restaurant, ready for the onslaught of revelers.

The rest of the night was nonstop and went by in a blur. The bar was packed right up until two a.m., keeping both her and Stephanie continually pouring and mixing.

By the time she stepped outside to walk home, she was thoroughly exhausted.

"Hey, bartender!"

She looked back at the three drunk frat boys she had just passed.

"We'd like another drink," one of them slurred.

She rolled her eyes and continued walking home, recognizing them from when they kept ordering shots of Jägermeister and Goldshlager up until closing time.

"Drinks at your place?" One grabbed her hand and walked along with her.

Pulling away, she snapped, "Don't touch me," and quickened her pace.

Another boy stepped in front of her. "Come on, let's have some fun tonight."

Emily tried to walk around him, but the third boy blocked her on the other side.

"Have you ever had three guys at once?" he sneered.

Just then, tires came screeching down the street, and Enzo jumped out of the car, wielding a baseball bat. "Get the fuck away from her!"

All three boys jumped back. "Whoa, chill dude! We were just playing with her. She told us she wanted to have some fun."

"Yeah?" Enzo's eyes were on fire. "I want to have some fun, too!" He charged them with the bat, and they took off running. "If I ever see your faces in my restaurant again, you won't be walking out!"

He turned back to Emily. "Are you okay?"

"Ummm..."

"Let's get you home." Enzo guided her into his car.

Pulling up in front of her building, the reality of the situation hit Emily, and tears began streaming down her face as she struggled to breathe.

Enzo reached over and placed his hand on hers. "Hey, you're okay. I'm here."

"But what if you weren't?"

"But I was. And I promise I'll always make sure you get home safely in the future."

"You can't do that every night."

"Sure, I can. It's one of the benefits of being the boss."

Emily nodded as she wiped away her tears.

"Are you going to be okay tonight? You're welcome to stay with Isabella and me."

"I'll be fine. I'm just a little shaken up."

He stared at her for a moment before opening his door and walking around to her side. He helped her out of the car and pulled her into him—just like he did on the last night of the Symposium.

"Are you scheduled to work tomorrow?"

"No."

"Good. I want you to relax and take care of yourself. And call me if you need anything. I'm here for you."

"I will, thank you." She wanted to ask him to stay with her, keep her protected in his arms all night. But instead, she walked into her dark apartment, alone, and immediately climbed into bed as the dam of tears broke through and she cowered under her down comforter.

***

"Oh, my god, Emily," Isabella reacted when she opened the door. Stepping out onto her porch, she grabbed Emily into a hug. "Enzo told me what happened the other night. Are you doing okay?"

"Better. I'm just so grateful Enzo was there."

"Me too. Come inside; let's get some coffee."

The two women had just sat down at the table to discuss the upcoming event when Enzo walked in.

"How are you doing, Emily," he asked, concerned.

"I'm okay," she responded. "I spent yesterday hanging out with Addison. We've decided to take a self-defense class together."

"That's so good to hear," Isabella said. "I also told Enzo he needs to send you home in an Uber when you get off work late at night. Women shouldn't be walking home alone, especially at that hour. We live in a different world than men."

"Absolutely," Enzo kissed the top of Emily's head. "But if you ever get cornered like that again, I hope I'm there to see you kick their asses. I have to head out. Have a good meeting, ladies."

Isabella patted Emily's hand before pulling out her notebook and moving on from the topic. "I'm so excited to do a casino-themed event for this upcoming birthday party. I've always wanted to do one of these."

"So, people will be gambling?" Emily asked, unsure how the gambling laws worked in Colorado.

"No. Anyone who wants to play will receive a stack of chips. It's just for entertainment," Isabella explained. "The poker tables are getting delivered at four o'clock on Thursday, and the dealers will be there at six-thirty. Since they've rented out the bar, you'll handle the drinks for the party, and Enzo will have Stephanie take care of the dining room. The guest of honor will be arriving with his family at seven sharp. It's a surprise, so I'll have you pretend to be the hostess up front and seat them by bringing them into the bar area."

"Sounds good," Emily agreed.

"But I'm not crazy about the work uniform," Isabella continued. "We want to make this feel like a high-end gambling club. Do you happen to have a little black dress you could wear instead?"

Why, yes, I do.

***

"How you show up in life began as something you decided," Enzo addressed the audience on Tuesday night. "You forgot, but you did decide. And just as it was then, it is still up to you every single day. You can choose to show up fearful and bitter, or you can create a new possibility.

"Bad things are going to happen in life. People are going to be jerks, including you. While we think we can control that, you have lived long enough to see it's not that simple. What you do control—whether you are noticing it or not—is your response. You get to take responsibility for how you react to upsets. Acknowledging that you have a choice is what allows you the freedom to take a stand for a new possibility."

Twenty-one

E mily pulled out her corset and smiled at the memory of the night she wore it. Placing it back in the drawer next to her crotchless panties, she picked up a simple black thong. Recreating her New York look, she texted Jack a picture of herself.

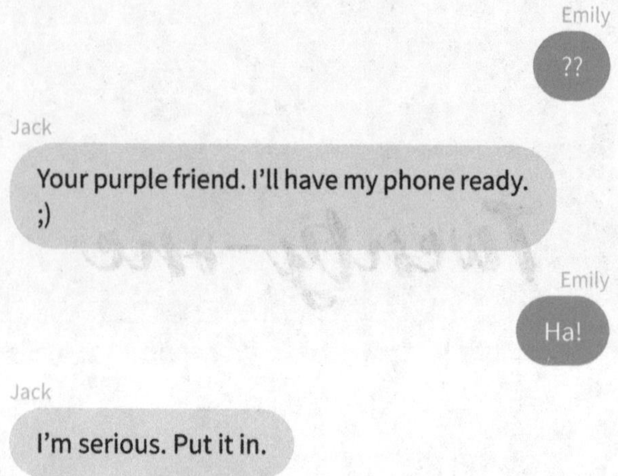

It had been three weeks since she had come home from New York, and they hadn't played with their little toy since. She was excited at the thought of what could lay ahead. Digging it out of her panty drawer, she slid it inside of her.

Her phone lit up with a FaceTime call from Jack. She answered and saw his sexy smile.

"I just wanted to see your face."

And then she felt it—the intense vibrations shot through her like lightning. She closed her eyes as a loud gasp escaped her mouth, instantly transporting her back to New York.

"God, I miss that," he growled.

She grabbed onto her dresser for support as the speed increased and almost brought her to her knees before it finally stopped.

"Keep that in tonight. I want to have more fun with you."

Emily caught her breath. "I can't handle that while I'm pouring people drinks."

"I promise I'll keep it gentle. Please keep it in."

Recovering from her orgasm while still throbbing from the vibrations, she breathed out, "How could I ever say no to you?"

She spritzed on Chanel No. 5 and headed back to the restaurant, feeling turned on and vibrant.

As she walked through the door of the already bustling Josephina's, she noticed a few of the servers doing double-takes.

Isabella was the epitome of elegance in her classic black sheath. "Wow, Emily! Where did you get that dress?"

"New York."

"I have a feeling more went on in New York than you're letting on," Isabella said to her with a knowing smile.

Emily pretended to zip her mouth closed, smiling mischievously.

"Well, you look beautiful." She handed Emily a bin of unused party decorations. "Will you please take these in the back and set them in the office?"

"Sure."

When Emily opened the door, she found Enzo working on his computer. He turned around as she set the bin on the chair next to him. "Sorry to bother you. Isabella asked me to bring these back here."

His eyes widened as they slowly traveled from her strappy heels wrapped around her ankles, up her bare legs, and over the curves of her body before finally meeting her eyes. His mouth opened slightly as if he were about to say something, but he remained silent.

Emily had to admit she liked the reaction she was receiving. She gave him a small smile as she turned around and slowly walked out.

As party guests began pouring into the room, Isabella greeted them and asked them to find seats.

"Okay, Emily, our guest of honor should be arriving any minute with his family, so why don't you head over to the hostess stand? His mother said he would be wearing a gold king's crown on his head."

While Emily waited, she greeted people as they walked in, passing them off to the real hostess. She finally saw a group of people walking up, surrounding a handsome man wearing a crown with a beautiful woman adorning his arm.

An older gentleman, his father, Emily presumed, stepped forward.

"Hello, young lady," he greeted her. "We have a reservation for tonight under Bennett."

"Yes, welcome, Mr. Bennett. Right this way."

She turned around for them to follow her into the bar. After taking them in through the doorway, she stepped aside as the group erupted into, "Surprise!"

As the party progressed, Emily felt a soft subtle vibration turn on in her panties. Walking around taking drink orders, she was sure her face looked flushed with pleasure.

The guest of honor approached her while she made cocktails behind the bar. The low vibrations continued.

She smiled at him. "I hear bourbon is your drink of choice?"

He returned her smile. "Yes, it is."

She poured him Blanton's and set it in front of him. "Happy Birthday."

"Aren't you going to pour one for yourself?"

"Not while I'm working." She smiled politely.

"Well, then, I'll just have to have one with you when you're not working."

She was not interested in more unavailable men. "I don't think your girlfriend would appreciate that."

"She's not technically my girlfriend. Besides, she doesn't have to know." He didn't take his eyes off her as he took a sip of his drink.

Dick. "No, thank you."

"Aw, come on, you can't turn the birthday boy down."

"Enjoy your party." She picked up her tray of drinks and walked back out to the tables where Isabella was mingling with the guests.

The soft vibrations continued, slowly building into what she knew would be an intense orgasm. Emily walked around the tables to quickly distribute the drinks, keenly aware she had to turn it off before she started convulsing and screaming in front of everyone. Setting down the last glass, she made a beeline to the restroom, but an elderly woman stepped into her path.

"Excuse me, is Enzo around? His mother and I are friends, so I want to say hello."

Emily glanced around the room but didn't see him. "He must be in the back. I'll go get him for you."

Her impending orgasm was now about to explode. She frantically threw open the office door, causing Enzo to spin around in his chair. "There's a woman out here who says she's friends with your mom and wants to see you." As she turned to leave, he quickly stood up and grabbed her hand. He pulled her inside and closed the door, pinning her up against it.

"I can't stand the thought of you with Jack. You're mine." He kissed her passionately, and as they both melted into the kiss, he reached around to grab her ass and pull her closer to him. Just as he did, her orgasm hit. She breathed out hard and shuddered against him, trying not to scream. Opening her eyes, she saw the look of shock on his face when he felt the vibrations against his pants.

"You are so fucking sexy!" Finding her lips again, he kissed her deeply. She could feel the waves of pleasure wash over her as she remembered holding on to Jack the same way outside of the theater.

Finally, pulling herself away, she said breathlessly, "I have to go!"

She opened the office door and quickly made her way to the restroom, ignoring Isabella's call for her from one of the tables. She had to make the vibrations stop.

Once inside a stall, she quickly pulled the toy out and turned it off, sitting down on the toilet to catch her breath. Realizing she had nowhere else to put it, she slid it back inside of her. After washing her hands, she looked at herself in the mirror and silently reprimanded herself for enjoying Enzo so much. Finally, after composing herself, she walked back out to the party.

Isabella approached her. "Is everything okay?"

"Yes, sorry. I just really had to use the restroom."

She placed an affectionate hand on Emily's arm. "It's almost time for us to do the dessert, but first, why don't you go take a break? You look a little flushed. And put some lipstick on before you come back out."

Emily walked into the back again. Thankfully, Enzo's door was closed. She moved quickly by his office to her locker, where she grabbed her purse. After reapplying her lipstick, she got out her phone to text Jack.

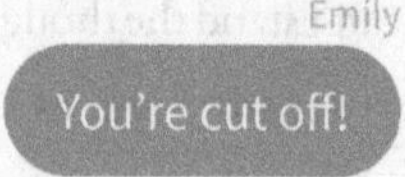

As she closed her locker, Enzo stepped out of his office to head into the dining room. Looking back at her, he smiled. "Coming?"

***

Emily stopped in to see Addison at The Market Saturday morning. "Are we still on for brunch tomorrow with Shelby?"

"Yes! I'm so excited for you two to finally meet."

"Me too. I've never seen you so happy."

"I really don't think I've ever been this happy before," Addison told her. "Everything is just so different now. Shelby is amazing. You're going to love them."

"I'm sure I will. Have you told your parents yet?"

Addison scrunched up her nose. "Not yet."

"How do you think they'll react?"

"I think my mom will probably be more accepting than my dad. He's pretty old-fashioned and religious."

"When do you plan on having that conversation?"

Addison sighed. "I don't know. Whenever the time feels right."

"Well, I hope it goes smoothly for you."

"Me too." Addison's eyes suddenly widened, and she looked nervous. Emily looked over to see Dylan walk through the door.

Shit.

"Hey," he said casually to Emily.

"Hi."

"Hey, Addison." He glanced up at the overhead menu. "Can I get a black coffee and a danish?"

There was an awkward silence as he paid and waited while Addison retrieved his breakfast. She practically threw it at him.

He picked up his food from the counter and looked at Emily. "So, how was New York?"

"Good." She recalled her conversation with Jack, where he pointed out Dylan owed her nothing, and that she needed to manage her expectations.

Dylan paused a moment and raised his eyebrows before nodding in acknowledgment. "Okay, well, see ya around."

"Are you okay?" Addison asked quietly after he left.

Emily breathed out as she kept her gaze on the door. "Yeah."

"What's going on in that head of yours?"

"I don't know. I guess I just wish he would have tried a little harder. But, honestly, I'm not even sure why he would."

"Because you're worth trying harder for Emily. Fuck, Dylan. He's an asshole."

Emily turned back toward Addison. "You're right. I was obviously just another groupie to him. And if I'm honest with myself, before New York, I think I really was looking for a relationship—like it was the end goal. But something in me has changed. I'm having fun exploring this whole new side of me."

"I think you need to keep doing that right now. Enjoy being young and single."

"That's easy for you to say," Emily smiled sardonically. "You're all happy in a relationship now."

"Well, I am a different breed than you, Emily. I've never been one to have a wild side. But you... it's like a fire that burns inside of you. Everyone sees that. You just need to embrace it right now."

"You sound like Jack."

Addison rolled her eyes. "I'm not really a big fan of Jack."

That statement surprised Emily. Addison had never given any indication of disapproval. "Why?"

"I don't know. Something about that whole situation just doesn't sit well with me. Maybe it's because he's so much older and in a position of leadership. Just seems a little... predatory."

"He's not a predator," Emily said defensively. "I wanted to go. I was very much a willing participant." She didn't like what Addison was implying. "I think Jack is amazing."

"I know you do," Addison said, her tone tinged with pity.

Emily grimaced as she contemplated her next words. "So, you probably wouldn't like hearing I kissed Enzo again?"

"Emily!"

"I know, I know! It just sort of happened during the event the other night." She looked down, trying to ignore the look of disappointment on Addison's face.

"A lot of things 'just sorta happen' to you, Emily. Have you noticed that?"

Emily stared at her, blankly. "Yes, I guess."

Addison sighed. "I don't think the thing with Enzo is going to end well, and I don't want to see you get hurt."

Emily knew she could never get Addison to understand her desire for Enzo. *I shouldn't have told her.* "I know. I appreciate that you're always looking out for me."

"Speaking of looking out for you," Addison infused her voice with sympathy and concern, "how are you doing since the whole Fourth of July incident?"

"Oh, I'm fine. Just trying to forget about it. Thank God Enzo was there, though."

***

That night at work, Enzo and Emily continued to flirt relentlessly with each other, just as they had the night before, with secret seductive glances and accidental brush-ups. Emily's skin sizzled from his touch, and she wanted more. Being careful not to let Stephanie notice their connection added more excitement to the forbidden game they were playing.

The previous night had been too busy for them to escape into his office, and since she didn't work the closing shift, there was no excuse to linger after hours. Tonight would be different.

"Hey, Emily, I can close for you tonight if you want to get out of here early," Stephanie told her towards the end of the evening. "I don't mind."

Hell, no. "Oh, it's okay. You've closed for me so much these past few weeks. And I'm off for the next two days anyway."

"I thought maybe you'd want to see your boyfriend?"

Emily was confused. "I don't have a boyfriend."

"Aren't you dating that guy from the band?"

"Oh, no... we're not seeing each other anymore." Emily was a little surprised Stephanie didn't realize that since he hadn't been around in over a month, and Emily never talked about him. Then again, Emily realized she never talked about much of anything with Stephanie. Stephanie kept to herself and never seemed interested in cultivating any kind of friendship.

Maybe I should try harder to be her friend.

Stephanie seemed concerned. "What happened?"

I flew to New York for a sex-filled weekend with a successful older man who opened up a whole new world to me, and now I find myself craving our boss.

Emily shrugged. "I'm not sure. Just lost interest, I guess."

"Okay, well, I'll go clock out then." A few minutes later, she returned, seeming agitated.

"Are you okay?"

"Yes," Stephanie replied hastily. "See you later."

Emily finished restocking, taking her time as the servers counted out their cash and left one by one. When everyone was gone, she walked into Enzo's office and closed the door behind her. Enzo spun around in his chair and looked up. They locked eyes and smiled like two teenagers who had just snuck into a closet. She immediately crawled into his lap, straddling him, and devoured his mouth, blocking Isabella from her mind.

Open marriage. Spontaneous. Living life passionately.

His hands caressed her body until his fingers found the buttons of her shirt, unbuttoning just enough to expose her chest and the soft mounds of her breasts. Reaching one hand up the back of her neck, he grabbed a handful of hair and pulled her head to the side. Kissing every exposed area of bare skin, his other hand cupped and squeezed her breast as she ground down onto his growing, covered erection.

"You belong to me," he growled as he continued kissing her.

Emily nodded in agreement. It was freeing to admit. He was her protector, and she felt connected to him.

"You are the sexiest woman I've ever known."

Empowerment feels good. Emily kissed him again and began unbuttoning his shirt, but his hand stopped her.

"I need to get home," he said reluctantly.

She pulled back, stunned. "You're kidding, right?" She leaned back in and breathed into his ear, her tongue circling the hollow. She nibbled on his lobe as she rocked her hips back and forth.

"God, please don't do that," he said, burying his face in her chest, his lips kissing the space between her breasts.

She had spent the last two days imagining what she would do to him—and what he would do to her. Was he really bailing? "I had big plans for tonight," Emily told him as she slowly extracted herself from his lap in the hope he would pull her back down.

"I'll make it up to you. I promise." He stood and buttoned her blouse. "Come on, I'll give you a ride home."

The minute-and-a-half ride to her place was quiet as she wondered why Enzo wouldn't take this opportunity to finally be with her. She wasn't sure if she should be pleased or disappointed with herself for being so bold.

When he pulled up in front of her building, he leaned over and kissed her. "Goodnight, mi amore. I'll be dreaming of you tonight."

Twenty-two

Sunday morning, Emily headed over to Pete's Kitchen on Colfax Avenue to meet Addison and Shelby. When she arrived, she found them waiting in line out front. Addison ran up to her and gave her a big hug. Taking her by the hand, she walked her over to meet her new partner.

"Emily, this is Shelby. Shelby, this is Emily."

Emily smiled and reached out her hand. "Hi, Shelby, it's nice to meet you finally."

"You too," they replied, shaking Emily's hand with a firm grip.

Shelby was taller than Addison—about Emily's height. They had short blonde hair and a dark tan. They looked very much like the outdoorsy type with their athletic build and make-up-free face.

"We just got back from a hike," Addison said excitedly.

Emily let out a laugh. "A hike?"

Shelby took Addison's hand into theirs. "Yeah, we got up early and headed up to Chimney Gulch in Golden."

"I've never known you to hike," Emily teased Addison.

"Shelby is part of a hiking group," Addison explained. "It's pretty cool. You should come with us sometime."

Emily laughed again. "I don't think I could handle it. My body would much rather sleep in."

Shelby didn't seem amused by Emily. "It's important to unplug and connect with nature regularly. Hiking helps you gain perspective on what really matters in life."

Emily couldn't quite pinpoint why, but she suddenly felt very judged. "Oh, I'm sure it does. I should probably try it sometime."

"Addison mentioned you were interested in taking a self-defense class?" Shelby asked.

Nervous pulses shot throughout Emily's body. *'Have you ever had three guys at once?'*

"Yes. I'd like to learn some self-defense. I just don't know where to begin. There are so many different types."

"I have a friend that teaches Jiu Jitsu up in Evergreen. I can ask if she knows anyone near you if you'd like?"

"That'd be great, thanks."

Addison beamed.

When they were seated, Emily ordered her usual breakfast burrito with bacon and green chili (the best in all of Denver) and some baklava for the table.

"Oh, none for us," Shelby interjected.

Emily looked at Addison, confused. "But you love their baklava."

"I'm trying to eat healthier. Make better choices, ya know?"

Shelby looked up at the server. "We're going to share a veggie omelet with a side of fresh fruit."

Emily darted her eyes to Addison.

"Their omelets are huge," Addison offered as some sort of explanation.

The server turned to Emily. "Would you still like the baklava?"

"No, thank you."

Breakfast was filled with blocks of uncomfortable silence broken up only by Addison's persistent attempts to spark conversation between her partner and best friend. Emily didn't get the impression Shelby liked her much, and she wasn't sure what to make of Shelby. But Addison remained blissfully oblivious. At the end of the meal, Emily hugged Addison goodbye and shook Shelby's hand—a little sad they didn't connect better.

***

The next morning, Emily knocked on Isabella's front door. After a moment, she found herself face to face with Enzo.

"Good morning, Emily."

"Good morning," she replied, refraining from grabbing and kissing him.

"I was just heading out." He stepped into the frame of the door and turned to allow just enough room for her to pass through. "Come in."

Squeezing past him, she let her hand graze the front of his pants. "Have a good day."

She heard a low groan escape him which pleased her.

Walking back into the kitchen, she found Isabella with the baby while the nanny was washing something in the sink.

"Ah, Emily," Isabella looked up at her. "Glad you're here. This morning is going to be quick as I have another meeting--"

The sound of breaking glass interrupted Isabella. Emily heard the nanny gasp.

"What happened, Carrie?" Isabella stood and held Chloe out to Emily. "Would you mind?"

"I... I'm so sorry," Carrie stuttered. "I was washing it with the dish soap like you asked, and it just slipped out of my hands when I picked it up."

Isabella retrieved part of the broken crystal candlestick from the sink and sighed.

"Okay, well, I just bought these. They were fifty dollars each, so I'll have to deduct one from your next paycheck."

Seriously?

Carrie looked like she was going to cry. "I'm sorry. It was an accident."

"I know, but you've got to be more careful. Please be sure to get all the shards of glass out of the sink." Isabella walked back to the dining table and sat down, leaving Chloe in Emily's arms. "Have a seat."

Surprised at Isabella's reaction, Emily awkwardly sat down with the baby on her lap.

"I have some great news," Isabella began. "Enzo and I have decided I'll take over the floor above the restaurant for events, so we'll have our own venue." She clapped excitedly.

"Oh, that's perfect."

"I know! We'll have a lot of work cut out for us in the next few weeks to get it ready."

"Just let me know what you need me to do," Emily said.

"Thanks, I will. I'm so happy I have you on my team." Isabella placed her hand over Emily's. "You're doing such a great job."

Emily smiled through the knots twisting in her stomach.

"Okay, so we just have this one event coming up next month." Isabella opened a Manila folder and pushed it toward Emily. "It's a bachelorette party. They want a live band, so I thought you could talk to your piano friend? Isn't he part of a popular band?"

Emily's stomach dropped. "Yes, the LoDo Dogs, but we aren't seeing each other anymore."

Chloe was squirming and grabbing Emily's hair.

"Well, you can't let that get in the way of business," Isabella smiled. "Just contact him on a professional level and see if they would be interested. The contract with the details is in the folder. Please take care of that this week so we can move forward or look for a new band."

Look for a new band.

Isabella must have noticed the anxiety on Emily's face. "You can do this, Emily," Isabella said to her reassuringly. "You've been through the Symposium. You're a powerful woman. Don't let a little uncomfortableness stop you from going after what you want."

How is this what I want? "Okay, I'll see what he says." Emily struggled to keep Chloe still while she tried to climb over Emily's shoulder.

"Great. Also, I need you to go by the restaurant today and ask Enzo to let you upstairs so you can take a look at the space. I'll need the two of you to come up with a plan to relocate everything currently being stored up there."

Well, that should be fun.

"Oh, and while you're there, in one of the cabinets, you'll find a box of glass vases. Can you grab those and run to the craft store to pick up some gilded gold paint and brushes and paint them all? We're going to use those as part of the centerpieces."

"Sure."

Carrie walked by them with a full trash bag. "Carrie, are you almost done? I need you to feed Chloe before she goes down for a nap."

"Yes, just taking the trash out since there's glass in it."

Chloe was trying to climb on top of Emily's head.

Turning her attention back to Emily, Isabella reached into her purse. "Let me give you my credit card, so you don't have to front the money. You can give it back to Enzo when you've got what you need."

"Okay," Emily took the card as she continued to wrangle the baby.

"Oh, for heaven's sake." Isabella stood up and reached for Chloe. "I swear that girl couldn't move any slower." She took Chloe out of Emily's lap and walked to the back door looking for Carrie.

Emily tried to straighten her hair and clothes. She saw herself in the mirror and looked as if she had been caught in a tornado.

When Carrie finally returned, Isabella handed over the baby. "I need to leave now, or I'm going to be late for my appointment. Please make sure to feed her right away and get her down for her nap. I want her rested for this afternoon when I'm home."

Isabella picked up her purse and turned to Emily. "Ready?"

***

Emily sat in her car and reluctantly pulled out her phone. Staring at Dylan's name, she contemplated just deleting his number and telling Isabella he was all booked up.

He did say that, right? 'Booked up for the next six months.'

Setting the phone back down, she drove to the restaurant.

"What are you doing here on your day off?" Stephanie asked Emily.

"Isabella is doing another event here next month. She wants me to check out the space upstairs. Is Enzo in his office?"

"Oh... yeah, I think," Stephanie said as she continued making drinks for the lunch crowd.

When Emily walked into the back, she found Enzo's door open. "Hello, Mr. Rizzoli."

He turned around in his chair. "Well, hello, Miss Bisset."

"I've been given instructions to have you show me around upstairs."

"Yes, of course." He grabbed a key out of his desk. "Follow me."

Once inside the room, Enzo closed and locked the door behind them. Butterflies jumped around in Emily's stomach.

Sunlight poured in from the large windows, and Emily gravitated toward them to look down at the people who were on their lunch breaks. She felt Enzo's arms wrap around her waist from behind. Kissing her neck, one hand slid up to cup her breast while the other reached down between her legs.

"Why are you wearing jeans," he groaned.

Emily turned around to face him so she could kiss his mouth. Wrapping her arms around his neck, she let herself surrender to him as his hands continued to explore her body. It felt so good to be in his arms and no longer deny her desire.

He took one of her hands into his and guided it down over his crotch. "I've been thinking of your touch all morning."

She stroked the outside of his pants, feeling the hard mass on the other side of the cloth. Enzo moaned as he lifted her t-shirt off over her head. He took a moment to stare at her breasts framed in a sheer pink demi bra.

"Beautiful," he whispered as he moved his hands over her nipples and kissed her again.

The door handle jiggled. Someone was trying to open the door. Emily quickly grabbed her shirt and put it back on. There was a knock. Enzo motioned for her to go to the door and pointed down to his obvious erection. He walked behind the bar area and rested his arms down on the counter to look as if he had been thinking. Emily walked over to the door and opened it to see Stephanie standing there.

"Why is the door locked?" Stephanie asked suspiciously.

"I don't know." Emily tried to sound surprised.

Enzo spoke up. "The bottom lock automatically locks when the door closes."

Stephanie didn't look convinced. "I need you to void out an order that was rung up incorrectly."

"Okay, I'll be right down."

Stephanie stood in place for a moment before turning around and leaving the door open behind her.

Enzo dropped his head into his hands.

"I'll finish up here," Emily said, aware that Stephanie may still be in earshot.

"Okay, well, I think most of the stuff should be able to fit in the closet." He straightened himself up and readjusted his pants before leaving.

Emily walked the room, noting the layout and opening the built-in cabinets to look for the vases. Finding them, she grabbed the box and headed downstairs. She stopped at Enzo's office to let him know she was leaving. She didn't dare risk closing the door since Stephanie already seemed on high alert.

"Thanks. See you tomorrow?" he asked.

"Yes, I'm opening tomorrow so I can attend your seminar in the evening." She smiled seductively.

"You should just ride over there with me after work," he suggested. "I can take you home afterward. It's the last one of the series—we can celebrate." The smile on his face made it clear what he meant.

Emily's pulse sped up. "My shift ends at four."

"Perfect. You'll have time to run home and change. Wear a skirt."

Twenty-three

After work the next day, Emily hurried home to take a shower and get ready for the seminar. Opening her panty drawer, she carefully sifted through her assortment before deciding on the crotchless ones Jack had gotten her in New York. She chose a short flowy red skirt and paired it with a white blouse that rested just off her shoulders.

Enzo smiled with approval as she slid into the seat next to him. "Lay your seat back."

She complied as he started driving. He reached over with his free hand and began caressing her inner thighs, encouraging her legs to relax open. When he realized he had complete access, he looked at her with amused surprise.

Just before they reached the seminar center, Enzo turned the car sharply and drove up to the top of an empty parking structure of a business complex. Leaning over, he grabbed her ass and kissed her hard, trying to pull her into him, but the center console made it impossible. As his tongue danced with hers, his fingers explored between her legs.

"We have to go," he told her as he licked his fingers and drove away, smiling.

Emily was breathless.

She had a hard time concentrating on what exactly Enzo was saying during the seminar. Something about being fully present in life. She noticed him take his hands up to his face a few times, acting as if he were itching his nose, but then his eyes would briefly meet hers and a smile would flicker across his face.

Afterward, Lucas, Clay, and Tonya all wanted to go up and thank Enzo for a great seminar series since it was the last one.

"Really appreciated this insight," Clay told him, shaking his hand.

Oh, my god, does his hand smell like me?

"Especially the part about designing our futures free from our past."

"Of course," Enzo replied. "You'll begin recognizing things more and more for how they really are, regardless of the filters you've put in place. Thank you all for participating." He went on to shake Lucas and Tonya's hands as well before turning away to greet others waiting for him.

Celebrity Seminar Leader. Just like Jack.

"You guys ready?" Lucas asked.

"Oh, I rode with Enzo tonight," Emily told them.

"Are we still on for dinner tomorrow at your guys' place?" Tonya asked the boys.

"Definitely," Clay responded. "I'm working on perfecting my Buffalo Wings. I hope you all like it hot."

Emily hugged them goodbye before walking to the front of the room to meet Enzo.

Looking up from his phone, he said, "Let's go."

The car ride back was Emily's turn to tease. She climbed up into her seat so she could lean over and lick his ear while breathing heavily and nibbling his lobe. Her hand descended to his crotch as she stroked him through his pants.

He groaned.

She undid his belt and pants and slid her hand inside, continuing to caress him.

Returning to his ear, she whispered, "I want you to fuck me."

Enzo inhaled sharply.

As they approached the restaurant, Emily pulled away and sat back in her seat, smiling at the look of shock on Enzo's face. He reached his hand across to caress her legs. "I need to stop at the restaurant first to drop off the key for them to lock up. Stephanie texted that she can't find hers."

Enzo parked in the back alley, and they both stepped out of the car. He was buckling his pants back up when Stephanie walked out from the trash bins. Everyone froze and stared at each other as they all assessed the situation. Finally, Stephanie went back into the restaurant. Enzo followed her.

Emily decided to wait in the car.

A few minutes later, Enzo emerged, looking visibly upset.

"What happened?" she asked tentatively.

"Nothing." He drove her home in silence. He pulled up in front of her building and turned to her. "I'm sorry. I need to go home."

Emily nodded, a pit forming in her stomach. "Okay, goodnight," and got out of his car.

***

When Emily went to work the next morning, Enzo wasn't there. She had been up all night wondering what happened between Stephanie and Enzo when they had gone inside. She wasn't looking forward to seeing Stephanie later that afternoon when she would be coming in for her shift.

How am I going to explain what she saw? Especially not knowing what Enzo told her?

Except, Stephanie never showed up. Neither did Enzo. Instead, the assistant manager, Michael, walked up to Emily just before it was time for her to go home and told her Stephanie had quit with no notice and asked if she could cover the shift.

"Oh, I can't. I have a dinner engagement I need to be at," Emily told him. She was starting to feel sick to her stomach. "What happened?"

"I have no idea," he said. "When she didn't show up, I texted her. She just texted back that she had to quit. Didn't give me any details. I'll see if one of the servers can cover. I know Joe used to be a bartender."

Emily wanted to reach out to Stephanie to find out what was going on but knew she needed to talk to Enzo first. As she was walking home, she texted him:

Emily

Is everything okay?

By the time she showered and changed and headed over to Lucas and Clay's place, she still hadn't received a response. She tried to shake it off and enjoy her evening. Tonight was about celebrating the completion of the seminar series. The four of them sat around the small living room, eating hot wings and playing Uno, laughing at how competitive they all were.

Emily's phone rang, interrupting their game.

Isabella.

She froze and stared at the phone as the knots twisted tighter in her stomach.

"Are you going to answer that?" Tonya asked her.

Isabella never called her, especially at night, preferring to text instead.

Emily took a deep breath. "Hello?"

"Enzo told me everything." She heard Isabella's angry tone on the other end of the phone.

Emily's heart dropped into her stomach. She was silent.

"How could you do this to me?!"

"I'm so sorry, Isabella," Emily whispered, closing her eyes.

"I trusted you! I thought you were my friend. I took you under my wing," Isabella broke down, crying, "and you saw that as an opportunity to seduce my husband?!"

That last part caught Emily off-guard. She opened her eyes. "I didn't seduce him, Isabella. I just gave in to him. I thought you had an open marriage?"

Emily saw Tonya, Lucas, and Clay staring at her. Tears of shame began streaming down her face.

"An open marriage? We have a baby! Whatever made you think that? Is that what you told yourself while you were with him? You could have any number of men. Why would you try to take mine after everything I've done for you?" Her sobs broke through again.

Emily felt like she was going to throw up. She now realized the full extent of her betrayal to Isabella, but she didn't think it was fair for Isabella to place all the blame solely on her. Especially since it was becoming clear Enzo had lied. She didn't like being cast as the seductress.

"Enzo pursued me. Why don't you see him as the one at fault here?"

"You don't think I see him as being at fault?" Isabella snapped at Emily. "We are talking about divorce! He didn't just do this with you! He was also fooling around with Stephanie!"

Emily felt as if somebody had punched her in the gut.

"I bet you didn't know that, did you?" Isabella snarled. "He only told me because Stephanie caught the two of you last night, and he wanted to tell me before she did."

Emily was silent as she processed Enzo's double betrayal.

She wasn't special.

There was no connection.

She didn't belong to him.

He belonged to Isabella.

"I want you to bring me my property right now," Isabella demanded. "Bring my credit card, my event folder, and my vases. I want you to face me in person."

Emily felt defeated. "Okay. I'm so sorry, Isabella."

"I expect you here within the hour."

Emily dropped her phone and began sobbing uncontrollably in her hands. Her friends gathered around her to comfort her. When she was finally able to catch her breath and calm her crying, she told them everything that had happened between her and Enzo.

"I can't believe that arrogant son of a bitch." Lucas shook his head. "He knew what he was doing going after you like that."

"Emily, what he did was wrong and illegal. He's your boss; that's sexual harassment," Clay explained.

"But I reciprocated," Emily cried. "He didn't force me into anything I didn't want to do."

"He should have never put you in that position," he said. "You should have been able to go to work without getting hit on by your boss."

Emily began sobbing again as they all held her. After a while, she pulled away. "I have to go to their house right now. Isabella wants her stuff back."

"There's no way in hell I'm letting you go there by yourself," Clay said. "I'll take you."

Emily nodded, handing him her car keys. "Thank you."

The drive over to Enzo and Isabella's house was quiet except for Emily giving directions through her sobs. Clay didn't say anything or press her for more information. He just let her cry.

Emily grabbed the manila folder along with Isabella's credit card, and Clay carried up the vases from the trunk. When they approached the door, he knocked, staying right by her side. Isabella opened the door, glancing at Clay before settling her eyes on Emily. Her face was red and puffy from what must have been hours of crying. She turned around, silently, leaving the door open for them to follow her inside.

When they walked into the dining room, they found Enzo sitting at the table, looking dejected. He didn't say a word.

I can't believe he did this to me. Why would he tell her? Why would he lie to me?

Isabella turned to Emily. "I've already heard from Enzo, but I want to hear from you directly. How long has this been going on?"

Emily's mind was racing. "Since the Symposium," she finally answered quietly.

Isabella glared at her. "And afterward, you let me take you to lunch, buy you clothes, and have you come work with me?"

It sounded so much worse to Emily hearing her lay it all out like that. "I'm sorry."

"Did you have sex with him?"

"No."

"Did he touch you anywhere?"

Emily started crying again. Clay placed his hand on her back to let her know he was there with her.

"You don't get to cry and feel sorry for yourself, Emily," Isabella said angrily. "Where did he touch you?"

Emily didn't know how to respond.

"Over your clothes or under?"

"Under," Emily whispered.

Tears returned to Isabella's face. "Did you touch him?"

Emily nodded, looking down at the floor.

"Did you suck his dick?" Isabella continued her interrogation.

"That's enough, Isabella," Enzo finally spoke up. "I've already answered these questions. It's not her fault. It's on me."

Isabella spun on her heels in a rage, her finger pointing directly at him. "You don't get to tell me when it's enough!"

Turning back to Emily, she asked, "Did he go down on you?"

"Okay, I'm sorry, Ma'am," Clay interjected. "I know you're hurting, and you got a raw deal, but I don't think this line of questioning is going to accomplish anything."

After an almost unbearably long moment of silence, Isabella said, with restrained anger, "Get out. Don't ever set foot in my restaurant again. Don't ever try to contact my husband. And don't ever show your face at the seminar center. I never want to see or hear from you."

"I'm sorry, Isabella," Emily managed to say one more time.

"Get out!"

When they went outside, Emily broke down crying. Clay took her into his arms and held her as she sobbed uncontrollably.

Back at her apartment, he told her, "You shouldn't be alone tonight. If it's okay with you, I'm going to stay here."

Emily nodded without saying a word. They climbed on top of her bed, and she cried herself to sleep in his arms.

Part Three

At some point, a woman just gets tired of being ashamed all the time. Then she can finally become who she truly is.

Elizabeth Gilbert, City of Girls

Twenty-four

Emily woke up to the muffled sound of the coffee grinder penetrating her dull headache through her closed bedroom door. Her swollen eyes were heavy to open after a night of crying, but when she did, she discovered her red throw blanket covering her. She was still wearing her clothes from the night before, having fallen asleep on top of the comforter.

She pulled a pillow over her face to block out the sunlight that had filled her room. She didn't want to get out of bed. She just wanted to fall back asleep, so she didn't have to think about anything.

There was a gentle knock before she heard her bedroom door open. "Emily? Are you awake?"

With the pillow still covering her head, she turned to peek through the small opening and saw Clay standing in the doorway holding two cups of coffee.

"You take cream and sugar in yours, right?"

"Yes, thank you," she said, slowly sitting up.

Clay walked over and handed her the mug while she kept her head down, ashamed and embarrassed.

"How are you doing?"

"I'm such an idiot," she said, shaking her head.

"Listen, you made a mistake. People make mistakes. Enzo on the other hand had taken vows. He's the one that lied about his wife having affairs. I don't doubt that he got in your head and led you to believe it was okay."

"But deep down, I knew it wasn't," she admitted. "I wanted to believe they had an open marriage because how else could he get up on that stage every week and say the things he says about relationships and integrity and yet pursue me?" She could feel the tears welling up in her eyes.

"May I?" Clay asked, gesturing to the spot beside her on her bed.

When she nodded, he sat down and took a sip of his coffee. "Men like that will say whatever they need to get women like you to fall for them."

"I thought I actually meant something to him," she said softly as the tears broke free. "I mean, not in the sense that I thought he would leave Isabella for me. I just thought..." She wiped her face dry. "God, I'm so stupid! Of course he was screwing around with Stephanie, too. I'm a horrible person. Isabella didn't deserve this from me. She was my mentor—my friend. How could I do this to her?" She broke down crying.

Clay stood up, taking Emily's mug from her, and placed both cups of coffee on the nightstand. Grabbing a tissue, he sat back down next to her and pulled her into him as he held her, letting her cry. When she had calmed down, he offered to make her breakfast. "How about some scrambled eggs and toast?"

"I'm not hungry." She reached over and took another tissue. "Don't you have to work this morning?"

"Well, unless you have somewhere else you need to be, I thought I'd take you rock climbing. I have plenty of vacation days to burn up."

Despite her tears, Emily laughed. "Seriously?"

"Yep, it'll help clear your head."

"I've never been rock climbing. It looks a little terrifying."

"As long as you have the right equipment and a certified climbing instructor, you'll be good." He smiled. "You've got both."

"You?"

"Yes, Ma'am." He stood up and extended his hand out to her to help her off the bed.

She reluctantly agreed and changed into yoga pants and a tank top. Slipping on her Vans, she grabbed a baseball cap as they headed out.

When they stopped at his house to pick up the equipment, he threw together some food and water and tossed them into a backpack. Looking at all the ropes and carabiners, Emily was a little nervous about what she had gotten herself into.

As they drove into Boulder, she spotted the majestic reddish-brown slabs that rose out of the ground at a slant, reaching high into the sky.

"We're going to climb the Third Flatiron." Clay pointed toward them as he was driving.

"Are you serious?"

"As a heart attack." He looked over at her and smiled.

"You realize I've never done this before, right?"

He laughed. "You'll be fine."

When they got out of the car, Clay grabbed a large coil of rope and had Emily slide one arm in and over her head, so it rested against her body diagonally. He clipped other equipment onto the bundle before slipping a backpack on himself that included his own coil bundle.

"Ready?"

"No."

"You got this. Let's go."

By the time they finally reached the bench of the Third Flatiron, Emily was already exhausted. "You didn't tell me we would have to hike in," she complained.

He laughed and handed her some water. "All right, let's get you geared up."

He took the rope from his back and then removed hers. Reaching into his backpack, he pulled out a couple of pairs of shoes. "Here, these should fit you. They're my sister's, but I think you guys might be the same size."

"What's wrong with my sneakers?"

"You'll get a better grip with specialized climbing shoes. Trust me. The right equipment makes all the difference."

Emily sat down on a rock to put the rubber shoes on while Clay put his on and offered instructions.

"You're just going to squish your toes and shove them up in there. Then grab the tabs on the heel and pull it out so you can get it around your foot."

Emily tried but couldn't get her foot in. "I think they're too small."

He walked over and picked up her foot to examine her efforts. Placing his hand around the bottom of her foot, he told her to push upward while he pulled the straps out over her heel.

"You want them to feel a little too small, no extra space to slip. That's what will give you the grip you need on the rocks."

After he finished helping her with the other shoe, he pulled a con-traption out of his backpack that consisted of nothing more than a bunch of black straps. "Okay, time to get you in your harness."

Emily stood as Clay squatted down in front of her, spreading the ropes open so she could step into them. As she steadied herself with her hands on his shoulders, she threaded each leg in through the waist loop and then the leg loop. He slid the harness up her body until it stopped at her crotch. Being sure to pull them up as high as they would go, he tightened each strap around her thighs.

Emily found herself holding her breath as his hands moved around her, his face inches from her navel. He stood up, brought his hands to her waist, and pulled the strap high above her hip bones. While he tightened it, he explained the importance of double-backing.

Keeping his eyes focused downward on his tasks, he told her, step-by-step, what he was doing. She tried to ignore the graze of his fingers along her body as he checked the tightness of each strap. He reached for a rope and tied a knot into a clip on the front of her harness, tracing it over itself several times and pulling it tight. He picked up the helmet and placed it on her head.

His crystal blue eyes finally met hers while he clipped it under her chin. "How's that?"

"Good, I think."

He stepped away to get on his own harness and ropes. As he walked back towards her, Emily couldn't help but notice how his harness squeezed around his groin area over his jeans, creating a large bulge. She looked away—sure she was blushing. She could only imagine what she must look like, with the ropes outlining everything on her as well.

Attaching a long rope from him to her, he explained that they would be "belaying" and showed her how to give slack on the rope and when to hold back. He had her rub chalk on her hands and went over the basics about using friction with her feet and placing her hands onto the bumps and cracks of the rock face to help pull herself up.

"Okay, I'm going to head up first while you release the rope," he instructed her. "I'll lock us in up there, and then you'll follow me up. Got it?"

"Let's hope."

Emily watched Clay effortlessly scale the rock, his Captain America body flexing with each reach, his rounded ass perfectly outlined by the harness. She was thankful he wouldn't be behind her.

"Okay, all locked in," he called down to her. "Your turn."

She placed her hands and feet over some bumps on the rock and began her climb. When she reached Clay, he gave her a high five and outlined the rest of the path. They continued their slow ascent with her following him. Emily felt strong as she moved upwards. Finding the right footing and the proper grip gave her the confidence she needed to keep going.

About halfway up, she couldn't find anything to grab onto. Everywhere she reached, she couldn't get a grip. She began to panic. Clay had stopped above and was trying to tell her where to place her hand, but she couldn't figure it out. She was on the verge of tears.

"There's nothing I can grab," she yelled, almost in a full-blown panic.

"Emily, look at me!"

She looked up and found his eyes.

"I want you to take a deep breath. Regroup."

Emily closed her eyes and took a long inhale through her nose and pushed out the exhale through her mouth.

"Now, look at me again. I want you to place your right hand on the rock and slide it up until I tell you to stop."

She did as he told her.

"Slide your right hand over a little more to your right, and you'll find a crack that your fingers can grab onto."

"I got it!"

As she pushed her foot off to begin the climb again, it slipped, slamming her body into the slab. She screamed as she struggled to find her footing, her fingers desperately clinging to the crack. Clay told her to push her heel down and her toes into the slab to create friction. Listening to his guidance, she finally found her balance again. She took another deep breath and looked up at him.

"You got this, Emily. You're strong. You can make it to the top if you don't give up."

She nodded.

"Okay, I want you to continue climbing toward me, but think of it as climbing a ladder. You're pushing with your feet, finding stable placement, and just using your hands to assist. Your strength comes from your foundation, got it?"

She nodded again and pushed up, reaching for the next rough edge or bump that could assist in her climb to the top. As she slowly began to move again, her confidence returned. She climbed more swiftly, knowing what to look for, finding the right spot to plant her foot and push off. When she made it to the summit, she did one final pull. Clay reached out for her hand and helped her stand up steadily.

"You did it," he yelled with a huge smile on his face, holding up both hands for her to hit in victory. He pulled her in and hugged her tightly. "See, Emily, you're stronger than you think."

She held onto him and stared out over the land below. The view was breathtaking. She felt safe in his arms until she looked down at the steep rock she had just climbed up.

"I need to sit down."

Clay unzipped his backpack and handed her a peanut butter and jelly sandwich and water bottle. "You need to eat and hydrate."

It was another perfect Colorado day, but this time, Emily saw it from a viewpoint she never had before. She stared out, taking it all in.

Clay rested his arms on his knees as he looked out, his short blond hair just long enough to blow in the wind. "When I'm up here looking at all of this, I don't understand how people can think there's not a God. I mean, this didn't just happen on its own."

"Maybe," Emily said, staring out at the majestic mountains against the blue sky. "Or maybe we have this need to put an authoritative figurehead over us so that we can wrap our brains around the amazingness of what just exists."

Clay took a bite of his sandwich, looking at her with a curious smile. "Hmmm... maybe. I guess it just makes sense to me that someone designed all of this—designed us."

"I don't really know what I believe anymore. I grew up in the church, but the more I start to think about things, the more things don't make sense, and the more questions I have."

"I think it's good to have questions. Having questions is an indication of wanting to learn. And learning is what ultimately leads to enlightenment, right?" He tossed her an apple.

The two of them sat on the summit for a while, talking about religion and human nature, trying to come up with the answers to save humanity from itself. They didn't discuss Enzo or Isabella, which Emily appreciated.

Eventually, Clay said it was time to head back down before the temperature dropped anymore. And just like that, Emily's relaxed state disappeared.

Clay helped her up and tightened her harness, tying ropes into new knots and threading through carabiners. He connected her to an anchor and showed her how the hand brake worked, explaining that she would be in total control of how slowly or how quickly she descended. "Turn around and face me. Now walk out to the edge and plant your feet as you lean back."

Emily felt her panic return. "I can't do this!"

Clay placed his hands on Emily's arms and looked into her eyes. "Emily, you didn't think you could get up here, but you did. You can do this. Remember, you're in control. You determine how much slack to let go of and when to put on the brakes. I've got you securely anchored. Trust what I say to you. The hardest step is the first one."

Emily nodded and took a deep breath. Looking down, she slowly stepped back to the ledge.

"Good. Now, lower your butt down like you're going to sit in a chair... good... lower... okay, perfect. Now push off, swing out, and let your feet land onto the wall of the rock."

Emily was terrified. Leaning back, she felt like she was going to fall. Her fingers hurt from gripping the rope so tightly.

"I got you," Clay said as he continued to look into her eyes, "You can do this."

She took a deep breath and pushed off slightly, just enough to get her feet below the ledge. Her heart almost fell out of her body.

Clay watched her closely. "Knees bent, back straight... good... when you're ready, start to release some slack on the rope and begin your descent. When you reach the bottom, I want you to disconnect from the rope and yell 'off rappel' so I know when it's safe for me to come down. Got it?"

"Got it." Emily's knuckles were turning white. She slowly began releasing the rope as she looked behind her to see where to place her foot next, one step at a time. She felt as if she could go crashing to her death at any moment, but once she found her groove, she realized she was actually enjoying it—even picking up a little bit of speed.

When she reached the ground, she disconnected and yelled "off rappel!"

She watched Clay bound down quickly and smoothly. When he made it to the ground, she jumped into his arms. "That was amazing!"

He held her tightly, laughing. "You were awesome!"

"Thank you so much. This is exactly what I needed today."

"I'm glad you enjoyed it. Let's get you out of this gear." He unbuckled her helmet and lifted it off.

Emily tilted her head back, running her fingers through her hair to loosen it from her scalp. As her eyes caught his, he quickly looked down, placing his hands at her waist.

He began quietly untying the ropes and removing the clips before unbuckling the strap. Emily held her breath again as he reached down to her thighs and undid the others. Sliding the entire harness down her legs, he squatted down in front of her. She placed her hands on his shoulders once again as she steadied herself to step out. Standing back up, he quickly turned around and removed his gear.

When they arrived back at his place, she helped him carry the equipment inside before hugging him goodbye. Lucas wasn't around.

"Thank you for everything today and for being such a good friend to me."

He held her, his face buried in her hair, before finally pulling away. "Of course. I'll always be here for you."

Twenty-five

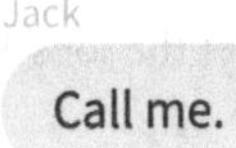

Emily looked at the text and set the phone down, rolling back over into bed. She had ignored his previous calls yesterday. She couldn't bear the thought of talking to him about everything right now. She knew he would be disappointed in her as well. For all the strides she had made in embracing her sexuality, she had just fucked it all up.

She picked the phone back up and texted Addison.

> Hi! Shelby and I are going out of town when I get off work. What are you doing right now? Come see me at the Market.

Emily

> OK… be down in a few.

"Are you all right?" Addison came around from the counter as soon as she saw Emily walk in. "You look like someone died."

Tears jumped into Emily's eyes.

Addison wrapped her arms around her. "What's going on?"

"It all blew up."

"What did? What happened?"

"Enzo. Isabella." Emily whispered, trying not to let the sobs escape her mouth.

Addison looked to one of the workers cleaning off tables. "Devon, can you cover the counter for me? I'm going on break." She took Emily's hand. "Come on, let's go back to the office."

Through her crying, Emily told Addison everything that had transpired over the last couple of days.

"Oh, Em," Addison embraced her friend once again. "I'm so sorry. Enzo is a lying, cheating asshole."

"Well, so am I, apparently," Emily sobbed.

Addison pulled away and took Emily's hands into hers. "Look, while I can't condone your behavior fooling around with a married man, there clearly were other factors at play here. First of all, he's your boss, and he took advantage of you. Secondly, he lied to you by saying they have an open marriage."

"But I should have known better," Emily said quietly, wiping the flowing tears from her face.

"Yes." Addison reached over and held her. "You should have. But there was also a power imbalance. He positioned himself as an authority figure in your life and then took advantage of that. And now you're the one left without a job."

"I don't know what I'm going to do now. Everyone must think I'm such a slut."

"Hey," Addison pushed Emily off her shoulder. "You say that word like it's a bad thing! And we don't disparage sexually liberated women in this century. Don't you remember what 'slut' stands for?"

Emily rolled her eyes and smiled as she recited in unison with Addison, "Sexually Liberated, Utterly Tantalizing."

"That's right," Addison squeezed her back into her arms. "So, if you're going to refer to yourself as a slut, at least say it with pride. We don't all have that gift."

Addison always knew how to lift Emily's spirits.

"Have you told your dad what happened?" She handed Emily a tissue to wipe her face.

"No. All it would do is validate to him how irresponsible I am. I need to find another job and tell him I just decided to finally move on. He doesn't need details."

"Probably true. Your experience at Josephina's should land you another job pretty quickly."

Emily smirked. "Not likely. I don't think that reference would go over very well."

"Emily, you've got the upper hand here. What Enzo did was against the law. I guarantee you he knows that. And I'm pretty sure he wouldn't risk you suing him by not giving you a good reference."

"I guess that's true."

"I can cancel my plans with Shelby this weekend," Addison told her.

"No, absolutely not, Addy. I'm glad you've found someone that makes you so happy. I'll be fine." Emily offered a smile.

Addison smiled back with sympathetic eyes. "You will too."

Not likely. "I went rock climbing yesterday."

Addison pulled back in surprise, laughing. "What? You don't do that kind of thing!"

"Clay ended up staying the night with me after the whole confrontation."

Addison raised her eyebrows as a slight smile appeared on her face. "Really?"

"It's not like that. I was really upset, and he didn't want me to be alone."

Addison let her smile spread.

"Anyway," Emily chuckled, "he thought rock climbing would help clear my head."

"And did it?"

"It did. It actually was pretty amazing."

"I think you're going to need some more of that in your immediate future."

***

"Hello?" Emily answered her phone, seeing it was her big brother, David.

"What's up, li'l sis," his exuberant voice bellowed through the phone.

"Hey, David!" Emily was happy to hear from him. They didn't often talk since he lived in California, but she always missed him. "How are you?"

"I'm awesome! Just wanted to call and say hi—see what you're up to?"

Fucking up my life. "Well, I just quit Josephina's. Looking for a new job. So, that's exciting."

"Why did you quit? I thought you loved working there?"

"Yeah… kind of a long story." She didn't want to get into it with him right now. "I miss you. I wish you were here."

"Funny you should say that."

There was a knock.

"Hang on." When Emily opened the door, David stood before her, grinning with the phone still to his ear.

Completely shocked, Emily threw her arms around him. "What are you doing here?"

"I'm making a delivery up in the mountains tomorrow and wanted to surprise you."

"Well, you succeeded!"

They grabbed dinner and drinks at My Brother's Bar, the oldest bar in Denver and David's favorite place to visit whenever he was in town. They spent the evening getting caught up on each other's lives, and she told him everything that happened with Enzo.

"What the hell were you thinking, Em?" He reprimanded her during the twenty-minute walk back to her apartment.

"I know, I'm an idiot."

"Yes, you are!" Seeing her pained face, he put his arm around her. "Come here. You see the world, and people, through rose-colored glasses, Em. You always want to believe people have the best intentions."

Emily wanted to change the subject. "So, you're no longer selling the coin-operated basketball games that dad designed?"

"No, I'm getting away from arcades. Focusing on more high-end stuff. I have a client who asked me to build them a couple of blackjack tables. They turned out really well, and I had a lot of fun with it. So, I threw a picture up on my website, and within a week, one of the casinos in Central City contacted me wanting to buy six of them."

"Wow, that's amazing! So, woodshop in high school paid off?"

He laughed. "Yes, it did. I built six more that I'm going to try to sell to other casinos while I'm up there. I figure if one is willing to pay that amount, it should interest some others."

"That party I was telling you about at Josephina's last week was a casino party. Isabella rented four poker tables and had them brought into the bar."

Saying her name out loud made her cringe inside.

"That's interesting. How did it go over?"

"People were crowded around them all night and seemed to be having a lot of fun."

"Hmmm..."

Emily could see his wheels turning. She knew that look. He and their dad were always coming up with new business ideas. "What?"

"Well, I'm just wondering how a casino table might do on a regular basis in a bar down here?"

"I'm pretty sure if people could gamble in bars, we would already see it happening," Emily told him.

"Right. But I'm thinking more along the lines of people buying in and playing just for fun. Like, they maybe pay twenty dollars and are given a certain amount of chips, and they play until they run out."

"I could see how that could work. It would be an opportunity for people to practice and hone their skills before going to do the real thing," Emily said.

"Exactly!" He lit up. "Em, this could be a great opportunity for you."

"What do you mean?"

"Why don't you look for a place down here that will let you try it out? Offer to give them a cut of what you bring in? I'd be happy to give you one of my tables if it could help get you started in your own business."

"Oh, wow, that would be incredible! You'd really give up a table for me?"

"Hey, any chance I get to be the hero big brother, I'm in."

"Actually, they would probably just be happy with the revenue from the alcohol that people order. At Josephina's, we paid live bands based on how much alcohol revenue was generated while they were playing."

"See? Perfect. You have the experience of working in a bar, so you understand these kinds of things. Talk to some places tomorrow while I'm making my deliveries. Dad and Amy want to get together for dinner tomorrow night. I'm assuming you're able to join us?"

"Oh, let me just check my busy schedule," Emily replied sarcastically.

"Awesome. Mind if I just crash here tonight? It was a long drive today pulling a trailer over the Rocky Mountains. Not really up for driving up to dad's tonight."

"Of course."

Emily stayed up most of the night writing out plans and ideas, creating a list of her favorite restaurants and bars that she felt would be a good fit. It was just the distraction she needed.

***

She spent the next day checking off her list of locations between lower downtown and Capitol Hill, avoiding Larimer Square. But everywhere she went told her they didn't see it working. A few were open to the idea but wanted to think about it and gave no commitments for a follow-up conversation. "Check back in a couple of months," seemed to be their go-to line.

After exhausting all other avenues, she walked into the Crimson Room to speak with the general manager.

"That's an interesting concept. How do you think it will do with gambling being legal in the mountains, though?"

"It's not really competing with actual gambling," Emily explained. "It's more for entertainment value while they're out for a night on the town. I think having a casino table would be the perfect addition to this place. It goes well with the whole prohibition-era vibe."

"It is unique. What the hell? Let's try it out and see how it goes. How about Friday and Saturday nights to start?"

"That's perfect. I'll make arrangements to have it delivered in the next day or two, and we can start next week if that's good for you?"

"Works for me." The manager shook her hand. "See you soon."

As soon as Emily walked outside, she texted David to let him know.

David

Way to go! I'll be at your place with the fam at six. Rezzies at Josephina's.

Emily

David agreed there wasn't a need to tell their dad and Amy what happened with Enzo. Together, Emily and David explained their idea over dinner and the opportunity it provided for Emily.

Emily recounted how she secured a prime location and said she gave her notice to Josephina's. David explained that once the table at the Crimson Room took off, Emily would be able to buy another from him and hire an employee to deal at the second location. She would continue to duplicate that. Their vision was for her to place them in popular restaurants and bars throughout Denver.

Being an entrepreneur himself, her dad was supportive of this idea since she had a clear plan. And he liked that she was getting guidance from David.

"I'm proud of you, Emily."

You wouldn't be if you knew everything.

Twenty-six

On her twenty-fifth birthday, Emily drove up the mountain to celebrate with her family. Amy prepared one of Emily's favorite dishes—green chili quiche topped with salsa and a mixed green salad tossed in homemade lemon-dill dressing. The early August mountain breeze rustled through the aspen trees as they sat out on the patio, enjoying the nature surrounding them.

"So, how's the new business going," her dad asked when Amy took the girls inside.

"Really well. People love it," Emily told him. "It's going to take some time to build up, but the manager at Crimson is happy with it."

"That's great. Are you making as much as when you were at Josephina's?"

Not even close.

"Not yet."

"But you're able to keep up with your bills?"

"Yeah. I got a job as a server at Snooze, so that helps."

"Why couldn't you just continue working at Josephina's then?" he pressed.

Because I fucked up.

"I wanted something I could do in the mornings, so my evenings were free to deal." Emily took a sip of her iced mint tea, hoping she sounded convincing.

The interrogation was interrupted by Summer and Rain walking back outside with Amy carrying their homemade carrot cake and singing Happy Birthday.

Thank God.

After Emily blew out her candles, the girls each presented her with their gifts. Summer had hers covered in blue tissue paper, tied with a green ribbon. After unwrapping it, Emily pulled out a small hand-painted ball of earth.

"I made it myself with modeling clay," Summer exclaimed, taking it out of Emily's hand and turning it around. "And look, I painted all the continents on there!"

Amy pointed to a cardboard box sitting on a small table by the back door. "Her fifth-grade class has been studying the solar system." The interior was painted black with Styrofoam planets hanging from fishing line.

"Wow, impressive! I love this, Summer."

"Look at mine!" Rain held out her gift. Emily unwrapped the tissue paper and discovered a refrigerator magnet of painted flowers in a vase.

"This is so pretty. Thank you!"

"She painted that," Amy told her.

"Wait, what?" Emily looked back at the Picasso-style art. "Really?"

"Mommy had it made into a magnet," Rain told her.

"This is amazing. I thought this was a store-bought magnet. You painted this all by yourself? At seven years old?"

Rain nodded her head emphatically, bursting with pride.

"Wow, you two are so talented. Thank you for my beautiful gifts." Emily pulled them back in for another hug. "I'll always keep them where I can see them every single day."

"Here you go." Her dad handed her a large box.

Emily looked at Amy to acknowledge the beautiful wrapping—a hand-sketched lion that Amy had drawn on cream-colored paper with "Leo" written in beautiful penmanship above the head. A thick green ribbon tied into a bow held a freshly cut sunflower.

"This is too beautiful to unwrap," Emily said.

"I can help," Rain offered.

When they peeled the paper away, Emily jumped up. "Really?"

"Every business owner should have a laptop. Happy birthday, sweetheart." Her dad stood and hugged her, kissing her cheek.

For the first time, Emily felt like her father was actually proud of her.

If only he knew.

***

The next evening, Tonya had the group over for her now-famous lasagna to celebrate Emily's birthday. Clay and Lucas brought a bottle of wine for the occasion.

"So good," Emily mumbled through a mouthful of Italian heaven.

"Did you see that email about the newest seminar at the center?" Tonya asked towards the end of the meal.

"I unsubscribed." Emily rolled her eyes. She saw Clay and Lucas glance at each other before glaring at Tonya.

"What?" Emily could tell they seemed to be keeping something from her.

Tonya suddenly looked like she realized she shouldn't have brought it up. "Oh, nothing. I just wasn't sure if you still followed that."

Tonya was a lousy liar.

"What's going on?"

"Well, I think she has a right to know," Tonya told them.

Clay and Lucas put their forks down and sat back.

Tonya looked at Emily. "The schedule for the new seminars came out, and Enzo will be leading the one on relationships and sex."

Everyone remained silent as Emily processed what she just heard. And then it hit her as she set her wine down and tried to focus. "Are you serious?"

Tonya nodded. "I couldn't believe it when I saw it."

"Wow." Emily sat back, letting it all sink in. "So, I get shunned like I'm some Jezebel while he's rewarded for his behavior? Unbelievable." Emily gulped down the rest of her wine. "Whatever. I'm over it."

"As you should be," Tonya agreed, standing up to clear the dishes. Emily stood up as well.

"No!" Tonya reprimanded her. "You sit. Clay and Lucas can help me."

Emily sat back as she poured herself more wine, still reeling from the news about Enzo.

The three of them suddenly burst back out from the kitchen, singing "Happy Birthday" very loudly and dramatically, making Emily laugh. They presented her with a cookie cake covered in frosting balloons.

After dessert, Tonya handed Emily a gift bag that held a beautifully framed picture of the four of them taken during their first dinner party at Emily's house.

"Aw, Tonya, I love it. Thank you!"

Next, Lucas handed her a small box wrapped in aluminum foil. "Sorry, I didn't have wrapping paper," he laughed as she stripped the shiny silver packaging away. "I thought you should have your own Uno deck."

"Yes," she grinned. "Now I can kick your ass at my place!"

The last gift was from Clay. It was wrapped in a brown paper bag from the Tattered Cover Book Store, tied with a small bungee cord that held a carabiner. She smiled, remembering their first day of rock climbing. They had also gone a couple of weeks ago, taking Lucas and Tonya with them. But once Clay explained how everything was going to work, Tonya opted to wait at the bottom of the rocks.

Unwrapping the package, she found a book entitled *Jonathan Livingston Seagull* by Richard Bach.

"It's about a seagull who wants more out of life than what's expected of him, and he refuses to conform," Clay explained. "It was my favorite book growing up. You remind me of Jonathan."

She opened the cover to see where he had inscribed:

Emily,
"The secret is to begin by knowing that you have already arrived."
Keep asking questions and you will soar.
Love, Clay

***

Emily continued her birthday celebration a few days later with Addison, Diego, and Todd at Cuba Cuba Café & Bar. The little historic turquoise house with yellow trim and a palm tree out front reminded her of being back home in Southern California. They sat on the patio listening to salsa music while eating Ropa Vieja and maduros.

"Happy birthday, Em!" Everyone raised their mojitos to toast her.

"So, how are you holding up through everything?" Todd asked.

"Fine," Emily responded. "Just trying to stay focused on building the new business." Emily appreciated her friends' concern for her, but she wanted to move on from the conversation about Enzo and Isabella. "When are you guys going to come in and see me at the Crimson Room?"

"Soon. We're so swamped right now with trying to get the rec center completed before winter. We've had so many delays. And six kids are going through the program right now."

"Are they responding well?"

"Yeah, really well, although the boys aren't crazy about yoga."

"They want something more aggressive," Diego interjected. "Yoga is great to manage their stress, but they're bored."

"Shelby's friend teaches Jiu Jitsu at the rec center in Evergreen," Addison said. "She'd probably love to teach at your camp. Emily and I spoke to her last month about taking classes. I'll put you guys in touch if you want?"

"That's not a bad idea," Todd said. "Yeah, have her give me a call."

Diego grabbed Emily's arm. "I'm so glad to hear you guys are doing that. I've always worried about you walking home so late by yourself, Em. I'd hate to think what could have happened if Enzo wasn't there that night."

Emily breathed in as she tried to push away the image of the three drunk men surrounding her. She also felt nauseous at the mention of Enzo. She hadn't talked about him directly with Diego and Todd.

She had relied on Addison to share that humiliating information with them.

Addison spoke up, deflecting the attention away from Emily. "We actually just signed up for Krav Maga in Denver."

"Isn't that like an Israeli army thing? The girl who played Wonder Woman was trained in that, right?" Diego asked.

"Yes," Emily said enthusiastically, bringing herself back into the conversation. "We just took a free introductory class a few days ago."

"About killed me," Addison said.

Emily laughed. "It was pretty intense. But I liked it. It focuses on real-world situations."

"That's perfect," Diego said. "When do you start regular classes?"

"This week."

"Hey, have you guys set a date for the grand opening?" Addison asked.

"I think we're going to push it into spring," Todd said. "It's just too stressful trying to get this build done. The added pressure of putting on an event at this time is too much right now."

"Understandable," Addison acknowledged. "We need to come up when it it's all done."

"Definitely! We'd love to show you all the changes we've made," Diego said.

After they finished their meal, and their server cleared the table, Addison ordered Diplomático rum for everyone. "So, I have some news. I did it!"

"Did what?" Diego asked.

"I told my parents." She beamed with pride. "I came out to them yesterday."

"Oh, my god, Addy, that's huge. How did it go?" Emily asked.

"Better than I expected. They told me they love me no matter who I choose to love. My dad even hugged me. I could tell he was uncomfortable, but he didn't get angry like I thought he would."

"That's amazing, Addison," Todd said.

"It really showed me that I live so much of my life concerned with what others will think, that I don't even give people the chance to love me for who I really am."

"We love you for who you really are." Diego reached his hand across the table.

"I know you do." She wove her fingers into his. "And I love you all so much for that. Which brings me to my next piece of big news."

"Wow, there's more?" Emily asked.

"Shelby just asked me to move in with them." Addison held her breath, eyes wide, waiting for their reaction.

Emily didn't expect that. "Really?"

"Yes!"

"What did your parents say about that?" Todd asked.

"Nothing yet." Addison's face fell slightly. "Shelby just asked me this morning."

"Is that what you want to do?" Emily was shocked by this new development.

"It is."

"It seems kind of sudden, though, doesn't it? I mean, you guys just met a couple of months ago. Do you think you know each other well enough?"

"I do," Addison tried to reassure Emily. "It's hard to explain, but when you meet the right person, you just know. Everything falls into place. Everything feels right. You don't have to try so hard. You know what I mean?"

"I get it." Todd smiled as he put his arm around Diego.

Emily sipped her rum as she mulled over those words. "Well, then I'm happy for you. I just want to do my due diligence as your best friend and make sure you aren't rushing into something you may regret."

"I may," Addison laughed. "But that's okay, too. I think it was Lucille Ball who said she'd rather regret the things she'd done than regret the things she hadn't done. That's my new motto."

"That's a good motto," Emily agreed and raised her glass in another toast.

Just then, a roaming Cuban band surrounded their table, playing the "Birthday Mambo." The server appeared with a mini Tres Leches cake with a huge shower of sparks shooting from its center.

He placed it in front of Emily. "Make a wish, Birthday Girl!"

Twenty-seven

Emily and her dad walked through the Denver Art Museum, listening to the audio tour as they absorbed the prolific career of Edgar Degas. When her dad had invited her to the exhibit, referencing a piece of art he saw hanging in her apartment, she had no idea who Degas was or that her garage sale find of ballerina dancers was part of a whole series of famous paintings.

At the end of the exhibit, they stopped in the gift shop where her dad purchased a pack of postcards featuring more of Degas' work and handed them to Emily.

"For you. I'm so glad we got to spend the day together," he said. "We don't get much dad/ daughter time, just the two of us like this."

He was right. They never really spent time together separate from the rest of the family, which made this outing all the more unusual. There had to be a reason he wanted to see her alone, and she couldn't ignore the growing pit in her stomach.

As they walked across the street to MAD Greens for a late lunch, he dropped the bomb Emily knew was coming.

"So, I had a conversation with Enzo."

Emily was quiet as she looked down, trying to figure out how to best respond. *Don't assume anything.* "Oh, yeah? About what?"

"Emily." Her dad stopped in front of the restaurant. She turned to look into his eyes, knowing they would be full of judgment. The unspoken words hung in the air between them as her breathing quickened and her eyes filled with tears. He reached out and pulled her into his arms, hugging her tightly. He held her—without saying a word—as she broke down and cried.

While eating their Buddha bowls, he told her how Enzo had called him a week earlier to apologize to him. Enzo assumed Emily had told her dad everything.

"I wish you felt you could have. I love you, Emily. I couldn't be there for you like I wanted while you were growing up, but I'm here now."

"I just feel like a constant disappointment to you."

"You are not a disappointment to me, sweetheart. And I'm sorry if I've made you feel that way. Frankly, I'm impressed you've turned out as well as you have given the raw deal you got with divorced parents and growing up with a bipolar mother."

"She's a good mom." Emily instantly felt defensive of her mother.

"Yes, I know, I know. But she did keep me from you most of your life. I'm just thankful and amazed we get to have a relationship now. And I hope we continue cultivating that. I've only ever wanted you to have an extraordinary life. One you can truly call your own."

Emily's tears returned. "I'm just so ashamed of how I hurt Isabella. I'm embarrassed I'm that woman. I never thought that would be me."

"We all have to live with the consequences of our choices. I made some pretty shitty choices when I was younger—when I was married to your mom."

"Mom told me you had an affair with your secretary."

Her dad nodded. "I did. That's true. I was caught up in the glamour of the advertising world, following in the footsteps of my mentor. It's just what was expected. And then one day, a friend of mine gave me hallucinogenic mushrooms, and they changed my life. I had a spiritual experience. There's no other word for it. I realized I was living a life I didn't want. I didn't want to be the hotshot advertising executive anymore. I actually had this sort of moral crisis about what I was do-ing—essentially tricking people into believing a lie about themselves and the only way to be better was to buy our product. So, the very next day, I quit.

"Your mom wasn't too happy about that. I mean, we had two kids to take care of, so I get it. But I just couldn't be a cog in the wheel anymore. I wanted off that ride. I wanted to invent things. Create and build things. Eventually, that's what led to the demise of our marriage. And as heartbreaking and devastating as it was, we both knew it was for the best. When we admitted we were living a life we didn't want, it gave us the freedom to begin living the life we did want. There was a time when your mom got that—before she found God, and I suddenly became the antichrist."

"Dad..." She hated when he made those little digs at her mom. He had no idea what it was like for a single mom struggling with mental illness.

"The point is, Emily, it's okay to make mistakes. But if you don't get complete about it, if you just ignore it, it will follow you into your future. What you resist, persists. Get complete about everything and leave the past in the past. Then choose who you're going to show up as in your future."

"How am I supposed to get complete about it," she asked, hearing the defensiveness in her voice. "Isabella made it very clear she never wants to see or hear from me again. And not to ever contact Enzo. I feel like I need to respect that."

"I agree,' he said. "Getting complete isn't the same as getting forgiveness. Your mom has made it clear she doesn't forgive me for what I did to her. But that doesn't prevent me from being complete about my past. Being complete is about taking full responsibility for your actions and acknowledging your role in the situation. It means to let go of any resentment and anger—or blame—that you may be holding onto."

Emily considered his words. "But how will I know when I'm complete?"

"When you no longer have any emotional reaction or attachment to it."

"How do I do that?"

"Say everything there is to say about it until there's nothing left to say, and it no longer holds any power over you."

***

"In Krav Maga, we want all ten toes pointing forward and palms open, facing out," the instructor reminded Emily. "The things we communicate with our body language can escalate or deescalate a situation. So, if someone is approaching you in an aggressive manner, keeping your palms open and facing toward them communicates that you're not trying to be aggressive while at the same time, providing you the opportunity to better defend yourself."

Emily nodded as she reset her feet shoulder width apart and raised her hands in front of her face.

"Now, tuck those elbows into your side, and as I come for you, strike my face with the heel of your hand." He took the bolster from Addison and held it in front of him as he lunged toward Emily.

Left, right. One, two, three, four.

"Perfect. Just like that. Keep taking turns with your partner."

Emily and Addison spent the next forty-five minutes kicking, punching, and screaming as they practiced the choke holds and counter attacks they had been learning for the past few weeks. As usual, they ended their session sweaty, exhausted, and energized.

After Addison dropped Emily off at home, Emily showered and climbed into bed for an early night of reading. She picked up *Daring Greatly* by Brené Brown—a book her dad had given her many months ago, and one she also noticed on Jack's bookshelf back in New York. As she read about shame and vulnerability, a particular passage stood out:

"Only when we're brave enough to explore the darkness will we discover the infinite power of our light."

She grabbed her phone and opened Jack's contact. She had ignored his multiple calls and texts over the last couple of months. When everything with Enzo first blew up, Jack called her two to three times a day every day that first week. Her thumb would hover over the green icon before hitting the red one. She couldn't bring herself to face him. His calls had started declining. His last text was a week ago: *Where you are in life is perfect, Emily.*

She stared at his picture in the little circle above his name. A picture she took of him the night they went to see *Phantom of the Opera*. And then she tapped his number.

"You've been avoiding me, Emily." His seductive voice came through the phone.

"I have."

They sat in silence.

"I'm curious," she finally began, "when you brought me on stage at the Symposium, did you know I worked for Enzo?"

"No. I didn't know of any connection between the two of you until afterwards. He told me in a follow-up call that you worked for him, and he was the one who enrolled you in the seminar. He also told me you were very special to him. Though I didn't realize just how special."

"I wasn't special."

"Okay."

"You know, what I really don't understand is how he stood on that stage every week talking about the importance of integrity while he pursued me and another woman claiming he had an open marriage."

"I get that."

"That's all you have to say?"

"Would you like me to say more?"

"Well, yeah... and not only that, but I hear he's leading a new seminar on relationships and sex. What the hell is that about?" Her anger was pumping through her veins, pushing the words out of her mouth. "That's so fucked up! Do you have any idea how stupid I feel for falling for all the bullshit you told me about needing to embrace my authentic self? That my power is in my sexuality? Is this some sick game you guys play? Find a vulnerable young woman at the seminar and tag team her?"

There were no tears. She had none left. All that was there now for her was anger and bitterness. Everything she had tried to suppress for the past two months came rushing forward, hitting her full force, and she wanted Jack to feel it. Because she realized she partially blamed him as well.

After a few moments, Jack spoke. "Here's the thing, Emily. We are all just spiritual beings having a human experience, and human beings fuck up all the time. Transformation occurs when we can acknowledge we fucked up, get off it, clean up our messes, and create a new possibility for ourselves. That's what Enzo is doing. He acknowledged his fuck-up, and he's working on cleaning it up with his wife and the center."

"What about cleaning it up with me? He could have talked to me first. He only acknowledged it to Isabella because he got caught."

"Sometimes it takes getting caught with our hand in the cookie jar before we realize how monumentally we've fucked up."

"So, that's it? He just has to say he fucked up, and all is well for him? Life is normal, and he gets to lead a seminar about relationships and sex? You really don't see the hypocrisy with that?"

"You once mentioned to me that you trained new bartenders," Jack said. "Have you ever noticed when you're training somebody how to run a bar, it gives you more clarity about actually running a bar? You might see something during the training process that was missing or that hadn't occurred to you before."

"Sure, I guess."

"Something to consider is that when seminar leaders teach a seminar, they're getting just as much—if not more—out of it than the participants. They have to confront ugly truths about themselves to stand in a place of transformation. What better person to lead a seminar about relationships and sex than someone who has discovered firsthand the intricacies of relationships that go way beyond sex? Enzo wasn't rewarded with leading the seminar. Enzo's training in becoming a leader of transformation requires him to lead the seminar."

"How can someone lead a conversation about transformation if they haven't transformed themselves?"

"Exactly."

"No, I'm asking you," she clarified.

"Human beings have an innate desire to figure things out and to understand. But to understand something, it must first mean something, right? So, we say what it means and then get to work on understanding it. Do you know who Henry Miller is?"

"'Tropic of Cancer?'"

"Yes," Jack said. "He said that life has to be given meaning because of the obvious fact that it has no meaning. And when we have the realization that life has no meaning, that opens up a world of possibility. That allows us to invent our own meaning, knowing of course that it really means nothing. That's when transformation occurs; when we recognize that none of it means anything."

"So, you're saying that Enzo cheating on his wife, my betrayal to her... means nothing?"

"It means whatever you say it means."

Emily sat with this as she struggled to comprehend the concept.

"And one more thing," Jack said. "I never told you your power was in your sexuality. I said your power lies in being authentic. Being authentic means being truthful about where you're being inauthentic in life. And how you know you're being inauthentic is when you experience a loss of power and self-expression. That's what came up for you in your Symposium. For someone else, it could be that they're being inauthentic about their health or career or relationship. Everyone experiences their own Symposium."

"I did enjoy discovering that authenticity with you," Emily admitted.

"I know you did," Jack said. "And I promise you, I got more out of that weekend than you did. Emily, you really are a force. Don't let this breakdown stop you from expressing who you are. Without a breakdown, you can't have a breakthrough. Of course you're more than your sexuality. You're a powerful woman. But you lose your power when you stop being authentic."

Twenty-eight

The throngs of drunk people invading downtown for Oktober-fest in late September was an annual tradition that no self-respecting pleasure seeker would let go by without participating. Emily closed down the table at The Crimson Room Saturday night after no one came in the night before because they were partaking in the festivities on the streets.

She slid on the sexy dirndl she bought a few years earlier when Diego and Todd first initiated her and Addison into the drinking fest. A small brown bodice tied together with pink ribbon held in the off-the-shoulder white blouse. Straps wrapping from around the front to behind her neck pushed up her small breasts into heaving mounds of flesh. A tiny white apron sat atop the short green skirt that covered a spray of pink crinoline, barely covering her green boy shorts underneath. White thigh-high stockings ended in black-and-white-checkered Vans.

When she opened her door to Clay and Lucas, they both looked momentarily stunned.

"Nice braids," Clay said. "The pink bows really pull the whole outfit together."

His sarcasm was not lost on her.

"Nice lederhosen." Emily didn't expect Clay to come dressed up in full costume, but he looked like he was straight out of Bavaria with knee-length leather shorts and suspenders over his green gingham shirt.

"And where's yours?" she asked Lucas.

"You wouldn't catch me in that ridiculous get-up!"

"Only because you know you're not sexy enough to pull it off." Clay slapped Lucas's back.

After Clay and Lucas dropped their overnight bags in Emily's apartment, the three of them headed up Larimer Street to the Ballpark District surrounding Coors Field, arm in arm, with Emily in the middle.

As they approached the beer hall, the crowds made it impossible for Emily to continue holding onto Lucas. He broke away and walked behind her and Clay.

"This is insane!" Lucas yelled up to them while they pushed their way through the revelers.

As soon as Diego spotted them, he pulled away from Todd, laser-focused on Clay. "Oh, my god, Emily! Where have you been hiding him?"

"She never lets me come out and play." Clay extended his hand and introduced himself.

"You really do look like Captain America," Addison said as she shook Clay's hand.

Clay laughed and side-eyed Emily.

Grabbing Lucas from behind her, Emily brought him forward to meet everyone.

"Where's Tonya?' Addison asked Emily.

"She's not twenty-one, so she can't drink with us which didn't sound very fun for her. We told her we'll bring her next year."

"Speaking of drinking, I'll get us some beer," Clay told Emily, seeing that everyone else had already started.

"Actually, I hate beer," Emily responded. "But if they have German wine, I'll take some of that."

Clay looked at her, horrified. "You're at Oktoberfest! How can you hate beer?"

"That's what I always ask her!" Addison laughed.

As the afternoon turned into evening, the drinks kept flowing while they snacked on bratwurst, pretzels, and German cakes and treats. Whenever the live polka band broke into the Chicken Dance song, hundreds of people in the street stopped what they were doing to dance and clap in unison. Emily and her friends swung arm to arm, passing from one to another.

Late into the night, they all wandered into a tent blasting rock music and selling mini bottles of shot-sized Feigling. Clay bought two bottles for everyone, followed immediately by Todd with another round before Emily dragged all her friends up onto the stage to dance to Pink's *Trouble*.

Grinding into Clay, she sang the words of warning as she wrapped her arms around his neck before breaking away and turning toward Lucas, dancing between both men. Clay spun her back around to face him. His hands held onto her hips as she moved seductively over his thigh, pressing into him, their faces dangerously close as their mouths held mischievous smiles. She was mesmerized by the droplets of sweat that had formed on the front of his neck. She wanted to lick them up, but on the final guitar riff, she pushed off from him, raising her arms high while she spun around to the music.

Suddenly, her ankle twisted, and she dropped, falling from the stage to the hard asphalt three feet down.

"Party foul!" A drunk group near her shouted.

Clay was the first at her side. "Emily! Are you okay?"

"No," she moaned as she rolled over onto her butt, looking at her bleeding knee through ripped stockings, tiny pebbles embedded in her skin. "Ow!"

He scooped her up from the ground and carried her to a nearby table, sitting her in a chair.

"Will you pull my stocking down?"

"Oh, um, yeah... sure." His hands wrapped around her thigh as he hooked his fingers into the top of the band. He slid the stocking down her leg, carefully peeling it away from her bloodied knee.

"Owwww!"

"Okay, party girl, you're cut off." Addison had Clay hold Emily's leg up while she poured water over the open wound.

Pulling up a chair, Clay propped her leg across his lap while Shelby placed clean napkins over the fresh blood that rushed to the surface. Clay pressed his hand over it, providing gentle pressure to stop the bleeding.

"Here, Em," Todd broke through the barrier of friends surrounding her. "Brought you a shot of tequila to help with the pain."

Emily smiled at Addison as she took the glass and shot it back. Addison shook her head in defeat.

"You certainly know how to close out a show," Diego teased. "I'm sorry you got hurt, baby."

"Don't stop the night because of me," Emily told them. "I'm fine. Just give me a few minutes."

Addison laughed. "I don't think so. It's after one in the morning. Last call is coming up anyway. I think it's time to call it a night."

"She's right, Emily," Clay said. "We should get you home and get ice on this. Can you walk?"

Emily slowly pulled her leg from Clay's lap and stood up with his assistance. When she took a step forward, the pain shot from her ankle up her calf, and she cried out.

"Well, that's not good," Lucas mumbled.

"Piggyback it is," Clay said as he turned around and squatted down in front of Emily.

"You can't be serious."

"It's only a couple of blocks. Come on."

Diego and Todd helped Emily climb onto Clay's back and straddle him, wrapping her arms over his shoulders and across his chest. He grabbed onto her legs and stood, hoisting her up a bit more.

"You good?" Clay asked.

"Yes. You?"

He looked over his shoulder at her and smiled. "I'm good."

When they reached her building, she instructed Lucas to get her keys out of the small crossbody bag she was wearing. Once inside the apartment, Clay took her into her bedroom and sat down on her bed so she could dismount. She fell backward onto the mattress when she released her grip, causing the room to spin.

"Do you have pajamas I can get for you to change into while I get the ice together?"

"I don't wear pajamas," she stated bluntly.

Clay laughed. "Okay." He looked around and spotted a red satin nightgown hanging from a hook on the back of her bedroom door. "How about this?" He brought it to the bed and removed her sneakers.

Emily struggled to get her costume off.

"I'll go get ice." Clay quickly headed for the door.

"I need help," she cried.

He paused. "Okay. What do you need me to do?"

"Unzip me."

Clay sat next to her on the bed and reached around her back to pull down the zipper.

The costume relaxed from Emily's body as he lifted the strap over her head while carefully keeping her covered. He placed her hand across her chest to hold the costume up.

"You got it from here?" he asked.

Emily nodded, and he made a beeline for the door.

Once she got the dirndl off, she slipped on her nightgown and undid her braids, running her fingers through her wavy hair to release the tension in her head. She stood up and tried to walk to the bathroom, but the pain was too much, and she stopped in place.

Clay knocked. "Can I come in?"

"Yes."

Stepping in to find her standing in the short negligee, he froze before averting his eyes to the wall.

"I really need to pee."

He set the icepack on the nightstand and wrapped his arm around her waist to help her hobble to the bathroom. Stepping inside, he pulled the second door closed that opened to the rest of her apartment before retreating back into her bedroom and closing the bathroom door behind him.

Emily pulled down her boy shorts, collapsing onto the toilet in pain. When she finished, she kicked her panties off to the corner and hopped over to her medicine cabinet, pushing things out while looking for Tylenol.

"Emily? You okay," she heard Clay ask.

She opened the door to the living room and saw Lucas sitting on the couch.

He quickly stood up. "Can I get you anything?"

"Water."

Clay opened the other door from her bedroom and came in to help her back to bed.

"It hurts," she cried out as she tried to hobble.

"Hang on." He pulled the covers back on her bed and picked her up to carry her the rest of the way. After he laid her down, he placed the bag of ice on her knee. "Do you have any first aid stuff?"

"I think."

As Clay left to go search, Lucas walked in with her water. "Here you go." He stood there watching Emily fumble with the medicine bottle before finally setting the water down and opening it for her, handing her two small pills.

"Three. I need three."

"Oh, okay, sure," he said, dumping one more into her hand.

She threw the pills in her mouth, washing them down with water as he stood there looking like a deer in headlights.

Clay returned with an armload of supplies and sat on the bed next to Emily. Pulling the sheet over the middle of her body, covering her up, he left only her injured leg exposed. "Lucas, why don't you get the blankets for us? I think she keeps them in the hall closet. I'm just going to get her bandaged up and settled."

When Lucas left, Clay cleaned her knee with hydrogen peroxide. After dabbing on some antibiotic ointment, he taped a gauze pad over her wound and placed the icepack back on top.

Emily winced.

"Your ankle is pretty swollen," he said. "My grandpa used to rub sprains with rubbing alcohol. It always seemed to make it feel better. Do you want me to do that?"

Emily nodded. She watched as Clay poured the alcohol into his bare palms and carefully picked up her foot, placing it in his lap. His hands firmly caressed her ankle, massaging the liquid into her skin. His warm touch countered the coolness of the alcohol as she felt herself drifting away.

"You're such a good friend," she whispered.

****

Her naked body intertwined with his as she felt the slickness from his sweat, his mouth kissing her neck, his firm hand kneading her breast. She wanted him; she needed him inside of her. She dug her fingers into his shoulders, pulling in closer, wanting to fuse their bodies. She was throbbing, her climax building, his other hand between her legs. Almost there. Her tongue was licking his skin, searching for his mouth. His lips teased her, bit her. His hand grabbed her ass, enveloping her in his embrace. Almost there. Throbbing. Throbbing. Her mouth on his. Her tongue trying to catch his tongue. More. His crystal blue eyes focused on her before he pushed himself deep inside, sending shockwaves through her body.

Emily's eyes shot open.

Her breathing was heavy, her body tingling.

What the hell was that?

She looked next to her and then to the foot of her bed. She was alone.

How can that be?

Daylight was pouring in through her windows. She placed her hand on her belly to slow her heart rate, feeling the satin negligee.

Did I really just orgasm from a sex dream?

She closed her eyes again, trying to calm herself, and saw Clay's face smiling at her as they danced, his hands on her hips, moving together rhythmically to the music.

Shit!

Throwing the covers off, she found her legs elevated on her yoga bolster. Two baggies of water lay on the sheets, one near her knee and the other by her foot. It was then that she remembered her fall. Propping herself up, she first noticed her bandaged knee before moving her eyes down to her swollen ankle.

Images of Clay taking care of her last night flashed through her head—carrying her piggyback, helping her to bed. But she didn't remember putting on that nightgown.

Did he undress me?

Swinging her legs to the ground, she stood up and took a moment to gain her balance before taking a step. There was pain, but she was able to hobble to the bathroom. The other door was open, and she saw Lucas asleep on the sofa. Peeking out, she found Clay crashed out on the giant beanbag. She quietly closed the door.

After brushing her teeth and washing her face, she picked up her panties from the bathroom floor and limped back into her room, changing into sweats and a t-shirt before opening her bedroom door.

"You're awake," Clay said as he slowly sat up, rubbing his eyes. He didn't have on a shirt, but her red blanket covered him from the waist down.

Emily blushed as she looked away. Even though she knew it was just a dream, she was still very much in the moment of it all feeling real, and she suddenly had an irrational fear that he knew what happened between them while they were asleep. Like maybe he had the same dream.

"I need coffee," she said as she headed toward the kitchen.

"Wait. I'll get it." Clay grabbed his t-shirt from the floor, putting it on before standing up.

Emily was relieved to see he was wearing sweatpants.

"You need to lay back down. I'll bring it to you."

"No, it's okay. I should walk it off. I have to work at Snooze tomorrow morning. Just glad I already asked for today off."

"Actually, you need to rest it for the first twenty-four hours. Stay off it and keep it elevated with ice. Otherwise, you could make it worse."

He helped her sit down in her dining chair and grabbed a sofa pillow that had been tossed on the floor. He propped her leg up on another chair. "How are you feeling?"

"Sore. But probably better than if you hadn't doctored me up last night. Thank you."

"I'm always up for playing doctor," he teased, heading into the kitchen.

Her dream flashed in her mind as she thought of his hands caressing her body, his mouth on hers. Her orgasm. She remembered the sensual, drunken kiss from a few months earlier and had a hard time looking at him now.

"Did you change me out of my clothes last night?" she asked while he put ice in a baggie. She had to know.

"What? No. I just... you asked me to unzip you, which I did, and then handed you your nightgown and left the room."

Relief.

"Sorry," she said. "Things are fuzzy for me. I guess I drank too much. I hope I didn't do anything else too embarrassing last night."

Flashes of her grinding into him, running her finger along his sweaty chest and wanting to lick him as she watched his tongue graze his lips. Her breath skipped.

"No... not at all," Clay said quietly as he placed the ice pack on her ankle.

He returned to the kitchen and pressed down on the coffee grinder, its deafening whir rousing Lucas.

While the coffee brewed, Clay stared into her refrigerator and asked, "How about some breakfast?"

Twenty-nine

"So, how is it living with Shelby?" Emily asked Addison as they drove to Krav Maga. "Is it as blissful as you imagined?"

"Better." Addison glowed. "I love them more every day."

"I'm so happy for you, Addy. How are things going with your parents? Have they met Shelby yet?"

Addison sighed. "Not as great as I'd hoped. My dad says it's hard enough accepting that I'm gay, but then throwing it in his face by moving in with Shelby is crossing the line. And don't even get him started on the pronouns."

"Oh, no."

"He refuses to meet them. He told me he could love me and accept that I'm a lesbian, but that doesn't mean he has to accept Shelby. My mom's been great, though. She comes over to visit at least once a week."

"I'm sorry about your dad. That must suck. Hopefully, he'll come around."

"I'm not holding my breath. But at this point, I'm just thankful he hasn't disowned me. It's something, I guess."

Addison kept her eyes on the road, but Emily noticed her grip on the steering wheel tightened. She could tell she was holding back tears and wanted to comfort her, but she didn't know what she could say to make it hurt less.

"On a happier note," Addison's voice perked up, "I love living in RiNo. Shelby's place is so cool. You need to come over and have dinner with us sometime."

I don't think Shelby would like that. Even though Shelby helped her when Emily fell at Oktoberfest, Shelby hadn't said a word to her that entire day.

"What does RiNo stand for? I realize I don't even know."

"Really? River North Art District. Sheesh, you act like you just moved here." Addison laughed.

"Well, in my defense, I only ever hear people call it RiNo, and I've always been too embarrassed to ask for fear of being shamed." Emily emphasized the last word to make her point.

"Fine, fine. So sorry. I didn't mean to shame you." Addison kissed the air toward Emily. "So, you really think your ankle is strong enough now to get back to Krav Maga? It's only been a couple weeks. Aren't you supposed to wait like six to eight?"

"I'm good. It was just a minor sprain, thankfully. And Clay made me stay off it the next day, icing it every couple of hours. So, I think that really helped. He and Lucas waited on me hand and foot. It was pretty sweet. Made me food. Watched movies with me. They even went down to the drugstore to get an Ace bandage so Clay could wrap my ankle."

Addison glanced over at Emily with a side smile.

"What?"

"Nothing."

"Oh, and Clay did this thing where he massaged my ankle with rubbing alcohol a few times, and I swear it made it feel better. Have you ever heard of that?"

"Nope."

"He said it's something his grandpa used to do for him. Anyway, it was like magic. And now I weirdly love the smell of rubbing alcohol."

Addison laughed. "Okay. I just don't want you to reinjure it, so the moment something hurts, please stop."

"I will. I really need to get back into the studio. It makes me feel strong, and like I can take on anything. I'm wearing an ankle support wrap that Clay brought over last week, so that should help."

Addison pulled the car into the parking lot. "Sounds like Clay is taking really good care of you," she said through a stifled grin.

***

Emily wanted to throw her laptop across the room. She had spent close to two hours trying to open a file her brother had emailed over. At her wit's end, she finally decided to call her personal IT department.

"Sure, I'll head over after work," Clay said. "I get off in about half an hour."

When he arrived at her place, he sat down at her desk to take a look. "You know, house calls are pretty expensive."

"Will you accept dinner as payment?"

"Only if it includes a beer."

Emily leaned over to show him how she had been trying to open the attachment from her email. "Look, nothing happens." She meticulously recounted everything she had done to make it work, so he wouldn't think she was completely computer illiterate.

When she glanced at him, she noticed him gazing at her with an amused smile, but he quickly moved his eyes back to the computer. She felt a flutter in her stomach and moved out of the way to let him try to fix it—which he did— in about three minutes.

"What the hell?"

Clay laughed. "You just needed a zip-file extractor."

"Are you kidding me?" she asked incredulously. "I assumed it already had that! I've had this laptop for over two months and have never had an issue opening a file."

"You probably haven't tried to open a zip file before. Are you sure this wasn't just an excuse to get me to come over?" He smiled wide, taunting her as he reclined back in the chair.

"I wouldn't need to make up an excuse," she replied sarcastically.

"No, you wouldn't," he chuckled. "You know I'd come running anytime you needed me—even in a snowstorm." He glanced out the window.

Emily looked over to see the flurries falling steadily.

"Oh my gosh... I wasn't even paying attention to the weather! I've been so wrapped up in this stupid computer." She felt horrible that she had him drive over to help her with such a simple problem. "Why is it snowing in October anyway?"

"It's been known to happen." He laughed, clearly entertained by her obliviousness. "The world could be falling down around you, but if you're focused on something, you'd have no idea. It's one of the things I love about you."

She smacked his arm. "Come on, let's go eat."

People packed into Rock Bottom Brewery for Happy Hour. Snowy days never stopped anyone from drinking, even on a Wednesday night. Emily and Clay grabbed their drinks at the bar before finally snagging a table.

"So, how's the new dealer doing over at the Cruise Room," Clay asked.

"Stressful. She called in sick at the last minute on Saturday, so since it was only the second weekend in that location, I had to go work it instead of Crimson."

"Yikes, that's scary. How did it do?"

"Decent. Not as well as Crimson, but it should pick up over time. I just wish I knew if this girl was really sick or just blowing off work."

"Ah, the downside of running your own business—flaky employees." He took a sip of his Guinness.

"Gives me a whole new appreciation for all those times I called in sick when I wasn't. There's a lot to figure out—a lot of moving parts."

"You seem to be handling it pretty well."

"It's all a façade," she smirked.

"I disagree. Where do you see yourself in a year?"

"I'm hoping to buy more casino tables from David and hire dealers over the next few months so I can quit waiting tables," Emily told him. "Hopefully, in a year, I'll be able to stop dealing myself and just manage the business. But who knows? It could never come together." She picked up her amaretto sour, uneasy with so much uncertainty.

"I don't doubt you'll get there. You just need to be patient."

"Not one of my strong suits."

"So, what about in five years? Where do you envision yourself?"

That's a good question. What would she be doing in five years at thirty years old? Still running casino tables or bartending? She was so focused on hustling right now just to pay her bills that she hadn't stopped to think about a bigger picture. The realization that her circumstances likely wouldn't be much different than today washed over her. She took another drink and looked away as tightness gripped her chest.

"Are you okay," he asked. "I'm sorry. I didn't mean to upset you."

She laughed, trying to shake off her sudden heavy emotions. "I'm fine. I'm sorry. I don't know what that's about."

Clay reached across the table and took her hand into his, interlacing his fingers with hers. Emily's breath skipped at his intimate gesture.

"Hey, you're young, Emily," he reassured her. "You don't have to have everything figured out at twenty-five."

She wiped a tear from her cheek that had escaped. "You did."

"Not really. Sure, I have a boring job right now, certainly not what I would call my dream job. And it's not a guarantee of anything. I could get laid off tomorrow and end up flipping burgers somewhere."

Emily laughed, trying to lighten the somber mood. "You can flip them, and I'll serve them."

"As long as I get to hang out with you, I'll be good." He smiled, staring into her eyes.

Emily felt her stomach flutter again. She didn't understand why he was starting to affect her like this after all these months.

We are just friends.

"I'll be right back," she smiled. "I need to use the bathroom."

As she was washing her hands, Stephanie walked in, locking eyes with Emily in the mirror.

Emily turned around. "Stephanie..."

But Stephanie ignored her and walked into a stall, closing the door. Emily stood there for a moment, contemplating what she should do.

On one hand, she was angry (and she hated to admit, jealous) that Stephanie was also involved with Enzo. But on the other, she felt compassion toward her, understanding the deep hurt of betrayal.

As a group of women came bursting in, laughing, Emily quietly slipped out.

Clay and Emily headed back to her apartment after dinner in the ever-growing snowstorm.

"This weather is crazy. I'm not letting you drive home in this," she told him.

"Well, I can't say I was looking forward to the drive. Let me stop at my car. I've learned to keep an overnight bag in the trunk, and I need to get out of these wet jeans."

Emily was a little nervous about how the evening would play out. Ever since Oktoberfest, the memories of them dancing and her sex dream about him would randomly pop into her head. Even though her feelings for him were starting to shift into new territory, she didn't want to compromise their friendship—or her friendship with Tonya who still had a massive crush on him.

She changed into warm pajamas and made hot chocolate with mini marshmallows. They sat down in front of her fireplace, side by side, leaning against the giant beanbag.

"I thought you didn't wear pajamas?"

Emily looked at him, unsure how to respond as she glanced down at her fuzzy pants covered in jack o'lanterns and black cats.

"Never mind," he laughed.

They talked late into the evening. Clay shared with her more about Lucas's brother's death. He said when Lucas called him, screaming that Marcus was dead in the shower, he thought it was a prank they were playing on him.

"I laughed. 'Call someone who cares,' I told him." Clay dropped his head and was silent for a moment. When he looked back up at the fire, Emily saw a tear stream down his face. "He was my best friend since we were two years old. I still can't believe he's gone."

Emily laid her head on Clay's shoulder to offer comfort. He draped his arm around her as she rested against him, listening to him talk about some of his favorite memories of Marcus.

She awoke in the morning to the sound of the coffee grinder. Sitting up from the beanbag, the red blanket that had been covering her slid off.

"Good morning, sleepyhead." He grinned. "Look at all the snow."

Emily turned around to see a winter wonderland outside her window. "Beautiful."

"Yes, it is." He smiled at her while preparing the coffee. The aroma quickly filled her apartment.

She noticed the blanket he used on the sofa was folded neatly, stacked on top of the pillow.

"I'm working remotely today, so I thought I'd head over to Tattered Cover while I'm down here. I love walking around that place, and I've wanted to pick up this book someone told me about. Want to join me?"

"Of course! That's my happy place."

They spent most of the day perusing the bookstore and reclining in the big comfy chairs to read their selections while Clay intermittently worked on his laptop. He left with *The Holographic Universe* by Michael Talbot, and Emily bought *Untamed* by Glennon Doyle—a book Jack had recommended in their last conversation.

When they returned to the front of her building, Clay pulled her in for a hug and held her tightly. "Thanks for everything. I had a great time."

Emily could feel her heart thumping in her chest and wondered if he could too. "Thank you so much for coming to my rescue... again."

"You absolutely do not need to be rescued. Look at everything you've been through. Most people would withdraw, stay on the ground after all those hits. But not you. You decide to start your own business and learn Krav Maga. You're a badass, Emily. Don't ever let anyone ever make you feel differently."

***

"Shelby and I are having a Halloween party," Addison announced when Emily walked into the Market to meet her for coffee. "We just decided last night. Can you come? You can bring Clay," she paused and smiled, "and Lucas and Tonya if you'd like."

"Ohhhh," Emily groaned with disappointment, ignoring her smiling implication. "I wish I could, but I'll be working at Crimson. It's also Lucas's birthday, so he and Clay are having a party, and I already told them I'd stop in before I head to work."

"I see how it is." Addison cut her huge pumpkin spice muffin in half and pushed a piece toward Emily. Her grin widened. "So?"

"What?"

"Did you sleep with him?"

"Addison!" Emily laughed. "Why would you ask that?"

"Because he just spent the night at your place... alone for the first time ever. And, literally, every time I see you, you talk about him. And the way you talk about him... you light up. It's clear you have a thing for him." She popped a piece of muffin in her mouth.

"I do not have a thing for him."

Addison stared at her like she was an idiot while she finished chewing.

"We're just friends," Emily insisted.

"Mmm-hmm." Addison took a drink of her tea, presumably so she could better lecture Emily. "Em, we have been friends for a very long time. You are my best friend. I know when you have a thing for someone. I have listened to you talk about Clay incessantly for the past few months. I could see this coming from a mile away—even when you were mired in all that other shit. When are you going to start being honest with yourself?"

"I don't... I just... The thing is..." Emily was trying to find her words.

"Stop it," Addison chastised her. "Stop making excuses. You like this guy, Emily. And from everything you've told me about him, he sounds like a really great guy. It was evident at Oktoberfest he's crazy about you. And you him, I might add."

Shit. She's right. Emily smiled in resignation. "He is a really great guy."

Addison smacked her hand on the table in victory. "I knew it!"

Emily laughed at her exuberant display. "But it's more complicated than that."

"No! No, it isn't. You deserve happiness, Emily. You deserve a good guy who adores you, not these assholes who take advantage of you and gaslight you."

"But Tonya has a huge crush on Clay. She's even asked me to teach her how to flirt with him. So, I would be betraying her, and I've betrayed enough friends in my life."

"Isn't she like, twenty? Has he ever given any indication he is remotely interested in her?" she asked pointedly.

"No, but—"

"Then, fuck her! Not to be callous toward her because I am a woman's woman, and I love that you value your friendship with her, but seriously—she doesn't have any claim on him. It's been like, what, five or six months? And if she were really a good friend to you, she wouldn't let that stand in the way of destiny."

"Destiny?" Emily laughed.

"Yes, destiny! You can't deny this is the stuff romance novels are made of."

"I wouldn't know. I don't read romance novels. I'm more of a realist," Emily teased.

"Emily." Addison sounded exhausted with her friend's defiance.

"I've made it abundantly clear to him that we are only friends. I wouldn't even know how to approach that conversation at this point."

"No conversation. Just kiss him. He's already made it known that's what he wants with you, and he would get very clear your feelings have changed."

"You really do read too many romance novels, Addy." Emily picked up her muffin and took a bite.

"I do read romance novels," she admitted proudly, "because I believe in romance. And just like I found it, you will, too. It's literally at your fingertips."

"But those romance novels aren't realistic. You don't fall in love with someone in a week and live happily ever after."

"Maybe not," Addy said. "But you can certainly have a 'happy for now' ending."

Thirty

Emily carefully painted snakeskin scales on her forehead and around her eyes before drawing on the liquid black eyeliner, extending the lines just below the inside corners and sweeping up the outside. She added black and gold jewels around her temples and applied long gold-flecked black lashes. After dusting bronzing powder over her face, she traced black lip liner around her mouth and blended it with MAC's deep red "Sin" lipstick.

The brown and black snakeskin crushed velvet dress hugged every curve of her body, from the high neck down to its long sleeves that looped around her thumbs. She slid on her matching thigh-high snakeskin boots that ended just a few inches below the hem of her dress, exposing a flash of black fishnet stockings. Delicate gold snakes dangled from her ears, and a gilded crown of serpents sat on top of her flat-ironed, silky straight hair.

Emily hoped Clay would appreciate her satirical costume. She also hoped it would make him drool. After her talk with Addison a few days earlier, Emily finally felt ready to move forward with Clay. She knew he was the one. He had always been there for her, respecting her boundaries and encouraging her growth. She liked how he made her feel about herself. She even liked that he was a "nice guy." She was choosing happiness and creating a new possibility for herself.

As she pulled up to their house in the University neighborhood, she was surprised to find it overflowing with people drinking out front. Plastic skeletons and translucent ghosts scattered the yard. Orange and purple lights dangled across the porch as she walked up the steps past zombies smoking pot. When she went into the house, she saw Rocky Horror Picture Show playing on the TV while a group of partiers danced to "The Time Warp." It was only a little after seven p.m., and people were already obviously drunk.

Emily was shocked. The scene seemed so incongruous to how she knew Clay and Lucas.

Then again, there are many things about me they don't know.

"Emily?"

She turned her head to see a green witch with bright red lips carrying a broomstick. "Oh, my god... Tonya?"

"I'm Elphaba from Wicked!"

"You look incredible!" Emily grazed Tonya's long black lacy gown.

"Thanks, so do you. Your makeup is amazing, and your hair—I love it! I've never seen it straight before." Tonya shouted above the music.

"Thanks. This is crazy! Who are all these people?"

"Right? I have no idea!"

"Where are Lucas and Clay?"

"I think that's Lucas over there." She pointed across the room to a guy with long black curly hair and a floppy top hat, wearing only a black leather vest over his bare chest and black leather pants. He had a guitar strung around his shoulders and round sunglasses covering his eyes. "I haven't seen Clay yet. I just got here a few minutes ago."

Lucas glanced over and left the group he was in when he noticed Emily and Tonya. "Holy shit! You guys look great!"

"So do you, Slash." Emily hugged him. "Happy birthday! This is for you." She handed him a gift. "I had no idea this many people would be here."

He laughed. "Yeah... we kinda started a little early. A few of my friends from school and Clay's friends from work came over this afternoon to help set up. Then others just started showing up."

"Happy birthday!" Tonya hugged him and gave him her gift.

"Thanks, ladies! I'll open these later if that's okay?"

"Of course. Where's Clay?" Emily asked casually.

"He's around here somewhere. Maybe in the backyard. Let's go find him."

Pushing their way through the crowd in the kitchen, they stepped out onto the back porch where she saw Clay on the other side of the yard, standing around a keg, drinking with people.

Pirate. A fucking sexy pirate.

He wore a long blond wig with a red bandana covering the top of his head. A large gold hoop earring hung from one ear, and a sword dangled from his side. A white billowy shirt, unbuttoned to his navel, disappeared into black leather pants.

Jesus, he even looks like he belongs on the cover of a fucking romance novel.

Clay's eyes locked onto Emily, and they stared at each other as if no one else was around—soaking in every detail of one another.

Maybe there's something to this romance novel bullshit after all.

Emily imagined herself walking up and kissing him without warning.

I can't really do that with Tonya at my side, but I can dream.

As she began her descent down the steps toward him, a sexy nurse jumped into his arms and pushed her tongue into his mouth. Emily froze as she watched him wrap his arms around the nurse and return her kiss.

Her heart fell out of her body.

"Emily, he's over here!" Lucas shouted, motioning for her to follow. Her eyes fell on Tonya, who also looked like she got punched in the gut.

As Emily carefully navigated across the lawn in high heels, Clay met them, his hand interlaced with the sexy blonde's. "A snake in the grass." He smiled. "Nice."

Lucas looked Emily up and down. "Oh, yeah. I get it. That's hilarious!"

"Who's this?" Tonya asked with false exuberance straining her voice.

"Oh, this is Amber. We work together." Clay and Emily held each other's gaze as Amber and Tonya shook hands.

"Nice to meet you." Amber's Southern drawl dripped out like honey through a sweet smile as she extended her hand to Emily.

Emily shifted her focus to the supermodel standing in front of her. "Oh, nice to meet you, too."

"Can we get y'all a drink?" Amber offered, resting her hand on Clay's chest as if he belonged to her. "We've got a keg here and liquor in the kitchen."

What is this 'we' shit?

"I could definitely use a drink," Emily smiled. "Tonya, want to join me?"

The girls turned around and left them in the backyard.

"Are you okay?" Emily asked Tonya once they were inside, pouring tequila shots. *Because I am not.*

"Yeah. I just had no idea he was seeing someone. Did you?"

"Not at all." Emily licked her hand and sprinkled on the salt before passing it to Tonya. "Drink up."

Emily spent the next couple of hours sipping water while she politely chatted with strangers in the house. Tonya continued drinking and was dancing in the living room to Shakira, so Emily walked out onto the front porch for some fresh air.

A few minutes later, Clay appeared. "There you are. I've been looking for you."

She smiled as she turned toward him. "You make a good pirate."

"You make a fucking amazing snake." His chuckle fell silent as the air between them momentarily stood still.

"This is quite a party." Emily broke the longing silence. "I had no idea you had so many friends," she teased.

"I'm a mysterious guy."

"Yes, you are. Speaking of which, how did I not know you were seeing someone?" She took a sip of water, hoping it seemed like a normal friend question.

"It's very new."

Look, I finally realize I'm an idiot and have missed the most incredible guy standing right in front of me the whole time. I want to feel your lips on mine again. I want to dance close to you again. I want it to be me that you hold at your side at a party. "Well, she seems very nice." Emily forced a smile.

"Thanks. She is."

I hate her. I hate that I'm not her.

"Can I get you a drink?" he asked.

"No, I actually have to head to work now. Will you tell Lucas and Tonya goodbye for me?"

"Yes, of course."

Emily stepped in to hug him. He wrapped his arms around her, pulling her in tightly. His hands held onto her waist as she breathed in his scent. *Please kiss me. Forget about Amber. You can have me.*

"Happy Halloween." She broke from his embrace, quickly turning away so he wouldn't see the tears in her eyes.

***

The Crimson Room was packed. Most people were dressed as gangsters and molls to coincide with the forties speak-easy vibe. Emily realized she vastly underestimated the transformative power of a Halloween costume as everyone really got into character. People stood three deep around the table most of the night, waiting for their turn to play. She had to explain to more than one gangster that this wasn't real gambling and to take their cash off the table.

The crowd surrounding her didn't prevent her from noticing Dylan when he walked down the stairs in a silk robe, looking very much like Hugh Heffner, complete with a Playboy bunny on his arm.

Well, this is just perfect.

Dylan led the young woman to the same booth he and Emily sat at months earlier—directly next to her blackjack table. She watched as Robert, the piano player, approached their table and removed the *Reserved* sign. Taking the woman's hand into his, he kissed it before sitting down at his bench and playing "Satin Doll."

A well-rehearsed act.

Emily had never conversed with Robert during her evenings at the bar. She wasn't entirely sure he even remembered meeting her. Now, she understood why.

One of many desperate groupies.

Dylan did a double take when he finally realized it was Emily dealing cards next to him. Their eyes briefly met before she took her attention back to her table. She noticed them leave just a short time later.

She was thankful the players kept her mind off both Dylan and Clay and his sexy nurse. Sometime after midnight, the crowd started thinning, and she looked up to see Lucas approaching her table, still in his Slash costume—minus the guitar and sunglasses.

"Hey! What are you doing here?"

"Can I buy in?" He pulled out his wallet and sat down at an empty barstool.

Emily pushed a stack of chips towards him. "It's on the house for the birthday boy. Why aren't you at your party? Did you drive here?"

"No, I took an Uber. I came to thank you for my present."

"You did not leave your birthday party just to thank me for Cards Against Humanity."

He laughed before taking on a more somber face. "I guess I'm drowning my sorrows. Katherine broke up with me."

"Oh, I'm so sorry."

"On my birthday, no less!"

"Aw, tough break, man." The drunk guy sitting next to him chimed in. "Let me buy you a shot!" He grabbed the server. "My friend and I will each have a shot of Fireball. And one for Medusa."

Emily grimaced as she began dealing the cards. "What happened?"

"She said she met someone else," Lucas shrugged his shoulders. "She called to wish me a happy birthday and then said we were over. After three years together, that's how it ends."

Emily went through the rounds of hitting or holding for the player's cards. "Well, she let a good man get away." She tried to comfort him as she flipped her cards to show a jack and a six. Drawing a third card, she busted with a nine and paid out the winners.

Everyone at the table bought shots for and toasted to Lucas and his newfound freedom until last call at one-thirty. Lucas ordered two more shots of tequila for Emily and another Fireball for himself. "You have some catching up to do."

"There's no way I could keep up with you and still deal cards." After closing out her table, she threw back her shots and grabbed her bag. "Come on. You can crash at my place tonight."

"You still walk home at this hour? After what happened over summer?"

"Sometimes I take an Uber. But I've got you to protect me if we get jumped." She looked over at him and saw the zoned-out drunkenness on his face. "Just kidding. I'll protect us. I've got skills now."

On the walk to her apartment, they started debating about whether Fireball was actually whiskey.

"Whiskey is eighty-proof," Emily insisted. "Fireball is only sixty-six."

"They couldn't call it whiskey if it wasn't whiskey!"

"I was a bartender. You have to trust me."

"Even bartenders can be wrong," he challenged her, laughing.

"Fine, I'll prove it to you." Once inside her apartment, she yanked off her boots and snake crown. Sitting at her desk, she opened her laptop to Google the information. Lucas suddenly swooped in and kissed her. Pulling away, she looked at him in disbelief. He stared at her, seemingly shocked himself, unsure what to do next.

Fuck it.

Standing up, she grabbed him and kissed him back. He quickly slipped her dress off over her head, exposing her black lacy bra, crotchless panties, and garter belt. His eyes widened as his mouth fell open.

After pulling down his leather pants, she pushed him back on the bed and climbed on top of him. "Do you have a condom?"

"No." He looked worried.

Emily rolled over to reach for the box in her nightstand drawer, thankful she had gotten them when she returned from New York. After she slipped the condom on him, she lowered herself, taking him inside of her.

As she moved up and down, the room began to spin. Dylan and glowsticks flashed across her mind, and she felt the sting of his aloofness when he walked out of the bar tonight. She pushed him out of her head and thought of riding Jack and how she felt sexy and powerful with him. But then the feeling of emptiness and loneliness that she experienced when she returned home hit her. Suddenly, the pain of betrayal penetrated her soul as Isabella's crying face burned in her eyelids, and Enzo's lies pierced her heart.

Then Clay's smile filled her head, reminding her of the warmth of his embrace, the touch of his hand holding hers, and the way he took care of her when she was hurt. He made her feel important. He made her feel safe. She imagined she was on top of him right now, making love to him, surrendering to him.

Lucas groaned loudly, forcing Emily to bring her awareness back to the man beneath her, tears streaming down her face. He pushed up while holding her in place, his stillness confirming he had just climaxed.

"That was amazing, Emily. Happy Halloween." He smiled and passed out.

She rolled off from him. Clay kissing Amber played like a reel in her head as she felt the torment of all her bad decisions lock around her like a prison cell.

What the fuck did I just do?

***

Emily was grinding the coffee, wearing her sweats and t-shirt when Lucas moaned from the bedroom. "Oh, my head…"

She brought him a glass of water and Tylenol. "Here, take this."

Walking back into the kitchen, she grabbed two cups of coffee and strategically placed his mug on the dining table while she sat in one of the chairs on the opposite side.

Lucas eventually stumbled out and walked over to Emily.

Play it cool. Maybe he doesn't even remember. Maybe he'll think it was all a dream. I can just deny it happened.

He leaned down and kissed her lips before grabbing his coffee and pulling up a chair next to her. "Last night… wow, Emily."

She felt nauseous. "Lucas, I…" she began, not knowing where she was going. "I need to head up to my dad's this morning," she lied. "I'm spending the day with my family."

"Oh." He set his mug down and placed his hand on her thigh. "I was hoping we could hang out some more so I could make up for passing out on you last night."

Shit!

She didn't know how to let him down. She didn't know how to get out of this. But she knew she had to. She knew she had to be truthful even if it hurt him. "Look, last night should not have happened. You're like a brother to me."

He pulled his hand away before glancing down at his coffee and slowly nodding as if he expected this.

"Lucas," she placed her hand on his, "your girlfriend of three years just broke up with you last night. On your birthday. You were so drunk. So was I. And I'm so messed up in my head right now about men. We don't want to go down this road with each other."

"I get it." He looked at her with resignation on his face.

"I really value our friendship, and I don't want to lose that."

He nodded again. Emily waited while he sat in silence, turning his mug around and around. Her stomach was churning.

"I know you're right," he finally said. "I guess I was just hoping we could be more. But knowing how Clay feels about you…"

She hated that she was hurting Lucas, but she was devastated at the thought of Clay finding out and the hurt it would cause him.

"I think we should keep this between us," she said. "The last thing I want is for our group to have any tension."

"It will just be our secret. I promise."

***

"You did what?!" Addison shrieked through the phone.

"I know, I know. It's bad."

"You think?"

"I had a few shots and was upset about Clay… which is mostly your fault, by the way."

"My fault?"

"Yes," Emily exclaimed. "You're the one who got me to admit my feelings, and then I couldn't stop thinking about him. It was like you opened the floodgates."

"Okay, well, let's pause right there for a moment and dissect that," Addison said. "Keywords: you admitted your feelings for him. I didn't create those feelings."

"I know," Emily replied, despondent.

"Oh, Em... why do you keep getting yourself into these situations?"

"Because I'm an idiot."

"Hard to argue with that. Look, I get it. You were finally ready to open your heart to Clay, and now—"

"Now, it's too late."

"You don't know that," Addison tried to reassure her. "He and this girl could be over in a week."

"But I've just ruined everything by sleeping with Lucas. How could he ever get past that?"

"From what little I know about him, he seems like the kind of guy that could."

Emily shook her head even though Addison couldn't see her through the phone. "I don't know how any guy could."

"I bet he'll surprise you." Addison took a beat. "Look, Em, I know you've come a long way these past few months shedding your shame and guilt surrounding sex, which is fantastic. No woman should be made to feel trashy because she wants to have meaningless sex. Men, of course, sleep with whoever they want without judgment. But as your best friend, someone having a front-row seat to all this, I'm concerned that you've placed your self-worth in your sexuality. Despite what Jack and Enzo told you, your sexuality doesn't define you any more than mine defines me. It's just a detail about us."

Emily had been so wrapped up in the freedom that came from claiming her power through sex, that she felt that was all she had to offer. The only success she had ever experienced was through the eyes of men who praised her sexual prowess.

But Clay wasn't like that. Clay encouraged her endeavors and took care of her when she needed solace. Clay made her feel seen for who she was separate from how she looked.

"I just wish I had never allowed myself to feel this way about him. Things were fine as they were. I was fine. I feel like I've put myself in such a vulnerable position now, and everything can blow up all over again. But this time, I would lose so much more."

"You did allow yourself to be vulnerable, Emily, but that's not a bad thing. Being vulnerable is scary—trust me, I know—I put everything on the line for love even when I could have lost it all, too. But you know what? I gained more than I could have ever hoped for, and I wouldn't have had I been too scared to expose my true emotions."

Emily was silent as she listened to Addison's words. "But—not to be negative about your relationship with Shelby because I am so happy for you—what if things don't work out and you guys break up? Then what? Will it have all been worth it? Risking your relationship with your parents?"

"Of course it will have been worth it," Addison told her. "Because me being vulnerable wasn't about Shelby; it was about being honest with myself and everyone else in my life."

Emily smiled at her friend's wisdom and self-awareness. "When did you become so enlightened?"

"It's not only reserved for the people who attend those seminars," Addison teased her. "The fact that you showed up to that party, ready to be honest with Clay about your feelings for him, shows a lot of courage. You can't always control the outcome, Em, but you can show up. That risk of uncertainty can ultimately lead to some of the best things in life."

Thirty-one

"Welcome to Friendsgiving!" Emily opened the door to Diego and Todd. "You guys are the first ones here."

"Of course we are!" Diego kissed her cheek. "Where do you want me to put my abuela's tamales?"

"Over on the breakfast bar. I'm setting up the buffet there."

"Hi, Sweetheart." Todd held out two bottles of wine for her inspection. "Beaujolais Nouveau."

"Perfect."

He set them on the table and hugged her. "How are you doing?"

"I'm doing well."

He pulled back and looked at her for confirmation.

She laughed. "I promise. Things are going great. I've even picked up a third location for a blackjack table. Now, I'm on the hunt for a reliable dealer. Know anyone?"

"Not in my line of work," he chuckled. "But that's so awesome. Congrats!"

"Thanks. It's really starting to take off. It's been interesting meeting with these bar owners. I'm definitely learning a lot."

There was a knock on the door just before Lucas and Tonya let themselves in. "Happy Thanksgiving," Lucas bellowed.

Emily greeted him with a quick hug. They had seen each other a couple of times since Halloween but hadn't talked any more about "the incident." She did catch him staring at her a few times when they all got together for dinner. She hoped Clay didn't notice, but he seemed oblivious to anything except Amber, singing her praises every chance he could.

Emily took the pumpkin pie out of Lucas's hands. "Thanks for bringing this. It's huge!"

"Costco. My mom got way too many pies, so I snagged one."

"Here's the mac and cheese." Tonya held up her casserole dish.

"Homemade?" Emily walked to the breakfast bar to drop off the pie while Tonya followed.

"Of course. With five kinds of cheese."

"That sounds decadent!" Diego walked up to them. "You must be Terri?"

"Tonya," Emily corrected him as she went to answer the next knock on the door.

"Happy Friendsgiving!" Addison beamed.

"You too! Come in." Emily hugged her before greeting Shelby. "I'm so glad you could come."

Shelby protectively held onto a huge bowl. "Thanks for having me. I made a salad."

"It's the best salad I've ever had," Addison said. "Shelby put in blue cheese crumbles, dried cranberries, and candied pecans and then tossed it in a homemade orange citrus dressing."

"Wow, that sounds amazing."

Addison held up a bag. "I brought some freshly baked bread from the Market. One loaf of sourdough and one loaf of pumpernickel."

"My favorites!" Emily walked Addison and Shelby over to the rest of the food and introduced them to Tonya and Lucas.

"It's so nice to finally meet you, Tonya, and you to see you again, Lucas." Addison hugged them both.

Emily loved seeing all her friends come together.

Todd had opened the wine and was pouring glasses for everyone when the final knock came. Emily's heart quickened, and she glanced at Addison, who stared back in solidarity.

After taking a deep breath, Emily put on a big smile and opened the door. "Happy Friendsgiving!"

Clay smiled back, holding up peanut butter whiskey and vanilla ice cream. "I hear there's a party going on here."

"Well, now that you guys have arrived," Emily teased as she forced down the lump in her throat.

"Thanks for inviting me." Amber smiled sweetly, holding a casserole dish. She looked effortlessly gorgeous in tight black pants and chic winter boots topped with a gray cashmere sweater. The plunging neckline highlighted her ample cleavage. A fuzzy black scarf wrapped around her neck, and her flowing blonde hair cascaded around her shoulders.

Barbie and Ken. The perfect match. How can I compete with that?

"Of course. I'm so glad you could make it." *Liar.* "Come in." Emily held the door open and stepped aside. "You can set the casserole dish on the breakfast bar. She took the ice cream and whiskey and told Clay to introduce Amber to the group.

Addison followed Emily into the kitchen. "You okay?"

Emily smiled and nodded, opening the freezer.

"Can I help you with the rest of the food?" Addison offered.

Emily was grateful that Addison knew how to give subtle support when she needed it most. "Would you mind grabbing the green bean casserole out of the oven while I get the Honeybaked ham?"

Emily had rearranged her furniture for the evening, pulling her desk and chair up alongside her dining table. Since her barstools were adjustable, she used those as well, providing just enough room for the nine of them to squeeze in and dine together. Before everyone had arrived, she covered the tables with white sheets and set centerpieces of white candles surrounded by greenery and fresh cranberries. Michael Bublé played softly in the background.

She stood at the head of the table and asked everyone to gather around with their glass of wine. "I just wanted to take a moment to say how grateful I am to have you all in my life." *Well, except for you, Amber. No hard feelings.* "Each of you is so special to me, and I'm so happy we could all get together tonight. I love you guys."

"We love you too, Emily," Todd said, raising his glass for a toast. "To new friends."

"To new friends!" Glasses clinked all around.

Over dinner, everyone chatted, getting to know one another. Still, Emily wasn't quite prepared when Shelby asked Amber how she and Clay met.

"I got transferred from our Kentucky office last month to help develop a new department within our company in partnership with Clay. We had a lot of long days and late nights working together. I guess it was inevitable." She giggled. "Anyway, he and Lucas had a big Halloween birthday party for Lucas, and I could tell Clay was stressed about getting everything set up because we had been working so much. So, I offered to come over the day before and help with everything. And the rest is history!"

A day? I was late by a day?

Emily's stomach twisted in knots. She didn't want to hear any more about how they got together. "These sweet potatoes are delicious, Amber," which was very true. "How did you make them?"

"Oh, this is my mammaw's family recipe that's been passed down through the generations. I cut up the potatoes into large chunks and put them in a pot with white sugar, brown sugar, butter, cinnamon, allspice, and cloves. The sugar and butter melt together while it simmers for about three hours. Very easy."

"Yeah, you should have smelled our house today. It totally smelled like the holidays," Lucas said.

Of course she cooked this amazing dish at Clay's house.

Thankfully, the conversation moved on from Amber's greatness to Todd and Diego sharing with everyone what they do for at-risk foster kids at their camp.

"That's incredible," Tonya said. "My mom grew up in foster homes too and had a pretty rough life when she was younger. She was a social worker until she passed away three years ago from lung cancer."

"I'm so sorry to hear that," Todd told her.

"Thanks. She started smoking when she was just twelve. My dad too. He's got emphysema and is on oxygen. I think it's great what you guys are doing. If my parents had people like you helping them out when they were younger, maybe things would have been different for them."

After dinner, they all helped clear the table. Emily made coffee and set out dessert plates for pie.

"Clay brought peanut butter whiskey to pour over vanilla ice cream. Everyone want some to go with their pie?"

It was a resounding yes from the group.

While Amber was wrapped up in conversation with Addison and Shelby, Clay came into the kitchen. "Need help?"

"That would be great. Would you mind scooping the ice cream into the dishes?"

"Not at all." He grabbed the scoop from the drawer and the ice cream from the freezer and got to work. "You remember how to make the little indents on top and pour the whiskey over it?"

Emily thought back to their drunken night when he spoon-fed the ice cream to her; the night she felt his lips on hers, and his tongue in her mouth.

"I'm pretty sure I can figure it out," she teased as she began using the back of a spoon to push down into the mounds.

"You look really nice tonight," he told her as he continued scooping. "I like your dress."

Emily bought the gold silk tank dress specifically for tonight. She wanted something classy and liked how it draped down her body and caressed her skin, stopping just above her knees.

"And those shoes are killer."

Her New York strappy black stilettos paired perfectly. She was thrilled Clay noticed.

"Thanks." She handed him the bottle of Skrewball. "I'll let the expert pour the whiskey."

Clay's fingers brushed Emily's as he took the bottle out of her hand, sending sparks through her skin. Sparks she was certain he didn't feel.

Emily placed the whiskey ice cream on the breakfast bar next to the pie and called everyone up to grab some while setting out coffee mugs and cream and sugar.

"So, Shelby, what do you do?" Clay asked over dessert.

"I'm a Virtual Assistant, so I do anything from social media management to admin work online, but I'll also occasionally pick up odd jobs here locally, like with Instacart or even walk people's dogs. Whatever it takes to pay the bills, you know?"

"Hey, Emily is looking for a blackjack dealer," Todd said. "Have you guys talked about that?"

Shelby looked over at Emily. "No. I'd be interested. Addison was telling me about what you do now."

"Oh, really? That would be great. Let's set up a time to talk next week." It had never occurred to Emily that Shelby would be interested. She always got the impression they were busy and didn't like Emily all that much.

At the end of the evening, everyone said their goodbyes to each other. Tonya left first, saying she had to get home to her dad. Lucas said he would catch a ride with Clay and Amber, but as they were leaving, he offered to stay and help Emily clean up.

"Oh, no, I'm okay." Emily was surprised he would even suggest that.

"I don't mind. I feel bad leaving you with this mess."

The knots in her stomach returned as Clay stood there looking at her with Amber's arms wrapped around him.

"Thanks for the offer, but I'm pretty tired. I'm just going to bed now and will tackle it all in the morning."

Lucas looked defeated. "Okay, well, thanks for everything." He hugged her quickly and walked out.

Amber thanked Emily and hugged her as well. She smelled heavenly. *Of course.*

Clay gave Emily a one-armed hug while Amber held onto his other hand. "It was a great evening. Happy Thanksgiving."

"Happy Thanksgiving, Clay."

Thirty-two

Emily wrapped herself up in her red wool coat, black scarf and hat, and cashmere-lined gloves to walk up to the Market. Even though there wasn't snow on the ground and the sky was bright blue, the crisp air stung her nose and eyes as she walked toward Larimer Square.

Downtown buzzed with holiday cheer. Festive decorations hung on streetlamps and threaded across buildings. Christmas songs played from hidden speakers as business people made their way into the surrounding office buildings.

When Emily walked into the Market, Addison handed her a flat white coffee and buttery croissant before taking her to join Shelby at a back table.

"I'm so glad you're interested in this, Shelby," Emily told them. "It's surprisingly difficult to find people who want to work on Friday and Saturday nights."

"I'm totally up for it. I need to make money to pay my bills. I'm drowning in student loans, so I'll pretty much do anything I can to get out of that as soon as possible."

"Do you know how to play blackjack?"

"I do. That's why I was so interested when Addison told me you were looking for another dealer. My brothers taught me so we could all play together when we were teenagers. Not much else to do on a farm in the middle of nowhere." Shelby chuckled.

It was the first time Emily had ever seen a flicker of vulnerability in them.

"Well, then you already have a head start. It's actually a lot of fun," Emily said. "And you can make pretty good money. It's a cash buy-in for the customer. There are different levels they can purchase. You'll need to stay after you close up to count the money with the manager. Once they sign off on it, you get to take home twenty-five percent plus any tips you make."

"What's an average night like?" Shelby asked.

"The Cruise Room at the Oxford Hotel is usually around five hundred a night. Lots of tourists and business people staying at the hotel, so it's a great location. Three to five hundred is more common at Crimson, but on Halloween, I did just over a grand."

"You're kidding?" Shelby said. "That's awesome. So, this will be your third?"

"Yes. This one is set to go into Nocturne next week."

"Right in our neighborhood!"

"That's why I was so excited when you said you were interested."

"Yeah, I love the vibe there," Shelby said.

"Wait," Addison said. "If we're talking that kind of money, I might need a job, too!"

"Oh my god, Addy... that would be amazing. I'd love to have you as a dealer. I'm actually planning on buying two more tables after the first of the year. I followed up with some of the bars I marketed to a while back. Showed them what we're doing at the current locations, and two of them said they're on board as soon as I get the tables and dealers."

"You're not concerned five tables in downtown is going to dilute the novelty, though?"

"That's a great question. I did think about that. But the locations are far enough apart, attracting different types of patrons, that it shouldn't affect the revenue. And the other two won't be downtown."

"Where are they?"

"The Church Nightclub in the Golden Triangle neighborhood and Roxy on Broadway. But if you're serious about dealing, I could give you Crimson or the Cruise Room."

"Oh, I'd love to work in Crimson! I'm so proud of you, Em. You've really made this happen."

"Thanks. I'm pretty happy with the way things are coming together. I just gave my notice to Snooze yesterday. I'm finally making enough money with this business that I don't have to keep waiting tables."

"So, do the venues get a cut?" Addison asked. "How does that work?"

"Yes. They all say since they have to give up a tabletop, they need to charge for the space, essentially. So, the venue gets twenty-five percent as well."

"Have you thought about offering blackjack lessons mid-week when it's slower?" Addison asked. "I would think there would be a market for that given the gambling up in the mountains."

"I hadn't thought of that, but that's a great idea."

Addison laughed. "At least my business degree is good for something."

"It really is a great idea," Shelby chimed in. "We could offer to teach not only the rules of the game but strategy as well. I bet that could really take off."

"Shelby has a degree in marketing. They could do a lot to help you."

Emily sat back, filled with possibility and a clear vision thanks to Addison and Shelby, and she was incredibly grateful. "I think we've just formed a new partnership!"

***

"So, how does this work?"

Emily's heart stopped as she lifted her gaze. Standing at the corner of the table overseeing the game, she hadn't noticed him when he first walked up.

Shelby answered before Emily could form words. "Buy-in is a twenty-dollar minimum. You play until your chips run out. There's no actual gambling."

"Interesting." He looked at Emily. "Hi."

"Hi, Dylan." She had seen the poster outside Nocturne promoting The LoDo Dogs tonight. She knew she would likely run into him even though the blackjack table was on the upper level, but he still caught her off guard. She took a deep breath, trying to calm her nerves.

"The owners told me they were going to start offering this. I wondered if it would be you."

Emily thought back to Halloween when they saw each other at the Crimson Room and how he had parroted their evening together with the new girl. She swallowed the lump forming in her throat. "Shelby will actually be working the table here on Friday and Saturday nights. I'm just training them tonight."

"That's cool." He held Emily's gaze for a moment before speaking again. "I stopped into Josephina's a couple of months ago, but they said you didn't work there anymore. I wondered what happened to you. How have you been?"

Apparently, you didn't wonder enough to text and find out.

Emily stepped away from the table so the players wouldn't be distracted and walked with Dylan to the railing. "I've been good. Just focusing on building this new business. What about you?"

"Oh, this is your own business? That's cool."

"Thanks. Yeah, I started it a few months ago. What about you? Things going well?"

"They are. I just got offered a record deal, so I'll be heading out to Los Angeles soon to meet with the bigwigs."

"Wow, Dylan... congratulations. That's amazing." She always knew he was bigger than downtown Denver.

"Thanks. Hey, I have to get on stage, but I'd love to catch up more. You'll be here all night?"

"I will."

"Great... can I buy you a drink in between sets?"

"Sure, that would be nice." She was curious what he would say to her after all this time.

"It's really great to see you, Emily." Dylan flashed his megawatt smile and winked at her just before he turned to walk away.

He definitely has that elusive star quality.

The table was attracting a lot of people, and Shelby handled them like a pro. Shelby cracked jokes with a dry sense of humor that Emily had never witnessed from them before. They lured people in by offering a couple of chips to play a hand for free. Of course, the new players were hooked and immediately bought in to continue playing.

Brilliant.

Dylan reappeared after his first set, precariously carrying three drinks in his hands. Setting one down on the drink ledge of the blackjack table, he put another in front of Shelby and handed one to Emily. "You still like Bee's Knees, I'm assuming?"

"Can't go wrong with that drink. Thank you."

He held up his glass and looked to Shelby to pick theirs up after paying out the players. "To your new business. May success follow you both." They all clinked their glasses and took a sip.

"Can you take a break from being a boss for a while and join me downstairs? I have a table."

Emily looked at Shelby. "Are you okay if I step away for a few minutes?"

"I got this," Shelby said confidently.

After they sat down near the stage, Emily and Dylan simply looked at each other for a moment. It was apparent neither of them knew where to begin the conversation.

Finally, Dylan broke the silence. "I've missed you."

That was the last thing Emily expected to hear, and it must have shown on her face.

"Things just ended kind of abruptly," he continued. "I wasn't sure what happened. I'm sorry if I did something to upset you."

Emily tried to articulate the words that were flying through her brain. She remembered her conversations with Jack and how he pointed out that Dylan didn't owe her anything because he never promised her anything.

"I'm sorry for not talking with you about what was upsetting me," Emily told him. "It wasn't fair to you for me to have certain expectations without having any communication about them."

Now Dylan seemed surprised.

At her candor? Was it too much? Just drink and shut up, Emily.

"I... I, um..." he stammered. "I guess I didn't realize you had expectations. I thought we were just having fun."

"We were," Emily assured him. "I was just hurt when you would rush off after being with me. And when you stood me up, and I didn't hear from you all week, I figured you had moved on to the next girl—which is totally fine, by the way, because I know we weren't exclusive or anything. But it still hurt to not hear from you. And then you showed up a week later like nothing was wrong."

"I stood you up?"

Seriously?

"If I remember correctly," *of course I remember correctly,* "you had invited me over for lemon meringue pie one night and then ghosted me."

He reached out and took her hand, looking deep into her eyes. "Emily, I'm so sorry. I don't remember what happened that night, but it was never my intention to hurt you. I was an asshole. Look, we may not have been officially exclusive, but I want you to know I wasn't sleeping with anyone else while you and I were hanging out if that's what you're thinking."

Emily slowly pulled her hand away and picked up her drink. "I appreciate you telling me that."

Even though she doubted his claims, she was reminded of her behavior with Jack, agreeing to fly out to New York for an erotic weekend even while she was still semi-involved with Dylan. All the while keeping Enzo in her back pocket. She was shocked at her ability to deflect her shitty behavior and blame Dylan when she was just as big an asshole.

Gaslighting at its finest.

"I hope you'll forgive me," he said.

She smiled. "There's nothing to forgive, Dylan. We're good."

"I'm glad to hear that. I have to get back for the second set. Will you still be here afterward?"

"Yes. I have to count out with Shelby and the manager at closing."

They both stood up, and Dylan kissed her on the cheek before walking away.

Back upstairs, Emily stood at the railing, watching the band perform below. As they began a jazzy rendition of "All I Want for Christmas," Dylan looked up at her often while singing and smiling. She felt her stomach flutter, but not the same kind of flutter as before. This was a nervous flutter that she was getting into something she didn't intend to.

After she and Shelby closed everything out, Shelby was thrilled to go home with two hundred dollars in cash that included generous tips from the players.

"It will only go up from here," Emily told her. "Especially once we get your marketing ideas rolling. You'll be earning an extra ten percent from all the tables across the board."

"Thanks so much for this opportunity, Emily. This is really amazing. I appreciate it." Shelby hugged Emily.

Emily had finally connected with her best friend's partner. "No, thank you. You were amazing tonight, Shelby. You did a phenomenal job—so much more than I could have hoped for."

When Shelby left, Dylan walked up to Emily. "Can I give you a ride home?"

"Oh, thanks, but I drove tonight."

"I'll walk out with you then." Dylan placed his hand on her back as she walked toward the door.

No, no, no, no.

When Emily reached her car, she unlocked it and tossed her brief-case inside before turning to say goodbye to Dylan.

He stepped in closer and placed one hand on her waist. "I'm so glad I ran into you tonight, Emily."

As she stared at him, trying to figure out how to respond, he leaned in to kiss her. But before his lips could meet hers, she stepped back. "Dylan..."

"Can we try this again," he pleaded. "I promise I'll be better."

This was all Emily wanted to hear last summer. But now... now, she was over him. Despite his sexy musician celebrity thing going on, she didn't want him anymore. She wanted something else. She had other things to focus on in her life other than hot men. And she wasn't going to let steamy sex derail her this time. Especially steamy sex that ultimately left her unsatisfied.

"Dylan, I'm happy we got to talk about things tonight, but I'm not the one for you. Besides, you're running off to L.A. to get famous, and I'll never hear from you again," she added with a teasing smile, hoping it would soften the rejection.

He laughed. "Well, I don't know about becoming famous. But I really would love to enjoy more time with you before I leave."

"As fun as that sounds, I'm just not up for it. I'm sorry."

After a few moments of silence, Dylan smiled softly. "I understand. Goodbye, Emily."

"Goodbye, Dylan."

Thirty-three

Grabbing her coffee and blanket, Emily curled up on the sofa to watch the snowfall outside while she tried to wake up.

The ring of her phone interrupted her peaceful silence, but when she saw Clay's face, she answered. "Happy New Year's Eve."

"Big plans tonight?" he asked.

"Not really. Since Shelby is working at Nocturne, Addy and I are just going to hang out there with Todd and Diego. What about you?"

He chuckled. "Well, I had planned this whole weekend thing with Amber at The Brown Palace, but she got snowed in back in rural Kentucky, and the roads from their house to the airport are closed. Guess they're having a pretty big storm right now, so she thinks it's going to be a few more days before she can get back here."

"Oh, that's awful. I'm sorry, Clay." Taking a sip of her coffee, Emily felt a little guilty at the small flash of satisfaction, knowing Clay wouldn't be with Amber tonight.

"Yeah. Well, so I know you already have plans, and I totally get if you can't, but I spent a lot of money on this fancy New Year's Eve bash, and I'd hate to have it go to waste."

Wait.

"Any chance you'd want to go with me?"

Emily's stomach dropped. "Oh, um," *Yes! Yes! Yes!* "Well, let me talk to Addy and make sure she'll be okay with me dropping out, but sure, that sounds fun."

Emily knew Addison would push her to go with Clay.

"Awesome, thanks. I was so bummed at the thought of missing it. Not every day I get to wear a tux," he laughed.

"A tux? Just how fancy is this?"

"Black-tie, baby! Oh, god, I'm sorry... do you have a dress you can wear?"

Emily thought about her little black dress from New York but wasn't sure if it was even fancy enough for black-tie. Besides, it didn't seem right to go out with Clay while wearing the dress Jack bought her.

"I'll come up with something," she told him.

"I know Amber went shopping weeks ago. It's so easy for guys. I didn't even think about that. I'm sorry."

She tried to imagine what Amber's gown looked like. *Probably something sexy and stunning—like her.*

"I can shoot you over some money if you have time to go shopping today?"

Emily smiled. "Well, that's very generous of you, Clay, but I don't need you to buy me a dress."

"I know. But you're really helping me out here, and I don't want to create any burden for you. I know formal gowns aren't cheap."

"I appreciate the offer, but I can afford to buy my own. Business has been good. What time does it start?"

"Dinner reservations at The Palace Arms are for 7:30, and then Big Band dancing in the atrium starts at 8:30. But I got a room there for the night, so I'll be checking in about four. You're welcome to come earlier and hang out before dinner—even get ready there if you'd like. I can pick you up on my way in so you don't have to deal with parking or the shuttle."

Get ready there?

Emily knew Clay wasn't interested in her anymore now that he had Amber. And she knew it would be wrong to come between them. She had learned that lesson the hard way and vowed never to get involved with someone attached to someone else. Still, she couldn't help but be excited at the thought of spending New Year's Eve with just Clay—even if it was only as friends.

"Sure. That should give me enough time to find a dress."

"Sounds great," he said. "I'm looking forward to this. See you soon."

Emily hung up the phone and stared out at the flurries gently falling from the sky before bringing the sofa pillow to her face to muffle her scream.

I have to call Addison.

"Of course I don't mind, Emily! This is so exciting. Just like something out of a romance novel."

"Well, except in this novel, the hero already has a girlfriend, so that kind of puts a damper on the 'happily-ever-after-ending,'" Emily reminded her.

"Hmmm, we'll see. So, what are you going to wear?"

"That's the thing... I need to go shopping. Would you and Shelby want to go with me? I need help finding the right dress."

"Shelby is working on a project for one of her virtual clients, but I can go. Todd is here. I'm sure he'd love to go, too."

"Oh, I didn't think they'd be down the mountain until later?"

"Diego is spending the day with his foster sister before we meet up tonight."

"Oh, nice... okay, I'll swing by and pick you guys up in about an hour to go shopping at Cherry Creek. Yay!"

Emily didn't bother with Nordstrom. She couldn't afford those gowns, and now that she was a business owner, she saw things differently—she could no longer, in good conscience, take back a dress she had worn to an event. Instead, they headed for the sales racks at Macy's. Gathering armloads of gowns, the three of them went into the large dressing room.

Todd and Addison helped Emily slip on and zip up several dresses before she found the one that made them all gasp. Silver sequins scattered over a charcoal tulle that was laid over silver satin. The strapless gown hugged the curves of her upper body and thighs before it cascaded down to the floor in flowing waves of fabric. Emily felt like a princess.

Todd smiled. "Well, that should do the trick."

Before they left, she bought clear slide-on high heels, cementing her Cinderella status.

***

Emily stood off to the side, holding her bagged gown and backpack while Clay checked in at the front desk. She had only been inside the historic hotel once a couple of years earlier when she met a guy from a dating app for drinks in the atrium. She walked out when he invited her up to his room fifteen minutes later.

The atrium was decorated for the big bash with garlands of white lights. Blue and silver balls adorned the Italian renaissance archways and the extravagant crystal chandelier. The small cocktail tables had been pushed to the outside perimeter, leaving only the grand piano, providing enough room for the live band and dancing.

"Ready?" Clay asked.

It was only as they were walking through the doorway into the room that it occurred to Emily how awkward this could be. It was one thing to be alone together as friends in her apartment. But another thing entirely to be in a small hotel room where the main centerpiece was a luxurious and inviting king-sized bed, especially when all she wanted to do was fall into it with him.

"So, what should we do for the next three hours," Clay asked, hanging her gown and his tux in the closet.

I have a few ideas.

She peeled off her wool coat, scarf, gloves, and knit hat. "Well, the last hour should definitely be about getting ready. I'll need time to shower and do my hair and make-up."

"What do you mean? You look great in jeans and boots with your wild hair."

"Now you tell me," Emily retorted. "Could have saved me all the trouble of shopping for a formal gown."

He laughed. "Okay, fine. How about we start with some drinks and snacks?"

"You brought snacks?" she asked eagerly.

He began pulling items out of a Hickory Farms gift box, setting them up on the vintage desk. "Christmas gift courtesy of my boss.

We have nuts, beef summer sausage, assorted cheeses and crackers, and some apples and pears."

"Yum!"

He pulled out a cutting board and knife and opened the little packages, creating a small charcuterie board.

"I'm impressed."

"You should be. Took me hours looking on Pinterest to figure out how to do this."

"Really?"

He looked at Emily like she was ridiculous and laughed, shaking his head. "Hey, in that other bag is a bottle of wine and a couple of glasses. Can you grab those? And the wine opener?"

They found an old John Cusack movie, *Serendipity*, just beginning on TV, so they propped up the pillows and climbed onto the bed with full glasses of Riesling. Their snacks in between created the perfect safety barrier as they watched.

"Really? She's not going to give him her phone number again?" Clay asked incredulously when the wind blew it out of Jon Traeger's hands. "Seriously?" He moaned when the little devil boy pressed all the buttons in the elevator, preventing Jon from finding his soulmate waiting for him on the twenty-third floor. "Yes! His phone number on the five-dollar bill!" And in the final scene, when they finally reunited ten years later and embraced each other in a kiss on the ice rink, Clay was quiet. But Emily caught the relaxed smile on his face when she glanced at him while taking a sip of her wine.

Maybe watching a romantic movie about two people destined to be together wasn't the best idea.

"It's a little after six," she said, turning to him. "Do you want to shower first? I'll probably take a little longer than you to get ready."

"Yep." He gulped down the last of his wine and rolled off the bed. Thirty minutes later, he walked out of the bathroom with wet hair and glistening skin, wearing nothing but a towel. "Sorry, I left my clothes out here."

It took everything Emily had to hold it together. His chiseled abs descended underneath the towel that hung low on his hips, exposing the oblique muscles forming a V and making Emily's mouth dry and thirsty. "Wow, look what you've been hiding."

"I'm full of surprises."

"Okay, Captain America." She grabbed all of her stuff, including her gown, and went into the bathroom to shower and get ready. She tried to stop herself from imagining him in there with her.

Using the barrel iron, she tamed her frizzy curls into soft waves. Smoky eyes and red lips completed her glamourous look before she slid on her sparkling gown and stepped into her Cinderella shoes.

When she emerged, she found Clay sitting at the desk scrolling through his phone. He looked up at her and stared before finally standing up. She tried not to hyperventilate, seeing him in a tuxedo looking like he wanted to devour her.

"Beauti—that's a beautiful dress. You look beautiful," he stammered.

"Thank you. So do you. I mean—handsome. You look nice." The words stumbled out of her mouth.

After a moment, he held out his elbow for her to take. "Shall we?"

The elevator doors opened to an elegantly dressed elderly couple. "Oh, look at you two," the woman gasped. "What a gorgeous couple you are!"

"Aw, thank you," Emily smiled as they walked in. "I love your dress."

"You're one lucky fellow," the gentleman said to Clay. "You better treat her right. Don't let her get away. I finally got this one to say yes after chasing her for years."

"One year, dear."

"Well, it seemed like years. But now, almost five decades later, we're still like newlyweds. You got to treat them right. Happy wife, happy life. That's my motto."

Clay nodded his head. "Sounds like a good motto."

"How long have you two been together," the woman inquired.

"Oh, I just met her in the lobby tonight," Clay deadpanned.

Emily smiled as the elderly couple stood silent, unsure how to respond. "He's kidding. He's my cousin who couldn't find a date for tonight, so he begged me to come with him." She stepped in closer and took his hand into hers, resting her head on his shoulder.

Clay continued looking straight ahead, working hard to conceal his laughter. The elderly couple fell silent. As they all stepped out of the elevator, Clay wished them a lovely evening and escorted Emily toward The Palace Arms restaurant as he continued to hold her hand.

"You're a little wicked, aren't you," he said quietly into her ear as they were walking.

Her heart quickened. "No more than you."

Walking into the restaurant was like being transported in time. Its old-world ambiance dripped with history and charm: Napoleonic artifacts and revolutionary-era American flags were on display between the tufted red leather booths. Red charger plates and crystal stemware sparkled on the white tablecloths under the glow of the ambient lighting.

Clay pulled out Emily's seat for her as she sat down.

"Wow, such a gentleman. Thank you."

"Sometimes." He smiled as he sat across the small table from her.

When the hostess asked if they would like tap or bottled water, Clay and Emily looked to each other for the answer.

"I'm fine with tap," Emily told him, having never been asked that question before at a restaurant.

Soon, an older man approached their table and introduced himself as Phillip, their server for the evening. He explained the special five-course wine pairing. Dinner would come with a glass of the sommelier's choice with each dish. First up would be Oysters on the half-shell paired with Muscadet, followed by Lobster Risotto with Gewurztraminer. Pinot Grigio would accompany their famous table side Caesar salad, and the main entrée, Beef Wellington, would be served with Pinot Noir. Finally, for dessert, Sauternes would complement the Bananas Foster.

"That's a lot of wine." Emily was already feeling the effects of the two glasses she had up in the room.

Phillip gently smiled. "We only pour three ounces of each for wine pairings."

When the server stepped away, the hostess returned with water and warm bread, along with butter in the shape of rosettes, stealthily setting them on the table before disappearing again.

"I feel very fancy." Emily picked up her water glass and took a sip, hoping to finish it before the wine arrived. She wanted to enjoy herself tonight, which included not getting sick from drinking too much.

"It suits you," Clay told her while struggling to slather the cold butter on his bread. "Why do places even serve cold butter?"

"So, they can make it into pretty little sculptures for you." Emily picked up a warm roll and split it, placing a rosette in between the slices. After a moment, she opened it and spread the softened butter with her knife before presenting it to Clay.

"You're a genius!"

Phillip returned, placing a small plate in front of each of them that held a silver spoon with something unrecognizable on it. "Foie Gras. An amuse-bouche before the first course."

Emily was the first to ask, "What's an amuse-bouche?"

"A single serving of an hors d'oeuvres, Miss."

After Phillip left, Clay looked at Emily. "Isn't Foie Gras duck liver?"

"Yes, it is," she said, staring at the vomit-colored ball rolled onto her spoon. The pretty little greenery on top couldn't disguise what lay underneath.

"Well," he picked up his spoon, "we're in this together." He waited for Emily to do the same.

They watched each other closely to make sure they swallowed it at the same time. Emily's taste buds were confused.

Clay had a pensive look on his face. "It kind of tastes like... buttery meat."

"Mixed with whipped cream," Emily added, scowling.

"Yeah, not my thing."

They both quickly took a bite of bread and drank water, laughing at their bravery trying something new.

The sommelier approached their table, presenting a bottle of wine before pouring a small amount into their glasses. "Pepiere, Muscadet de Sur Lie, Clos des Briords."

Neither Emily nor Clay understood what he said, so they nodded and smiled politely. Phillip swooped in and set down the oysters. "An aphrodisiac to get the night going." He winked at both of them before walking away. Emily raised her brows in astonishment while Clay laughed.

Squeezing lemon juice over the oysters, he asked, "Ever had these?"

"Yes! I love them. How about you?"

"One of my favorites. With or without cocktail sauce?"

"Definitely with."

He placed a tiny dot of sauce on two oysters and handed her one. "Cheers!"

They each slurped up the meat and let it slide down their throats before taking a sip of wine.

"Mmmm, that really does pair well," Emily said. "Kind of lemony."

Soon, Phillip brought the second course: chunks of mouth-watering lobster sat atop a bed of creamy risotto.

"What exactly is risotto? Pasta?" Clay asked Emily.

"It's an Italian dish made with Arborio rice. My stepmom makes a mushroom risotto. It's one of my many favorite meals of hers."

He took a bite. "Mmm. Oh, man, this is delicious. Do you know how to make it?"

"No. I've never attempted it. It seems pretty complicated."

Next, Phillip stood table side while he prepared the Caesar salad for them, throwing in extra garlic. "It's the magical ingredient."

Emily had never had Beef Wellington. It seemed odd to wrap steak in a pastry puff. But she couldn't argue about the taste. It was one of the best things she had ever had, and Clay agreed.

After the dishes were cleared away, Phillip rolled up a cart that held a gas burner and pan. "Ready for your Bananas Foster?"

Emily was most excited about this. The only time she had it was as a teenager when her brother made it for her and her mom in his first apartment. He had just returned from New Orleans and was excited to show off his newly acquired culinary skills.

Phillip quartered the bananas, adding them to the pan of butter and brown sugar, followed by a pour of banana liqueur. After sautéing everything for a few minutes, he added in the rum, sending flames jumping into the air. Reaching underneath the cart, he pulled out two bowls of vanilla bean ice cream and spooned the bananas and sauce on top. "Voila! Enjoy!"

"Have you ever had this?" Emily asked Clay.

"No, but it smells incredible."

Emily watched him take a bite. His eyes got big as he mumbled, "Oh, my god."

"Right?" She took a bite and closed her eyes with gastronomical pleasure.

When they finished dessert, Phillip brought the bill along with coconut macaroons.

Emily imagined the dinner must have been extravagantly expensive and felt bad sticking the whole thing on Clay. "Let me pay for my half. I'll Venmo it over."

"Absolutely not." He didn't look up until he finished signing. "You're my guest. Besides, it was included in the package. I just left him a tip. But thank you for your offer."

"Well, thank you for an amazing dinner. And the wine! So fun to get to try all of those. Now, I'll have to see if I can walk out of here."

By the time they made it into the atrium, the live band and dancing were in full swing, with a Sinatra sound-alike singing "The Way You Look Tonight."

"Up for some dancing?" Clay asked, extending his hand out to hers.

"Of course! You know how to dance?"

"Four years of Cotillion made sure of that." He spun her around.

The lower part of her gown fanned out, just like a Hollywood starlet. Clay pulled her back into him and wrapped his other arm around her waist. They continued to dance and laugh over the next couple of hours, stopping only to drink water or champagne between songs.

A female singer had joined the band, and when they started singing "Baby, It's Cold Outside," Emily playfully sang the words as Clay spun her out and pulled her in over and over. She felt like she was in a fairytale when he turned her around, bringing her backside against him, his hand resting on her stomach while he sang in her ear before he twirled her out again and pulled her back to face him, holding her tightly. On the last line of the song, he spun her three times before bringing her back into a dramatic dip for the finale.

The band segued into "At Last," and the two of them settled into an embrace for the slow dance, staring into one another's eyes. Emily's heart raced. She wanted nothing more than for him to kiss her, tell her that it's her he wants. Before he could read her thoughts, she averted her eyes to his shoulder. His arm tightened around her waist, bringing her closer. If she turned her face back toward him, she knew their lips would meet, so she continued staring straight ahead. She could feel his head turn ever-so-slightly into hers, feel his mouth brushing against her cheekbone, causing her to momentarily stop breathing.

She had never really listened to the words of this song before, but it seemed like they were written just for them. As their bodies gently swayed to the music, Emily remembered the night he kissed her. How tender it was, how his sensual tongue played with hers. And how naturally her body responded to him before she stopped it. She wished she had realized then what she knew now.

When the song ended, they slowly pulled back, holding each other's gaze as the MC began the countdown.

"Ten…

"Nine…

"Eight…

"Seven…

"Six…

"Five...

"Four...

"Three...

"Two...

"One...

"Happy New Year!" Everyone cheered as champagne bottles popped, and the band began singing Auld Lang Syne.

The two of them stood frozen in the moment before Clay finally spoke. "Happy New Year, Emily."

"Happy New Year, Clay."

Their faces seemed to slowly gravitate toward one another when Clay suddenly stopped and grabbed his phone out of his pocket, displaying Amber's beautiful face. Pulling himself out of Emily's arms, he took a step back and turned away to answer the phone. "Happy New Year!"

Ripped out of her fantasy, Emily was left standing by herself while couples surrounded her in happy kisses.

"Happy New Year, dear."

Emily looked over to see the elderly woman from the elevator smiling at her sympathetically. She tried to smile back.

"He's not really your cousin, I take it?"

Emily let out a sad chuckle as she shook her head.

"I've been watching the two of you tonight, and you're breathtaking together. There's no doubt that man loves you. And you, him?" She looked at Emily for confirmation that she didn't give.

"Don't feel the need to rush things. You two are so young. The best relationships are always built on a foundation of friendship. And that takes time. That's why I wouldn't marry my Hugo right away. I made sure we built that solid foundation first because that's what will get you through anything."

Emily wiped away a tear as she nodded. "Thank you."

"You'll be okay, dear. Hang in there. He'll come around. May I hug you?"

"Yes," Emily smiled. "I could use that."

"Happy New Year."

"Happy New Year to you and Hugo as well."

As the woman walked away, Clay approached. "What was that about?"

Emily shook off her heartbreak, trying to sound cheerful. "Oh, she came over to tell me how much she liked our dancing."

"Nice. Sorry about that." He gestured his head back, indicating the phone call that had taken him away from her. "I forgot I told Amber I would call her at midnight her time, so she stayed up to call me instead."

Emily took a deep breath. "That's sweet. I'm sure she's very disappointed she couldn't be here tonight." Guilt flooded through Emily as she pictured Amber wrapped in Clay's arms. *This was her evening. I'm an imposter. And I don't want to be the other woman, again.* "Thank you for such an incredible time. I'll just call an Uber after I grab my stuff from upstairs. I don't want you to have to deal with parking again."

"What? Why not just stay here tonight?"

It's too hard. She was trying to come up with a plausible reason. After all, they had spent the night together as friends on many occasions. "Oh, well, I didn't even bring anything to sleep in. And there's no sofa for me to sleep on."

"Yeah, that part was a surprise. I figured there would have been a sofa bed—which I would have slept on, of course. But I'm sure we can find you something to change into, and I promise not to bite. Maybe." He smiled.

I couldn't resist you if you did.

"Plus, I've paid for two massages tomorrow, and it would be a shame for one of them not to get used."

"Massages, huh?"

"Swedish."

"Well, since you threw that into the deal…"

"Great! Besides, look out the window at the snow. It's cold outside, baby!" He paused, waiting for her reaction. "See what I did there?"

Emily laughed in resignation as she accepted his hand and headed back out to the dance floor.

Thirty-four

"Okay, well, I have the t-shirt I wore earlier today, but it might not smell so great," Clay said, offering her the crumpled fabric he pulled out of his duffle bag.

Emily was kicking herself for not realizing he would be expecting her to spend the night. She should have known better and brought something to change into. She really didn't want to sleep in her jeans and sweater.

"Or you could wear this shirt," he told her while taking off his jacket and bow tie. "I don't think I ruined it too much tonight." He unbuttoned and slid it off to inspect it, sniffing the armpits. "The t-shirt underneath kept it pretty clean."

"Thanks. I need to take off my make-up and brush my teeth." She took the shirt and headed into the bathroom.

When she emerged a few minutes later, Clay was lying on top of the bed wearing his t-shirt and pajama pants. She had hoped he would have turned out all the lights already, but his bedside lamp was on while he flipped through the local tourism magazine. Pretending not to notice him slyly watching her out of the corner of his eyes, Emily hung up her gown in the closet. She walked to the far side of the bed and climbed in, hoping her shakiness and short breaths weren't outing her.

Clay jumped up. "I'll be back."

When he returned from the bathroom a few minutes later, he flicked off the light and got under the covers. The two of them lay there in silence until Clay finally spoke. "Thanks again for coming tonight. I had a great time."

"Me too. Thanks for inviting me. I'm sorry Amber couldn't be here with you." *Not really.*

Emily was thrilled to be the one to spend New Year's Eve with Clay. Still, she felt bad that Amber had missed out on such an amazing night with her boyfriend.

Boyfriend. Clay is her boyfriend. He has a girlfriend. And I have to respect that.

"Goodnight."

"Goodnight."

Emily rolled over onto her side, facing toward the window and away from Clay. Closing her eyes, she could smell the remnants of cologne emanating from his shirt she now wore as she drifted off to sleep.

When she woke up in the morning, her head was on his shoulder—like he was her pillow. His arm held her in an embrace while her hand rested on his stomach under his shirt. The covers had been pushed off, and her bare legs intertwined with his. She didn't want to move. She wanted to stay here forever. But she knew this was going to become awkward very quickly.

When she tried to carefully extricate herself, Clay rolled onto his side, toward her, still asleep. Wrapping his other arm around her, he pulled her in tightly and threw his leg over hers, pinning her down. With her face now smashed into his neck and her lips resting on his skin, she couldn't move under his grip. All she could do was breathe in his delicious scent.

She knew the moment he woke up. She felt his body jump slightly as his arms loosened around her, breaking the spell she was under. Slowly removing his leg and unraveling himself, he mumbled, "I'm sorry."

Emily didn't know what to say. She had no witty comeback as she watched him roll away from her and head to the bathroom. After a few minutes, she got out of bed and opened the curtains to let the sunshine pour in. That was the beautiful thing about Colorado weather—there could be a raging storm one day, but the next usually brought bright blue skies.

Grabbing a water bottle, she filled the coffee maker and started brewing coffee.

"Good morning," Clay said as he walked out of the bathroom. His smile was warm, but his eyes seemed to avoid her. "Here's a robe from the bathroom. Thought you might feel more comfortable. Thanks for making coffee."

"Sure." Emily was feeling very exposed, standing around wearing only his tuxedo shirt, but she also felt pretty damn sexy and knew she should probably cover up. "So, what's the plan today?"

"Check-out is at noon, and then massages at 12:30. Are you hungry? Breakfast is included in the package. We can either head downstairs or just order room service." He picked up the menu and scanned over it. "Looks like they stop serving in half an hour—at 10:30."

"Let's do room service, so we don't have to rush."

"Great idea. How do French toast and eggs benedict sound?"

"Divine! I'm going to take a shower and get ready."

Emily heard room service at the door when she turned off the shower. She quickly brushed her teeth and threw on yesterday's clothes. When she walked out, she saw the bed was semi-made and the trays of food laid out.

"Breakfast is served."

They sat on the bed eating and laughing, the morning's awkwardness having disappeared.

After checking out downstairs, they left their belongings with the concierge and headed into the spa.

An older woman greeted them. "Welcome. Do you have an appointment with us today?"

"Yes. Clay Olson. We have two massages booked."

"Yes, Mr. Olson, I have your reservation right here for you and Amber Mills." She looked up and smiled at both of them.

Gut punch.

"Would you mind having a seat while I escort Miss Mills to the ladies' lounge?"

"Actually—"

"It's fine," Emily told Clay, saving him the embarrassment of explaining she was a different woman.

His smile conveyed gratitude. "Enjoy."

Emily followed the woman into an elevator that took them up one level to the lounge, where she was given a locker and robe with slippers. "After you undress, have a seat and enjoy some cucumber water and fresh berries. Your massage therapist will be up shortly to get you."

As promised, Emily was fetched and taken back downstairs to the treatment room. When she walked in, she was surprised to see two beds and a soaking tub. Just then, Clay and his masseuse walked in behind them.

As Clay and Emily stood there in their robes staring at each other, Emily's masseuse said, "We'll step out while you disrobe. You can hang the robes here." She pointed to the hooks on the wall. "Please lie face up under the sheet." Both therapists stepped out, closing the door behind them.

"I, um, I didn't realize it was going to be like this," Clay stammered.

Emily started laughing.

"I'm glad you see the humor."

"Well, go on then. Disrobe," Emily told him, smiling.

"You first."

They stood in a stalemate, waiting to see who would break first.

Emily did. "Okay, I'll turn around while you go get on your table. Then close your eyes, Mr. Olson, while I get onto mine."

"How can I trust you?" he teased.

"You can't." Emily shrugged her shoulders before turning around and waiting, struggling not to peek.

"Okay, all set."

"Eyes closed?"

"I guess."

Emily discarded her robe and quickly ran to her bed before the massage therapists reentered.

Gentle spa music played in the background, and the scent of lavender-infused oil filled Emily's nose, immediately sending her into a state of deep relaxation. When it was time to roll over onto her stomach, she was grateful her masseuse held up the sheet, blocking Clay's view.

The massage was heavenly, and she was disappointed when it was over fifty minutes later.

Her therapist spoke in a soothing voice. "When you're ready, you can soak in the tub. We'll come get you in twenty minutes."

The therapists walked out, leaving Emily and Clay alone again.

Soak in the tub. Together.

After a few moments of silence, Emily asked, "Are you alive over there?"

"Barely."

"I'm going to get up now," she warned him.

"Mmm-hmm."

Wrapping the sheet around her, Emily walked over and slid on her robe. She grabbed Clay's and laid it across his body.

His eyes fluttered open and fell on her. "You look... relaxed."

"I am so relaxed."

He sat up, strategically holding the robe in his lap, and glanced over at the filled tub. He looked back at her and tilted his head with a smile, cocking his brow.

Emily rolled her eyes. "Get dressed." She returned to her table and sat facing away from him, imagining herself dropping her robe and leading him into the tub.

He brought her some of the cucumber water served in a glass dispenser on the counter. "Did you enjoy that?" he asked, standing in front of her.

"Immensely. Thank you. That's the first professional massage I've ever had."

"Me too. I'm so glad Amber booked them."

And another gut punch.

Another reminder this was Amber's weekend, and Emily was just the stand-in.

After Clay dropped her off at her apartment, Emily unpacked her backpack, pulling out her clear high heels from the night before. Just like Cinderella—the magic ended when the ball was over, and she was back to her real life.

Thirty-five

E mily stared at the unopened email sitting in her inbox.

⟹**Isabella RizzoliCompletion9:17 am**

Her throat constricted as a lump took over the space that held her breath. Her stomach went into freefall. With shaky hands, she clicked the mouse.

Emily,

I'd like for us to get complete. Are you available to meet Saturday morning at The Market? Enzo would also like to get complete, so after our conversation, he can take my place. I understand this is likely very uncomfortable, but I don't want to keep dragging the past along with me as I create a new future for me and my family. Please let me know what time works best for you.

> *Thank you,*
> *Isabella*

***

"Are you sure this is a good idea?" Addison asked as she handed Emily a chai tea latte and sat down.

"Thank you," Emily said. "I owe it to her. It's the least I can do. And frankly, I'd like to put this all behind me, too."

"But isn't it already behind you? It's been six months and you're thriving. Why not just continue to live in the present instead of revisiting the past?"

"When I spoke to Jack, he reminded me of a conversation in the Symposium about how the future we're living into is what makes us who we are in the present."

"That makes no sense. You still talk to Jack?"

"Not often. He just checks in with me once in a while, but I called him when I first got her message because I wasn't sure how to respond," Emily said. "And I know it's confusing. I'm still trying to understand it myself. But it's kind of like when I went to New York. Before I knew I was going, I was upset about Dylan, confused about Enzo, and just stressed out about my life. But the moment I had the plane ticket to New York, none of that mattered because I knew I would soon be in one of the most amazing cities in the world with this incredibly sexy man."

Addison rolled her eyes.

"Despite the crap I was dealing with, I was giddy because all I could think about was being in New York with Jack. So, fast forward, there I am on the last day, lying in his arms. I should have just been basking in the bliss of the most epic weekend I've ever had. Instead, my stomach was in knots, and all I wanted to do was cry because I knew it was going to end in just a few hours. I would be back in Denver, and my New York experience would be over. I couldn't enjoy the moment. Does that make sense?"

"I think I get it. Kind of like how I dread getting together with my whole extended family on the holidays because I know from past holidays it's going to be a shit show."

Emily laughed. "Right! So, then you don't have room for the possibility of having an amazing time with your family because you've already decided it's going to suck based on your past. That's what they mean by having our past in our future. So, the idea is to get complete with it so we can leave it in the past because if it's in the past, what's in our future?"

Addison thought for a moment. "Nothing?"

"Exactly! And with nothing there, we can create anything." Emily smiled at the realization that she was finally understanding the concept after all these months. But her confidence disappeared the moment Isabella walked through the door.

Addison grabbed Emily's hand. "You got this. I'll be right over there behind the counter if you need me."

Isabella approached their table as Addison stood.

"Hello, Addison. It's nice to see you."

"Hi, Mrs. Rizzoli. You too. Can I get you something to drink?"

"I'd love some Earl Grey tea if you have some. With lemon and sugar?"

"Of course." Addison nodded and walked away.

Emily stayed seated, unsure if she should stand to greet Isabella.

Isabella's eyes fell to Emily before she quietly took the empty chair across from her. The two women sat in a moment of silence as they acknowledged one another's presence.

Emily held back her tears of shame that immediately threatened to escape. She didn't want her emotions to get in the way of their conversation. She waited for Isabella to say the first words so she could assess her tone.

"Thank you for meeting me, Emily." Her lilting voice immediately calmed Emily's racing heart.

"Of course. I'm so glad you reached out."

Emily missed Isabella's guidance and mentorship in her life. She wondered if they could restore their friendship, truly move beyond this and love each other again like family... like before.

"To be clear, this is something I'm still struggling with," Isabella began. "It saddens me to have lost what we had. You were a big part of our lives for over five years. I watched you grow from an aimless college kid into a beautiful young woman. I was honored that you considered me a mentor, and I didn't take that role lightly."

Emily's throat constricted as she blinked to hold back her emotions. She wanted to let it all out, beg for Isabella's forgiveness, cry to her that she didn't mean it... she didn't know what she was doing. She was a stupid girl who got caught up in a fantasy, and she would never let it happen again. But she knew that's not what Isabella was here for. She knew she needed to give Isabella the space to say what she came here to say.

"When I found out about you and Enzo, I was shocked... but only because it was you." Isabella took in a deep breath and then said, "The truth is, I lied to you. Enzo was right. I was involved with someone else."

Emily's mouth fell open. *What. The. Fuck.*

"Enzo and I had decided that we would try an open marriage. I was feeling stifled and unattractive being a new mom, always trapped at home while he got to go to the restaurant every night. I knew he had every opportunity to be with beautiful women. And he was hardly ever around at home. So, I started spending more time chatting with an old boyfriend. He reminded me of who I used to be."

Addison walked up and gently set Isabella's tea in front of her. She caught Emily's wide eyes before stepping away.

"When things turned flirtatious, and I found myself fantasizing about being with him, I made the suggestion to Enzo that we declare an open marriage. We talked about it for a while, what it would look like. In hindsight, we should have set clear boundaries and expectations. It just never occurred to me that he would pursue you. Or how much I would hate him being with another woman." Isabella looked down at her tea.

Emily watched Isabella in stunned silence tear open the little sugar packet, dump it in, squeeze the lemon, and stir it all together with the demitasse spoon. She brought the teacup to her mouth and took a small sip before setting it down and bringing her attention back to Emily.

Emily was frozen. Sadness, shock... anger all at once. *She lied to me? It was her idea? And she let me and Enzo take the blame? What a fucking bitch!* She wanted to jump up and throw her latte in Isabella's face. Scream at her. Humiliate her the way she had been humiliated. Instead, she continued to stare at Isabella in disbelief.

"I take responsibility for this entire situation," Isabella said. "And I'm here to tell you I'm sorry. I know my actions had a huge impact on you as well as my family."

Emily slowly nodded, not taking her gaze off of Isabella as she contemplated how to respond.

"I know it's a lot to take in, but I'd like to give you the opportunity to say what's there for you."

This is the moment of transformation. Emily could hear Jack's voice in her head.

She spoke slowly. "I got it." And she did. "Thank you, Isabella. I'm sorry I hurt you. Despite you and Enzo having an agreement, it was still a betrayal on my part, and I know that."

Isabella wiped away the tear trickling down her cheek. "Thank you." She stood up. "I'll send Enzo over now. Take care of yourself, Emily."

"You too."

Emily watched Enzo approach Isabella and lovingly take her hand in his as they shared a quiet moment. He broke away and walked over to Emily, sitting down across from her in Isabella's seat.

"Hi, Emily."

"Hi, Enzo." She was surprised to discover she had no physical reaction to his presence. No racing thoughts. She was able to just be with him.

"Here's what I want to say to you, Emily. I'm sorry. I'm sorry that I took advantage of our relationship. And I'm sorry for how my actions have impacted you."

"Why did you kiss me?"

"The truth is, I had no idea Isabella felt the way she did. I thought she was happy. I took her for granted. When she first came to me with this proposal, it devastated me. I told myself I had failed as a husband. And then the night of the fundraiser, when I saw you... something shifted for me. I knew I wanted to experience you, and it occurred for me that it would have been inauthentic had I not acted on that. But it was a line I shouldn't have crossed. I get that now."

"But there was also Stephanie."

Enzo sat back and sighed. "Yes. Stephanie. Another line I shouldn't have crossed. When I realized you were going to New York to see Jack, I was upset. Wildly jealous. And Stephanie was just... there. I did clean things up with her, by the way."

"Why did you tell Isabella before talking to me? I was blindsided, and that wasn't fair."

"You're right. It wasn't fair. None of this was fair to you. When I was standing there with you and Stephanie in the back alley, I was confronted with how much I had really fucked things up. At that moment, the only people I could think of were my wife and daughter, and my commitment to my family. I needed to restore my integrity with Isabella which included letting her know an open marriage is not okay with me."

"I guess I can understand that," Emily said. "I'm happy that you and Isabella are able to move beyond this."

"Emily, you are so very special to me, and I can't apologize enough for causing you so much pain and grief. You are an amazing young woman. I really admire how resilient you are and your tenacity for transformation."

Emily took all this in and realized there was nothing else left that needed to be said.

"I appreciate that, Enzo. Thank you."

She knew she could let it all go now because it was finally complete.

Thirty-six

Emily threw herself into her business. Her five tables were all performing well, especially now that Shelby and Addison were helping with the marketing. Shelby had a reporter-friend at the Denver paper, Westword, do a write-up on them. The lessons Shelby offered were booked solid, and on the weekends, every table was packed all night long with players.

Despite her busier schedule, Emily held open Tuesday nights for weekly dinners with Clay, Lucas, and Tonya. The boys hosted a few days after Valentine's Day, at which point Emily learned Clay and Amber broke up on Valentine's night.

"She wanted more than I could give," was all Clay said about it. When Emily heard that, she lit up inside but quickly realized her one-night stand with Lucas had likely sealed the nail in that coffin already. She didn't want to be the one to destroy a lifelong friendship between the boys, so she resolved to ignore her feelings for Clay and appreciate the friendship they all had.

Tonya seemed to have gotten over her Clay crush as she talked about a different guy almost every week. The University of Denver provided no shortage of boys to distract her. Clay and Lucas had become like big brothers to her—giving her dating advice and explaining how men's minds worked.

Emily would take Tonya shopping periodically to help her pick out new clothes, being sure to visit the cosmetics counters so Tonya could get expert advice on how to wear make-up to enhance her already beautiful features. Emily could see Tonya's self-confidence blooming as she started to grow into herself.

At the beginning of March, they all took Tonya out barhopping on her twenty-first birthday to celebrate reaching her new level of adulthood. Of course, the night ended in a slumber party at Emily's, as many of their weekly dinners did.

In mid-May, Emily met a reggae band at Retrograde while checking in on her newest location and dealer. They gave her two tickets to the music festival for the next day at Red Rocks Amphitheater, where local musicians would be showcased. Emily loved going to concerts at Red Rocks. The open-air amphitheater, built into a rock formation, sat high above Denver, looking out over the sprawling city. It was one of the most beautiful venues in the country.

Knowing that Clay loved reggae music, Emily texted him Sunday morning:

Emily

Are you free today? I was given two tickets to the Red Rocks music festival. Want to go with me?

Clay

***

The hostess seated Clay and Emily out on the cozy patio where a local musician strummed his guitar and covered classic rock.

"So, big news. I won't be flipping burgers after all. I just received a promotion today," Clay stated matter-of-factly before taking a swig of his Dos Equis.

"Oh, my god, that's amazing! Congratulations!" Emily beamed.

His smile broke across his face in unbridled happiness, causing Emily to lose her train of thought momentarily.

"They made me a manager. I've got a whole department I'm responsible for now."

"I'm so happy for you. You've worked really hard to get there."

"Thanks. And you... look at how far you've come in your business. Six tables! I told you I had no doubt you'd be successful. You've got a lot of drive and intelligence. It was only a matter of time."

Emily blushed as he gazed at her warmly, the air standing still between the two of them. She felt herself getting lost in his ethereal eyes.

Snapping out of her trance, she raised her skinny margarita for a toast. "Well, we have much to celebrate. To us!"

***

They grabbed seats at the top of the amphitheater. Only a handful of people sat up high with them, which allowed Emily to dance all around while Clay watched her, laughing.

When the sun went down, the night skies suddenly opened up, dumping rain on them. Emily spread her arms wide as she looked up, letting the large drops fall over her face. Late spring and early summer rainstorms in Colorado were one of her most favorite things ever. As it continued to pour, the band announced intermission, and they blasted out Rihanna's "Umbrella."

Emily started laughing at the song choice and looked over at . They were both drenched from head to toe as he stood there smiling at her.

His smile always made her feel safe. Made her feel important. And made her feel loved. Before she could talk herself out of it, she stepped in and kissed him. He didn't miss a beat. His hands slid around her waist as he pulled her closer into him, his tongue diving deep into her mouth. She wrapped her arms around his body and melted into him.

Her stomach wouldn't stop somersaulting. 's kiss was electric and passionate as if he couldn't get enough of her. And she couldn't get enough of him. She had never felt this kind of energy in any other kiss. She had never felt this much emotion for the person she was kissing.

The rain poured all over them as he held her tightly while his mouth continued to explore hers. She noticed how perfectly her body fit into his, how in sync their tongues danced with one another. She never wanted to let go. Finally, their kiss slowed as she pulled back and looked up into his eyes.

"Emily," he whispered, staring back as he let his forehead rest against hers.

She leaned in to kiss his neck softly. Tasting the saltiness of his skin, she wanted more. "Take me home," she said as she gently bit his lip. Grabbing her hand, he quickly led her out of the venue until they found his Jeep in the dark parking lot. He swiftly picked her up and placed her on the hood of his Wrangler. Kissing her neck and chest, he was chasing the rain pouring down in between her breasts. She wrapped her legs around him as he pulled her hips into him.

Emily wanted him to take her on the jeep. She didn't want to wait any longer. Her fingernails scratched along his back as she tried to pull her body closer to his.

As if reading her mind, he placed his hand on her chest to gently push her back, directing her to lie down. Emily's stomach fluttered as he took command and dropped his head in between her legs.

The rain continued to pour over her body. Clay slid his hands under her dress and pulled off her panties. Kissing the inside of her wet thighs, he slowly moved from one side to the other, teasing her as his mouth moved closer to her center. She squirmed, pulsating with anticipation.

Finally, his tongue slowly slid from the bottom up, over her lips, and found her clit. She almost came right then. His mouth was warm against the coolness of the rain as he continued to lick slowly, lapping up the drops as they fell between her legs. Her body was already quivering and shaking.

He stood and pulled her up into him. "Mmmm... I want to do that all night, but I think people are starting to leave. Let's go." Helping her off the jeep, he walked her around the car and opened the door. When he jumped in behind the wheel, he leaned over and kissed her again. "That was... spontaneous."

"Yes," she smiled.

"I like spontaneous," he said softly and pushed her wet hair from her face. They stared into each other's eyes. There was so much Emily wanted to say, but she didn't.

"I'm sorry... I have no idea what happened to your panties."

They both started laughing.

Clay focused on carefully driving out of the increasingly busy parking lot and down the winding road. Once they made it safely to the highway, he reached his hand over and began caressing her bare thigh. Emily closed her eyes and held onto his arm, enraptured by his touch as John Mayer filled the silence.

Clay parked his Jeep in front of her building and ran to the other side to open her door. Dashing out of the rain, they headed inside, laughing as their drenched clothes left puddles in the elevator. As soon as they made it into her apartment, she unbuttoned his shirt, sliding it down his muscular arms. Running her fingers along his chiseled chest, she grinned. "I haven't been able to stop thinking about these abs since New Year's Eve."

"I haven't been able to stop thinking about you since the day I met you." He lifted her dress over her head as he stared into her eyes. "You are so beautiful, Emily. And intelligent and kind. The whole package." He pulled her wet, naked body against his and kissed her deeply.

She unbuttoned his wet jeans and worked with him to quickly pull them off. When his beautiful cock sprang out in front of her, she couldn't help but take him into her mouth. Hearing him moan turned her on even more. She loved making him feel good. She loved having him in her mouth and tasting him.

"Oh, my god, Emily... I want you now." He helped her up and kissed her again before grabbing a condom out of his wallet. She took the package out of his hand and tore it open, sliding it onto him as she caressed him before leading him to the giant bean bag in front of the fireplace. Flipping on the switch, the gas flames snapped on, creating a warm glow in the room.

She laid down, bringing him with her. She wasn't nervous. And for once, she didn't feel like she was putting on a show for someone. She truly wanted this, wanted him. This was the kind of connection she had been searching for but always came up short.

Clay took his time kissing her belly, discovering every curve as he slowly moved upwards and found her breasts. He pulled himself higher as his body spread her legs. Leaning down to kiss her mouth softly, she felt the tip of his cock against her eager opening. Emily's whole body was on fire. Kissing her ear, he whispered, "Do you want me now, Emily?"

She thought she would burst into flames. "I want you so much, ."

He pulled back and stared into her eyes, "God, I love you," and plunged deep inside of her.

Wait... what?

He took Emily's breath away. She wrapped her legs around him as he slowly moved in and out while kissing her. They kept their eyes open, staring into the other's soul, silently committing their hearts. Their bodies meshed together perfectly as if they were made for one another.

Did he just say he loves me? He loves me.

Emily wrapped her hands around his shoulders, holding on to him, while they continued to move in a graceful rhythm, their mouths nibbling at each other's faces and necks.

As he raised himself on his hands to pump faster and harder, she ran her fingers along his sides and back, caressing his ass, appreciating every bulging muscle. Each thrust pushed her upper body off of the bean bag and onto the floor, hitting her g-spot like a target. Entangling her fingers in the hair around the base of his neck, she pulled hard as she came in an explosive wave at the same time he did. Tears flowed down her face.

"Why are you crying?"

She laughed, embarrassed. "I have no idea!" She had never experienced such an intense, emotional orgasm. "I think I'm just really happy!"

He kissed her tears before he softly kissed her mouth. Pulling back, he looked into her eyes. "Well, you blew any fantasy I ever had about you out of the water."

"You too."

"Ah... you've had fantasies about me," he teased.

She shrugged. "Maybe a couple."

"You were killing me on New Year's Eve."

"You were the one with the girlfriend."

"And do you have any idea how conflicted I was about that?"

Emily stared into his eyes for a moment before responding. "I appreciate that you kept your integrity and didn't try anything that night."

"It was incredibly hard."

"I know. For me too."

He took her hand and placed it on his cock. "This was incredibly hard. For you. I had to go into the bathroom just to calm down. And then, when I woke up with you wrapped in my arms, I had to force myself to pull away. I just wanted to kiss you, make love to you... but I couldn't do that to Amber. She didn't deserve that. And neither did you. But I was ruined after that night. It wasn't fair to Amber to continue." He kissed her again.

"How did it end with you guys?" She had been curious to know but was too nervous to ask before now.

"I tried to keep it going after New Year's Eve. I guess I felt guilty. So, when Valentine's Day came around, she wanted to plan another weekend getaway at The Brown Palace to make up for the one she missed out on. But when I got there, when we got into the room, all I could think about was you and our time there. She could tell something was wrong—that something had been off for a while. So, we talked over dinner, and I went home that night. Every day, I thought about calling you, but I had no idea how you felt about me, and I didn't want to mess things up between us."

They eventually moved into her bedroom to climb into bed. She loved feeling her sweat mix with his as she placed her head on his chest and traced her hands along his body—exhilaration coursing through her veins.

They spent all night exploring each other and discovering what made the other quiver. In between, Clay held her in his arms while they talked for hours about their life goals and dreams of the future.

They were surprised when the sun began filling her apartment with its morning light. Clay picked up his phone to check the time. "I'm supposed to be at work in two hours." He rolled on top of Emily and kissed her. Even though her body was exhausted, she still couldn't get enough of him before they drifted back to sleep.

Thirty-seven

They were startled out of their slumber when her alarm went off at nine a.m. Emily grabbed her phone to turn off the intruding noise.

"Oh, shit! I forgot I have meetings scheduled all day!" She turned to . "Aren't you supposed to be at work right now?"

He laid there with his eyes closed. "I'm taking the day off."

Emily curled up into him, laying her head on his chest. "Mmmm... I wish I could take the day off with you."

"Me too." After a few more minutes of sleepy silence, Clay kissed her on her head, sitting up. "Let's get you in the shower."

As Emily let the warm water run down over her, he poured shampoo onto her head and gently massaged her scalp before rinsing it out. Grabbing the conditioner, he ran his fingers through her long hair and let it sit while he meticulously lathered up her body. She was falling asleep against him as his hands caressed her skin. Tilting her head back under the stream of water to rinse out the conditioner, he stroked her head before letting his hands find their way back to her breasts.

"All clean," he whispered, kissing her mouth. "I'll finish up in here while you get ready for work." He pulled the shower curtain and helped her step out. She wrapped her towel around her body and set out a clean one for him before brushing her teeth and washing her face.

As he stepped out of the shower, she admired his physique once again while reflecting on the night. "You definitely are not what I expected."

He gathered her up in his arms. "I'm afraid to ask," he laughed.

"Let's just say I don't think I'm the only one who's been a snake in the grass," she teased as she squeezed his ass, pulling him into her while she kissed his chest.

"You better stop, Emily, or you won't be making it to your appointments," he warned her playfully.

Emily moaned. "I don't want to leave you." She kissed him and then pulled back, looking up at him. "You could always hang out here today and wait for me," she suggested, smiling hopefully.

"I like that plan."

"You should sleep, though, so you'll be all rested up when I come home." She ran her hand seductively down his chest and grazed his cock, feeling it flinch.

"I kind of feel like a kept man," he laughed.

"You are for today, which means I get to do whatever I want to you when I get home." She nibbled on his lower lip.

"Promise?"

Emily smiled as she pulled away to get dressed. "If we leave soon, we can stop by The Market for coffee and croissants. I desperately need those to get me through this day."

"Well, get going." He smacked her bare ass as she walked out of the bathroom.

Emily and Clay walked hand in hand down Larimer, passing by Josephina's. Thankfully, they were never open this early. When the two of them walked through the door of the Market, Addison immediately saw them and noticed their hands intertwined. Her eyes widened as she raised her brows.

Emily's grin was ear to ear. "Good morning!"

"It must be," Addison agreed, her confusion not easily masked. "You look like the Cheshire cat."

"Sooooo... Addison, you remember Clay?

Addison shook Clay's extended hand. "Of course. Nice to see you again."

"It's been a while." He smiled.

Emily knew Addison's brain was in overdrive, and she wanted to help her out. "We have some catching up to do."

"Since yesterday?" Addison teased.

"A lot can happen in a day."

"Apparently. You both want a cappuccino?"

"I'll just take regular coffee. Thanks," Clay said.

"And two croissants, please," Emily chimed in.

After handing over their breakfast, Addison walked out from behind the counter to hug Emily goodbye while Clay put cream and sugar in his coffee. "What the hell is going on?" she whispered.

"I took a risk and made myself vulnerable."

"Well, I need details," Addison told her as Clay walked up to them.

"Details?" He smiled mockingly. "It was all her." He wrapped his arm around Emily's waist, kissing her cheek.

"Oh, I don't doubt that," Addison laughed.

Clay and Emily headed back toward her apartment, drinking their coffee and eating croissants as if this had always been their regular morning routine.

"So, tomorrow should be interesting," Clay said.

It took Emily a moment to figure out what he meant. And then she felt the pit in her stomach.

"What do you think Lucas and Tonya will say about this new development in our friendship?"

Emily suddenly felt like she was going to throw up. She had been so immensely happy these past few hours with Clay that she had completely put the reality of the situation out of her mind. She had betrayed him before she even slept with him; she had sex with his best friend. And she knew it would crush him. As soon as he found out about her and Lucas, he would probably hate her, and it could likely end his friendship with Lucas. She also knew she had betrayed Tonya, despite Tonya's interest in other boys. Her entire world was about to be destroyed again because of her impetuousness.

"I don't think we should say anything yet."

"Why not," he asked, clearly surprised by her response.

"I'm just concerned about how it will affect our group." She was reaching for excuses. "We should give it some time. Just keep it between us for now."

"I get that," he acknowledged thoughtfully, "But at some point, it has to come out."

That's what I'm afraid of.

They stopped in front of her building, and she reached up to kiss him. "I know. Let's talk about it when I get home. I'm interviewing dealers this morning and then meeting with a couple of new locations. I should be back around three.

"Look at you, making shit happen." He leaned down and kissed her, taking the key. "I'll be waiting with bells on."

Emily had a hard time focusing on her meetings. All she could think about was the conversation she needed to have with Clay when she got home. She had resolved to tell him about Lucas. She knew it was the right thing to do. She just hoped he would understand that they had both been drinking, and it happened over six months ago—before anything between her and . He technically didn't have a reason to be mad at her. *Right?*

"On my way," she texted.

As Emily walked through the door, a naked Clay accosted her and began peeling her clothes off, devouring her mouth. Taking her to the sofa, he told her to lie down on her stomach. She noticed he had it covered with a sheet. Climbing on, she curled a throw pillow underneath her as she watched him pick up a new candle from the coffee table. After blowing it out, he dropped to his knees and hovered it above her back.

She looked over her shoulder at him. "What are you doing?"

"Relax," he smiled.

"No, seriously, what are you doing?"

"It's not actually wax. It melts into edible massage oil," he assured her. "I found it in a little store today while I was out." She felt the warm liquid drop onto her back as he poured it along her spine. Setting the tin back on the table, his firm hands spread the oil over her body.

"Mmmm..." She relaxed as he glided down her sides and over her ass, tensing up at the unexpected touch of his fingers brushing in between her cheeks before he began kneading one leg and then the other. Moving to the end of the sofa, he picked up her feet, massaging each one, starting at her heels and ending on her toes. Emily had her eyes closed, enjoying the tenderness of his sensual massage with Billie Eilish playing in the background. "That feels so good."

"Turn around," he whispered.

Dropping back down to his knees, Clay positioned the throw pillow under her hips and drizzled warm oil over her breasts and belly, massaging it into her skin. He coaxed her legs open and began massaging her mound. When his thumb slipped in and out, slowly gliding over her clit, Emily gasped. The intensity of the massage increased around her clit, harder and faster... her soft moans getting louder and louder. He slipped his fingers inside, thrusting into her g-spot, pulling out the orgasm.

He quickly retracted his hand. With her body coiling up around him at the sudden withdrawal of pleasure, he buried his face between her legs, sucking up her clit hard. Emily screamed out in ecstasy, but Clay was relentless until her hips pushed toward the sky, forcing his mouth to detach from her body.

She was in a new realm having an out-of-body experience. With every nerve ending lit up, her entire body convulsed in waves of pleasure from her eyelids to her toes.

When she was finally able to regain control of her shaking body, she looked up at . He was staring down at her with a soft smile.

"Did you like that?" he asked.

Emily started giggling. And then her giggling turned into full-on laughter, and she couldn't stop—which made Clay laugh.

"You know, it's not the best thing for a guy's ego when the girl he's trying to turn on laughs in his face."

"Oh, my god... I don't know why I can't stop laughing!" Emily managed to get out.

"You do look like a little whimsical kitten." He sat down on the sofa, pulling her on top of him as she calmed down. "My kitten."

"All yours, " she breathed out, looking at him with awe. "That was amazing. I've never experienced anything like that before."

He pulled her closer into him and held her tightly.

She felt safe with him. And she never wanted to leave his embrace.

After a few minutes, he asked if she was hungry.

"I am, actually. I've only had that croissant today."

"Good... I made an early dinner."

"You did?" She lifted her head toward the kitchen, where she noticed a beautiful bouquet of wildflowers in a vase placed in the center of her dining room table. Two place settings surrounded a bottle of wine and a baguette.

"Oh, my... wow," was all she could say. He kissed her neck. "I hope you like pesto."

They cleaned themselves up, and she grabbed her silk robe while he wrapped a towel around his waist. He pulled the Caesar salad out of the refrigerator and tossed it with the dressing. Taking the lid off the pot, he revealed fettuccine in pesto with roasted red peppers.

"You made all of this?"

"Well, I put it all together out of packages. Does that count?"

"Thank you." She kissed him. "I thought you were sleeping today?"

"I did for a bit but figured you'd be hungry when you got home."

She helped carry the food to the table and sat down, watching him pour the wine. "Why are you so good to me?"

"Because you let me." He smiled as he sat down, taking a drink.

Emily took a contemplative sip. "I don't deserve you."

"Now, why would you say that?" He furrowed his brows.

"I just... when I first met you, I put you in the friend zone pretty quickly."

Clay laughed. "I remember. But as I told you then, I could be patient."

"But why?" She wanted to know. "Why would you bother being patient with me? Especially after what happened with Enzo."

"Because I was drawn to you from the moment I met you. You're different from any other girl I've known. You're so raw and open about everything—about who you are as a person and what you struggle with."

But I'm not. I'm a liar.

"That's rare to find in someone." A mischievous smile spread across his face. "Plus, you were sexy as fuck up on that stage during the Symposium."

Emily smirked at his comment. "But I haven't exactly made the best choices this past year," an obvious reference to her fling with Enzo. However, she knew she was tentatively leading up to the dreaded conversation about Lucas.

"Emily, none of us are exempt from making bad choices," he told her. "Believe me, I've made plenty."

"Yeah, like what?" She flirtatiously challenged him.

He raised his brows while he ate his pasta, seemingly trying to decide if he was going to confide in her. Finishing it with a drink of wine, he said, "Well, last year, when I went home to visit my parents over the weekend, I ended up sleeping with our neighbor."

"Ohhh, scandalous!" Emily teased, bringing her glass to her lips.

"She's a forty-seven-year-old single mom who used to babysit me."

Emily practically spit out her wine. "Oh my god... what?!" She started laughing again.

"And she's friends with my mom," he added to her amusement. "Her son is one of my best friends."

Her laughter increased before she stopped herself. "Oh, my god! Is it Lucas's mom?"

"No! No... another neighbor. But, yeah, we all grew up together."

"That's amazing!" Emily resumed her laughter. "You totally are a snake in the grass, too!"

Clay laughed with her. "Ha... yeah, maybe. But I gotta say, I never did get that whole bit the Symposium leader did with you. He was wrong about you."

She stopped laughing as she relaxed into a comfortable smile. "Well, he was certainly wrong about you."

Shit!

"What do you mean?" Clay asked curiously.

Emily stared at him blankly as she tried to formulate the words in her head.

Clay set his fork down and sat back in his chair, waiting for her to explain.

She took another drink of wine to try to calm her nerves. "Ummm... So, Jack Fletcher and I sort of got involved after the Symposium."

Clay didn't respond for a moment. "Well, that's interesting. How did that come about?"

Her stomach was twisting. "At the end of the seminar, I went to thank him, and we got to talking. He said he wanted to give me some homework and would follow up with me..."

Clay rolled his eyes. "Of course."

"So, we started talking on the phone about relationship stuff, and that's when you came up because you had just asked me out for a drink."

"Hmmm, so what did he say about me?"

Emily took another sip of wine. "Just that you were a nice guy, and he didn't think..." She didn't know how to finish the sentence without offending him.

Clay nodded his head, taking in what she was saying. "So, are you guys still involved with each other on any level?"

"No," Emily assured him. "It was really just... we just spent a week-end together. That was it. I haven't spoken to him in months." She looked down, embarrassed.

Clay eventually reached out and took her hand. "Hey, it's okay. I mean, honestly, it seems kind of predatory on his part, but I don't hold it against you if that's what you're worried about." He lifted Emily's chin to look at him. "I'm just happy you're here with me now. Come here." He tugged at her hand, so she rose from her seat and straddled him on his chair. Kissing her, he untied her robe to caress her body.

How am I supposed to tell him about Lucas now?

She kissed him back deeply, wanting to swallow him up and stay here forever. She loved how he touched her and how he kissed her. He was so different from what she initially assumed. Jack *was* wrong. Clay did know how to fuck her hard and dirty, but he also knew how to make her feel loved and special.

Thirty-eight

Emily met up with Addison, Diego, and Todd on Saturday afternoon for lunch. She hadn't seen them much lately because everyone's lives seemed to be going in different directions. It was a rare treat for the four of them to get together.

"The grand opening for the rec center is finally next week," Diego gushed. "I can't believe how long it's all taken. You girls are going to be there, right?"

"I wouldn't miss it for the world," Emily promised.

Todd grabbed Addison's hand, "And bring Shelby. We adore them."

"Of course." Addison turned to Emily with a sly smile. "Will you be bringing Clay?"

"Clay from Friendsgiving?" Diego asked.

"Yes!" Addison practically jumped out of her seat. "Emily, catch them up so we can get on with the current situation." Addison sat back in her chair with an excited grin on her face.

"Why is your face turning red, Emily?" Todd goaded.

Emily sat there silently, shaking her head, smiling at her friends.

"Oh, can I tell them? Please?" Addison practically jumped out of her chair.

Emily laughed.

"You can't not tell us now!" Diego insisted.

"Fine—"

Emily barely got the word out of her mouth when Addison blurted out, "Clay has been totally in love with her since they met last year at that seminar, but she friend-zoned him because she was seeing the guy from The LoDo Dogs—"

"Wait, Dylan Holt? You were seeing Dylan Holt?" Diego's jaw dropped. "How could I have not known this?"

"It was very brief," Emily told him. "We went out a few times after the fundraiser."

"Well, I'd say it was more than going out," Addison teased. Emily playfully rolled her eyes.

"Okay, well, I'm going to want the dish on that later," Diego said. "So, Clay has been in love with you..."

"Clay has not been in love with me," Emily corrected.

Addison picked up where she left off. "Yes, he has. She just doesn't want to believe it. But, by Halloween, she finally admitted her feelings for him—well, to me—and she was going to tell him that night, but then she—" Addison stopped herself, looking to Emily for permission to continue.

"It's okay," Emily told her.

"She went to their Halloween party where she was going to finally tell Clay she loved him—"

"I wasn't going to tell him I loved him."

"Okay, whatever. She was going to tell him how she felt about him, but that's when she saw him kissing Amber!"

"Oh, no..." Diego whispered. "I remember Amber."

"So, she left the party upset, and then Lucas showed up at her blackjack table all sad because his girlfriend broke up with him—"

"It was also his birthday," Emily interjected, hoping that would somehow help explain her behavior.

"So, he and Emily got drunk, and she ended up sleeping with him!" The boys both gasped.

"Emily, no!" Todd reprimanded her.

"I know." Emily agreed, dropping her face in her hands.

"So, how did that play out with him?" Todd wanted to know. "You guys seemed fine at Friendsgiving."

"We talked about it the next morning and agreed it would be best to keep it to ourselves."

"Have you hooked up since then?" Diego asked.

"No. It was one drunken, sad night. It should have never happened."

The boys both nodded their heads emphatically in agreement over that statement.

"So!" Addison jumped back in. "Remember how she ditched us to spend New Year's Eve with Clay? They had this amazing night together, but he was still with Amber."

"Did you sleep with him?" Todd's eyes got big.

"No," Emily assured him.

"But he broke up with Amber on Valentine's Day." Addison's smile got exponentially larger. "So, the other morning, Emily and Clay come strolling into the Market for breakfast, holding hands, and being all lovey-dovey to each other!"

The boys' faces perked up as their smiles spread, too.

"You should have seen her," she told them. "She was beaming."

"We want the deets," Diego demanded. "Fill us in!"

Laughing, Emily obliged, telling them how she was the one to initiate the first kiss.

"And there was no alcohol involved?" Todd asked in disbelief.

"Well, one drink each over lunch a few hours earlier."

Todd waved his hand, dismissing that as counting for anything.

"So, what made you finally make your move," Addison asked.

Emily sat back and thought. After a moment, she said, "I think when I saw him standing in the rain, smiling at me, I was just so overwhelmed by him. I just got it. I felt this... I don't know. I don't want to say *love*—"

"Oh, my god!" Diego clasped his hands together in excitement. "This is like a romantic movie."

"Right?" Addison grabbed his arm. "That's what I've been saying!"

Laughing, Emily continued. "Not love... well, maybe love... just... I don't know how to explain it. I just feel at home with him. Does that make sense? I realized he is the one guy who really gets who I am."

"So, love," Todd confirmed.

"I told you he was the one." Addison playfully pushed her.

"Yes, you definitely knew before me." Emily laughed.

"I knew it the moment you told me how he took you over to face Isabella and Enzo and stayed with you that night."

"Oh! Is he the rock-climbing guy?" Diego was finally putting it all together.

"Yes."

"I remember now." Diego's grin lit up his face. "You talked about that day—a lot."

"You've had quite a year, Emily." Todd chuckled. He meant it to be funny, but tears sprang into Emily's eyes.

Addison grabbed her hand. "What's wrong?"

Trying to keep her composure, Emily finally found her voice. "As soon as he finds out I slept with Lucas, he's going to hate me."

"Who says he has to find out," Diego asked.

Todd threw him a pointed look. "You don't know that, Em. You and he weren't even a thing when you slept with Lucas."

"But it's his best friend and roommate."

"I think you should talk to him, Emily. Tell him," Addison said.

Emily shook her head. "I was going to tell him the other day, but then the whole thing about Jack ended up coming out, and that seemed to rattle him a bit. I can't imagine how he'll react when he hears about Lucas."

"Who's Jack?" Diego asked, confused again.

"The seminar leader," Addison told him.

"I thought Enzo was the seminar leader?" Diego was still confused.

"Jack led the Symposium Intensive the first weekend," Emily told them.

"Okay." Diego nodded his head slowly. "So, what happened with Jack?"

"That's who she went to New York with," Todd explained, getting exasperated.

Addison continued holding onto Emily's hand. "You have to be the one to tell him, and you two will just have to deal with it. I think you guys have a special connection. I really believe you can get past this."

"But it doesn't just affect him." The tears continued streaming down Emily's face. "I'm sure Lucas won't be happy that I told him I only think of him as a brother while I think of Clay a lot differently."

"But you said Lucas had a girlfriend for years, so, of course, you wouldn't think of him like that," Todd pointed out.

Emily continued. "Tonya had a huge crush on Clay. Ever since we all met, she confided in me and asked for my advice to help them get together. This will hurt her, too."

"Yeah, maybe," Addison said. "But, Emily, you don't just let this kind of relationship go before you've laid all your truths out on the table."

Emily knew they were right. She knew she needed to have the conversation with Clay soon, but it would have to wait until after his birthday dinner with Tonya and Lucas tomorrow.

***

The knock on her door was an hour early. Opening it, Emily found Clay smiling.

"Sorry, I couldn't wait any longer." He walked in and wrapped his arms around her, pulling her in for a long kiss. The butterflies in Emily's stomach danced around.

"God, I've missed you," he growled, kissing her neck. Chills went down her spine. She wanted to strip off his clothes.

"Happy birthday." She held him tightly.

"It is a very happy birthday." He kissed her again. "And I already got my wish."

Her stomach twisted in knots. "I thought you'd be coming with Lucas," she asked casually.

"I told him I had some stuff to take care of first." He attempted to take off her shirt.

Emily laughed as she stopped his hands. "No... you can't! I have to cook dinner. I'm making you mushroom risotto, and it's very labor intensive," she chided him.

"You got the recipe!" He pulled back and sighed with a resigned smile on his face. "Okay, fine. I can wait. How can I help?"

Ravel's *Bolero* blared through the apartment on repeat as the two of them stood side by side in the kitchen. While Emily wiped down the portobellos and passed them to Clay, she watched as he gingerly held the mushrooms down with his fingertips, taking his time to meticulously slice with the same care and precision as when his hands explored her body.

While she sauteed the portobellos, he chopped the shallots and chives. Setting the mushrooms to the side, she drizzled more olive oil into the pan and instructed him to toss in the shallots. He stood behind her, his hands on her hips, his body inches from hers, as she added the Arborio rice. She could feel the heat emanating from him.

Reaching for the white wine, Emily poured it over the rice, steam springing up out of the pan. She continued stirring as the rice absorbed the wine. Clay gathered her hair in his hand and kissed her neck, sending shivers throughout her body.

She reached for the vegetable broth, trying not to leave his grasp, and slowly added it to the pan.

"What can I do now," he whispered in her ear.

She felt her heart quicken. "Nothing. I have to stir this continuously for the next twenty minutes. There's Guinness in the fridge if you'd like to sit down and relax."

"I can think of something else to help me relax." He kissed her neck again, and she extended her hand behind her to hold onto his hip. His mouth traced an invisible line from one side of her neck to the other. His hands slowly inched up her skirt, and one slid in between her thighs to dip his finger inside. He nibbled on her ear, "You are so wet," and began slowly massaging around her clit.

As she tried to focus on stirring the risotto, a whimper escaped her mouth. The throbbing desire between her legs was too distracting.

Clay slid her panties off as he dropped down to the floor, leaning his back against the stove and settling between her legs. He ducked his head under her skirt and held her ass while he licked up her flowing juices. His tongue moved faster and faster as she struggled to keep herself standing. She was trying not to scream, knowing their friends could be walking up to the door at any moment. Just as she was about to collapse, he stopped and slid out from between her legs to stand up.

As she continued to stir the risotto, she felt him raise her skirt from behind and pull her hips back toward him. She placed one hand on the counter to steady herself as he entered her and slowly moved in and out. As the lengthy piece of music built to its crescendo, she was lost in the moment, so close to her own climax. She absentmindedly stirred the food until a loud knock on the door startled her out of her bliss.

She felt Clay slip out of her and heard the lid of the trash can close. He came around to stand next to her, turning her face toward his, kissing her softly on her lips. "That was fun." Reaching down, he picked up her panties and tucked them into his pocket before he walked to the door. The music ended, and there was another knock.

"Hey, guys." Clay greeted Lucas and Tonya as he let them in, wiping at the corners of his mouth.

"Jesus, that music was loud," Lucas exclaimed as he walked inside. "We knocked a few times."

"You did?" Clay asked, surprised.

"Yeah... when did you get here? I've been calling you."

"Just a few minutes ago."

"Happy birthday!" Tonya reached up to hug Clay. Emily felt like a horrible friend.

"Hi, guys," Emily greeted them. "Sorry, I love to cook to *Bolero*. I'm just finishing up the risotto. There's beer in the fridge and wine on the counter."

"Thanks." Lucas turned to Clay, noticing his empty hands. "You don't have a birthday beer yet?"

"I just haven't had a chance to get something. Want one," he asked Lucas.

"That would be great."

"Tonya, can I get you some wine," he asked her.

"Yes, please."

Emily felt like she and Clay were throwing a dinner party together. As if he belonged here in her home offering their guests drinks. She liked it.

Lucas and Tonya sat at the table.

"These are beautiful wildflowers. Where did you get them?" Tonya asked Emily.

"Oh, someone was selling them on the corner the other day."

She saw Clay crack a slight smile as he walked into the kitchen. "Did you guys come together?"

"Yeah," Lucas responded. "Figured it's better since parking sucks down here."

Clay walked up next to Emily to grab the unopened bottle of red wine from the counter, his body brushing up against hers. "Do you want anything, Emily?" He smiled as she glanced at him from the side.

An orgasm.

Emily was still trying to clear her head as she felt the tingling between her legs linger. "Would you mind pouring me some wine?"

"Not at all. Where's your bottle opener?"

"In the drawer to the left of me."

He walked around her, his hand skimming her ass as he reached into the drawer. "Glasses?"

"Above you."

Continuing to stand next to her, he opened the wine and poured her and Tonya a glass.

"Thank you," she said, trying to sound calm when all she wanted to do was kiss him.

Clay joined Lucas and Tonya at the table, the three of them talking while Emily finished cooking. She already felt her stomach twisting into knots. She imagined Clay and Lucas confiding in each other about how they had slept with her on their birthdays.

On their birthdays! Oh, my god, I'm such a fucking cliché.

She pictured their faces as the realization of what she had done washed over them. The hurt on Clay's face burned in her thoughts. The betrayal he would feel crushed her heart.

"Dinner's ready. Why don't you guys come in here, and I'll dish it up from the stove?"

Clay stepped up for his plate. "Smells delicious. I hear risotto is very labor intensive."

"I hope it isn't burnt," Emily responded. "I kept getting distracted while I was stirring."

Throughout dinner, Emily tried to carry on a conversation with the three of them as if nothing had changed—as if she hadn't just imploded the group. As if this wouldn't be their last meal together.

For dessert, Emily pulled out a chocolate-peanut butter cake she had picked up from the Market. Chocolate ganache dripped down the sides while peanut butter cups adorned the top. After they sang "Happy Birthday," she pulled out vanilla ice cream and peanut butter whiskey. The look on Clay's face was one of surprise and gratitude. As she served him, she felt his finger ever-so-gently graze her leg.

"Time for his gift," Tonya asked as they carried dishes into the kitchen.

"I get gifts, too?" Clay asked.

"Of course," Emily said. "Your twenty-seventh birthday needs to be celebrated properly. Especially when it comes with a promotion."

"But I've already gotten so much." He smiled at Emily as she walked to her closet and pulled down a big gift box. She had spent all of Friday finding just the right present.

"Sit," she told him, setting the gift on the table. "This is from all three of us."

Lucas and Tonya weren't aware that she paid for the majority of the expensive gift. She knew they weren't in a position to contribute much, and her casino table business was bringing in more money than she could have imagined.

Clay's face lit up like a little boy as he unwrapped the paper and lifted the lid off the box. As soon as he saw the quality dark brown leather, he looked up at Emily with shock, understanding this was her doing. She knew that he would appreciate the handcrafted Bosca briefcase.

"It took some digging to find out your middle name, Clay Everett Olson," Emily said, rolling her eyes. "You'd think one of your oldest friends who grew up with you and currently lives with you would know." As those words came out of her mouth, she felt a jab through her heart.

Lucas laughed, "I'm sorry! I'm a guy... we don't pay attention to that kind of stuff."

"It's true," Clay agreed. He lifted the briefcase out of its box. "This is gorgeous."

"We went with the dark, distressed brown because its ruggedness seemed more your style over the shiny black," Emily explained.

"I especially like how your initials spell CEO on the front," Tonya pointed out.

Clay flashed that same grateful smile as earlier. "Thank you, guys, so much, for this. It means a lot." He leaned over and side-hugged Tonya and fist-bumped Lucas across the table. With Emily standing right next to him as he was sitting in the chair, he reached his hand up and wrapped it around her hips, pulling her toward him to hug her. She placed her hand on the side of his head as he rested against her. Without giving it a thought, her hand gently caressed his hair.

Emily didn't realize just how intimate that gesture was until she saw the mild looks of surprise on both Lucas's and Tonya's faces. Stepping back, she picked up the discarded wrapping paper to throw it away.

Tonya followed behind her. "You guys seem pretty cozy," she whispered. Emily was grateful the music was still playing over by the boys.

"What do you mean?" Emily asked, feigning ignorance.

"Is there something going on with you and Clay?"

Emily's stomach dropped. She didn't know what to say. She didn't want to blatantly lie to Tonya, but she was worried about how she would react. Nevertheless, she knew she had to be honest with her.

She let out a sigh as she nodded her head. "I'm sorry, Tonya. I didn't mean for it to happen; it just did."

Tonya stared at her for a moment as she processed what Emily said. "Sorry? Why are you sorry? I think that's incredible!"

That is not the reaction I was expecting.

Emily tried to understand. "You do? You're not mad?"

"Mad? Emily, I love you both so much. I think you're perfect together."

"But I thought you really liked him?"

Tonya laughed. "Oh, my god... that was so long ago! He's like my big brother now."

"Really? You're okay with this?" Emily was shocked to learn of Tonya's change of heart. Even though Tonya never really spoke longingly about Clay anymore, Emily assumed she still felt the same way about him.

"I'm so okay with this. It makes so much sense." Tonya hugged her.

"What's going on in here?" Lucas walked into the kitchen with Clay trailing behind.

"Apparently, we aren't the only ones sneaking around." Tonya smiled mischievously as she wrapped her arms around Lucas.

Emily and Clay's jaws dropped open.

"No shit?" Lucas laughed. "It's about time."

"When did this happen?" Emily asked, still trying to comprehend what was unfolding in front of her.

"Just after my birthday," Tonya told them.

Emily was stunned. "That was almost two months ago!"

"I know." Tonya glanced up at Lucas nervously.

Lucas took her cue. "We just didn't really know how to tell you guys. We didn't want anything to get weird between all of us."

"I think we can appreciate that," Clay said, taking Emily's hand into his.

As soon as the door closed behind Tonya and Lucas, Clay advanced in, pushing Emily back against the wall, pinning her arms. "I've waited for this all night."

His tongue inhaled her as her soul lit on fire. Every nerve under her skin stood on end, begging for his body to fuse with hers. He quickly undid his pants and pulled himself out to slip on a condom. Hoisting her up, he immediately entered her, taking her breath away. Her long legs reached across the entryway's short width, her feet resting on the opposite wall. His strong arms held onto her body while he buried his face into the curve of her neck. She wrapped her hands around his head, grasping onto his silky soft hair while his body convulsed as he came.

In that moment, she knew she loved him with every ounce of her being. She loved him for everything he stood for—and everything he was against. She loved him for how he made her feel—both emotionally and physically. She loved him for his friendship—and his patience. He connected with her spirit like no one else ever had. But mostly, she loved him because she chose to love him.

After they had spent hours making love, Emily sat up in front of the fireplace, staring at the glow of the flames as they flickered along the wall. She thought Clay had fallen asleep until she felt his hand reach up and caress her back.

"There's something you should know," she said softly.

He pulled her back down to him, taking her into his arms as he brought her head to his chest. "What is it?"

Have the courage to choose what's right over what's easy, even when you can't control the outcome.

"Last Halloween, I came to that party ready to open up to you. Ready to admit that I had completely fallen for you." Her body started trembling. "I wanted to run into your arms and kiss you—tell you that I finally got it. And then I saw you with Amber. Every hope and dream that I envisioned with you had been ripped away. I was devastated and heartbroken. But mostly angry with myself for losing you."

Tears fell from her face onto his skin as she collected her thoughts to continue. "Later that night, Lucas came to see me at work. His girlfriend had just broken up with him, and he was sad, too. We had a lot to drink." It was getting harder for her to get the words out as the crying took over.

Clay didn't loosen his hold on her.

"He came back to my place because he couldn't drive. One thing led to another—heartbreak mixed with alcohol—and we ended up sleeping together."

There. She said it. It was out.

Silence filled the room as Emily lay still, not wanting to remind him she was in his arms for fear that he would push her away.

Clay took in a deep breath and exhaled slowly. "You left out the part where you told him it shouldn't have happened because he was like a brother to you."

He knows!

Emily bolted upright and looked down at him in disbelief. "You know?"

Clay smiled.

"I can't believe you already know! And you're smiling! You're smiling?!"

He sat up and wiped the tears from her face, sweeping her hair back behind her ears.

"Yes, I know," he said gently.

She looked at him, dumbfounded. *What does this mean?*

"Lucas is not good at keeping secrets," he chuckled. "He told me that day he came home. But I really appreciate hearing it from you now."

Emily was stunned. She had spent all these months beating herself up over it, convincing herself he would hate her, and Tonya would hate her. She was almost ready to walk away from Clay because she was too ashamed to admit to him what she had done. But now he sat before her, confessing that he's known all along.

"And you're okay with this?"

"Obviously, I wasn't happy about it. Actually, I was pretty pissed. But at him—not you. You had made it clear to me you only wanted to be friends. Lucas, on the other hand, knew how I felt about you. It took us a while to get past it. That's a large part of why I threw myself into Amber. I was hurt and angry. I didn't even think you cared, honestly. But I couldn't stay away from you. It was like this invisible cord tethered me to you. And, ultimately, that's why I had to end things with Amber. Because she wasn't you. I am madly in love with you, Emily."

Emily's heart practically burst open. She couldn't believe she had denied herself this kind of happiness for so long because she didn't feel worthy. She had let the shame of all her past mistakes dictate her future, assigning meaning to everything and convincing herself it was the truth.

In that moment, she got it. She got that she could choose to be complete and leave her past in the past. She could choose happiness and create an entirely new future for herself. She finally understood everything Jack and her dad—and even Enzo—had been saying.

She crawled into his lap. "I love you, too, Clay."

Clay kissed her deeply before pulling back. "There's something I need to talk with you about, also."

"What is it?"

"When I went into work on Friday, they told me they're sending me to Tokyo to help open the new office."

"Wow, that's amazing! Congratulations!" She leaned in and kissed him. "When do you leave?"

"They want me out there by June first."

She smiled and took her hands into his. "You really deserve this, Clay. I'm so happy for you. How long will you be gone?"

Emily saw the glisten in his eyes from withheld tears. He took a deep breath before he spoke. "It's for an indefinite amount of time. I'll be living there."

Emily's heart stopped. She had assumed he would be gone a couple of weeks.

All the air had been sucked out of the room as the reality sank in.

"I had no idea they would choose me, Emily. It's something I put in for a few months ago without really believing I had a shot."

"But you just got promoted," Emily whispered, trying to find her voice.

"And that's why. My boss wanted to surprise me. They threw an office party for me on Friday to celebrate my birthday and promotion. And that's where they announced I had been hand-selected by the president to go to Tokyo."

Emily slowly pulled out of his embrace and climbed off his lap. "Why are you just now telling me if you've known for two days?"

"Honestly, I've been trying to figure out how. I even considered declining the promotion."

"Oh, my god, no, Clay. You can't do that. Not for me."

"I know. The timing of everything just really sucks."

"June first... that's less than a month away."

He looked at her for a long moment, contemplating. "I don't suppose you would go with me?"

Emily smiled. "You know I can't do that."

"Why not?"

She opened her mouth to provide a reason but had too many thoughts racing around in her head.

"Marry me."

That was not one of them.

"What?"

Clay gathered her back into his arms. "Marry me. I love you, Emily. And, for whatever reason, you love me. I want to spend the rest of my life with you. And I want that to start now."

"Clay..."

He kissed her. "Please say yes," he whispered.

She held his face in her hands as tears slid down her cheeks. "I can't marry you right now. I do love you, and I'm heartbroken that it's taken me so long to figure that out, and now you're leaving. I think of all the time I wasted. But I'm just starting to build the life I want for myself. And as much as I want you to be a part of that, I can't commit the rest of my life just yet. This is so new between us."

"But we can build it together. I can help you."

Emily kissed him. "Oh, Clay. As romantic as that sounds—and trust me, it's very tempting—I'm just not ready for that. I feel like I'm finally coming into my own, and I like that. I like who I'm becoming and the success I'm creating. And I want to keep building on that. I wish we could do it together here while we pursue this relationship, but you know we aren't ready for marriage."

He held onto her tightly, resting his face against her chest. "I know you're right," he said in resignation. "I just hate the thought of losing you now that I've finally got you."

Emily kissed him, pouring her longing and hope and heartbreak into him before she took her lips from his. They stared at each other, breathing in the silence as they came to terms with their situation.

"So, do we try a long-distance relationship?" Clay asked.

"I think even that level of commitment is too much pressure on us right now," Emily told him. "You're going to be on the other side of the world focusing on your career. And I'll be doing the same. We don't have to define this just yet. Let's just enjoy our time together this month and see where life takes us after that."

Emily knew now that only she had the power to create the life she wanted. She no longer would let life just happen to her. And even though she knew there was no guarantee for a "Happily Ever After," she did know she could choose to be happy for now.

Thirty-nine

It was practically one year to the day since the fundraiser and the Symposium. Emily took stock of her growth from irresponsible party girl to business owner, blazing her own trail. She was also pretty impressed that she could now afford to drop three hundred dollars on a cocktail dress and not have to hide the tags to return it after the grand opening of the new rec center.

Standing in front of Clay's mirror, she slipped the cherry red dress over her naked body, the scoop neck being held up by thin, delicate straps that disappeared underneath her dark curls. Her entire back was exposed to her sacrum as the rest of the fabric hugged her curves down to her mid-calf, separated by the high slit showing off her toned leg. The matching red strappy stilettos and painted toenails topped off her look.

Clay walked up behind her, slipping his hand around her waist as he kissed her neck. "You are the most beautiful woman I've ever laid eyes on. How am I going to make it through the night knowing you've got no panties on underneath this amazing dress?"

She turned in his arms, facing him so she could kiss his mouth, drinking him in. "I can't wait to feel you inside of me when we get home," she breathed in his ear. As they pulled apart, she looked at him in his black suit, running her hand down his chest. "Yummy. You wear this look very well."

Stepping into the living room, Clay called for Lucas that it was time to go as Emily grabbed her small purse and reapplied her lip gloss. After standing there waiting for a minute, he called out again. Finally, Lucas and Tonya came stumbling out of his bedroom, giggling. Clay shook his head. "You two are like children."

"Thanks, Pops," Lucas teased and planted a kiss on Tonya's mouth.

Tonya wore a sapphire blue short slip dress that showed off her petite body. She had let her blonde hair grow out to her shoulders and started highlighting it. And her make-up was on-point. She, too, had grown into herself, and her confidence shone through.

When the four of them walked into the brand-new recreation center, Emily saw Diego and Todd chatting with Addison and Shelby.

"Oh, my god... look at you!" Diego squealed as he rushed over to them with the rest of the group following. "You all look like you belong on the cover of Vogue!"

Clay shook everyone's hands. "It's nice to see you, again."

"Jesus, Emily, what took you so damn long to make up your mind about him," Diego asked.

Todd punched Diego's arm as Clay graciously chuckled.

They all dispersed to mingle while enjoying appetizers and drinks. Clay stayed close to Emily's side, protectively keeping an eye on Enzo and Isabella, who stayed on the other side of the room. They each gave Emily a smile of acknowledgement but never approached her.

Addison and Shelby spent most of the evening with the jiu-jitsu instructor and her girlfriend, while Lucas and Tonya immersed themselves in conversation with Diego and Todd.

On the drive back down the mountain, Lucas told them that Diego and Todd wanted to set up an interview with him after graduation to discuss him taking on a Counselor role in the program.

"And I'll be volunteering up there this summer," Tonya exclaimed.

"That's incredible, you guys!" Emily was thrilled for them. "The psychologist and the social worker... sounds like a perfect match."

"Kinda sounds like a cheesy romantic movie," Clay laughed.

"Graduation is in a week!" Lucas yelled from the backseat, making them all jump. "And then it's party time!"

"It's going to be a huge blowout celebrating your graduation and Clay's promotion." Tonya pulled Lucas in for a kiss.

Emily took a deep breath, not wanting to think about Clay's departure that would come two days after the party. Clay reached over and took her hand into his as she stared out at the bright lights flashing through the fast moving highway.

***

The week seemed like hours. And the party was epic. This time, Emily was the beautiful woman on Clay's arm offering people drinks. But it was fleeting.

Monday morning, Clay stood with his suitcase outside Emily's apartment, waiting for an Uber to pick him up and whisk him out of her life.

Emily held onto him tightly. "I wish I had given you a chance the first night you asked me out. I wish I had realized my feelings for you the day you took me rock climbing. You snuck up on me. You got into my head and my heart, and I didn't even realize it until it was too late."

"It's never too late." He kissed the top of her head and stroked her hair. "I love you so much, Emily. This isn't the end of us."

A silver Kia pulled up in front of them. Clay removed one of his arms from Emily's body to wave to the driver.

She squeezed him into her, tears flowing freely down her face. She never wanted to release him and questioned if she made the right choice to not follow him. "I will always love you. I'll probably live the rest of my life knowing you are the one I let get away."

"I will come back to you, Emily. I promise." He tilted her head up, and she saw the tears in his eyes before he gave her a long, slow kiss. "Goodbye, Kitten."

She released her grip on him when the driver popped open the trunk and got out of his car.

Emily stepped back watching everything in slow motion.

He turned his attention to the man who grabbed the luggage and tossed it inside. Clay opened the back door and turned to look at her one final time.

And then he was gone.

Forty

"**H**ey, sis!"

"Hey, bro!" Emily and David spoke often these days. He had been out several times, delivering tables to her and other casinos up in the mountains. He not only gave her business advice but also listened to her lament about Clay all those months, celebrated with her when they finally got together, and comforted her when she broke down after he moved to Tokyo three weeks ago.

"So, I've been thinking—"

"Oh, no," she teased him.

"Ha… listen. My business out here is going through the roof. Ever since expanding into high-end games for large corporate events, I can't keep up with everything. I need someone to manage and grow the accounts throughout Southern California, and I'm beyond impressed with what you've done out there with those tables. What would you think about coming back here and bringing some of that magic with you?"

Emily was stunned. "Move back to California?"

"Yeah. Well, I figured maybe it would be nice to have a change of scenery, get your mind off certain things."

Like the love of my life moving to the other side of the world? "But what about my business out here?"

"Offer to sell the tables to the locations. They can keep your dealers and take them on as employees. Or sell the business to someone who would want to take over. Or simply walk away, and I'll pick up the tables. Whatever you do, I guarantee you'll be making at least six figures out here... and, oh, did I mention, you get to live at the beach? Malia and I just bought a place with a guesthouse above the garage."

"That's crazy!" She laughed.

"I know, right? But, seriously, hiring you is a slam-dunk. I know I'm getting someone with a strong work ethic who will bust her ass and do whatever it takes to be successful. That's hard to find in an employee. I'd rather have my baby sister out here working alongside me than some schlub who I have to worry about constantly."

"When?"

"How soon can you be here?"

***

"You're just giving me your business?" Addison asked in disbelief.

"If you want it. I mean, it wouldn't be what it is if it weren't for you and Shelby. You guys helped build it just as much as I did."

"Of course I want it!" Addison beamed. "I just hate that it means you're leaving me."

"Me too. But I'm leaving you with something magical we created together. You always stood by me, even when I was being a little shit," Emily laughed. "And despite all my stupid choices, you still loved me and pushed me forward. I'm so grateful for that. You've got a good partner in Shelby. I don't doubt the two of you will continue to grow the blackjack empire."

"I love you, Em. You'll always be my best friend."

"And you mine, Addy."

***

Emily's sisters cried, begging her not to leave, but perked up when she told them they could come out and visit her and David, and they would take them to the beach and Disneyland.

"I wish you weren't going, Emily," her dad told her. "I feel like we were finally getting closer."

"I know, Dad. I appreciate everything you and Amy have done for me. You've impacted my life so much. I'm sorry I didn't listen to you earlier, but I've now devoured every book you've ever given me. Thanks so much for loving me. I promise to keep in touch."

"I love you, Emily Rose.

"I love you, too, Dad."

***

Emily caravanned behind David as they cruised down Pacific Coast Highway in the late afternoon of July Fourth. Oingo Boingo's "We Close Our Eyes" blasted through her stereo. She reflected on the lyrics about the world turning around again as she drove past the familiar sights of her teenage years.

They pulled into a parking lot above Crystal Cove in Newport Beach. When Emily stepped out of the car, the salty air and warm sun hit her face, welcoming her home.

David checked his phone. "Mom and Malia are meeting us at the Beachcomber for an early dinner before the fireworks show. Figured a nice walk after a long drive would be good."

"Perfect." Emily smiled, remembering all the times her mom dragged her to the little shack on the sand.

They followed the footpath from the parking lot to the tunnel that took them under PCH, leading them into the Historic District of rustic cottages from the 1930s and 40s.

As they made their way toward the restaurant, David checked his phone again. "They aren't quite here yet. I want to run in and see if my buddy is working today. Will you wait for them out front?"

"Sure."

David sprinted up the steps, leaving Emily in the sand. She stared out at the vast ocean before her, listening to the sound of crashing waves. She hadn't realized how much she missed all of this until now. It immediately soothed her soul. She took in a deep breath, letting the ocean air fill her lungs.

"California really is as beautiful as you said."

She snapped her head to the left.

"I think I might stay awhile."

Emily stood frozen trying to comprehend who she was seeing. "Clay..."

"I couldn't let you go that easily, Kitten." He pulled her in and kissed her.

"But... Tokyo... How..."

"After I got everything in place over there, I convinced the company Amber should take over the position so I could focus on our growth and retention from our headquarters in Los Angeles." Clay kissed her again. "I can be very persuasive."

"You're moving to California?"

"Got here late last night thanks to your family's help." He nodded toward the raised patio above them.

Emily looked up to see her mom, David, and his girlfriend Malia smiling down at them.

"So what do you think? Are you up for continuing this dating thing until I use my skills to persuade you to marry me?"

She couldn't contain her smile. "You better never stop dating me... even when we're married."

"I wouldn't have it any other way, Kitten."

Emily's mouth closed in on his as she surrendered completely to the man she loved, knowing she had created a world where she had everything she ever dreamed of.

Just like a fucking romance novel.

The End.

Acknowledgements

This story wouldn't be what it is today without the inspiration, support, and encouragement from so many people throughout this journey.

Lisa Beverly-DuFloth, LeslyAnn Collins, and Linda Williams—I can't thank you enough for reading my earliest chapters and then re-reading them a few dozen times as I went into endless revisions trying to get them just right! Your patience is deep. I'm so blessed to have you in my life as my best friends forever!

Steven Zapiler, thank you for knowing me to be someone bigger than I had been being. You created the space for a new possibility that allowed me to add so much more depth to the story. I am eternally grateful for you. I can't wait to see our vision come to life with Richelle Martinez portraying Emily on the big screen! Richelle, you are a rockstar, and you encompass all of Emily's best qualities. Thank you both for being such amazing humans.

Ronel Kelmen, I appreciate your keen eye and attention to detail while copy editing and proofreading my manuscript. But more importantly, I appreciate your friendship! Our daily calls keep me accountable to what I say I'm up to in life (even on the days when I don't want to do anything).

To my coaches at Landmark: your leadership has opened up my world. Thank you Niranjan, Elana, and Jerry for your commitment to creating a world that works for everyone.

Greg Renne, thank you for believing in me early on and always motivating me to keep moving toward my dream.

Dana Kring... without you, there would be no story. I will always cherish our friendship and hold you in a special place in my heart.

Thank you Kathy Ver Eecke at How To Get Published for your expertise and guidance in the publishing world. I'm so grateful for all the fellow writers I met in the Pitch to Published community who were in the trenches with me as we honed our skills. Nel, your feedback and suggestions have been invaluable. You are such a talented writer! I'm thrilled I get to call you my friend (I'm sorry I still use way too many exclamation marks)!

I so appreciate the countless beta readers and ARC readers who gave me their brutal feedback about what worked and what didn't. You all made me a better writer and helped me create something I can be proud of.

To my parents and siblings: Shirley, Foster, Jill, Fos, Eric, Sierra, and Annie—thank you for your grace and love. Each of you has been a guiding force in my life, pushing me to always be better and do better. I love you.

And lastly, to my children: Thank you, Jeremy, for not being too embarrassed by your mom's writings and always being happy for my small wins. You going after your passion in life inspired me to go after mine. Thank you, Levi, for allowing my constant distraction and obsession with writing. You bring such joy to my life. And thank you,

Lauren, for calling me out when I wanted to hide behind a pen name! You are a fierce young woman with a wisdom that often challenges me and others to see what many don't. The three of you are my world. I love you with all my heart and all my soul. I hope I make you proud.

ABOUT THE AUTHOR

JUSTINE BRASHEAR'S obsession as a little girl with making up stories led her to study Creative Writing during her college years in downtown Denver. As a mother, daughter, sister, friend, and breast cancer survivor, she is passionate about inspiring women to live life unabashedly self-expressed. She currently lives in Southern California with her two big dogs, Joey and Biscuit, while she plots out her next book and living life as a best-selling author.

Listen to Emily's playlist and sign up for Justine's newsletter (if she ever gets it off the ground) at justinebrashear.com

 tiktok.com/

instagram.com/

 facebook.com/